death by the river

Other Books by Alexandrea Weis

To My Senses
Recovery
Sacrifice
Broken Wings
Diary of a One-Night Stand
Acadian Waltz
The Satyr's Curse
The Satyr's Curse II: The Reckoning
The Satyr's Curse III: Redemption
The Ghosts of Rue Dumaine
Cover to Covers
The Riding Master
The Bondage Club
That Night with You
Taming Me
Rival Seduction
The Art of Sin
Dark Perception: The Corde Noire Series Book 1
Dark Attraction: The Corde Noire Series Book 2
His Dark Canvas: The Corde Noire Series Book 3
Her Dark Past: The Corde Noire Series Book 4

By Alexandrea Weis with M. Clarke

Behind the Door

By the Multi-Award-Winning Duo
Alexandrea Weis with Lucas Astor

Blackwell, Prequel to the Magnus Blackwell Series
Damned (A Magnus Blackwell Novel, Book I)
Bound (A Magnus Blackwell Novel, Book II)

Forthcoming from Vesuvian Books

By Alexandrea Weis

The Secret Brokers
Realm

By Alexandrea Weis with Lucas Astor

The Chimera Effect
4 for the Devil

death by the river

ALEXANDREA WEIS
AND LUCAS ASTOR

Death by the River

This is a work of fiction. Names, characters, places, and incidents either are the product of the author's imagination or are used fictitiously.
Any resemblance to actual persons, living or dead, or locales is entirely coincidental.

Cover design by Michael Canales
Photograph by Carolina Heza

ISBN: 978-1-944109-14-1

VESUVIAN BOOKS

Published by Vesuvian Books
www.vesuvianbooks.com

Printed in the United States of America

10 9 8 7 6 5 4 3 2 1

some truths are better kept secret.

some secrets are better off dead.

Chapter One

Beau Devereaux stared at the clock, watching the minutes tick by. The only noise in the stuffy classroom was the monotonous, raspy voice of his teacher. Like a thoroughbred chomping at the bit, he waited to bolt.

The jarring bell couldn't have come soon enough. Not even taking time to put his book in his bag, Beau headed for the door. He turned a corner on his way to the gym and spotted a familiar dirty-blonde messy ponytail.

"Leslie." Beau cornered her in the hall, pinning her between a break in the lockers. "How's it going?"

Her blue eyes ripped into him—just what he expected. "What do you want, Beau?"

What did he want? He almost laughed. He drank in her flawless, porcelain complexion, the regal curve of her jaw, her small, perfectly shaped nose, and enticing full lips. His attention settled on the notch at the base of her neck. It fluttered like a scared little butterfly.

"Can't a guy say hello to his friend?" Beau put his arm on the wall behind her, trapping her between the lockers. "We see each other in the halls but never speak. Why is that?"

He loved watching her eyes dart about, searching for a rescue, but no one would challenge him. No one ever did.

"I'm not your friend." She shoved him back. "Go talk to Dawn."

He curled his hands into fists. If he couldn't have Leslie, her twin sister, Dawn, was the next best thing. He'd started dating her to get his mind off Leslie, but it hadn't worked. They were alike physically, but Dawn wasn't Leslie. She didn't have her sass. That he still wanted Leslie infuriated him. He always got what he wanted.

Beau leaned in, letting his breath tease her cheek. The scent of her skin, like fresh spring clover, filled his nose.

"One day, I'm going to take you to The Abbey and set things right between us."

"Is there a problem?"

The deep voice tinged with pseudo-macho angst buzzed in his ear like a gnat. Beau turned around, knowing who he would find— her trusty watchdog, Derek Foster. The brown-haired son of a waitress, Derek spent way too many hours studying with the geek patrol and not enough partying with the popular crowd.

"No problem, Foster," Beau said in a reassuring tone. "Your girl and I were just talking about next week's biology test."

Leslie edged around him. "Do you even know how to spell biology?"

He bristled at the question. That smart tongue of hers begged to be tamed.

A few students gathered next to the set of lockers to his right, taking in the encounter.

Beau gave his best wholesome grin. "That's really hostile, Leslie. I'm trying here, for your sister's sake."

Derek was about to pull her away when Beau wheeled around, stuck out his elbow, and landed a perfect shot right to Derek's cheek.

He stumbled back, bouncing off some freshman girls.

"Derek!" Leslie went to his side, pushing Beau out of the way.

Holding in his satisfaction, Beau displayed a fretful frown as he rushed up to Derek. "Oh, man. I am so sorry." He put a hand on his shoulder, avidly checking the red spot on his right cheek and suppressing a smug grin. "That was my fault, Derek. I didn't see you there."

Leslie shot him an icy glare. "You're an ass, Beau."

He gave her his best wide-eyed expression, reveling in her

reaction. "I'm sorry, Leslie. It was an accident. I didn't mean to hit him." Beau spoke loud enough for onlookers to hear. "Stop making me out to be the bad guy here. I know you dislike me, but can you give this attitude of yours a break?"

Derek took Leslie's hand. "I'm fine. It was an accident. Let it go."

Beau smiled sweetly at her. "You should listen to your boyfriend."

"What's going on here?"

Ms. Greenbriar's screeching voice made all three of them spin around. The middle-aged principal of St. Benedict High stood with her hands on her hips.

"Mr. Devereaux?"

Beau presented the principal with one of his winning smiles. "Nothing, ma'am. Just a misunderstanding. I caught Derek with my elbow when I turned around. My fault entirely."

Ms. Greenbriar shifted her beady brown eyes to Derek. "Mr. Foster, anything you want to add?"

Derek nursed his cheek. "No, ma'am. It was an accident, just like Beau said."

She tapped her high-heel on the tile floor, glancing from Beau to Derek. "My office, Mr. Devereaux."

Beau backed away from the lockers as his stomach tightened with anger. "Yes, ma'am."

* * *

"That bastard!"

Leslie bolted out of the wood and glass double doors to St. Benedict High School, tugging Derek behind her. The strong October sun shone down, highlighting the red mark covering Derek's right cheek and sending a sharp pain through her chest.

Damn Beau Devereaux.

For almost a year she'd tolerated his comments and lewd glances, but since she'd started dating Derek, he'd stepped up his game.

"I can't believe he punched you like that."

Derek wrapped his arm around her waist and ushered her down the stone steps to the school parking lot. "He didn't punch me. It was an accident."

She halted and stared at him numb with disbelief. "You don't buy his bullshit, do you?"

"No, but what am I going to do about it? Punch him back?" Derek urged her along. "Then I would be the one in Greenbriar's office, not him."

She searched the parking lot while students on the grassy quad outside the school entrance sat on benches, tossed footballs, studied their laptops, or listened to music.

"Does anyone in this town stand up to him?" Leslie shook her head. "He's got everyone believing he's Mr. Perfect and I'm the crazy bitch."

Derek slipped the book bag off her shoulder to carry it. "No one thinks you're crazy, least of all me."

The simple gentlemanly gesture melted her heart. Leslie touched Derek's dimpled chin, feeling fortunate. "Maybe we should go have you checked out. Just in case."

"It's just a bruise. I'll be fine." He stopped on the sidewalk at the bottom of the steps. "What did he say to you, anyway?"

"The usual."

A car turned on a monster bass, blasting the park-like setting with hard rock.

Derek glanced at the source of the noise. "I still don't get how the guy can be crazy about your twin sister and not like you at all."

Leslie removed the band holding her ponytail. "Sometimes I think she went out with him to spite me." She ran her hand through her shoulder-length hair.

"What makes you say such a thing?"

She shrugged and fell in step beside him. "We aren't exactly the closest of sisters. It was always a competition between us when we were younger. I joined the swim team, and then Dawn joined. Dawn wanted to join Brownies, so did I. Except I gave up competing with her when we got into high school." She gazed down at the neatly trimmed grass beneath her feet. "Dawn never stopped. Sometimes I think that's why she became a cheerleader and started seeing Beau—to show me she could."

Derek put a protective arm around her shoulders. "I can't see her dating Devereaux to get back at you. He's the richest and most popular guy in town. Isn't he every girl's dream?"

Leslie stopped short, shuddering. "Not mine. There's something off about him."

"He's just a guy used to getting his way. My guess, it comes from two hundred years of inbreeding. Don't all those old, rich Southern families marry their cousins? Maybe that's his problem. Too many crazy relatives in his family tree."

A brisk wind stirred as they crossed the blacktop to the white Honda Accord she shared with her sister. The chill wrapped around her, seeping into her bones. She wasn't sure if it was a change in weather coming, or something else.

Derek nudged her. "Hey, you okay?"

She came out of her daze, shaking off the bizarre feeling. "Just really sick of dealing with Beau."

Derek smiled at her from across the roof of the car and her heart skipped a beat.

"I know what we could do. Want to sneak up to The Abbey? I could show you around. It's pretty cool."

She didn't like the idea of crawling around the derelict abbey. She'd never been to the abandoned St. Francis Seminary on the banks of the Bogue Falaya River but had heard stories from friends.

"I don't want to go there. We should get you home and see to your cheek." She hit the remote on her key chain and unlocked the doors.

"Stop worrying. I'm fine." He climbed into the car, brandishing a wicked grin. "We can skip The Abbey tour and hang out at the river."

She put her book bag in the back seat. "I have no interest in going to the river. I've told you that before."

"No. You told me you used to go there but stopped around the time we met."

Leslie wanted to jump all over him for pursuing the subject, but she didn't. Her life had been empty before she'd met Derek. They had shared classes for almost a year before getting the courage to talk.

"Do you remember the first time you spoke to me?" she asked, warmed by the memory.

"How could I forget?" He leaned over the console. "I left class early and found Beau pinning you against a locker. Seems to be a thing with him. Anyway, you threatened to tell everyone his dick was the size of a number two pencil. I was impressed."

She laughed as Beau's horrified expression came back to her. "And you told him to leave me alone and then offered to buy me a soda. Never realized how thoughtful you were."

"Then why did it take you two months to go out with me?"

Leslie started the car. "Because I wanted to see how serious you were."

A bit rough around the edges, Derek reminded her a little of James Dean, with his bashful glances and soulful brown eyes. He was from, what some would call, "the wrong side of the tracks." The total opposite of the polished Beau Devereaux. But Leslie didn't care where he came from or how he dressed—Derek Foster was the most perfect boy in the universe. Cute, smart, and funny, when he'd finally asked her out, she hadn't wanted to ruin her daydreams of him with the disappointment of reality. But she'd taken a chance, and six months later, here they were.

A funny fluttering cascaded through her stomach with one glance at his contagious smile. "If I agree to go to the river, what did you want to do there?"

Derek sat back in his seat, his eyes on the road, his smile beaming. "I'll come up with something."

Chapter two

Beau sat on a wooden bench outside of Ms. Greenbriar's, aka *Madbriar's*, door in the austere administrative offices of the school. He tapped one finger methodically on his elbow while staring out the window as students rushed by in the hall.

He waited, keeping a lid on the anxiety rising up his spine.

The occasional stares of the other students did not bother him, but he needed to get to practice. Coach Brewer hated it when any of his players were late, and Beau made it a point never to show a lack of discipline. Next to his father, Coach Brewer was the only man whose anger he tried never to incur.

"Beau," Ms. Greenbriar called from her office.

He stood from the bench, raked his hand through his hair, and put on his best smile.

Once in the tiny room, jam packed with bookcases, he took in her crummy desk and outdated computer.

This will be fun.

"You want to tell me what that was about with Leslie Moore and Derek Foster?"

"I was speaking to Leslie when Derek came up. I accidentally hit him with my elbow when I turned around." He cleared his throat, turning his eyes to the floor. "I know how you feel about fighting, and I completely understand if you want to punish me for hitting Derek Foster."

Madbriar took a seat behind her cheap desk, her chair squeaking. "Relax, Beau. You're an exemplary student and an upstanding member of the community. No one is questioning your behavior." She sat back, staring at him for a moment. "I was wondering if you could tell your dad to give me a call when he can. I want to talk to him about having Benedict Brewery donate beer for the fundraiser the school is having for the new gym addition."

Beau folded his hands, keeping the tips of his index fingers together, a thrill of amusement running through him. Everyone always wanted something from him or his family. Being the town's biggest employer, his family was expected to donate to every fundraiser in St. Benedict. He sometimes wondered how his father put up with all the parasites.

"Sure. No problem. I will let him know, but he's always happy to help out."

She pointed at the office door. "Now, you'd better get to practice."

His tension eased, and he stood from the chair. Beau wanted to pat himself on the back for an impeccable performance.

"Thanks, Ms. Greenbriar."

"And Beau, do yourself a favor," she called when he reached the door. "Stay away from Leslie Moore."

He gripped the door handle, squeezing it with all his might.
"Ma'am?"

She picked up an open a folder "That girl is trouble. The kind you need to stay away from."

He nodded then hurried from her office, chuckling.
Trouble is my middle name.

* * *

A load lifted from Leslie's shoulders the moment she put the red-bricked walls of St. Benedict High School behind her. The place felt like a prison and made her stomach turn every time she pulled into the parking lot. She knew the reason—just the idea of running into his six-foot-two, muscular frame made her tremble. The months of putting up with Beau had taken their toll.

She relaxed her hands on the steering wheel, the cool afternoon breeze running through her hair as she drove toward Main Street.

She took in the rustic storefronts set between modern buildings. The hodgepodge of styles reminded her of the people in the town, an interesting blend of old families who had lived in St. Benedict for several generations, and new families running away from the urban sprawl taking over the larger nearby cities.

Derek reached over and gently touched her leg. "Why don't you like going to the river? You never told me."

Leslie glanced at a thick swath of honeysuckle vines on the side of the road, her unease returning.

"All you ever said was you went to the river with Dawn junior year, ran into Beau and his friends, and swore you'd never go back."

Leslie's shoulders drooped. "Dawn and I got invited to the river by some seniors. Being asked to party on the river at night was a big deal to me." Her stomach twisted. "Beau started out talking to me, and I knew he was interested, but Dawn didn't like that. So when I went to grab a beer, she stepped in and pretended she was me. She hit on Beau, hard. They hooked up and disappeared. I got stuck fighting off his football buddies who wanted to bring me to The Abbey and show me a good time."

Derek's face scrunched. "What did you do?"

Leslie raised her nose in the air, giving him her best snarky smirk. "I started spouting feminist literature and they ran for the hills."

Derek shook his head. "I bet that was a scary situation for you."

"It was." Her voice cracked. "When three guys start manhandling you, you want to run away. I tried to get Dawn to go with me, but she refused and stayed with Beau. So I headed back to the road and walked to town."

"At night?" His voice edged up. "That was dangerous, Leslie."

She took in the sunlight skipping over the tops of the buildings along the street. The smell of grilling hamburgers from Mo's Diner lingered in the air.

"Staying at the party was dangerous. A virgin hanging around a bunch of drunk and horny football players would only end badly."

Derek edged closer. "I don't want you to put yourself in that situation again. The only guy I want drunk and horny around you is me."

Leslie considered the inkling of possessiveness in his voice. "But you never try anything with me when you're drunk or horny."

He sat back. "That will change one day."

Near the edge of town, the buildings retreated and tall oak trees covered with Spanish moss replaced them. The gentle breeze ruffling the treetops eased her tension.

Leslie turned off Main Street and headed down Devereaux Road toward the remains of St. Francis Abbey.

Derek hooked his hand around her thigh. "I want your first time to be special. But that doesn't mean we can't fool around at The Abbey." He bobbed his eyebrows. "What do you say?"

She let her foot off the gas, slowing as the road narrowed, her sense of dread returning. "Are you sure you want to go to those ruins? The place is so eerie."

Derek flashed a boyish grin. "Hell yeah."

The trees around them dipped and the spires of St. Francis Abbey peeked out. The car cruised along the road and the ruins of the towering white marble and brick structure rose behind a patch of trees. A horrible chill enveloped her. Leslie slammed on the brakes, not wanting to go any farther.

Derek leaned in front of her. "Is something wrong?"

Tearing her gaze away from the ghastly structure, she sought refuge in his eyes and the feeling passed.

"Can we skip the tour of The Abbey? I don't think I'm in the mood."

"We can do whatever you want." He lightly kissed her lips. "I only want to make you happy."

* * *

The smell of sweat and freshly cut grass greeted Beau as he strutted onto the practice field in his jersey and warm-up sweats. He tightened his grip on his practice helmet. The team, already on the field, was in the middle of their stretches. He was late.

Coach Brewer, his protruding belly hanging over his gym shorts, walked between rows of guys, blowing his whistle to keep time with the exercises he insisted on before and after every practice.

Beau's attention drifted to the metal bleachers and the cheerleading squad working on their routine. Dawn was there, in a short, white cheerleading uniform accentuating her tiny waist. He loved how the bright red St. Benedict cougar hugged her breasts. The other girls on the squad, whose names eluded him, shouted their silly rhymes for victory and team spirit as Dawn watched them kick, split, and jump with enthusiasm.

She turned to the field and, spotting him, waved.

The wind caught her long blonde ponytail and brushed several strands over her shoulder, making it appear shorter like Leslie's. Though they were physically identical in every way except for their hair length, Beau wished Dawn was the smart-mouthed bitch he really wanted.

Before he could turn away, Dawn came running out to greet him. It was the last thing he needed. Coach Brewer would be pissed.

"Hey, baby." She frowned at him. "You okay? I heard Madbriar called you into her office."

Her voice wasn't Leslie's. He'd memorized the husky, sexy sound of her sister. The way she raised her tone ever so slightly when she was about to say something sarcastic. Dawn had none of Leslie's nuances—her voice was utterly lifeless. Unlike her sister, Dawn worked hard on portraying a wholesome image by avoiding cursing and smoking, which he admired. But her love of red lipstick and clumpy mascara aggravated him. He had told her more than once not to wear so much, but she didn't listen. She just put on more, thinking he liked it. Beau longed to wipe the color from her mouth, to make it clean and pure.

He gave her a warm smile, hiding his thoughts. "She wanted to talk to me about my father contributing to the gym fundraiser." He glanced at his buddies, who were warming up on the field.

"I heard it was because you were giving Derek and my sister a hard time."

He snapped back around to her. How dare she contradict him? "No way, baby." He laced his voice with extra charm to sound convincing. "Why would I waste my time on that loser Foster and your sister? I already have the sweetest Moore girl."

She squealed. Putty in his hands, Dawn melted against him, wrapping her arms around his neck.

"I knew it wasn't true," she whispered, nuzzling his cheek.

He smelled her skin. It wasn't there—the heady aroma of clover always lingering on Leslie. Another difference between them, but one he was sure only he noticed.

"Beau, get your ass over here," Coach Brewer yelled from the center of the field while walking between players.

"Gotta go." He unwound her arms from his neck. "See you after practice."

"I love you," Dawn barely managed to get out before he turned away.

He pretended not to hear her and hurried to the field while putting on his helmet.

Love wasn't what he was after with Dawn. He was saving that for someone far more deserving.

Chapter Three

Leslie turned her car down a tree-lined street composed of tired old homes, with peeling paint, sagging porches, and varying degrees of disrepair. It saddened her to see the residences crying for attention. One of the older neighborhoods in St. Benedict, the atmosphere reflected the work-weary attitude of the people struggling to hold on to their dreams.

She pulled into the cracked cement driveway of a familiar yellow wooden house. With a rusted tin roof, broken white picket fence, and bent mailbox, the residence mirrored others on the street. Despite its unsettling appearance, the home contained happy memories.

She shut off the engine. "Is your mom still working doubles at the diner?"

Derek shoved open his door. "Yes. Thank goodness."

Leslie got out of the car, astounded by his comment. "What makes you say that?"

He pointed to the bruise on his cheek. "You know how she feels about fighting. She's going to kill me when she sees my face."

"You can barely—"

The chug of an approaching engine cut off her reassurances.

A blue pickup truck, with a bent front fender and cracked windshield, pulled into the driveway alongside her car.

Leslie blocked out the sun with her hand, a sinking feeling settling over her. "I guess you're going to find out real fast."

"Thought I might beat you home." A waiflike brunette stepped out of the truck.

Leslie decided it was the polyester yellow waitress dress that made Carol Foster look a lot older than her forty-two years. It accentuated the deep crow's feet and circles rimming her eyes. She saw little of the pretty young girl her father told her once made the male hearts in St. Benedict beat faster.

Derek went to his mother's side and helped her unload the groceries from the back of the truck.

"What are you doing home early, Mom?"

"I got the afternoon off." Carol nodded to Leslie. "How have you been, dear?"

She went to Derek's side, nervous about what would happen. "I'm good, Mrs. Foster."

"I told you to call me Carol, sweetheart." She ambled up the drive next to her son. "No need for all the—" Her eyes honed in on her son's cheek. "What happened to your face?"

Leslie's insides clenched, and she winced.

Derek coolly kept going to the porch steps, ignoring his mother's reaction. "It's nothing."

"Nothing, my ass." Carol dashed up to him and turned his chin to get a closer look. "Who did this?"

He tugged his head away. "It was an accident. I ran into Beau's elbow."

Carol's cheeks paled. "Gage Devereaux's son? Why were you fighting with him?"

"I wasn't fighting." The dejection in Derek's voice cut across Leslie's heart. "He turned around and caught me with his elbow in the hall. No big deal."

Carol wheeled around to Leslie. "Were you there?"

Leslie cautiously approached, twisting her fingers as her guilt grew. "He was coming to my rescue."

"Your rescue?" Carol marched to the porch steps. "What did Beau do to you?"

Derek waited for Leslie to climb the steps before following her with the groceries.

"He's been stopping Leslie in the hall a lot lately. Saying upsetting things."

Carol's green eyes widened. "Beau Devereaux? Why would he pick on you?"

"Because he hates me." Leslie rolled her eyes, the sick feeling she got whenever thinking of Beau resurrected. "Always has, ever since the night he got with my sister. He keeps telling everyone he wants to be friends, but I don't buy it. The way he looks at me, the things he says … He doesn't want to be friends, not by a long shot."

Carol yanked her keys from her handbag. "Sounds like you need to steer clear of him, Leslie." She opened the front door, but it stuck halfway. Leaning her shoulder into the warped wood, she shoved hard to get the door to budge. "I've been meaning to fix this."

A single mother working twelve hours a day deserved a break, but Leslie didn't know how to help Derek or his mother. Getting ahead in St. Benedict took more than a strong work ethic; it took the good graces of the town patriarch, Gage Devereaux.

Leslie followed Carol and Derek inside. The sparsely furnished living room had a simple green sofa, a wobbly oak coffee table, and a cream oval rug covering the dull hardwood floors. The only new item was the flat screen TV mounted on the wall above the dusty mantle.

"I haven't cleaned." Carol ran her hand over her forehead, hiding her worry lines. "But you've seen the place messier than this."

Leslie put on a reassuring smile, her heart aching for the woman. "You should see my room. My mother's always complaining about it."

Carol set her five-gallon purse on a rickety, round table next to the kitchen. "And what about your sister? Do you two share your propensity for messy rooms?"

Leslie shook her head as she considered her sister's OCD-like ways. "No. Dawn is the perfect one. Her room is always spotless."

Derek took the groceries to the kitchen counter. "But her

personal life is a mess."

"That's not a kind thing to say." Carol slapped her son's shoulder, frowning at him.

"Why not?" Derek tossed the book bag from his shoulder to the kitchen counter. "She's well aware of how he feels about Leslie, but still, she says nothing to him."

"You don't know that." A pensive line across her lips, Carol went to the kitchen and flipped on the lights. "Right now, Dawn is caught up in having the attention of a guy she thinks is the catch of St. Benedict. Dating the football star and heir to the Devereaux fortune seems like a dream come true. She's probably afraid to speak up and risk losing him."

Carol's expression bothered Leslie. She sensed the woman was hiding something.

"You seem to know an awful lot about what Dawn is feeling, Missus ... I mean, Carol."

Carol lifted a milk from one of the grocery bags. "I was in your sister's shoes once."

Leslie swallowed hard. "You were?"

Derek removed eggs from a grocery bag. "Mom dated Gage Devereaux in high school. Didn't I tell you that?"

Leslie gave him a wide-mouthed *no you did not tell me that* look.

"So, what happened?" More than a little intrigued, Leslie moved into the kitchen. "Why aren't you the one living in their big plantation house outside of town?"

Carol tossed her head. "There isn't much to tell. Gage and I dated for a couple of years, and then we went off to separate colleges."

"That's when she met my dad." Derek put the eggs in the fridge. "After she quit college."

"Don't remind me." Carol sucked in a ragged breath. "We weren't even married two years when your father took off for California."

Derek shook his head and headed back to the counter to finish unpacking the grocery bags.

Leslie observed the interaction between mother and son. She knew Derek's father skipping town was a sore spot. He never talked about him. Her curiosity about Carol's past with the Devereaux family got the better of her.

"Is Beau like his father?"

A slight smile added a touch of warmth to Carol's sad eyes. "I don't know Beau, but Gage was very kind and considerate of other people. Even though he was the richest boy in town, he never acted like he was above anyone else." Her smile vanished. "I'm going to take a shower." Carol nodded to Leslie. "Good seeing you, sweetheart."

Derek waited until his mother disappeared down the narrow hall to her bedroom before he approached Leslie.

"Did she seem upset to you?" Leslie hooked her pinkie around his. "When I asked about Mr. Devereaux, she changed."

"Nah. She's upset about me getting hit. I'll get an earful after you're gone."

She rested her head against his chest, wishing she could stay, but she could hear her mother's voice in her head. "I should go. My mother wants me home for dinner."

Easing away from him, Leslie went to the freezer and found a pack of frozen peas. She returned to his side and gently pressed the bag against his bruised cheek.

"Keep this on for a few hours. I can't have my boyfriend walking around school and looking like the other guy won."

Leslie kissed his good cheek and scurried to the door. It took a stiff yank to open.

She strolled down the driveway, rehashing what she'd learned about Carol's connection to Beau's father. She knew there were secrets buried in their small town, especially about the Devereaux family. Hints about their nefarious past had circulated among the residents of St. Benedict as long as she could remember. But Carol's disclosure about her history with Gage Devereaux had not been one of those tales.

Images of Beau's father and Carol filled Leslie with a strange sense of foreboding. If Dawn continued dating Beau, would she end up like Derek's mother? A broken woman, struggling to survive.

The chill she'd experienced on the road to The Abbey resurfaced. She didn't know why, but the daunting thoughts about her sister's future made her think of the sinister spires of the abandoned abbey. Unnerved by the sensation, Leslie made a beeline to her car.

She backed out of the Fosters' driveway and decided to take the long way home, avoiding The Abbey altogether.

Chapter Four

The beauty of the sunlight filtering through the oaks lining Leslie's street offered a moment of distraction as she drove through her upper-middle-class neighborhood. Nestled in a quiet part of St. Benedict known as The Elms, her house wasn't far from the entrance to the lands owned by the Devereaux Estate.

Leslie pulled up to the three-car garage. She cringed when she looked at the clock on the dash.

Late again.

She grabbed her book bag and headed toward the back door, hoping her mom wouldn't be downstairs.

"You were supposed to be home ten minutes ago, Leslie Elise," Shelley shouted from the kitchen.

Leslie sighed and shut the garage door. "Yeah. Sorry."

Her mom rounded the corner, her honey-blonde hair back in a clasp.

No doubt about it. Shelley Moore could intimidate Satan himself if she wanted to.

Her mother's blue eyes sparkled with irritation. "You were at that boy's again, weren't you?"

Leslie scowled. "His name is Derek, Mom. Not *that boy*. I hate when you call him that."

"And I hate when he makes you late for dinner." Shelley pointed a spatula at her daughter, her lips nothing but a thin, angry line.

Leslie followed her mother into the kitchen. She crossed the threshold, her tennis shoes squeaking on the brick floor. She hiked her bag onto the counter with a heavy thump.

"I was only ten minutes late. It's not a big deal."

"We have rules for a reason." Her mother wielded the spatula again, pointing it at Leslie like a sword. "And you know better. Books on the floor, not the counter."

Leslie deposited her bag next to the breakfast bar. "Where's Dawn?"

"Not home from cheerleading practice yet." Shelley carried a bowl of vegetables to the table in the open dining room.

Leslie gritted her teeth. "Is Beau bringing her home?"

"Of course. You know he always brings her home after practice."

Great. The princess gets to be driven home by her asshole boyfriend and I get crap for spending ten extra minutes with mine.

A few choice curse words slipped from Leslie's lips.

"What was that, young lady?"

"Nothing. Dad home yet?"

Shelley pointed her spatula to the family room next to the kitchen. "In his office. Go tell him it's time for dinner."

Leslie hurried through the family room toward her father's office. She knocked and gingerly pushed the door open.

Soft overhead lights stretched across a paper-strewn desk. His head bowed in concentration, John Moore's slight frown told her he wasn't happy with what he read. A stack of manila folders lay neatly on the corner of his mahogany desk, each representing a case.

Leslie leaned against the doorframe and smiled. The only attorney in St. Benedict, she couldn't remember a time when he had not been working on a case.

"Hey, Dad."

John glanced up from the file, his glasses slightly askew.

"What are you working on?"

He ran his hand through his thinning hair and leaned back, resting his head against the leather seat. "I'm finishing up one of the contracts for the brewery."

Lately, he'd been working a lot for Gage Devereaux's company.

Benedict Brewery was on the verge of breaking nationally, which meant a lot of late nights for her dad.

"How was school? Did you have a good day, Leelee?"

She smiled at the nickname. All her life she'd been Leelee to him, never Leslie. "School was good." She slouched her shoulders. "Well, not good. Beau hit Derek."

John set his glasses on his desk. "Why? Is he okay?"

"He claims it was an accident, but Derek's got a bruise on his cheek." She rested her hip on the corner of the desk. "Daddy, can you sue Beau or something on Derek's behalf? Emotional cruelty or perhaps assault?"

John folded his hands on his desk, a deep crease spreading across his brow. "You know the law. Derek has to file charges, or at least seek compensation. Were any charges filed?"

She shook her head. "No. Ms. Greenbriar took Beau to the office, but I doubt she will do anything to him."

He sighed. "And I doubt Carol Foster would pursue any legal fight with the Devereaux family."

Leslie perked up, intrigued. "Why? Because she dated Beau's father in high school?"

John narrowed his gaze, appearing somewhat menacing. "Where did you hear that?"

"Mrs. Foster told me a little about it. I got the impression Mr. Devereaux meant something to her."

John picked up his glasses, redirecting his focus to his paperwork. "They were very close in high school. I remember seeing them holding hands everywhere they went, but everyone knew the Devereauxs never liked Carol."

She scooted up on his desk, hoping to distract him. "Why not?"

John hesitated, staring into his daughter's eyes. "Her father was the brewery foreman at the time, and they were uncomfortable with their son dating the daughter of an employee. I'm sure they discouraged the relationship."

A whole new perspective on the Devereaux family popped into Leslie's head. She'd always thought of them as stuck up and pretentious, sort of like her mother, but had never considered them cruel.

Concern for Dawn weighed on her. "Do you think they will do that with Dawn? I mean, you work for the brewery like Mrs. Foster's father."

He chuckled, and his brown eyes lit up. "No, sweetie. Things are different now."

"Are they? Mom wants me to stay away from Derek because she's a snob and doesn't think he's good enough for me."

"I heard that." Shelley barged into the room. "And just because I don't like your boyfriend, young lady, does not make me a snob."

Leslie stuck out her chin. "Then what other justification do you have for the demeaning remarks directed at my boyfriend, Mother?"

Shelley angrily squinted at her husband. "You see what your influence has done? Now she's even talking like a lawyer."

John held up his hands. "Don't drag me in the middle of this. It's your argument, not mine."

Shelley folded her arms, smirking exactly like Dawn. "After raising twin girls, I think I'm better at winning arguments than you'll ever be."

John scanned the paperwork on his desk. "I have no doubts about that."

"Ah, hello!" Leslie stood and waved her hand, angrily redirecting her parents' focus to her. "I still have a question awaiting an answer."

"Oh, for God's sake." Shelley turned for the office door. "Dinner is ready," she announced before heading out of the room.

"Why does she always do that?" Frustrated, Leslie folded her arms and plopped down on the corner of his desk. "I ask a question, and she totally ignores me. But Little Miss Perfect can ask a question about the weather in Cleveland and Mom will give her a three-page report, complete with pie charts and a website."

"Leelee." His voice softened as he rose from his chair. "Don't you think you're exaggerating?"

"No, I'm not. She hates Derek just because he's not all rich and popular like Beau. But she won't even get to know him. She never lets him come over, or even bothers to talk to his mom. And whenever I want to go out with him on a date, I have to give her an itinerary, ten personal contacts, and a freakin' urine sample."

John chuckled. "Your mother has her faults, but she isn't that bad."

"Then why does Little Miss Goody Two-Shoes get to go everywhere with Beau while I get to face an interrogation just to go out for pizza with Derek?"

He stood from his chair. "Because your mother knows Beau. Knows his family, and she feels comfortable with him." He held up his hands before she could shout a reply. "He's known as an upstanding kid."

Her hopes of ever getting her mother's approval for Derek sank like a stone in a shallow pond. "And what about Derek? What do I do to make her see what a good guy he is?"

"I'm sure she will come around. You know how resistant she is to change, just like your sister." He patted her shoulder. "Give her some time."

Leslie pouted, doubting her mother would warm up to Derek. "Didn't you ever want to spend time with your girlfriend in high school? I'm not talking about having sex, Dad, just hanging out."

John rubbed his forehead. "Leelee, please. You're going to give me a heart attack. The idea of either you or your sister—"

"Hey, Daddy." Dawn bounded into the room. "I can't wait to tell you what happened to me at school today."

"Aaaaand I'm outta here." Leslie stood and headed for the

door.

Dawn frowned at her sister. "What's up your butt?"

Leslie spun around. They looked so alike yet were so different on the inside. While they had been inseparable when they were little, somewhere along the way they had grown apart. Now she didn't even know Dawn anymore. Beau had driven a wedge between them as wide as the Grand Canyon. Why bother telling her what Beau had done? She wouldn't believe her.

"Nothing's up my butt."

Dawn rocked her hip to the side, frowning just like their mother. "Is this about Beau and Derek going at it today? Just so you know, my boyfriend told me what happened. You were flirting with him in the hall. Derek got jealous and then accidentally walked into Beau's elbow."

Leslie's fury heated her cheeks. "You little toad! Why in the hell would I want a scumbag like Beau when I have Derek?"

"Girls," John edged in.

"You're kidding, right? Beau is so much more than the loser you're dating."

John's voice rose higher. "Girls!"

"Derek's not a loser!" Leslie got right in Dawn's face. "He's got a better GPA than your Neanderthal and will make something of himself one day."

"What's going on in here?" Shelley burst through the door.

Dawn pointed at Leslie. "She called my boyfriend a Neander … something."

Leslie crossed her arms. "Neanderthal, you idiot."

Shelley rushed between the two girls. "Enough. There will be no name calling in this house. Between each other or of Beau Devereaux."

Leslie scoffed. "And what about Derek? I can't call Beau names, but she can make fun of my boyfriend? That's not fair."

"She has a point, hon." John eyed his wife.

"You're not helping," Shelley grumbled, and then shifted her focus to Leslie. "I think you could learn from your sister's example. Dawn has a future with Beau. What do you have with that … that boy?"

Gutted, Leslie trudged toward the door. Her mother just didn't get it. She stopped halfway across the hardwood floor and glanced back at her mother.

"You're unbelievable."

She sniffled as she crossed the room.

Would it even matter to her mom if she knew all the horrid things Beau had said to her? The torment she'd suffered for months? If she said anything, her mother would twist it around and she would end up shouldering the blame. Leslie couldn't stomach that. So, she would keep her mouth shut, no matter how much it ate at her.

"What about dinner?" Shelley's voice echoed behind Leslie.

"I've lost my appetite."

She ran up the steps, anxious for the sanctuary of her bedroom.

Chapter Five

Beau strolled down the elegant curved mahogany staircase. He stepped onto the hardwood floors and caressed the newel post at the end of the steps. Shaped like the head of a horse, the bit pulled taut in its mouth, he admired the pain carved into the creature's bulging eyes.

He headed along the hallway, tugging his book bag over his shoulder, the occasional moan of the floor echoing around him. He glanced at a massive gold painting of New Orleans he liked, bought by some dead relative a century ago. Family portraits of other deceased members of the Devereaux clan littered the white wainscoting covered walls. He passed the tall cypress door to his father's office, not bothering to check inside. His old man was an early riser and probably on his way to the brewery.

At the end of the hall, he turned down a slender corridor to the kitchen and the entrance to the five-car garage. He enjoyed the quiet in the morning after his father went to work and before his mother crawled out of bed. It made him feel like it was all his, for a little while anyway.

In the kitchen, Beau went around the beaten copper-covered breakfast bar to the refrigerator.

His father appeared, holding a coffee mug.

Beau froze, almost afraid to move when he spotted him.

Gage Devereaux rested his hip against the black granite countertop. Tilting his head slightly, he inspected his son. In his usual attire—a long-sleeved shirt and slacks—he came across more like a casual businessman than a ruthless capitalist. Except for their height and physical prowess, Beau felt he had nothing in common with his father.

He attempted to relax by shifting his book bag on his shoulder. "Didn't expect to find you still home."

Gage set his mug on the counter. "I wanted to speak to you before you left for school."

The hint of condescension in his father's voice tightened his chest—it usually signaled a lecture.

"I got a call from Ms. Greenbriar yesterday afternoon. She said you visited her office after a run-in you had with Carol Foster's boy."

Beau's fingers twitched, the way they did when his aggravation got the better of him. Great. The idiot woman had called his father. The last thing he needed was Gage Devereaux up his ass.

"Derek is dating Dawn's sister, so I often see him at school." He tempered the irritation in his voice, not wanting to annoy his father. "I was talking to Leslie when Derek walked up. I accidentally caught him with my elbow when I turned around. I apologized and everything is fine."

He waited, analyzing every move his father made, searching his hard eyes for an inkling of his mindset.

"I've spoken to you before about this." Gage came around the breakfast bar. "This family is in a precarious position with everyone in town. I don't want your actions threatening our business or our good name." He gripped Beau's shoulder. "What have I always told you? What is our rule?"

Beau cringed as the words he'd spent a lifetime dreading screamed through his head. He faced his father, standing at attention. "Self-control in all things. Never let anyone see who you really are."

Gage leaned closer. "No matter what anyone says, no matter what they do, you walk away. This includes your girlfriend. Do you understand?"

Beau stiffened at the low, menacing tone in his father's voice. "Yes, sir."

Gage lifted the left side of his mouth ever so slightly. "Go to school."

Beau stood by the breakfast bar, not moving a muscle as his father headed to the garage. The door clicked shut and a trickle of sweat ran down his temple. His jaw muscles cramped from clenching, his heart rate slowed, and he glanced at his fists. His father's warning spinning in his head, Beau slammed his hand down on the copper bar.

Anger like molten lead ran through him. Beau sucked in deep breaths to calm himself—something he remembered from a long-ago therapy session. Then he relaxed his hand on the bar, checking the dent he'd left in the copper. He wiped the smudge away, stepped back, and raised his head.

I am the master of control.

* * *

Low clouds fat with rain hugged the sky above the student parking lot. Beau turned at the chain-link fence surrounding the lot and eased his silver BMW onto the blacktop. His father's words in his head, he tightened his grip on the steering wheel as he pulled into his usual spot beneath a shady oak.

Students milled around, chatting and laughing. A few guys tossed a football over the tops of cars. It was a relaxed and playful atmosphere, just what he needed to dispel the last remnants of his father's warning.

Beau spied Leslie and Dawn's white Honda pulling into the lot and grinned. Leslie was driving, as usual.

Dawn was out of the car as soon as it stopped. He waited until he saw her heading to the steps of the main entrance before he opened his door.

Leslie took her time getting her books from the back of her car, and he studied her movements, intrigued how she kept pushing a stray hair behind her ear.

She's nervous. Could it be I'm getting to her?

Beau enjoyed seeing her this way. It made him feel as if he had some mastery over her, giving him hope for more in the future. He stayed in the shade, clenching his fists as Leslie clutched the bag to her chest. Her head down, she walked toward the side entrance to the school.

Here was his chance.

He jogged across the green quad as a clap of thunder shook the air. Leslie stopped at the door, searching her book bag for something, giving him enough time to reach her.

She had left her hair down, just caressing her slim shoulders, and her light blue blouse set off the paleness of her skin.

She raised her head from her book bag and veered left, heading back to the parking lot, and ran smack into him.

He gripped her arm to keep her from falling over, enjoying the opportunity to touch her soft skin.

"Whoa, hey there." He kept his voice deep and seductive. "Just the girl I've been waiting for."

Her full, unpainted lips turned down. Beau pulled her close against his chest.

Leslie jerked her arm, trying to break free. He dug his fingers into her tender flesh.

He loved the fight in her. It made him feel alive.

"What's wrong, darlin'?"

"You're scum, Beau. You know that?"

As a few students rounded the corner, Beau let go of her arm and stepped back. A group of sophomore girls passed by, and he made sure to give them a dazzling smile. They giggled and quickly slipped in the side entrance.

Leslie pushed past him, heading toward the door, but he placed his hand on the side of the building, blocking her.

He leaned in, taking in the sweet smell of her. "What's wrong,

Leslie?"

She arched away from him. "Leave me alone."

"Why? What have I done?" He feasted his eyes on her figure, lingering on her breasts. "I would never think of harming anyone close to my girl. You know that."

Leslie glared at him, her blue eyes on fire. But before she could respond, Dawn ran up and got between them.

"Back off, Leslie."

Her low growl surprised Beau. *Where had she been hiding that?* Beau slipped his arm around Dawn's waist, eager to let her know she was his.

"I think you need to set your sister straight, baby. If I didn't know better, I'd swear she's mad at me about something."

Leslie shook her finger at him. "Stay away from Derek, Beau."

He flashed a brilliant smile; the one he used to get out of trouble, especially with female teachers. "I think you need to check your facts, counselor. I don't give a rat's ass about your geek boyfriend."

Dawn curled into his chest, her strong perfume stinging his eyes.

"See?" She did everything but stick her tongue out at Leslie. "He doesn't give a rat's hiney about Derek. So just drop it."

Beau hated the childish approach Dawn used with her sister, but it proved to him he had nothing to worry about when it came to her loyalties. That was good. The bigger the divide between them, the closer he could get to Leslie.

Beau took Dawn's book bag from her shoulder. "We on for the river Friday night? It's only gonna be a great party if you're there."

"The river is lame." Leslie tossed her bag over her shoulder. "All everybody does there is drink and screw around."

Her condemnation of the river stoked Beau's hostility. His nails dug into the strap of Dawn's bag. How dare she bash the one place he had total freedom?

"I think you have the wrong idea about what goes on at the river. We just hang out and have fun. There's no parents to annoy us, no rules to follow. We can do what we want without anyone telling us we're too loud or too wild." He rolled his neck, relieving the tension created by Leslie's presence. "I think you would enjoy yourself."

She shook her head. "No thanks."

Dawn smirked at her. "Leslie's creeped out by The Abbey. She never wants to go to the river because of it. Doesn't even like me talking about the place."

Leslie, with her wide stance and tightly pressed lips, reminded Beau of an Amazon warrior. Dawn had obviously hit a nerve, and he could guess why.

He sensed an opportunity. His heart sped up at the prospect of adding to her fears.

"Are you talking about the ghost?"

Dawn snickered, grating on his nerves. "What ghost?"

Beau kept his attention focused on Leslie while he spoke, eager to take in her terrified expression. "The lady in white. She wears a white-hooded cloak and haunts The Abbey grounds. Some say she appears when something bad is going to happen, but others think she's the lost love of a priest who lived at the seminary. You have to be careful in The Abbey. She's also said to take revenge on those who cause harm."

Thunder rolled across the sky and both girls flinched. He couldn't have asked for better timing, but their frightened reactions fascinated him. If only he could recreate the fear in their faces—what a turn on.

Dawn was the first to break the spell, slapping his arm and giggling. "Beau. Cut it out." She took his hand and pulled him toward the door. "Let's get to class."

He let Dawn lead him away, but not before glancing back at the reason for all his misery.

* * *

Leslie stared as her sister and Beau walked away, holding hands. She hated seeing Dawn manipulated by the sadistic shit. But how he acted one way with her and another with her sister disturbed her even more. Why couldn't Dawn see it?

Lightning raked across the sky, and she headed inside, spooked by the weather and Beau's eerie story. Leslie had watched his expression as he told the tale about the ghost. He'd almost seemed to enjoy her fear. But why?

Inside, students casually strolled through the gray locker-filled hallway, chatting and checking their phones. Leslie's cell buzzed in her back pocket. She grabbed it as she shifted her bag.

A text appeared on the screen.

Running late. Love.

A warm blanket of emotion wrapped around her and chased away the anxiety Beau had caused. Since dating Derek, Beau's choking effect on her had lessened. Knowing she had Derek to talk to, hold, and share her concerns with helped tremendously.

Once past the chemistry lab, the students in the hall thinned. Before she went to her first-period class, she sent off a quick text to Derek.

She wasn't paying attention to her surroundings when someone grabbed her from behind. Heart pounding, Leslie dropped her phone, and images of Beau made her cock her arm back to confront him with a quick punch to the throat. She spun around, ready to face him, when Derek smiled at her.

She almost crashed to her knees. Leslie sucked in a few deep breaths, overcome with the realization of what her encounters with Beau had done to her.

I'm losing it.

"Hey!" He held up his hands, eyeing her tight fist. "What is it?"

Leslie unclasped her hand. "I thought you were someone else."

He retrieved her phone from the floor. "Who else would be grabbing you in the middle of the hallway?"

Leslie took her phone, debating what to say. She didn't want to tell Derek how shaken she was. It would only make him go after Beau, and that was the last thing she wanted.

"I ran into Beau this morning." She touched the bruise on his cheek, glad it had not turned black and ugly. "It's looking better."

"Never mind about that." Derek took her hand. "What happened with Beau?"

The tension in his voice made up her mind. She couldn't share her fears with him or anyone. She had to keep Derek safe and not break her sister's heart, no matter how much it killed her to let Beau get away with his bullying.

"Nothing happened. He just pulled his usual crap. I can handle it."

"That guy has some sick obsession with you."

She waved off Derek's concerns. "He's dating my sister, so how could he have an obsession with me?"

Derek took her elbow and urged her along the hall. "Who knows? Maybe he hates that you're smart, independent, and the complete opposite of Dawn."

"Or he just has a sick fantasy of doing twins." She tucked her head against his chest. "Isn't that what all you guys want?"

"Guess again." He stopped outside her English classroom door. "I have you, and I would rather jump off a bridge than spend ten minutes with your sister." He kissed her cheek just as the first bell rang.

A frenzy of activity erupted as the shouts of students, bang of lockers, and the squeak of tennis shoes signaled the last-minute chaos before class.

Derek smiled at her before joining the mad rush for first-period.

He disappeared behind a sea of students, but the peace he brought to her, and the happiness he rallied in her heart, eased her apprehensions about Beau Devereaux.

Chapter Six

The final bell rang, and the front doors burst open. A wave of students poured out of the school. Caught up in the tide, Leslie went with the flow until they reached the bottom of the stairs, and the students sprawled onto the quad. The clouds had vanished, and the afternoon sun filtered down on the side of the building. She stepped toward the wall, anxious to soak up some warmth and wait for the crowds to thin.

Behind the school was the recently renovated athletic field. New metal stands lined the oval track, which encircled the turfed football field. All a generous gift from Beau's family during his freshman year—along with the announcer's booth and updated state-of-the-art video equipment.

Leslie kicked off the wall and stood, adjusting the weight of her books. She used to enjoy going to the games and watching her sister cheer, but everything had changed the first time Beau had cornered her after his first night at the river with Dawn. He confessed he had slept with the wrong Moore girl.

Your sister is a cheap imitation of the girl I really want, he'd said in his smoky voice.

For months she had kept quiet about his offensive comments. Her sister would never believe what a sick shit Beau was after so much time, and the rest of the school viewed him as the perfect catch. What in the hell was she going to do?

A loud bang to her left startled her. A handful of guys dressed in red football jerseys and gray warm-ups rushed out of the gym. Hollering and giving each other high fives, the players jogged to the field for their afternoon practice.

Leslie searched the jerseys looking for number four—Beau's number. She had it memorized after all the times Dawn had gone on about him.

"Isn't he the greatest guy," her sister used to say after every home game.

Coach Brewer, wearing his usual shorts, high tube socks, and St. Benedict Athletic Department knit shirt, trotted down the steps with a player at his side.

His gravely laugh resonated between the school building and the field. He patted his player's shoulder and his smile seemed sincere.

Then she noticed the number four on the back of the jersey. Leslie pressed against the wall, desperate not to be spotted.

Beau's attention remained on his coach, and as the two men hit the edge of the field, other players came up to them. They all laughed with Beau, knocked his shoulder pads and appeared genuinely friendly.

To Leslie, it was just another example of the Beau other people saw and not the one who haunted her day and night.

Arms wrapped around her and scooped her into the air. Derek's musky scent engulfed her, and Leslie tilted her head, giving him access to his favorite spot on her neck.

He nuzzled the soft hollow. "Let's get out of here."

"Great idea." Leslie took his hand, threading her fingers through his.

They crossed the green grass to the parking lot and wove through the remaining cars. She hit the remote on her keys, and her little car's headlights flashed as if it was glad to see them.

The stress of her day evaporated when she got behind the wheel. She turned over the engine, anxious to get away from the school.

Once out of the parking lot, she headed toward Main Street. "Where do you want to go?"

Derek leaned over and grinned. "Somewhere we can be alone.

How 'bout The Abbey?"

Beau's words came back to haunt her, and Leslie's knuckles whitened as she gripped the wheel.

"Did you get any applications in yet?" She stopped at a red light.

"Yeah. Two." He avoided her eyes. "One from LSU and the other from USL."

She frowned as she met his gaze. "None from out of state?"

Derek rubbed the back of his neck. "I'm not sure out of state would be a good fit for me."

"But you talked about going to UT in Austin before. It's your dream college."

"The cost will be twice what staying in state would be. If I stay close, I could come home on weekends and check on Mom. I hate to leave her alone for too long."

A car honked behind them, and Leslie glanced at the green light. She waved an apology and started through the intersection. "Maybe we could go to LSU. They have a great law program. We could even get a place together and save on expenses."

"No way. We're not living together until we're engaged. I've got my reputation to consider."

"If that's how you feel, Mr. Foster."

He playfully slapped her thigh. "Just wait until I get you to The Abbey. I'll make you pay for that."

Anxiety nipped at her. She couldn't keep refusing to go to The Abbey with him. Derek would want to know why she feared the place so much, and eventually, she would spill the beans about Beau and his taunting about taking her there. Leslie had to protect him and there was only one way to do that.

Suck it up and go.

She glimpsed the picturesque shop windows displaying everything from clothes to baked goods to art. The quaint, small-town charm of Main Street was occasionally interrupted by modern, sprawling structures, such as the new drugstore and Rouse's grocery.

She turned off Main and headed along the single lane road. The storefronts gave way to homes with bright gardens and oaks draped with tendrils of Spanish moss. Then the homes grew sparse and disappeared as greenery hugged the side of the road. Leslie slowed to avoid a pothole and heard the rush of the Bogue Falaya River through her open windows.

The trees thinned, revealing the two stone spires of The Abbey. Apprehension snaked through her as she pictured Beau, her sister, and all the unsettling things she associated with the derelict church.

A wall of dense red buckeye bushes swaying in the breeze shrouded a gravel path. Leslie finagled her car onto the path, weaving between an opening someone carved out long ago. A cleared, gravel lot lay hidden beyond the dense hedge, surrounded by thick pines and oaks with paths leading down a steep embankment to the river's edge.

The lot served the visitors who came to this spot in the summer months to visit the river for tubing, swimming, and small watercraft fun. Many parts of the river could barely accommodate a canoe, but the portion at the bend was wide, shallow, and offered a great place for families to gather.

Leslie climbed from her car, listening to the sweet refrain of the birds in the trees. "No cars here today."

"It's still too early. Everyone from school likes to come after dark."

He took her hand and led her to one of the pine straw-covered paths heading to the shore of the rushing river.

Something moved in the dense underbrush to the side of the lot. Leslie went ahead, trying to get a better look.

"What's that?" She crossed several broken branches until she stumbled on something nestled in the foliage. The stench of rotting flesh hit her nose. She gagged and slowed to a stop.

"Wait, Leslie, be careful." Derek came to her side and swept aside a few leafy twigs to get a better look.

Flies covered the bloated belly of a white-tailed deer, its head at an odd angle. Deep grooves slashed into what was left of the deer's neck. The poor animal's hindquarters had been completely torn away.

Derek grabbed her shoulder. "Don't get too close."

Leslie crept closer. "What did that?"

Derek covered his mouth. "This animal was taken down by a large pack. There are hundreds of bite marks."

"What could do such a thing?"

He took her hand and backed out of the brush. "I bet it was the wild dogs."

Leslie let him lead her away from the stench. "What wild dogs?"

He stopped outside of the brush. "They're around here. A couple of weeks ago, Mom said some hunters came in the diner and reported seeing them."

"Where did the dogs come from?" Leslie's voice shook.

Derek guided her to a path curving down a long slope. Up ahead, the rush of the river grew louder.

"There are lots of stories. I heard they were left behind when the priests abandoned The Abbey and the seminary school around it. Legend has it, when you see them, death is near."

A strong shudder ran through her.

Derek tugged Leslie's hand. "Come on."

The path widened, and a beach came into view. The outcropping of white sand had a collection of green picnic tables, red barrel trash cans, and a few black fire pits along the rivers' edge. Around the beach, thick brush covered the shore with limbs from pine trees dipping into the water. The sun snuck in through the gaps in the canopy and sparkled on the gentle waves in the river.

"This way."

Leslie followed him along the shoreline until they came to a rusted iron gate with a *No Trespassing* sign secured to it. Decorated with crosses and swirls, the sign marked the entrance to The Abbey grounds. Stepping through the open gate, she peered up at the imposing structure.

Two spires of white limestone, shaped like the tip of a sword, cut into the blue sky. The structure of red brick and limestone, the front windows and doors secured with loose scraps of plywood, sat in the middle of a field of high grass. The squat stone building of cloisters behind The Abbey remained intact. The Benedictine monks who had run the seminary school demolished the dormitories, refectory, and library after the site had been abandoned.

"Some place, huh?" Derek let go of her hand and trudged his way across the high grass.

Leslie's apprehension bloomed in her chest. The grounds, unkempt after years of neglect, were a hodgepodge of weeds, overgrown trees, and green vines. On the way across the thigh-high grass, they passed a beautiful triple-tiered fountain with an angel on top, raising her arms to the heavens—a silent witness to the past.

How do people come here at night?

"You ever wonder why those priests just up and left it?" she asked, uncomfortable with the eerie quiet. Even the birds had stopped singing. "I know everyone in town says they got a better offer from the seminary in New Orleans, but it seems funny a bunch of people abandoned the place for no reason."

"They left because it's a wreck." Derek parted a thick pile of tall grass with his shoe. "My mom told me it was falling apart when she was a kid, and the Archdiocese didn't have the money to fix it. So they packed up the seminary school, the priests, and all the staff and shipped them to New Orleans."

"Seems a shame, though. I read once that the structure dates back to the early 1800s when the Devereaux family built it as a private church." Leslie eyed the frame of the empty belfry atop one of the square-shaped towers. "You'd think they'd want to save it."

Derek nudged her with his elbow. "Maybe the ghost drove the priests away."

Beau's tale had been in the back of her head the whole time, but Derek's comment spooked the crap out of her. "By ghost, do you mean the lady in white?"

"Yep." He scanned the land around them. "They say she wears a glistening white cloak and wanders the priests' cells. She only appears when the moon is full or during storms."

The thought of being alone in such a disturbing place terrified her. "Have you ever seen the ghost?"

Derek searched the thick foliage ahead of them. "Nah. I've come here a few times with Mark and Andrew to hang out, but we've never seen anything."

Granite steps rose out of the high grass as they drew near the entrance.

Leslie kicked herself for letting him talk her into coming to the remote location. "What about the wild dogs? Have you seen them around The Abbey?"

"Not to worry, baby. I'll protect you from ghosts, wild dogs, and Beau Devereaux." He climbed the granite steps, encouraging her to join him. "But I have to draw the line at your mother. There's no way I'm taking her on in a fight."

On the porch, beneath the cracked and chipped stone arch over the front doors, she waited while Derek wrestled with the plywood covering the entrance. She scanned the landscape, searching for any hint of trouble. But despite the creep factor, the lush green trees encircling them did have a soothing effect. Leslie breathed in the fresh pine scent and mossy aroma of the tall grass. Then a fly zipped past her face.

Thud.

She spun around to the source of the noise. Derek had pushed one of the large pieces of plywood securing the door out of the way, leaving a nice sized gap to crawl through.

"How did you do that?"

Derek held the plywood to the side for her. "The loose boards have been rigged to open easily. Found out about it the first time I came out here with Mark."

Leslie dipped her head and looked through the doorway. "You sure it's safe?"

His smile won over her fears.

"Baby. I wouldn't bring you here if it wasn't."

Leslie gave him one last smirk and then stepped inside.

It took a few moments for her eyes to adjust. The first thing she saw were pinpoints of light on a floor covered with clumps of debris. She raised her head to the source. In the roof, thousands of holes, some big and some small, littered the space between the bare beams where parts of plaster had fallen away. Birds' nests of light-colored hay and twigs nestled against blackish beams, shadowy eaves, and were tucked in murky archways, creating a patchwork design on the ceiling, reminding her of the quilt her grandmother made for her as a child.

Derek appeared, shining a beam of light down on the floor.

She pointed to the flashlight in his hand. "Where did you get that?"

"I told you, me and the guys have been here a few times. We've stashed stuff around the place. We've even got a sleeping bag and a couple bottles of water socked away."

Here she was a nervous wreck, and his friends had turned it into their personal campground. Leslie's skin crawled at the idea of spending the night in such a place.

"I don't know how you guys can come here."

He took her hand and the flashlight beam bounced on the dusty floor. "I don't know why you're so freaked out about being here. It's just an old building. There's nothing sinister about it."

Perhaps not with the building, but ...

Beau's words about bringing her to the remote location sent a shiver down her spine. Any girl would be at his mercy in such a place. She questioned her sister's choices, knowing she'd been there with

Beau. Had she been afraid? Did she regret her decision?

Leslie doubted she would ever discover the truth. She and her sister had a propensity for keeping their troubles locked away.

The flashlight illuminated their way across the floor, shining on dozens of rotted pews, leaves, twigs, crumbled plaster pieces from the ceiling, and a few skeletons of dead birds. "There are lots of animals using this place as a shelter. I've seen possums, raccoons, deer, and once, Mark and I swore we saw a black leopard running out the back as we came in."

The disclosure made Leslie feel even more uneasy about being in the building. "You wouldn't happen to have a shotgun in your stash."

"The animals don't bother me, just the people."

Their footfalls echoing through the vast structure, they ventured farther. Expecting someone or something to jump out from the shadows, Leslie's heart raced. Her only distraction was the intricate carvings on the walls and atop the arches. Men and angels exchanging timid glances as rays of light from parting clouds shined down on their interactions.

Paintings of Noah and the flood, Adam and Eve, and other Genesis stories were barely visible on the white plaster covering the arches along the central aisle. In one spot, where the roof remained intact, she could make out the image of Moses carrying the Ten Commandments. His eyes stood out the most. It was like they carried the burning wrath of God.

Shivering, Leslie looked ahead to a white archway, marking the entrance to the altar. The gleam of the limestone appeared pristine. She got closer to the most sacred part of the old church, and her sense of dread rose. The hairs on the back of her neck rose, and she gasped, spinning around to face the open floor of scattered, rotting pews behind them.

"What is it?" Derek asked, taking her hand.

His voice rattled inside the hollows of the church, adding to her anxiety. They stood under the circular dome where the altar had once been, and then a soft low growl came from one of the shadowy corners.

The air left her lungs; her insides clenched in terror.

What was that?

Her senses heightened, seconds ticked by while she listened for any other sounds.

"Tell me you heard that?"

Derek raised his finger to his lips and nodded to a door on his left.

She wanted to run for the door but followed his lead, slowly moving across the debris-laden floor, careful not to snap any twigs or make a noise. Leslie cursed her decision to come.

She held her breath as he reached for the rusted doorknob. It turned and, fortunately, the old warped door gave way without a creek. Once they were on the other side, Derek gently shut it.

Her heartbeat slowed, and she relaxed her shoulders while letting out a breath. "What in the hell was that?"

"Wild dog, maybe? I don't know." He put his ear to the door. "I've never heard anything in there before."

"Maybe we should go."

"I'm not going back through the church." Derek glanced around the short hallway, brandishing his flashlight. "We can get out through here." He motioned with the beam down a narrow corridor. "There's an opening up ahead."

Leslie clung to him, wishing they were outside. "What is this place?"

"The cells." Derek kept his voice low.

She squeezed his bicep. "I've never been inside The Abbey." Leslie peered into the dim, cavernous corridor ahead, with only patches of light coming through the thick stone walls. "I wish we hadn't come."

"It will be fine, I promise." He patted her hand. "Nothing will hurt you. I won't let it."

They crept along, their feet hitting sticks and fallen pieces of plaster from the crumbling walls around them. Puddles of water dotted the uneven stone floor and dampened Leslie's tennis shoes. Mounds of dead leaves lay swept to the side. The low ceiling had roots coming through it, and the walls were cold and slimy to the touch. Derek shined his flashlight into the first room on the left. It was a depressingly small space composed of four walls and no windows.

It reminded Leslie of a jail cell rather than a place where a person would choose to live.

Scraps of paper littered the ground of the next cell they came across; another had a rusty metal frame of a bed. Several of the rooms had cracks in their plaster ceilings along with patches of mold. When they stumbled on a few rat skeletons, Leslie turned her head into Derek's shoulder.

At the end of the passageway, sunlight snuck through a break in the wall. The intrusion of light was a welcome sight and Leslie's fear abated. The jagged opening allowed green leaves from the plants outside to reach in, and a few creeping vines jutted up toward the ceiling. Along the floor, a thick pile of dead leaves hid the lower part of the opening.

"There was a cave-in along the wall here." Derek brushed the leaves aside, revealing a fairly large breach able to accommodate one person at a time. "The other cells past this point are too dangerous to explore. We can get out here and avoid going back through The Abbey."

Derek turned off his flashlight and handed it to her. He pushed the leaves back, pulled the vines down, and kicked the debris at the bottom away, trying to clear the opening.

While he worked, a glimmering light from inside one of the cells farther down the corridor distracted her. She flipped on the flashlight and angled it into the tight quarters beyond the cave-in.

The walls in this portion of the cells had deeper cracks than the rest of the structure. The fissures ran along the entire ceiling and down to the floors. Patches of black mold were everywhere. What struck her as odd was the lack of debris. It appeared as if it had been freshly swept without any leaves or rat skeletons littering the ground.

Derek came up behind her. "What are you doing?"

Leslie headed toward the room where she'd spotted the strange light. "I saw something."

The smell of rot and mold filled her nose. Her skin brushed against the slimy walls, and she cringed. But something compelled her to keep going into the section Derek had deemed too dangerous to explore.

"Leslie, stop."

Naturally, she ignored him and pressed on, testing the floor with the toe of her shoe as she carefully progressed. Her heartbeat kicked up a notch, but this time a tingling sensation of excitement went with it. She felt like Indiana Jones exploring a lost tomb and waiting for a booby trap to jump out at her.

Her beam of light filtered into the room, and her heart crept higher in her throat. She rounded the edge of the wall and halted.

The cell was small without any windows, but this room appeared lived in. Along the far wall, below a pair of rusted pipes where a sink had once been, a green cot—army issue—had a pillow and green blanket neatly stacked on top. At the foot of the cot was a blue ice chest; on top of it, an assortment of red and white candles.

Leslie went up to the cot and caressed the blanket and pillows. Her foot tapped something beneath. She bent down and discovered an old CD player.

What's this?

Footfalls came from behind her. She swerved the flashlight around to Derek, fuming.

"Did you do this?"

"Do what?" He shielded his eyes from the light and stepped

inside.

She wanted to believe he had no idea any of this was here, but her suspicions couldn't be silenced. The whole scenario seemed so well-planned.

"What the hell?" Derek came up to the cot and lifted the pillow.

She stood back, studying his reaction as he browsed the contents of the room. "I thought you said this portion was dangerous."

"It is." Derek went to the ice chest and moved the candles to check inside.

She couldn't picture Derek pulling a fast one on her, setting up a rendezvous in such a desolate place. It wasn't the guy she knew.

"You sure you're not just trying to get me alone so you can finally have your way with me?"

The ice chest closed with a *thunk*. "I have to admit, the thought had crossed my mind." Derek chuckled. "But it's not exactly romantic. If I wanted to have my way with you, I would pick you up, serve you champagne, and take you to a very nice hotel."

"But you can't afford a hotel, let alone a bottle of champagne." She sighed, taking in the room. "I don't know, maybe if you fixed it up, fumigated, and—"

"That's not a good idea." He guided Leslie's flashlight to an array of mazelike chinks scarring the plaster-covered wall. "It's not going to collapse today, but I wouldn't want to stay here for long."

"Should we leave them a note, 'Hey stupid, move your crap or die'?"

Derek pulled her to the entrance. "No. Let's get out of here before whoever did this comes back." He ushered her to the gap in the wall.

Derek pushed the leaves aside and eased his shoulder through until he disappeared into the sunlight. His hand came back through the gap and he wiggled his fingers at her. She took his hand, smiling, and followed his lead, working her right shoulder into the mass of leaves. They brushed against her face, and she closed her eyes. When she opened them again, she was in the midst of an overgrown camellia bush.

Derek tugged her forward and she soon stood in thigh-high weeds. A breeze brushed the tops of the long stalks against her hand. She eyed the fountain with the angel on top. Sunshine hit her face, and she raised her head, soaking up the warm rays, thankful to be outside.

Once the rush of relief passed, Leslie glanced back at the hidden opening and wondered how anyone had found such a remote spot. Her fear of The Abbey returned, but this time it wasn't related to ghost stories or talk of wild dogs.

This trip had made Beau's threats all the more poignant. The isolated locale, and the helplessness any girl would feel if trapped alone would make her an easy target. The only problem was, who would believe her if she tried to warn them? How did she get her sister, and everyone else, to see the dangerous predator lurking beneath the brilliant smile and good looks of St. Benedict's star quarterback?

Chapter Seven

Hunched over a bowl of homemade mac and cheese, compliments of their cook, Beau sat at the copper breakfast bar in his parents' kitchen, watching a zombie movie on his laptop. The only light in the room came from above the gourmet stove his mother never touched.

He couldn't remember a time when his mother had ever cooked or cleaned. He'd even had a nanny until his father insisted Elizabeth Devereaux take an interest in her son.

Family dinners were something he'd seen on TV shows but never experienced. He'd gotten a taste of it at Dawn's house when he'd eaten dinner with the Moores, but after his incident with Leslie earlier in the week, he wanted to give her some space.

He preferred to break her slowly, tearing her apart a bit at a time. Rushing her to the end he had in mind would only take away from the pleasure of the experience.

A soft overhead light above the kitchen island came on, the copper pots hanging from the rack above twinkled.

"What are you watching?"

Elizabeth glided into the light from the outer hallway, wearing her favorite yellow robe. Her drinking robe, as Beau called it.

Noticing the black coffee mug in her hand, he guessed she'd run out of ice to go with her whiskey.

"A zombie movie." He went back to his mac and cheese, not bothering to turn down the volume.

Her slippers shuffling across the floor were like fingernails on a chalkboard. He couldn't remember a time in his life when she hadn't dragged herself around the house like one of the zombies in his movie.

He watched her out of the corner of his eye. After getting ice, Elizabeth walked back to the counter and stood staring down at him.

He tried to ignore her, but her damned gray eyes were like crab claws when they dug in.

"What?" He paused the movie.

Her expression was flat—not a hint of happiness, sadness, remorse or concern lifted the muscles in her face. She'd been that way for the past two years.

His mother used to smile. He remembered how her full red lips would ease back, highlighting her dimples and carved high cheekbones. When she smiled, her eyes reminded him of the light at dawn spanning the night sky.

"Is that all you're eating for dinner?" A tapered finger tapped on the counter close to his bowl.

"What else would you recommend?" He grinned, feeling cocky. "The brisket you cooked?"

No reaction. Nothing. The same dull stare she gave him night and day. He didn't know if she was rubbing off on him, but lately, a certain emptiness had permeated his ability to give a shit about anything his mother said or did.

"Leah also made roast chicken. And there's steak with baked potatoes in the fridge. Your father grilled tonight before he went back out."

Her deadpan delivery irked him more than missing out on the steak.

"Who's he with tonight?"

A hint of life shone in her eyes. She pulled the lapels of her robe closed.

"What are you talking about?"

Suddenly, beating his mother up over his father's screwing around didn't appeal to him. He had a new interest, one who would be a hell of a lot more satisfying.

"Forget it." He stood and took his bowl to the sink.

Elizabeth stepped toward him and swept the hair from his brow. Beau jerked back. "Don't touch me."

His growl came out more menacing than he'd intended, but he was glad. It would keep her away from him.

The eyes frantically searching his face were not the lifeless ones he'd grown used to. Fear dilated her pupils, almost covering the gray.

"What's wrong with you? Every time I think I know you, you turn into a stranger."

Beau leaned against the kitchen counter, a smugness surging through him. "That's good." He pushed away, and his mother took a cautious step back, which pleased him. "Because if you don't know me, then no one else ever will."

"What is that supposed to mean, Beau?"

The fake motherly concern in her voice pissed him off.

"You know what it means." He went back around the counter to his computer. "Isn't that what you and Dad want? Don't let anyone know who I really am." He picked up the computer and, needing to destroy something, threw it against the far wall.

His laptop exploded into shards, plastic clinking against the floor until silence blanketed the kitchen once more.

Beau closed his eyes, avoiding his mother's terror-stricken gaze, furious with himself. He'd lost control. He had one ironclad rule, and he'd broken it.

"Beau, baby, perhaps we should talk to your father about—"

He willed his sense of discipline back into place, fighting the urge for more destruction.

"No. I won't talk to him." He could not look at her and stepped away to the pantry.

Her shuffling slippers followed him. "You need to talk to someone."

Mindful of his still-seething rage, he gently opened the pantry door and got the broom.

"Take your ice and go back to bed, Mom." Clutching the broom, still not able to face her, he went around the counter to what was left of his computer. "I'll clean up my own mess."

* * *

Leslie poured soap into the sink, preparing for dish duty. Her mother had demanded she hand-wash every dish as penance for coming home late, covered in mud and dust. Her parents were already in bed—both early risers, unlike their night owl kids. Leslie enjoyed having the kitchen to herself. She could eat leftovers in peace without the usual Shelley interrogation.

The abandoned abbey bothered her more than ever. The room in the cells gave her a weird vibe. Something wasn't right about the place. She could see why Beau was so fond of The Abbey—it reminded her of him. An empty shell with a hell of a lot of secrets.

When is everyone going to see what I see in the guy?

Leslie cursed while cleaning one of the pots from dinner, ready to pitch it across the room.

Dawn came sauntering through the garage door, nearly scaring her to death.

She dumped her book bag on the kitchen countertop. "You haven't done the dishes yet? Mom will be so pissed."

"She'll be even more pissed you put your books up there."

Dawn's ponytail, secured with her signature red ribbon, swung over her shoulder as she moved her bag to the floor. She tucked part of her shirt into her jeans as she stood, rubbing her red lips together, smearing her freshly applied gloss.

Leslie shook her head. Didn't take a genius to figure out what her sister and Beau had been doing.

"Why do you have that stuff on your lips?"

She popped her lips together. "Because it turns Beau on. He says he doesn't like it, but I can tell he does. Especially red lipstick. It drives him mad."

Leslie made a mental note never to wear makeup again. "So where did you go with Beau?"

Dawn twirled her hair around her finger. "Carl's for pizza, and then we went to the river."

"The river?" Soap dripped from her hands. "Who with?"

Dawn giggled when a glob of suds landed on the floor.

Leslie hated when her sister laughed like a little girl, which sounded fake and was something she did for attention. It seemed like forever since she'd heard anything genuine come from her sister—another side effect from hanging out with Beau.

"What makes you think we were with anyone?" Dawn yanked a paper towel from the dispenser next to the sink.

"You two went alone?" Leslie returned to the dishes. "You need to be careful out there. A pack of wild dogs took down a deer at the river. They could go after a person."

Dawn scrunched up her face, every inch Shelley Moore's daughter. "I already know about the dogs, and so does Beau. He brought his daddy's shotgun with us tonight. We hung out on the beach and made love under the stars."

Leslie ignored her sister's dreamy expression. "I don't know which image is scarier: you screwing Beau on the beach or him with a shotgun."

Dawn wiped up the floor and pitched the paper towel into the garbage. "Why don't you like him? You know he's tried to reach out to you plenty of times to be friends, but you just blow him off."

Leslie set a dish aside, struggling with what to say to her sister.

"Maybe I don't like how he talks to me. Makes me wonder what you see in the guy."

"What I see in him?" This time, Dawn's laugh was genuine. A roaring chuckle, reminding Leslie very much of her own. "My God, Leelee, are you blind? Beau is rich, great-looking. His family owns the whole damned town. He's a great athlete with a banging body, treats me like a queen, and to top it off, he's great in bed. What else could I want in a guy?"

"Did you ever speak to Beau about waiting to have sex?" One of Leslie's soapy hands came out of the sink and rested on her hip. "You slept with him that first night at the river. Before Beau came along, you always talked about waiting until you were sure about a guy—like me."

Apprehension flickered in Dawn's eyes. Leslie had seen her look that way a million times before whenever she tried to lie her way out of a bad situation.

"Beau did want to wait," she finally got out. "I was the one who wanted to do it. I wanted him more than any guy I'd ever known. Maybe I didn't go about it the right way, but it all worked out. I've got Beau."

Leslie went back to her dishes. "Every time you talk about him, you go on and on about his family, his money, and all his skills, but never once do I hear you say you love him."

"I do love him."

Leslie raised an eyebrow. "But does he love you?"

Dawn's pert smile slipped and anger brimmed in her eyes. "Beau was right. All you want to do is break us up."

Leslie set the last of the dishes to the side to dry. "Did he tell you that?"

"He told me I can't trust anything you say about him." Dawn picked up her book bag and marched out of the kitchen.

She was almost through the den when Leslie stopped her. "Has Beau picked out his college yet?"

Dawn halted in the den. "Yeah, Tulane."

Leslie went around the breakfast counter, eager to make her sister see some sense. "Has he asked you to apply there?"

Dawn played with the strap of her bag. "No matter what you say, you're not going to talk me out of seeing Beau. I trust him more than anyone I've ever known, including you. He loves me and wants to make me happy. What do you want to make me?"

"I'm just trying to keep you safe, Dawn Marie—like I've always done." Leslie softened her voice, hoping it would get through to her sister. "Remember when we were little, and you used to have those bad nightmares about fire, and I said I would always protect you from the flames?"

Dawn glared at her. "We were six, Leelee. I stopped having nightmares a long time ago."

"But I've never stopped protecting you. That's what I'm doing now."

She tossed the bag over her shoulder. "I don't need your protection. I'm all grown up and can make my own decisions."

"Just watch your back with him. That's all I ask."

Dawn shook her head and turned away, heading to the stairs.

Leslie sagged against the counter, wishing she could make her sister understand about Beau. Time would prove her suspicions right, and when Dawn learned the truth about her boyfriend's troublesome behavior, Leslie vowed to be there to pick up the pieces.

Chapter Eight

The sky clear, the wind barely a whisper, and the stands filled with families and students. Beau jogged out onto the St. Benedict High football field, surrounded by his teammates. He raised his voice once or twice, joining in as the other guys whooped and hollered getting fired up for the game, but he didn't need such antics to get in the mood to play football. The aggressive, tough-hitting, unfettered violence spoke to his soul. He'd been playing football all his life, if only in his head.

Red and white banners decorated the bottom of the bleachers with slogans cheering his team to victory. They clashed with the opposing team's bleachers across the field. Swathed in blue and white, St. Paul's High School hoped to *trounce the cougars*.

On the sidelines, Beau set his helmet on the bench and glanced at the bleachers, checking for his parents. His father was there; always the avid football fan, he never missed a game, or an opportunity to give Beau pointers. His mother was with him. Another command performance insisted on by his father, no doubt.

He scanned the crowd for Leslie, found her parents, but didn't expect to see her. Force of habit made him search for her at every game, in every hallway, and around every corner. He pictured her snuggled up somewhere with Derek Foster. Fantasies about ripping the geek's head off with his bare hands helped dispel the flow of anger raging through him. Leslie would regret the time she'd wasted with Foster once she understood the depth of his devotion.

Dawn's high kicks distracted him. He liked watching her, especially when she wore her cheerleading uniform. The thick red lipstick on her lips sent a shudder through him. He would wipe it away later.

Another girl on the squad, with long, lean legs and a pretty face, intrigued him. She looked like the kind of girl who was sweet on the outside, but once you got them alone, turned into a real slut. He liked those kinds of girls. They always made things interesting.

"Mitch," he called to his buddy just a few feet away.

Towering over the others, the dark-eyed player with ebony skin removed his football helmet and revealed a head of curly, black hair. "What's up?"

Beau pointed to the cheerleaders' line up in front of the home team's stands. "Who's the girl next to Dawn? The cute little brunette."

Mitch Clarkson studied the line of girls shouting, Go Cougars! "That's Taylor Haskins. She moved from Los Angeles a few weeks ago."

Beau nodded with approval. "California girl. Nice."

"Dude, you better not let Dawn catch you checkin' out another girl. She's gonna rip you a new one."

"I'm just curious. Not interested. What else you know about Taylor?"

"Her dad took that PR position with your Dad's brewery." Mitch rubbed a grass stain off his helmet. "He's gonna handle your father's national campaign for Benedict Beer. I thought you knew about that."

"I tune out when my dad talks about business."

He kept his eyes on her, examining the curve of her legs and her energy. She would never compare to his Leslie, but Taylor exuded a snobbish quality, something reminiscent of how his mother, the ice queen, handled herself. The cheerleader would be worth getting to know.

"I envy you, havin' your whole life planned. I have no idea what I'm gonna do with mine."

Mitch's deep voice tugged him back from his fantasies.

Beau picked up his helmet. "Yeah, well, maybe my old man's plans and mine don't quite gel."

Mitch punched his shoulder pads. "Yeah, but you got your family's business in the bag, so you can pursue other interests. Nothin' wrong with testin' the waters. You never know, could make you appreciate what you've got." With a lighthearted smile, Mitch backed away.

Beau returned his attention to the St. Benedict High cheerleading team as Mitch's words ignited an idea. Perhaps it was time to test other waters in preparation for the day Leslie would belong to him. Nothing wrong with feeding his fantasies with a few appetizers to hold him over for the big meal. It wasn't cheating if he had his fun before he possessed her, right?

He reached for his helmet, keeping his eyes on Taylor as the refs blew the whistle signaling the start of play.

I'm gonna like this game.

* * *

The aroma of freshly baked chocolate chip cookies hung in the air of the dimly lit den while one of her favorite rom-coms played on the big screen TV. A few strategically lit candles set the mood for Leslie's date night with Derek.

At the refrigerator, she caught her reflection in the stainless panel before pulling out the iced tea. She would greet Derek as she had every day at school: fresh-faced and with only a touch of mascara. Dawn's recent obsession with red lipstick had turned her off cosmetics altogether.

I can't be seen imitating her.

She'd spent her entire life working to become the complete opposite of her twin. It was the only way to guarantee people saw her as an individual and not part of a matched set.

After she poured the iced tea, Leslie set the cookies on a plate and put a bowl of popcorn on the coffee table. She did one last check of her favorite jeans and the knit top hugging her figure. *Perfect!*

The doorbell chimed, and Leslie's heart skipped a beat. She looked out the window. Moonlight streamed across Derek's distinct features as he patiently waited on her porch.

She opened the door, and, overjoyed at seeing him, ran into his arms.

He embraced her, and the world went away. There was no pesky Shelley in her head, warning her away from Derek. No fights with Dawn, no sick stalker images of Beau. All she sensed was peace and contentment.

He nuzzled her cheek with his scratchy stubble. "I didn't expect this kind of welcome."

"I missed you."

He held her back. "You saw me two hours ago."

"Yes, but we weren't alone."

She took his hand and led him into the kitchen.

Derek went straight to the chocolate chip cookies. He crammed three in his mouth before Leslie could blink.

"I love these things," he garbled with a full mouth.

Leslie laughed. "Try and save a few for me."

He hugged the plate to his chest. "No way. If you want a cookie, you'll have to earn it."

Leslie's brow crinkled. "Earn it? How?"

Derek just grinned.

Chapter Nine

The screech of a whistle echoed across the field. Beau's adrenaline surged as people in the bleachers roared for the St. Benedict Cougars. Football players crowded around him, hitting his helmet and patting him on the back, and celebrating their victory over the St. Paul Panthers.

After shaking hands with the losing team, many players ran to the stands to greet family members and fans.

Before Beau could find his father and mother, Dawn leaped into his arms.

"You were fantastic."

"Thank you, sweetheart." He kissed her lips, put off by her thick lipstick, and then put her down. "I got to find my mom and dad."

"Oh, they already left," Dawn told him. "I saw them walking out with my parents. I think they must have been in a hurry to get back home."

Beau's disappointment cinched his stomach into a tight ball, but he kept it from Dawn and put on an easygoing smile.

"Yeah, Dad mentioned something about a late meeting at the brewery."

Dawn gripped his hand. "Come on. I'll walk you back to the gym so we can change and get ready for the party. I can't wait to get to the river."

Beau's gaze drifted to the line of cheerleaders gathering up their pompoms and jackets in front of the stands. Taylor was deep in conversation with a cornerback on his team, Wade Farris.

His anger churned. He'd set his sights on her and couldn't

afford to have another guy mucking up his plans. It was bad enough watching Leslie with that idiot Derek. He couldn't handle the nerdy cornerback messing with Taylor.

I'm gonna shut that shit down tonight at the river.

* * *

The crescent moon peeked through a veil of thin clouds while crickets chirped from the azalea bushes. Leslie took a deep breath, appreciating the crisp, clean fall night.

"I had fun." Derek's voice deepened as they descended the porch steps.

Leslie walked Derek to his mom's beat-up truck. "Me, too. I think hanging out at my parents' is better than The Abbey. No wild dogs."

Derek chuckled and pulled his keys from his pocket. "Sure, but there we didn't have to duck out before your parents arrived home."

Her guilt tainted the glow of their evening together. "I'm sorry."

He turned the key in the lock of the truck door. "I'm used to it. I just wish we didn't have to sneak around so much. Might be nice to spend some time with your family."

Come on. Think of something. You've got to change this. He deserves better!

"I'll talk to Dad about inviting you to dinner. I'm sure once my mother gets to know you, she will love you as much as I do."

Derek slipped his arms around her. "What you mother thinks doesn't matter to me. As long as you love me, I've got the whole world." He kissed the tip of her nose. "We still on for dinner tomorrow night at Carl's?"

"You betcha."

He let her go. "I'll call you in the morning after I pick Mom up from the diner. She's pulling an all-nighter." He nodded to her front door. "Best get inside and clean up the evidence that I was here before

Shelley finds it."

Leslie peered down her quiet street, mad at fate for dealing her and Derek such a lousy hand. She didn't understand why a dick such as Beau Devereaux got to visit whenever he wanted and sit down to dinner with her family, while her boyfriend—the better guy—was left out in the cold.

Frustrated more than ever, Leslie headed back inside.

"This sucks."

* * *

A cool breeze whipped through the open windows of Beau's silver BMW 535i while the steady beat of a banging rock song blasted through his speakers. He got green lights all the way through town and with his two best buds in the car with him, he couldn't wait to get to his favorite place on earth—the river.

Mitch did a drum roll on the front dash. "I hope we get to meet some girls at the party tonight."

"Did you see the ass on the new girl, Taylor?" Josh licked his lips.

Beau squeezed the steering wheel picturing Josh Breeland's small brain in his hands. The big defensive end for the team—what he lacked in brains, he made up for in stopping power.

"You should be more considerate when talking about girls, Breeland." Beau sounded cold and hard like his old man whenever he screwed up. To add to his warning, he glowered in his rearview mirror at Josh.

"Dude, what? You talk that way about Dawn." Josh's usually gruff voice crept higher. He leaned in, sticking his head between the bucket seats. His wide shoulders wouldn't fit. "What difference does it make how we talk about them when it's just us?"

In the front, Mitch turned around and, with an exuberant chuckle, slapped Josh on the shoulder. "You know how our boy is.

He likes everythin' nice and shit. No nasty talk about women. He's got his rep to protect."

Josh punched the back of Mitch's seat. "But how does any of that help me score with girls?"

Beau eased up on the gas and the car slowed as the illuminated white sign to Rouse's Grocery Store drew closer.

"Because, dickhead, I pay for the booze you need to get the courage to talk to girls, so until you can buy your own booze, you have to act appropriately in my car."

"Yeah, booze you never drink." Josh shook his head. "I'll never get that. How can you not drink?"

Beau coolly appraised his friend in the rearview mirror, not about to admit the truth. "Because I'm always driving you two boneheads to the river. What do you think my old man would do to me if I got caught driving drunk?"

Mitch glanced back to Josh. "He's got a point. Someone's got to drive."

Beau pulled onto the sleek blacktop parking lot and veered to the left, away from where the shoppers left their cars.

He cruised around the side of the long cinderblock building, security lights glaring into his car, and came to a rear loading dock and another blacktopped parking lot, which was completely empty.

"You let Eddie know what we need?" Mitch eyed the raised loading dock.

Beau put his car in park right next to a pile of wooden pallets. "Yep. Called him from the gym after the game. Told him we're going all out tonight."

"I just hope you didn't get any more of that cheap rum. I got sick as a dog on that last time."

Beau removed his wallet from his back pocket and took out two, one-hundred-dollar bills. "Stop whining. The rum was good; you were the lightweight."

The creak of a door carried through the lot. Light swept across the blacktop until it covered Beau's car in a swath of fluorescent haze.

A single stout man, with curly hair and wearing a Rouse's black shirt and white apron walked outside. In his arms was a box packed with bottles.

"My man, Eddie Bishop." Beau stepped from his BMW. "You got my order?" He popped the trunk.

Eddie gently set the box in the trunk and the tinkling of bottles carried in the air.

"I got it." Eddie faced Beau, a little winded. "I'll sure be glad when you're old enough to buy your booze, Devereaux. This crap could cost me my job."

Beau handed him two hundred dollars. "When it does, I'll have my old man get you a job at the brewery. But until then, I need you to keep me stocked with party supplies."

Eddie flicked through the money. "Just keep paying me. My girl's pregnant and I need the cash. Just make sure your guys don't leave the bottles lying around on the beach. The barcodes can get traced back here."

Beau shut the trunk. "We'll hide the evidence, Eddie. Not to worry. And congrats on the baby."

"Thanks." Eddie stuffed the money in his pocket. "Call me a little sooner next time with your order. I had to do some fast talking with the evening manager to pull the bottles off the shelves."

Back inside his car, Beau kept a wary eye on Eddie as he strutted up to the loading dock and climbed the steps. The light in the lot retreated and when the rear door finally closed with a thud, Beau sat back in his seat, his mind buzzing.

Mitch turned to him. "Is there a problem?"

"Nah." His engine hummed to life. "Just glad we got everything we need for our party."

Once back on Main Street, Beau steered to the end of the last row of quaint shops, their darkened windows lit by the antique arched street lamps set up at the edge of the sidewalk. He passed display windows touting bakery items and clothes. At the old town hardware store, he took a left on Devereaux Road.

When he turned in to the cleared lot hidden behind the thick shrubs, he itched to get to the party.

The thump of a deep synthesized bass echoed throughout the trees surrounding him. He got out of the car and glanced at the steep embankment leading to the beach.

"Sounds like they started without us." Josh wiggled out from the back seat.

Beau went around to the trunk. "That's just a warm-up. The real party doesn't start until we deliver the goods."

The thick muscles in Mitch's arms bulged as he lugged the heavy box of alcohol down the pine needle-covered trail from the lot. Beau followed, breathing in the night. He cleared the last swath of trees blocking his view of the beach and saw three roaring bonfires. Logs pointed in a teepee sat in freshly dug sand pits along the beach. Their fire reflected on the murky water, creating eerie shadows on trees next to the narrow waterway.

The instant his toes hit the sand, the heat from the closest bonfire caressed his skin, chasing away the chill in the air. The music rocked around him, loud enough to get everyone in the mood, but not so overbearing it drowned out conversation.

His teammates had set the green picnic benches close to the fires while leaving the round metal tubs, packed with ice, farther away. It kept the ice from melting too quickly and the drinks from getting warm. He'd long ago discovered the best set up to create the maximum enjoyment for everyone. That was important to him. His friends needed to have a good time and remember he was the guy who had provided it.

A swell of pride and excitement careened through him. This was his realm, his world where he could be who he wanted and there was no one to rein him in.

The river rules and I rule the river.

Beau patted Mitch's back as his friend checked out two girls sitting on a bench by the fire. "Put the stuff on ice." He reached into the box and retrieved a bottle of vodka. "This is for Dawn."

A roar went up from the handful of revelers on the beach when Beau stepped out from the shadows. They raised their beers to him, cheering.

"Our main man is here," a voice called.

The adoration fed the black fire in his soul. He had created this, not his old man. Here, he wasn't Gage Devereaux's son. He was Beau and could make whatever life he desired.

"Hey, baby." Dawn slinked into his arms. "You got my drink?"

She kissed him hard on the lips, smearing her lipstick over his mouth.

"Would I forget my best girl?" He handed her the bottle and took a step back from her, feeling a little hemmed in. "But go easy. I don't want to bring you home drunk. Your parents won't be happy with me if I do. And you have an image to keep up, remember?"

"I remember your rules." She rolled her eyes. "I can get tipsy sometimes, but never drunk."

The touch of sass in her voice reminded him of Leslie. He wiped the remains of her red lipstick away and thought of her sister. "We on for our special place?"

Her eyes twinkled in the firelight, but their lack of anger cooled his desire.

"Let's socialize first. We've got to be seen by everyone to keep up appearances." She grabbed his hand and urged him closer to the nearest bonfire.

The gesture made him feel akin to a Prada backpack flaunted on the first day of school. He balked at her plan to wear him like a fashion accessory and let his hand slip from hers.

Beau was about to set off across the beach to one of the picnic benches when a pretty blue-eyed brunette sauntered up to them.

"Hey, Dawn, aren't you going to introduce me to the man of

the hour?"

Taylor grinned at Beau, not a sheepish smile, but an inviting smirk announcing her interest in no uncertain terms. The brazen gleam in her eye, and the way she dipped her noticeable cleavage in his direction sent a zing right to his crotch.

Gutsy move.

He liked Taylor already.

Dawn must have noticed the blatant flirtation because she cuddled against him, tucking her vodka bottle under her arm. She patted his ass with her hand—a sure sign she was marking her territory.

"Taylor Haskins is our newest cheerleader. She was impressed with your game."

"You like football?" He'd never met a girl interested in the game before.

"Love it. My dad used to take me to Raiders' games when we lived in LA. I think you've got a real talent for pulling it out in a fourth down situation and converting. You got a knack for reading the defensive line up on the field."

Beau could not help but laugh out loud. "You sound like a commentator."

Taylor kept her eyes on him, never acknowledging his girlfriend. "My dad worked with the Raiders organization doing PR before your dad hired him. I grew up on the game."

Dawn moved from his side, dragging her hand from around his back. She scratched across the stubble on his chin, her eyes glaring up at him.

"Didn't you say something about our special place?"

Her insistent tone did nothing to distract him from Taylor. He wanted to have a little fun with the defiant girl.

"Yeah, baby, in a minute. I'm being social." He kept his attention on Taylor, knowing it would make Dawn jealous. "So, your father's going to put together the national campaign for Benedict

Beer."

"Yep." Taylor nodded. "From what he tells me, this is going to be a big jump for your family's company. Lots of national press. You'll be famous real soon."

Her zeal for his family's company tagged her as another acclaim junkie looking to attach her star to his. He would have preferred she stick to football.

After giving him a smoldering glance, Dawn turned on Taylor. "We'll be back in a while."

Taylor blushed. "Ah, sure. I'll just go and get a beer."

She sauntered away, her hips swinging like a bell, captivating him.

Dawn pressed his chin between her thumb and forefinger, forcing his eyes to her. "Why are you looking at her like that?"

Beau recognized her deep growl. When she sounded like a threatened pit bull, she was pissed.

"I'm not looking at her any certain way." Her jealousy had worn thin. "Just wondering what she's about."

The rigid muscles in her jaw relaxed and she exhaled a long breath. "Yeah, weird, isn't it? I've been trying to introduce her around, but she sure is different."

Beau caught a peek of Taylor rummaging through a metal tub over Dawn's shoulder. She was different. Her bold behavior reminded him of Leslie. They even shared a few of the same physical traits. She'd never replace Leslie, but perhaps she could be a fun diversion.

"I guess all those LA types are strange."

"Enough about Taylor." Dawn cozied up to him. "You want to slip away?"

Beau detected the longing in her blue eyes and his interest in sex soured. Taking Dawn to his special room in the cells didn't appeal to him anymore. He wanted to try something new, but with Dawn around, enticing Taylor would be difficult.

He took the vodka from her as an idea percolated. "Sure, darlin'. Let's get out of here."

He escorted her along the sandy beach, away from the music and bonfires to a remote spot surrounded by dense trees and hidden beneath sinister shadows.

He'd stumbled on the isolated section before meeting Dawn when he'd used it as a make-out spot. Since then he'd upped his game and moved his activities to the cells. But the strip of beach, littered with dried twigs and dead leaves, would come in handy for what he had in mind.

With the faint beat of the catchy dance tune floating past them, he kicked a few sticks out of the way and cleaned off a swath of sand.

"Voila," he said, waving to the spot.

She raised her gaze to the smattering of branches overhead, blotting out patches of moonlight. "Why are we here? What about our room in the cells?"

He had a seat, setting the vodka in the sand. "I picked out this place special just for us." He snapped up a small rock and tossed it across the gentle waves of the river. "The cells are starting to feel dirty to me. I want to make you feel like a princess because you are one to me."

He thought it was a bit lame, but it would be something she would want to hear. Romance wasn't his thing, but he'd learned to embrace it to keep Dawn interested. Until he had Leslie, he would have to play her silly games.

Dawn settled next to him, softly squealing as she did when she was happy.

"Any place you take me is special. You know that."

He eased back on the sand, taking her in his arms, and encouraging her to recline next to him.

"I always want to make it perfect for you." Beau reached for the vodka and cracked the seal. "Here's a toast to us." He handed her the bottle and waited as Dawn stole a small sip.

That's not gonna be near enough for what I have planned.

"Baby?" He tipped the bottle up to her lips. "That was a toast. You're supposed to take a big sip. Otherwise, it's bad luck."

She twisted her mouth into a funny smile. "Bad luck? I never heard that before."

He put his lips to her ear, nuzzling her lobe as he spoke. "Take another sip, a bigger one for me."

Dawn gave in and he felt his power over her growing. He was glad she didn't argue. Nothing aggravated him more than when she started with the questions.

After she gulped down a small portion of the bottle, she coughed and covered her mouth.

"That's my girl." Beau took the bottle from her and pretended to take a sip. She needed to feel comfortable.

That was the key to girls, as far as he was concerned. Make them comfortable with you, and they're yours.

He handed her the bottle, frowning a bit to rouse her worry. "You'd better drink some more. You look uptight."

"I'm not uptight." She pushed the bottle back to him. "Why do I look uptight?"

Beau put his arm around her, his lips against her neck—the hollow spot under her ear where she loved to be kissed.

"You always say it feels better when you have a slight buzz on." He nipped her skin. "I want tonight to be so good for you. I want to make you scream."

She tentatively eyed the bottle, biting her lower lip as if having a great internal debate. "But what if I get drunk? You always say not to get drunk when we go out because you don't want my parents—"

He pressed his finger to her lips. "Tonight is about us. No parents and no rules." He set the bottle in front of her. "For me, baby."

She looked at the bottle and wrinkled her brow. "I don't need to be buzzed to have sex with you."

The hitch of anger caught in his chest. *Stay in control. Don't let her see who you really are.*

He took a breath and regrouped. "But you need to relax more. I thought you were the one who wanted to try different positions." He traced his finger over her lips to coax her to drink. "Well, I can't do what I have planned unless you're real relaxed."

The wrinkle in her forehead smoothed away as she took the bottle. "What did you have in mind?"

"Something I know you will love, so drink up." He tilted the bottle back to her mouth, very pleased with his work.

Dawn pulled the bottle away. "Can I ask you something?"

He clenched his fist behind her head, then ran his fingers over the red ribbon securing her ponytail.

"Anything, baby?"

"Did you ever think about what will happen after graduation? I know you're hoping to go to Tulane, but I was thinking … it might be nice if we went to the same college."

Where had that come from?

"You don't have the GPA or connections to get into Tulane."

She set the bottle in the sand. "I know, but have you ever thought about LSU? They have a great football team, and you could get picked up there and eventually go pro like you always talked about."

Beau considered her face in the faint light. How dare she try and change his plans? What made her think she had the right to even discuss his future? He settled the storm raging inside him, not wanting to frighten her away.

"What brought this on? You never talked about us going to college together."

"I was just thinking. That's all."

Beau leaned into her, studying her face. Dawn never came up with ideas on her own. That's what he liked about her—her gullibility. But who would put such a ludicrous thought into her head?

Then it struck him. The only person who fed her sense of inferiority was the same one who had driven her to sleep with him the first night they'd met—Leslie.

"Is this about Leslie and Derek? I've heard they're planning on going to LSU together. Is that what you want for us?"

"Haven't you ever thought about us after we graduate?" She tugged at the collar of his T-shirt. "Might be hard with me at LSU and you at Tulane. We won't be able to see each other every day."

Beau decided to turn the conversation to his advantage.

He kissed her lips. "I'd love that idea, baby, but I was afraid you wouldn't want to have me around all the time."

"I would, Beau. Every day. You know I love you."

A nudge of victory careened through his bones. "Then prove to me how much you love me, Dawn. Knock back more of the vodka so I can do all the wonderful things I've been dreaming about."

She eagerly chugged down two more big sips, and he turned his head away, smirking.

Dawn coughed, coming up for air. "If I drink much more, I'll be too drunk to enjoy anything."

"You're not a lightweight." He pushed the bottle back toward her. "I've seen you drink lots more than this."

She smacked her lips together. "You have?"

A mischievous smile spread across his lips. "Baby, would I lie to you?"

It didn't take long for the vodka to hit her. She had a hard time staying upright, and her words slurred.

Beau kissed her neck and waited until she drifted off to sleep against him. Then he gently rested her head on the sand.

Satisfied that she was out, he stood and wiped the sand from his jeans. He arched over Dawn, shaking his head.

"You sleep it off. I got somewhere else I got to be."

DEATH BY THE RIVER

Back at the party, Beau mingled. There were a lot of faces he didn't recognize and figured quite a few St. Paul's students must have heard about the party. He didn't care who showed up on the river, as long as they knew he was the king.

He made his way to the tubs filled with beer and drinks and spotted Taylor. She was with another girl Beau recognized—Zoe Harvey. The cute girl with the creamy mahogany skin and wonderful ass was one of Dawn's friends and a real blabbermouth. Whatever Beau wanted to do with Taylor, he'd have to get her away from Zoe; otherwise, his every movement would get back to Dawn.

He put on a smile and strolled up to them. "Hey, ladies."

"Beau." Zoe's hazel eyes glanced around him. "Where's Dawn?"

"She's not feeling well, so I took her back to my car to lie down for a while."

Zoe's small red mouth turned downward. "That's odd. She was fine on the ride over here. Maybe I should go and check on her."

Beau clasped her arm, giving it an encouraging squeeze. "Let her sleep, Zoe. I think the vodka just made her sick. She said she didn't eat anything today."

Zoe pulled against his grip. Her eyes shot to his, a glimmer of displeasure burned in them and then fizzled out.

"Yeah, she skipped lunch today. She was too busy in the gym getting all the banners ready for the game."

"I'm sure she'll be fine in another hour or so." Beau let her go and shifted his focus to his new objective—Taylor. "There's a guy from St. Paul's asking about you, Zoe."

Zoe's brassy smirk challenged him.

"Sure there is."

Beau pointed to a bonfire on the far side of the beach. He selected a random guy with thick shoulders, buzzed dark hair, and nursing a beer.

"His name is Mike, and he thinks you're cute."

She squinted as she followed his finger. "Mike?"

Beau pushed her ahead. "Go talk to him, if you don't believe me."

Zoe gave him one last cautious side-glance and then walked away.

Beau turned all of his attention to Taylor, ready to make his move. "I thought she'd never leave."

Taylor tucked a lock of hair behind her ear. "So where is Dawn, really?"

For a cheerleader, she wasn't a total ditz, but he doubted she was as sharp as Leslie. "She's passed out a little farther up the beach." Beau moved in closer. "We just had a big fight."

Curiosity twinkled in her eyes. "About what?"

From the way she rocked her hips, hinting at her haughty ego, to the aggressive manner in which she flirted, Beau sensed she was ready for more.

"You." He lowered his smoky voice, hoping she would move closer. "She's jealous because she knows I like you."

She dragged the tip of her tongue over her unadorned lips, wetting them. "But you're Dawn's boyfriend and she's the captain of my cheerleading squad. If she wanted to get even with me—"

"She won't know." He took the opportunity to get real close and put his lips next to her right ear. "I've been wanting to end it for some time now. With you at my side, I could walk away from Dawn for good."

The aroma of salty sweat mixed with her heavy floral shampoo disappointed him. Why did no other girl smell like Leslie? It just proved how special she was, and how worthy of his adoration.

He stood back, waiting to soak in her reaction.

There was no blush of embarrassment, no openmouthed surprise. What greeted him was a cold, calculating stare of a huntress closing in on her kill.

Desire like the flames from the nearby bonfires danced in her eyes. He had her.

"Is there some place we can talk?" she whispered.

Beau glimpsed the revelers around them. Some sat around the bonfires chatting, others played in the water at the river's edge. A few brave souls danced and swayed to techno-pop music, while the hardcore party-goers sat on picnic benches playing drinking games. No one would notice if they slipped away.

"Come with me."

He took Taylor's hand and guided her along the beach, leading her to the rusted iron gate of The Abbey.

Chapter Ten

Moonlight danced across the top of the high grass and crept up the cracked wall in the cells. Beau was glad he had forgotten to bring a flashlight. Mother Nature had set the mood for his tryst with Taylor.

He'd enjoyed flings behind Dawn's back, but none had been with her circle of friends. This could be an exciting challenge.

"What is this place?"

The ethereal light shimmered in her hair. She glanced at him with a slight crease in her brow. He ignored her concern and pictured how her hair would feel in his hands.

"This is the remains of the seminary school used by some monks. They abandoned it years ago. Just behind The Abbey is the priests' cells. I've got a place in there."

Right before they reached the fountain with the angel on top, Taylor yanked on his hand, stopping him.

"Are you kidding me? Priests' cells?"

He hadn't expected someone from Los Angeles to be as skittish as a high-strung racehorse. He thought West Coast people were mellow.

He put his arm around her. "It's real cozy and very quiet."

Her hands twisted and she eased away. "Sounds creepy."

Instead of getting angry, he remained the picture of calm, honing in on a possible way to make her trust him.

"I know it sounds creepy, but it's not. I've a cot and music, candles and even an ice chest. For me, it's a place to get away—a sanctuary. I only bring special people here." He gauged her reaction and decided to give her something to win her over completely—honesty.

Well, she would think it was honest.

"I just want to be alone with you without all the noise and interruptions of the others around. You ever just want to get away from all the bullshit? The constant pressure to be one way, act a certain way. Please your parents, your teachers, your coach—all of it. I get so sick of fighting to be the person they want me to be. So, I created this place where I can be me. Can you understand that?"

She hugged herself and slowly nodded. The aggressive tigress retreated and the quiet girl fighting to fit in came to light.

"I understand a lot better than you think." Her smile was tentative but genuine. "I didn't want to move here. I was happy in LA. My dad made us move."

He inched closer, encouraging her to open up to him. "My dad wants me to take over the family business. No matter how much I hate it."

She unwound her arms and walked to the fountain. "Yeah, well, your dad is successful. Whereas mine …"

He detected a slight sniffle as she kept her face hidden in the angel's long shadow.

He went up to her as she gazed into the black water. Beau placed his hand on her shoulder. "What is it?"

She faced him and the faint light revealed her trembling lips. "I can't say anything. My dad works for your dad."

He lifted her chin, antsy to discover her secret. Anything could be twisted and used against her, guaranteeing her complacency.

"They're not us. What they do has nothing to do with you and me." He gently kissed her lips. "Whatever it is, it will never affect us."

Her eyes searched his. "My dad couldn't get a job in LA. He's had problems before … with alcohol. He's sober now, but his reputation was ruined. That's why we came here. He needed a fresh start. But I sure didn't."

He put his arm around her and crushed her to his chest, feeling empowered. "Your secret is safe with me." He nodded to the crack in the wall just ahead. "Let's go inside."

She slid her arms around his neck. "What does a guy like you see in Dawn Moore? I would never have pegged you for the mousy kind." She bit his lip. "I'll bet you like a woman who knows her own mind."

Unlike other girls who had fallen into his arms because of his name, looks, or money, Taylor offered a different kind of challenge—a mental one. She made the game of seduction a whole lot of fun and gave him a taste of things to come with Leslie.

Done with waiting, he picked her up and her squeals carried across The Abbey grounds. Hiking her over his shoulder, he pressed on for the crack in the cell walls.

He remembered the first time he'd stumbled on the opening. Crammed with cobwebs and dead leaves, the numerous cracks in the walls had given him pause about the integrity of the site, but the dilapidated condition had a plus side—no one would ever venture there. It would be his place, untouched by others.

The first girls he had brought there balked at the conditions; after a few days of cleaning, and some homey touches, they seemed more intrigued than put off.

At the narrow opening, he put Taylor down. "Stay here and I will get some light, so you can see where you're going."

She stubbornly crossed her arms and turned her lips downward. "You want me to stay out here alone?"

He kissed her, biting her bottom lip. "There's nothing out here that can hurt you. The only person to fear is me."

Taylor relaxed, and her arms fell to her sides. "I don't scare easily."

Oh, yeah. He liked her. "I'm counting on it."

Beau ducked inside the wall, pulling a slow-moving Taylor

behind him. The blackness of the cells took a moment to adjust too, then ribbons of moonlight seeped in through cracks in the wall, allowing just enough light to help him make his way.

He crept along, keeping a firm hold on her hand until a remnant of light caught on the metal frame of his cot.

He let her go. "Wait here."

In the room, he shuffled across the floor to where he'd left the candles on top of his ice chest. Feeling around the uneven surface, he found the box of matches.

The brilliant flare of light took a second to get used to.

He lifted one of the candles and checked the contents of his cell. Everything was where he'd left it.

"Are you sure this is okay?" She came inside, inspecting the room.

He went to his cot and reached underneath where he kept his CD player and a flashlight. "Everything's fine."

She caressed the cracks along the doorway. "How'd you find this place?"

"One of the first parties I attended at the river was when I made the varsity football team as a backup quarterback. I got bored when everyone got drunk and went exploring. When I found the opening in the wall, I decided to check it out and discovered this." He flipped on the flashlight and pointed it around the room. "Cool, huh?"

She nodded, not appearing as enthused about the locale as he was. "It has potential."

Done with waiting for her, he put down the flashlight. "I promise you will grow to love it. I'm going to give you the night of your life in this very room."

Taylor faced him, her apprehension all but gone, her lips spread into a wide grin. "I like the sound of that."

He flipped her around, curled into her back, and wrapped her in his arms. He kissed her neck as he ran his hands up and down her chest. He liked the feel of her. She had curves and sweet-smelling skin.

His kisses became more urgent, and then he bit her neck, hoping she liked it.

Taylor sighed, sounding bored. "Is that the best you can do?" She turned around. "I thought you were into playing hard to get."

Beau pinned her arms behind her. "I always play hard."

She rocked her hips into his crotch. "Then play hard with me."

The request did more than excite him; it freed him. The girls he'd known didn't ask for it rough. They wanted sweet and gentle, the way Dawn always liked it. But this was an invitation to be who he really was; to let the true Beau out and allow him to run wild.

"Are you sure you want the real me?"

Taylor tilted her head. "The real you?" Her lips lingered temptingly in front of his. "Yes. I want to see who's hiding behind that popular, rich boy persona you do so well."

He tightened his grip on her wrists, squeezing just enough to hurt. "Then let's have some fun."

She wiggled against him. "Hey, no bruises." She got her hands free and pushed him away, not hard, but hard enough to make him angry. "We're gonna do this my way."

Like a rubber band pulled to the breaking point, his self-control snapped. Beau gave in to his rage.

"No, we're gonna do this my way." He picked her up and threw her to the ground.

She hit the floor and immediately looked up at him. Fear—dark, cold, and brutal—widened her eyes. The thrill of seeing her huddled on the floor, no longer the assertive flirty girl, her terror charging the air in the room, made him hard.

This is my kind of fun.

He crawled on top of her. "Let me explain something to you. You're in my world now. I own you, your family, your reputation, all of it. After I'm done with you, we'll see if you're still in the mood for games."

He tore at her blouse, ripping the silky material to shreds.

"Get off me!" Taylor tried to crawl backward to get away from him.

Beau held her down and struggled to get her bra off when she punched him in the stomach.

He used the back of his hand to slap her across the face. "Hard enough for ya?"

The sound of her head smacking against the floor sent a satisfying tingle through him.

She quieted down, rolling her head around, groaning.

He got her bra off and used it to tie her hands behind her. Then he dragged her across the floor to the wall.

She struggled a little when he lifted her onto the cot and secured her hands on the sealed off pipes jutting from the wall above.

Taylor glanced up at the pipe holding her and fought to free her hands.

He slapped her again, determined for her to comply. "You had the opportunity to do this the easy way. Now you'll do it my way."

Beau wrestled her jeans and underwear over her ankles. He noted the way her blue eyes bulged as her exasperation turned to abject horror. He even found the blush of her cheeks attractive.

"Stop it!" She writhed beneath him.

"Scream all you want; no one will hear you." He licked her cheek, tasting her sweat and fear. "You're mine. I'm going to make sure you never forget tonight."

Taylor fought against him, kicking at his head. Aroused by her spirit, he snapped up her underwear and shoved it in her mouth so he could have fun without bite marks.

He backhanded her one more time, and she crumpled against the cot. Beau laughed and patted her cheek, eager to make sure she was awake when he took what he wanted.

When he spread her legs apart, Taylor stopped fighting him. He didn't like that. He wanted her to struggle like he'd pictured Leslie would.

She turned her head and closed her eyes as he put on a condom. Then he slammed into her. He thought she would whimper or at least make a noise, but she didn't. So he did it hard to make sure it hurt.

When he was done, Beau untied her hands and took the underwear out of her mouth.

Tears stained her cheeks, and a trickle of blood ran down her lower lip. Every muscle in her body quivered. Her whimpering echoed around the room, adding to his sense of achievement. He'd shown her his true self, and she'd been too weak to take it.

His Leslie wouldn't have acted like such a blubbering mess. She would have looked up at him with her surly eyes and begged for more.

"If you mention this to anyone, you'll lose more than that fine ass of yours. I'll make sure your father gets fired, and his reputation as a drunk smeared across the country. No one will ever hire him again." He tossed her shirt in her face, and she flinched. "And when I come to you wanting another go, you will give it to me, without the struggle." He grinned. "Well, not completely without it. I liked it when you fought back."

Taylor grabbed her jeans and bra. With her hands trembling, she held her torn shirt to her chest and stood from the cot.

"Go on. Find your way back to the party. And don't let the dogs get you. They hunt around The Abbey at night."

Her bloodshot eyes glared at him.

"Oh, I forgot to mention the wild dogs roaming the grounds." He smiled, taunting her. "You'd better make a run for it. They'll make a meal of you."

She didn't even put on her clothes before running out of the room.

Beau stayed behind, blew out the candles and straightened up. The rush of power, the pure pleasure coursing through his veins, was better than the sex. More uplifting than the strongest opioid—he would have to have it again.

Once the blanket was neatly folded, and order restored to his little room, Beau put his flashlight back under the cot and quickly checked the corridor outside.

Quiet. Not a sound slipped through the night.

The air was crisp and not chilly against his sweaty skin when he stepped out from the opening in the wall. He felt strong, powerful, and like a king.

He returned to the isolated scrap of beach where he'd left Dawn sleeping. She was in the same position—on her side with her hand tucked under her chin. He settled in next to her. How could he go from so much fun in the cells to this?

With a sigh, he spooned behind her, his arm around her shoulders.

She stirred at his touch and rolled over.

"What happened?" She pressed her hand to her head.

"You just had a few too many." He patted her shoulder, already bored. "I've been here watching over you the whole time. Do you know you look like an angel when you sleep?"

Dawn rubbed her eyes, smudging her black mascara. "Did I miss anything? I mean, did we have a good time before I passed out?"

He sometimes wondered why he put up with her heavy makeup and lackluster mind, but through her, he was getting closer to what he really wanted.

"We had a great time." He sat up, wiping the sand from his long-sleeved shirt. "One of the best evenings I can remember."

"I'm glad you're pleased." Dawn snuggled into Beau's shoulder.

The weight on his shoulder got heavier.

He shrugged. "Dawn?"

She didn't move.

He put his arm around her. The play of moonlight on the water brought back a memory of the terror shining in Taylor's eyes.

Why was hurting her so much fun?

The rush of power awakened something in him.

He glimpsed Dawn's silky hair tucked against his chest. Would she like it rough with him? She would do anything to please him, and he could try different things with her to see what he liked. The surprise, the fire in Taylor, had made the sex worthwhile. He wondered how to introduce Dawn to new things. Might be worth looking into.

The chill in the air slipped under his shirt. Beau grew restless. He needed to get back to his party.

"Baby, get up." He nudged her shoulder. "I have to get you home before your curfew."

Dawn sat up, a little woozy. "Mom doesn't mind if you bring me home late."

He stood and tugged her to her feet. "No, but your dad minds. And I don't want him to think less of me."

Dawn tossed her arms around his neck. "I'm the luckiest girl in the world."

Beau loosened her suffocating grip. "Lean on me."

He guided her off the beach and helped her through the thick brush back to the path, leading to the party.

The music pounded in his ears by the time they returned. Couples danced in the water, some with clothes, some in their underwear. He checked the tubs of beer and wasn't surprised to find most of the stuff already gone.

Beau negotiated Dawn through the crowds gathered around the bonfires to stave off the cold. She stayed tucked into his side, not putting up any protest.

He had to help her up the slim path. Her footing wasn't so good on the slope, and she slipped on the pine needles twice, but he caught her in his arms before she hit the ground. He carried her the rest of the way, gazing down at her raccoon eyes as she tucked her head against his chest.

There were times he did find her appealing. Like a lost puppy in need of love.

When he reached the clearing, Beau searched for his BMW. Thank goodness he wasn't blocked in by other cars.

He set Dawn in her seat. Her head wobbled, and she leaned back, closing her eyes.

"I feel sick."

Beau cursed under his breath. "Don't puke in my car. I'll leave the door open while I'm gone."

She grabbed the sleeve of his T-shirt. "Where are you going?"

He pried her fingers off, hating when she got clingy. It reminded him of his mother when she drank too much.

"I got to find Josh and Mitch and tell them I'm taking you home. They can catch a ride with someone else."

Dawn wiped her hand over her face. "I should tell Taylor I'm leaving with you. She gave me and Zoe a ride here."

He patted her shoulder and stood. With no intention of finding Taylor, he said, "I'll let her know. I'm sure she's still at the party."

Her head rolled to the side, and he guessed she had fallen back to sleep. Good. He didn't need her getting together with Taylor, but he believed the girl would be too afraid to tell Dawn anything.

Intimidation would keep her quiet. It worked on everyone else in town.

Beau left Dawn and headed back to the beach. He wished he could stay, but he had to get her home. He made it a point never to give her father any reason to doubt his integrity. The last thing he needed was John Moore speaking to his father.

His feet hit the sand at the edge of the beach and he set out for the bonfires, checking out the faces lit up by the flames. He found several members of his football team, all pairing off with girls, but there was no sign of Mitch or Josh. At the picnic tables, he searched the revelers gathered there. Some were sober, most were drunk. A few lay passed out in the sand or strewn across the picnic tables.

No discipline.

He found Mitch and rushed up to him. A redheaded cheerleader from Dawn's squad was all over Mitch, but his friend's glassy eyes and clumsy movements bothered Beau more than the girl.

"Hey, there." Mitch slapped his shoulder. "Where you been?"

Beau pulled his arm off the girl and dragged him away. "Have you seen Taylor?"

Mitch nodded. "Wise choice, my friend."

Beau checked a few picnic tables around them. "No, I was just wondering if she's still here. Dawn got a ride with her, and I'm taking her home. I just wanted to let Taylor know."

Josh stumbled onto their spot, hooking his arm around Mitch's waist. "Dudes. Great party, huh?" He then fell to his knees, gripping a can of beer.

Mitch giggled like a little girl as he pointed at Josh. "You're drunk."

Beau snatched Josh by the shoulders to keep him from tumbling forward. "Josh, have you seen Taylor?"

Josh's face sobered. "Yeah. I saw her headin' to her car a while ago. She was upset about ripping up her shirt. She said she got caught on a branch or somethin'."

Beau contained his grin. He loved being right about people. "Can you guys get home without me? I need to see to Dawn."

Mitch waved his hand and almost fell backward. "We'll be fine."

Idiots! Why do I waste my time?

He knew why. They were part of the Beau Devereaux package. He'd spent years meticulously cultivating his outward persona—the good student, considerate son, best friend, football star, and respectful hometown boy. Suddenly the self-restraint he had fought so hard to maintain had slipped, and an addicting outlet for his ever-present rage had presented itself. From now on, the parties at the river wouldn't give him the thrill they once had.

Beau headed back to the parking lot, wearing an exuberant grin.

I've found a much better game to play.

Chapter Eleven

Thud!

Leslie popped up in bed, gaping around her darkened bedroom. She sat perfectly still, her heart pounding.

What the hell was that?

She tossed aside her comforter and a chill engulfed her. She stood, staring at her bedroom door and debating whether she should check out the noise.

A faint groan came from the hallway.

She hurried to the door and flung it open. Dawn fell into her room.

The pungent aroma of alcohol was all over her. "What are you doing?"

Dawn went to rub her face but half-slapped it. "I'm so wasted. Beau gave me vodka at the river."

"I thought your boyfriend didn't drink."

"He doesn't. He wanted me to drink so I was relaxed before we did it, but I don't think we did do it."

"That's way too much information, Dawn." Leslie pulled her inside and shut the door.

Dawn stayed on the floor, looking up at her. "I think I fell asleep, but even then, Beau stayed with me. Isn't that so sweet?"

"Yeah, he's a regular Casanova." Leslie knelt and helped her sit up. "I hope Mom and Dad didn't hear you. They'll ground your ass if they see you like this."

Dawn struggled to stay upright. "No, they won't. They think Beau is a stand-up guy. Everyone thinks Beau is a stand-up guy. Even the pope loves him."

"You're drunker than I thought." Leslie hoisted her up from the floor.

"No, it's the truth. Everyone in town loves him. Everywhere we go, people talk to him. It's kind of like dating a celebrity."

Leslie sat her down on a brass day bed, disgusted everyone in town couldn't see what she did—the monster lurking inside Beau Devereaux.

"I have to practically sneak around with my boyfriend, and you get a parade every time you go out with—"

"It's not always fun with Beau," Dawn cut in.

She sat back, not sure if she had heard right. Dawn gushed about Beau twenty-four seven. Was this the booze talking?

"What did you say?"

Dawn let out a loud sigh and flopped back on the bed. "There are times when I'm with him and I'm glad he has to take me home."

Her life had been turned upside down by Beau's unwanted attention, and to finally have her sister give even the slightest hint that all was not right with her "perfect" boyfriend was a huge breakthrough.

"I thought you were madly in love."

A small frown spread across Dawn's lips. "I am, but aren't there days when Derek gets on your nerves and you just want to get away from him?"

"No." Leslie shook her head, flooded with the warm, comforting sensation Derek gave her. "I could spend every day for the rest of my life with him and never regret a minute of it."

Dawn pushed up to her elbows. "You really do love him, don't you? But how? He doesn't have a dime to his name. His mother is a waitress. All he has to drive you around in is that beat-up truck, and all he can ever hope to be—"

"You're only looking at him from the outside in, Dawn. I see Derek from the inside. Can you say the same about Beau?" Leslie took her hand, knowing any meaningful conversation was pointless in her condition. "Come on. I'm putting you in your bed."

"Can't I sleep in here with you? Like we did when we were little?" Dawn relaxed, becoming a dead weight, and impossible for Leslie to move. "We used to talk about the kind of wedding we would have and—"

"You were the only one who talked about weddings." Leslie waited at the foot of the bed. "You've always wanted to live like a princess and find Prince Charming to whisk you away to his castle. Beau isn't him. He's no good."

Dawn's sweet countenance changed, and with a slight wobble, she rose from the brass bed. "You're wrong. One day, I'll be Mrs. Beau Devereaux. We'll live in his big plantation home, and I will be a loving wife, standing by him as he runs his father's brewery. Everything will be perfect." With a toss of her ponytail, Dawn strolled, rather haphazardly, into the connecting bathroom.

Prior to Beau coming into Dawn's life, Leslie would have run after her sister and begged her to see reason. But something her father once said came back to her.

"People are like windows, Leelee. They have to crack and shatter before they change their view."

* * *

"I mean it. I can't drink like that again," she told him on the phone.

Dawn kept the pillow over her eyes as she held the phone in front of her. She'd spent all day nursing the mother of all hangovers. Just the idea of drinking again made her nauseous.

"Just meet me there, baby. I want to spend time with you tonight."

She liked the insistence in his voice.

"My girl can't stay home and leave me all alone. What would everyone think?"

Ugh! He was right. They had to keep up appearances. Her rep as the head cheerleader would be in serious jeopardy if she didn't attend any party at the river. Sometimes high school could be so hard.

After hanging up with Beau, she wondered why Leelee never seemed stressed about her credibility at school. Her sister didn't care what anyone said about her, which seemed really weird. How could you not want to be popular? If they didn't look so much alike, she would swear someone had switched them at birth.

What really bugged her was ignoring the gossip from her friends about Leelee's choice in men. It hurt sometimes to listen to them talk about Derek's mother and the run-down house they lived in. She wondered if Leslie's problem with Beau was because of Derek's influence. She understood her sister's jealousy of Beau—he was the catch of the century—but she didn't get why she hated him. Leelee had never been a spiteful person. Growing up, she had been Dawn's rock, but lately, she'd changed. Maybe Derek was a bad influence. It would explain a lot.

After downing more Advil, Dawn put the finishing touches on her makeup.

Leslie walked into their shared bathroom.

"You going out?"

Leslie's condescending tone almost made her stab her mascara wand in her eye. Yep, Beau was right. Total bitch.

She reapplied the layer of mascara she had just messed up.

"Beau and his friends are partying at the river. I'm picking up Zoe and heading over there."

Leslie took a seat on the edge of the bathtub. "Are you going to spend your entire senior year at the river?"

Not another holier than thou lecture! Dawn's hands shook with rage. "What's wrong with the river? No, wait. Let me guess." She brandished the mascara wand like a microphone. "'It's nothing but a bunch of mindless drunks screaming and screwing to music.' Isn't that what you said?"

Leslie sat back on the edge of the tub, holding her knee, appearing calm—too damn calm.

"I'm surprised you remembered."

"How could I forget? I'd just started dating Beau and you were all pissy about it."

Leslie stood and cautiously approached her. The epitome of a cool, confident girl.

"He's not good enough for you. When are you going to see that?"

Dawn swallowed back the hurtful things she wanted to say about Derek. But she wouldn't stoop to Leslie's level. For months, Leslie had taken cheap shots at Beau, even hitting on him to steal him away. Dawn knew why; to prove a point—she wasn't good enough for Beau. She knew her sister ached to be proven right. It was her drug. She'd always been the smartest, the brightest, the twin everyone admired, but now people admired Dawn because of the guy she'd landed.

"Go away, Leelee. Don't make me say something we'll both regret."

Leslie left the bathroom without flinging another insult, which was odd for her. Dawn was used to hearing her jabs and one-liners, getting in her point no matter what. Leslie just walking away was unusual.

Pride swelled in her chest. *Maybe she's finally starting to see things my way for a change.*

* * *

A gentle gust from the river's breeze caught in Dawn's hair as she stepped from her car. The faint backbeat of a zippy dance tune wafted by. She smoothed out the wrinkles in her tight jeans and made sure her cashmere sweater showed off her boobs.

The slam of her car door reverberated around the gravel lot.

There weren't nearly as many cars as the previous night. Fewer people meant fewer girls to tease Beau. Lately, she felt like all she did was see who was checking out her boyfriend.

"Sounds like the party is rockin'."

Zoe came up to her side, wearing a big smile, her hazel eyes scanning the lot. She adjusted her light-yellow sweater and raised her head to the path to the river.

"Let's go!"

Dawn followed her, catching glimpses of the ghostly trees surrounding them. The shadows beneath their boughs came alive in the faint light from the rising moon. The shade shifted and tossed in time with the wind circling her. She got a creepy vibe from the darkness at the edge of the parking lot.

Zoe grabbed her hand. "Would you come on?"

Dawn hurried to keep up as they came to the edge of the lot, and gingerly maneuvered the steep path.

Before the lot disappeared behind her, she glanced back at the shadows. Nothing.

I'm losing it.

Dawn touched down on the sand and familiar faces lit by the glow of the bonfires erased her unease. A lot of the same people were back, members of the football team, her cheering squad along with the popular kids she hung out with at school. The music playing stirred her headache.

She spotted a head of curly, black hair by one of the bonfires amid a slew of girls she didn't recognize. Mitch Clarkson turned his round face to the guy next to him. It was the other guy Beau couldn't seem to live without, Josh Breeland. He grinned and blushed when one of the girls pecked his cheek.

She leaned over to Zoe to be heard above the music. "I'm gonna find Beau."

"Sure thing. I'll get us something to drink." Zoe took off in the direction of one of the tubs filled with ice and beer.

Dawn trudged across the sand, eager to spot Beau's sun-streaked hair. He usually met her first thing when she arrived at the river. So where was he?

A tingle in her belly ignited an inkling of concern. Was he with another girl? It was always a fear, probably because she never felt good enough for him. Sometimes she couldn't believe the most popular guy in school wanted her. What she hadn't realized was how stressful keeping him would be.

The music grew fainter as she made it to an obscure corner of the beach. Then a very familiar, musical chuckle drifted by.

Beau?

A breeze shifted the branches, allowing light to shine on an isolated picnic table. Beau was there, nursing a bottle of water and wearing a long-sleeved T-shirt that hugged his broad chest. Next to him was a girl in a pair of black leather pants. Big-boobed and platinum blonde, she had her arm wrapped around Beau's shoulder and gazed longingly into his eyes.

Dawn became so angry she felt like a bulging volcano about to blow.

Beau, seemingly captivated, raised his hand to brush the hair from the girl's face—a gesture he had done a thousand times before with her.

Dawn dug her heels and stormed across the sand. When a beam of moonlight caught the girl's face, jealousy quickened her pace. It was Sara Bissell—the smart-mouthed bimbo who told everyone she loved bondage, but no one actually believed her.

"Beau, what are you doing? Get away from her. She's trash."

Sara sat back from Beau, a broad sassy smirk on her bright red lips. "Who you callin' trash, bitch?"

Beau stood, his gray eyes hooded, and his mouth a thin, angry line. "Dawn, enough!"

His hard voice sent a chill through her. He scared her when he got mad.

"Why are you hiding back here with this whips and chains freak? What are you up to, Sara? He's mine!"

"I'm not up to nothin'!" Sara stepped down, appearing ready to claw Dawn's eyes out. "Your boyfriend asked to talk to me. Seems he's looking for pointers."

Beau's eyes darted around the beach. He took Sara's arm and walked her past Dawn. "Why don't you go back to the party?"

Sara gave Dawn one last steely-eyed stare. "You know where to find me."

Dawn wanted to hit someone or to tear Sara's dyed hair out by the roots. How could he have been talking to her out in the open where all their friends could see? What would everyone think?

In her head, a small voice sounding like her sister kept repeating, *"I told you so."*

"What the hell, Beau?" She spun around to him, seething. "You want to tell me why you were with Bondage Bissell?"

Beau remained aloof as he stood in front of her. One hand slipped into the pocket of his jeans, and the other holding his water. His expression was a mixture of amusement and discontent. The calculating way his gaze skidded up and down her figure made her feel like a rabbit caught in the sights of a wolf.

"You need to lower your voice." He sipped his water.

She charged up to him. "I will not lower my voice. What were you doing with her?"

He took her arm and dragged her back to the picnic table, his fingers digging into her skin. He pushed her onto the bench and set his water next to her. He took a moment, rested his hands on either side of her, pinning her in.

"We were only talking." Beau put on the boyish frown she had never been able to resist—until now. "She's been very forthcoming about her lifestyle and I had questions. Things I wanted to know about her world."

The disclosure hit her with the force of a tsunami. "What? You don't actually buy she's into that stuff? It's an act."

He eased his head lower until his lips came to a halt right before hers. "This isn't about her. It's about us. I've been thinking about trying some new things with you. To find ways to please each other."

She didn't recognize the way he spoke or the strange distance in his voice. This wasn't her Beau.

Her explosive anger trickled to a steady drip. "But why talk to Sara? Why not me?"

He kissed the tip of her nose. "I wanted it to be a surprise."

Part of her didn't buy it. "You were hitting on her. Admit it."

He chuckled softly, filling her with doubt.

"Baby, why would I want to be with her when I have you? Sara's a nobody. She isn't the head of the cheerleading squad, or very cute, or smart, or funny. All the things you are."

He'd described all the things she fought to be every second of every day. But still, she still didn't feel good enough.

"Yeah, but Sara's got big boobs, and all the guys think she's hot because she talks about bondage all the time."

Beau stood back and kicked the sand, looking too damn cute for her to resist. "You know I'm not a boob man. I'm an ass guy, and there isn't an ass in the entire school as fine as yours." He came up to her, grinning. "And as far as the bondage stuff, well, we could try it. Experiment with some things. What do you say?"

Dawn searched his face, hoping to find the truth. Instead, she became more confused. Was love supposed to be this hard? Was giving in all the time the norm in a relationship? And bondage— she'd just gotten the hang of sex. How was she supposed to feel about something that made her uncomfortable?

"What are you, drunk, Devereaux?" Zoe waltzed up to them, wrinkling her nose at Beau. "That bitch, Sara Bissel, is announcing to everyone you two are back here having a fight because of her."

"This is all I need." Beau ran his hand through his hair. "You can tell everyone at the party we're not fighting." He waved Zoe away. "Go on. I'm still talking to Dawn."

Zoe planted her feet. "What am I, your social director? Don't you be thinking you can shoo me away, boy. I'm here to protect my friend from your cheatin' ass."

Beau tossed his head back and held up his fists. "I'm not cheating!"

His smoky voice had been replaced by a touch of panic. He didn't sound anything like the boy Dawn had come to know.

What is going on with him?

Dawn got up from the bench, the nervous tickle in her belly growing stronger. She didn't want to be left alone with an angry Beau. She went to Zoe's side, ready to put some space between them.

"Let's go back to the party."

Beau slapped his chest, indignation burning brighter in his eyes. "What? You're leaving before we've finished our discussion?"

"Can you blame her?" Zoe stood protectively between Dawn and Beau. "You're a piece of shit, Devereaux."

"Shut up!" He smoothed out the tension in his face and shifted his focus to Dawn. "You need to chill, baby. I've done nothing wrong."

"Yet," Zoe edged in with a smirk.

"Damn it, Zoe, stop it." He raised his hand, looking as if he might strike her, and then lowered it. "Don't you dare make Dawn doubt me."

His reaction sent a gut-wrenching jolt through her system. Beau had never laid a hand on Dawn, but she'd never seen him teetering so close to the edge. With his fists clenched, and his jaw muscles quivering, he looked downright dangerous.

"Leave Zoe out of this." Dawn stepped away from her friend. "This is between you and me."

His deadly stare gutted her. Where were the kind eyes of the guy she loved?

"How can I compete with people who keep trashing me? I'm

your boyfriend. You need to believe me and not your so-called friends."

Her heart wanted to believe him, but her head urged caution. He was different, and she couldn't put her finger on what had sparked the change.

"I'm beginning to believe Leslie was right about you."

"You're going to listen to that twisted bitch? After all the times I reached out to her, only to have her throw it in my face?" Beau's voice ticked higher, sounding scary. He held up his hands and backed away from her. "That's it. I'm done. Believe who you want, Dawn."

Dread cascaded through her. She couldn't lose him. What would happen to her reputation? Last night things had been great between them, and now this? What the hell?

"Are you serious?"

He raised his head, a cruel sneer on his lips. "I've never been more serious in my life. I can't hack your drama anymore."

My drama!

The nightmare scenario she had dreaded was here. Her fear morphed into a crushing weight, sucking the air from her lungs.

I can't lose him!

Desperate to save their relationship, she got angry. "Beau Devereaux, if you walk away, I will never speak to you again!"

"That's fine by me." He turned his back on her and strolled toward the party.

The air thinned, and despite her deep breaths, she felt suffocated. Dawn bent over and grabbed her knees.

"It's all right." Zoe patted her back. "He didn't mean it."

Her cheeks burned. Dawn needed to get away. She took off for the party.

"Wait up!" Zoe shouted behind her.

She reached the beach where the partygoers swayed to the soft sounds of a ballad and sipped their beers. Faces blurred as she rushed past, her gaze focused only on the pine-needle strewn path returning her to her car.

By the time she was halfway up the embankment, Zoe caught up to her.

When she stepped out on the gravel lining the lot, her only thought was to get home and climb into her bed so she could cry without anyone seeing. But the heaviness in her heart got to be too much, and once she slid into the driver's seat, tears trickled down her cheeks.

"You'd better let me drive." Zoe took the keys from her hand.

Sniffling, Dawn opened her car door. "I can't go home. Not like this."

Zoe patted her hand. "We'll go to my house. You can stay over. Everything will be better tomorrow."

"Will it?" Dawn didn't think her life could get any worse.

* * *

The fire swirled and weaved around the pine logs in the pit, the crackling of wood carrying across the beach. Beau pictured the red and orange embers running through his bloodstream, flecks of rage surging into his muscles and igniting his desire for pain.

Dawn had ignited his fury. No one ever questioned him. No one.

"I think you blew it with Dawn." Mitch came alongside him, holding on to a can of beer. "She looked pissed."

"I'll smooth things over." Beau grinned at his friend. "We just had a misunderstanding."

Mitch popped open his beer. "Chicks are hard to figure out."

"Some are harder than others." Beau wiped his mouth with his sleeve. "Like Dawn's sister. Now there's a real tough nut."

"She's not so bad." Mitch's dark eyes flickered in the firelight. "She helped me get through freshman English. Would have failed without her."

Beau's fingers twitched. What other information had his friend kept from him?

"You never told me that."

Mitch's shrug was meant to reassure Beau. It didn't.

"You've always been down on her so I never wanted to say nothin'." Mitch sipped his beer.

Beau arched an eyebrow. "So, you like her."

Mitch's color turned ashen and he edged backward, sweat beading his brow. "No, man. It was freshman year. Before she got bitchy."

Beau tilted his head. "I wouldn't blame you if you did like her, but I'd stay away. You might end up cut off from everything. Like Derek Foster. Know what I mean?"

"Yeah, I hear ya." Mitch weighed the beer in his hand. "What you gonna do the rest of the night without a date?"

Beau surveyed the partygoers. "I'm going to hang out with my friends and have fun."

Mitch wiped his brow and toasted him. "You're the king!"

Josh came up to him, offering Beau a beer. "I saw Dawn busting out of here. You need to drink, heavily."

Tempting, but his father's mantra came back to him. "No. Gotta drive my best buds home sober." He slapped Mitch and Josh on their backs.

"Next weekend, I'll drive." Josh popped the beer he had brought for Beau. "Least I can do after all the times you've brought us."

The idea of Josh driving him anywhere almost made him break out in hives. He could trust his defensive lineman to cover his ass on the field, but not on the road.

"We'll see. I'm gonna change the tunes. I think we need some dance music."

He left the orange glow of the bonfire and passed through a mass of giggling high school girls. Then someone patted his back.

"You and Dawn okay?"

Sara's blue eyes came into focus as she stepped in front of him.

He reined in his irritation. "She's a little mad at me, but she'll get over it."

She rubbed her hand along his chest. "Anything I can do to help?"

Beau removed her hand, turned off by her aggression and her red lips. "Don't you think you've done enough?" He pressed into the soft spot of her hand, the space between her thumb and index finger. "I heard you were telling everyone Dawn and I were fighting." He squeezed harder. "Is that true?"

She recoiled from his grip. "Beau, you're hurting me."

He enjoyed the way she squirmed. "I thought you said you were into pain. That's what you told me before?"

"Not like this."

It was what he figured. Another girl who claimed to crave whips and chains, but when confronted by real pain, turned tail and ran.

He pressed on her flesh a little more. "What did you tell everyone about me and Dawn?"

Then he saw it. That captivating twinkle of fear in her eyes. Much less than the horror Taylor had fed him, but enough to awaken his thirst for more.

"I might have told a few people you were fighting." She twisted her arm, trying to get away from him.

The confession was what he wanted. He let her go. "Do yourself a favor, Sara. Don't spread lies about me." He wiped his hands, wondering how loud she would scream if he raped her. "I don't like it when people tarnish my image." He leaned into her. "Be careful what you say about me to anyone. It might come back to haunt you."

He thought he saw her lower lip quivering, but then it vanished. The light from the bonfire flashed in her eyes.

He held out his hand, eager to see if she was worth pursuing. "Now why don't you let me buy you a beer and we can talk some more."

"About what?" she asked, still appearing leery.

He smiled. "Anything you like."

Chapter twelve

Beau folded his arms, studying the trace of morning fog hovering above the blacktop of the school parking lot, his irritation gnawing at him.

Where in the hell was Dawn? She always rode with Leslie, but this morning they were late. Had something happened to her? It would explain why she hadn't returned any of his calls or his texts.

Sometimes she annoyed the shit out of him.

"Any sign of her?" Mitch asked, appearing next to him.

Beau rested his hip against the hood of his car. "She'll be here soon enough, and I'll convince her to forgive me."

Mitch kicked at the mist around his feet. "You know, sooner or later, she's gonna wise up about the other girls. She's not stupid."

Beau offered a playful smirk. "What other girls?"

"I'm just sayin', they all find out." Mitch stroked the hood of Beau's car. "My old man tried to keep his cheatin' hidden from my mom for years, but she found out. It's the reason I ended up in this damn town after the divorce. Workin' at the brewery was the only job my mom could find."

Beau leaned into him. "Yeah, well, Dawn better not get wind of any of the other girls from you or any of the guys on the team."

"I hear ya." Mitch hurriedly backed away. "I'd better get to first-period before the bell. Mr. Santos can be a ball-buster if you're late."

Beau sighed, disappointed. He'd always believed Mitch to be a friend, but what if his favorite wide-receiver was just another ass-kisser?

Aren't they all?

A familiar white Accord entered the lot. Beau uncrossed his arms and stood.

The car pulled to a stop and Dawn emerged from the passenger side.

He counted to ten before jogging across the lot.

I hope this damn woman appreciates the ass I'm making of myself.

"Hey, baby."

Dawn ignored him and made a beeline for the school entrance.

Leslie climbed out the other side of the car. The look in her eyes dug into his soul. He took in her sweater and jeans and pictured her naked body covered with bruises. She was curvier than her flat-chested sister, and, he suspected, a lot feistier in the sack.

"Leslie. How are you today?"

"Get away from me, asshole."

She started to walk away and he fumed, undone by her brush off. He so wanted to teach her a lesson.

"It won't always be like this between us."

Leslie stopped in mid-stride and turned to him. "What's your problem?"

He moved in closer, analyzing the turn of her head, the way her blue eyes never wavered. The rush she gave him sometimes made it hard to think.

"My problem is you." Beau's voice degenerated into a guttural rasp. "You haunt my dreams every night. I see me doing incredible things to you." He brushed the bangs from her eyes. "And I plan on making my dreams come true very soon."

She slapped his hands away. "Touch me, and I'll cut your dick off and shove it up your ass."

Enthralled, Beau licked his lips. "I love it when you talk dirty. If you could teach some of that to your sister, I would appreciate it."

"You're disgusting!"

Before he could blink, Leslie slapped him.

The sting brought a slow, smoldering smile to his lips. He

stepped toward her, relishing his anticipation of the day when she was helpless, stretched on his cot, and at his mercy.

"So, you like it rough. I'll remember that."

He drank in the crimson of her cheeks, the rapid rise and fall of her chest, sensing he was right about her.

"Hey, what's going on here?"

The magic of the moment slipped away when Derek stepped between them.

The stupid geek poked out his chest as he took a defensive stance in front of his girlfriend.

Beau found the gesture pathetic.

"Is there a problem, Devereaux?"

Derek's icy glare fueled Beau's hate. He yearned to rip his head from his skinny stick of a neck and squeeze it until his brains squirted on the blacktop, food for the crows. But the parking lot teemed with students and teachers—all eyes were on them.

Beau had spent too many years tending to his image to destroy it for the sake of one nerd. He needed to stay focused on the end result, and not let anyone interfere in his pursuit of his Leslie.

"I was just asking Leslie to help me with Dawn," he said in an easygoing manner. "She's mad at me and I could use some advice."

The air was so brittle between them, he thought at any second it would snap, and Derek would charge, defending his woman. Seconds ticked by and then Derek's caustic gaze withered. Beau knew then he would always back down.

A real man fights for what he wants.

From that moment on, Derek Foster would be an inconsequential blip in his pursuit of his perfect woman.

"Are you okay, Leslie?" Derek put his arm around her.

Derek's pseudo-manly gesture of ownership sickened him. "She's fine, Foster."

Leslie gripped Derek's arm. Beau admired her slender fingers, picturing them squeezed in fists of pain.

"Forget about it. Let's just get to class."

Derek got in Beau's face, squaring off like a contender in the ring. His tough guy act amused Beau.

"You're never to touch her, you hear me? I'll kill you if you try it."

Students gathered around, checking out their confrontation. He needed to turn the tables on Derek. Gossip could kill a rep faster than any action witnessed by one person. Beau had used such methods in the past to shut down challenges to his parties at the river and to dispense with a few old girlfriends, but this time he needed to make sure the crowd took away what he wanted them to remember.

"I think you should have a chat with your girl, Foster. I tried to have a conversation with her about her sister and she flew off the handle." He smirked at Leslie. "If you ask me, that's not normal. People are talking about how strange she's acting. Even the teachers are wondering what's up. Perhaps you should take her to the nurse to get checked out. Maybe she's pregnant. You guys practice safe sex, I hope."

The snickers from those around them let Beau know his arrow had hit the bullseye. By afternoon, the whole school would be abuzz with Leslie Moore's pregnancy.

"You asshole!" Leslie came at him, but Derek stepped in, boxing her arms and holding her against him.

Beau took a moment, wishing he could have been in Derek's shoes, holding her as she fought back.

All in good time.

He turned away, confronting the eager faces of those students behind him. He loved how they whispered amongst themselves. With her rep in a free fall, she would eventually need rescuing, and he would be there, her knight in shining armor.

A girl in a thick black sweater and a cap on her head of long brown hair cut in front of him. When her blue eyes zeroed in on him, Beau was thunderstruck by the change in Taylor's appearance.

Her hunched shoulders, lack of makeup, and layers of thick clothes were a far cry from the flirty girl he had met on the beach. The only thing he recognized was the hate stewing in her eyes. The look she gave him was the same one she'd given him in the cells.

"Taylor, nice to see you again." He kept his tone condescending. "Love the outfit. I hear bag lady is in this year."

A few chuckles from those in earshot assured him Taylor's rep would go down in flames with Leslie's. Even better.

Taylor never said a word. She stood, glowering, and he didn't like it one bit. If she kept this up, people might ask questions.

Leslie went up to her and put a friendly hand on her shoulder. "Taylor, you okay?"

He wanted to give Taylor a reminder of their night together, and a warning.

"Perhaps you shouldn't party so hard on the weekends, Taylor. You never know where it may lead."

The chuckles from those around him helped dispel his unease at seeing the stupid girl. Deciding not to push his luck, he strutted toward the school entrance. His heart raced and sweat beaded on his upper lip.

"Chill, dude, chill," he muttered while jogging up the front steps. "She won't talk. She wouldn't dare."

* * *

The din of conversation and rushing students circled Dawn as her jittery hands rummaged through her locker for her chemistry book. The image of Beau coming across the lot to her played over in her head, making her forget what book she needed.

Why do I feel like I'm in the wrong? He's the jerk.

She'd expected a lot of stares and whispers as she entered the halls of the school that morning, but the gossip hounds were already deboning their next victim. She refocused on chemistry and just as she retrieved her book, she spotted Beau.

His arm against a locker, he leaned into a girl, pinning her between him and a water fountain. Dawn couldn't make out her face, but from the protective way she hugged her book bag to her chest, she appeared frightened.

Beau, on the other hand, seemed angry. She had seen this before—his fists clenched, stiff posture and pressed lips—right before he yelled at her for doing something stupid.

The girl attempted to dart around Beau.

Dawn gasped. It was Taylor Haskins.

"What the hell?"

Did he have something going on with Taylor? By the looks of their encounter, she thought not. But why was he so upset?

Dawn's imagination got the better of her as she pictured the two of them making out at the river.

She must be why Beau was so odd the other night. He's sleeping with her!

She was about to march across the hall and confront Beau when Taylor dashed away. Then Beau coolly adjusted his book bag over his shoulder and strutted down the hall. The cocky grin on his face was the one he got when he felt powerful and in charge like at the river or a football field when he passed a touchdown. He never used such a face with girls; that was a different smile altogether. One Dawn had memorized.

Her anger melted into confusion.

Zoe jumped into her line of sight.

"Hey, you ready for the chemistry test?"

Dawn peeked over her shoulder to see what Beau was doing.

"Hello?" Zoe moved her head, blocking her view. "Are you listening to me?" She glanced behind her and then back to Dawn. "Oh, for the love of God. You're not mooning over him, are you?"

Dawn shut her locker. "No."

"After the night you spent at my house, crying your eyes out, I hope not. He showed his true colors. Why can't you see that?"

Dawn tucked her chemistry book in her bag. "I know he's a two-timing louse, but I saw …"

"Saw what?" Zoe inched in closer, her voice almost a whisper.

"Nothing." Dawn put on a smile. "Ready for chemistry?"

"Am I ready to fail another one of Mr. Elbert's tests? Yep."

"We have a test?" Dawn's mouth went dry.

Zoe shook her head. "Girl, sometimes your mind even amazes me."

* * *

Leslie tensed as she snuck in the back door of her home from the garage. The hall dark, the house quiet, and the kitchen empty, she held her breath, waiting for her mother to jump out from a shadowy corner and interrogate her about where she went after school. When she finally reached the newel post, she relaxed.

How had her life come to this? Between Beau, her sister, and fighting with her mother about Derek, Leslie had not had a moment's peace. The stress got to her, people at school had noticed, and even one or two of her teachers had asked about her life. But what could she tell them?

Upstairs, she hurried across the hall carpet to her bedroom, eager to hide from her mother. Lately, she had spent more and more time there.

Yellow light spilled on the cream-colored carpet from Dawn's open bedroom door. Leslie peered inside, not expecting her sister to be home so soon from cheerleading practice. But she was there, sitting on her pink princess bed, her brow wrinkled, and holding her cell phone.

"Hey." She leaned against the open door, spying the pink walls decorated with posters of boy bands and puppies. "Where's Mom?"

Dawn never looked up. "Out."

Okay. Let me ask another question.

"What are you doing home so early?"

Her attention stayed glued to her phone. "I called off practice and had Zoe bring me home."

Leslie couldn't remember a day when her sister had missed practice. Cheerleading had been her life. Well, cheerleading and Beau.

"You still upset about Beau?"

Dawn raised her head and revealed her bloodshot eyes. "What do you think?"

Her first impulse was to rush to her side and hold her. She never wanted to see Dawn upset, but her support would be unwelcome. The great divide Beau had created between them had taught her to keep her distance.

"Are you going to get back together with him?"

Dawn slammed her phone next to her on the bed. "Why do you care?"

For months, her sister had seemed so happy, so in love and swore Beau pampered her, so Leslie had kept quiet about her boyfriend's abuse. But now the relationship appeared stalled, and Leslie sensed an opportunity. Perhaps Dawn was ready to listen.

"There's something you should know about Beau." Leslie came into the room and shut the door. "He says things to me, awful things. He hits on me and promises to bring me to The Abbey one day. It's been going on for a while. He said some pretty disgusting things today."

Dawn narrowed her eyes. "Is this a joke? I heard about your argument at school. Everyone did. You're the one who threatened Beau. How am I supposed to believe anything you say? Is this part of your plan to get us to break up?"

Leslie tossed up her hand, disgusted. "I shouldn't have said anything. You're right."

Dawn jumped from the bed. "You're just saying this because

you want Beau for yourself. You know Mom can't stand Derek, but she loves Beau. And if you get him, then she will go easier on you."

Leslie's jaw dropped. "Are you out of your mind? Like I could care less what Mom thinks of me or who I date. I don't need her approval, and neither do you." She held up her hands. "You know what? I'm done. I don't care what you do when it comes to Beau Devereaux. Marry him. See if I care!"

"Fine. I will marry him and be the richest girl in town."

Dawn's smug expression sent Leslie running for the door.

See if I ever lift a finger to help you again!

* * *

The slam of the bedroom door knocked a picture of Beau off her dresser. She rushed to rescue the silver frame. She replaced the image of Beau, flashing his charming smile and hugging her, on the dresser.

How could Leelee understand what he meant to her? Years of living in her perfect sister's shadow had been forgotten the first time Beau kissed her. He was special, and he made her special by loving her. With Beau, she was an individual, and not Leslie Moore's twin. All her life she had been second best. Now she was somebody and her sister couldn't stand her newfound sense of self.

For Leelee to stoop so low as to attack Beau like that had been unexpected.

Of all the cheap shots.

Back on the bed, Dawn toyed with the idea of calling Beau. She was a better person with him than without him. Perhaps she had acted harshly, probably too much Leslie in her head. Listening to anything she said about Beau was a mistake.

With a shaky hand, she reached for the phone.

Beau answered on the first ring. "I've missed you, baby. Why haven't you called me?"

"I was mad." She cradled her phone against her cheek, wishing she was in his arms. "When I saw you with Sara, and then the way you acted ..."

"Nothing happened." He sounded so sincere. "You mean the world to me and I was such a fool to let you walk away. Please forgive me, Dawn."

Her heart melted, but the things Leslie had told her still ate at her. "What did you say to my sister at school today? I thought you were going to stay away from her."

An unexpected silence arose. It didn't last long but struck her as odd.

"I asked her to talk to you for me, but you know Leslie," he said in a matter of fact way. "She hates me. She got weird on me then her boyfriend showed up. I'm sure you heard the rest."

"I can't understand what her problem is." She considered how far apart they had grown in recent months. "It's like I don't even know who she is anymore."

His voice took on a gruff edge. "Forget about your sister. Let's talk about us."

She reclined on the bed, happy they were back on solid ground. "Just promise me you didn't have anything to do with Sara after I left the river?"

"Nothing at all, baby. I was so upset after you left. I actually drank with the boys. Ask them, if you don't believe me. Don't you know by now you're my number one girl?"

Dawn's doubt could not be so easily smoothed over. "I'm more concerned about being your only girl."

"Baby, you are! You will always be."

Dawn's grip on her phone tightened. "Promise me I'm the only one, Beau."

"I more than promise, I guarantee. You're my girl, now and always."

Leslie's words faded as Beau's declaration won her over. "I've missed you," she whispered. "Not being with you today was hell."

"When can I see you?" Desperation hung in his voice.

"Tomorrow, after school." She relished the idea of being alone with him. "We can spend time together then."

His sigh felt like a caress against her cheek. "Sounds great. It seems like we've been apart forever."

Dawn giggled. "Well, what are you doing tonight? You could come over?"

"Ah, I can't, baby. I've got a bitch of an English Lit paper to tackle and I've got to get an A or I'll blow my GPA. You know how I suck at Shakespeare."

"I know. Well, don't stay up too late. I want to see you first thing in the morning at school. We can walk in the front entrance and show everyone we're back together. I'll bet the whole school was talking about us today. Probably wondering why the quarterback of the football team and the captain of the cheerleading squad weren't together."

"I don't care what people think. I only care what you think."

"I'll be waiting at the entrance for you." She hesitated, then added, "I love you, Beau."

"Ah, gotta go, sweetie." Beau suddenly sounded rushed. "See you tomorrow."

He hung up.

Dawn stared at her phone, euphoric at first, and then she reconsidered the conversation.

Why am I always the one saying I love you?

She tried to push the thought back, but it was too late.

He does love me. Right?

Chapter Thirteen

Streetlamps nestled between tall oaks guided Beau to his parents' gate. A crisp fall breeze whipped his hair as the tall, arched gates of black wrought iron with romantic swirls loomed ahead.

He hated those gates. To the outside world, they marked the entrance to the Devereaux Plantation, but to him they represented prison.

At the gate, he pushed his security code into the keypad. The lights of the brewery in the distance lured him away from his doldrums.

The evening shift would be in full swing, and after them, the minimal night crew would check in. He couldn't remember a day when the brewery hadn't crept into his life. He'd worked every shift, in every building and after years of attending benefits, holiday parties for the employees, and sometimes traveling with his father to promote their brand, he hated the brewery almost as much as his home.

After the gates slowly swung open, Beau maneuvered his car along the long cement drive to the front of the prized three-story home. Built when the nation had been on the brink of the Civil War, the house had the customary sweeping galleries and temple-fronted facade attributed to the Greek Revival movement that was popular at the time. With four Corinthian columns, and painted white to resemble marble, the home boasted balconies trimmed in the same fancy wrought iron design as the arched gate, and a porch decorated with rocking chairs. His mother had insisted the chairs gave the house a homey feel.

Homey, my ass.

When he passed the cover of oak trees along the driveway, the light from the french windows and double front doors doused him with warm yellow light. It reached into the darkness around his car and created sinewy shadows in the Spanish moss-covered oaks and flowerbeds of gardenias. Beau used to believe ghosts haunted the trees when he was little because of the strange way the lights would make the moss undulate.

His father had insisted on the light display and made sure it burned until dawn. He even had the lights in the round cupola located atop the red-slated roof turned on. Beau thought the whole thing a waste of electricity and swore he would stop the silly tradition when he inherited the place.

Hate the house as he did, it had been in his family for ten generations, and he could not fathom giving it up completely. Ever since the Frellson family had purchased the land, a male heir had lived under its roof. The acreage had begun as a cotton farm and by the time electricity became available, turned to farmland. By then, the name had changed to Devereaux—for reasons still unclear to Beau—and the family fortune had expanded to gold, railroads, and banking. The brewery had been his great-grandfather's hobby and had eventually grown into a lucrative source of income. But it was his grandfather, an infamous state senator, who had given the family their political clout in the state. Beau hoped to follow in Edward Devereaux's footsteps, but only after his career in the NFL had ended.

After passing the edge of the porch, the drive followed the side of the home to the five-car garage at the rear.

Once safely inside the mudroom door, he passed through a set of etched glass french doors decorated with peacocks to a tile floor that traveled to the rear of the kitchen. Along the walls were framed magazine covers featuring his family home. There were six in all, and none captured the feel of the house. He figured no amount of rocking chairs would change that.

In the kitchen, the green digital lights from the numerous appliances cluttering the countertop cast an eerie glow. There were an array of cookers and coffeemakers his father had given his mother with the hope she'd take an interest in something other than drinking and shopping.

He yanked open the door of the onyx built-in refrigerator and retrieved a bottle of apple juice. He perused the containers of freshly prepared meals arranged neatly on the shelves by Leah—the only person in the house who seemed to care what he ate. Turned off by the selection, he closed the door and opted for a bowl of microwavable mac and cheese.

Study material in hand, he repositioned his book bag over his shoulder and took the short cut to the staircase through the cypress-paneled dining room, wanting to avoid his father's study door.

The dining room had numerous painted portraits of former Devereaux men. Arranged according to the years they lived in the home, the portraits started at the entrance off the main hall with the builder of the plantation, Gerard Frellson. The most recent addition, his father's painting, hung toward the back entrance by the kitchen. Beau felt the likeness exactly like Gage Devereaux—cold, ruthless, and lifeless. An empty spot sat on the wall for his portrait.

Yeah, that's another tradition I'm getting rid of.

He walked across the room and swore the eyes of each family member followed him, criticizing his choices. For years, he'd refused to go to the kitchen at night by himself, no matter how hungry he was, for fear the pictures would come to life. Now they meant nothing, but he was thankful for the discipline his fear had taught him.

Self-control is everything.

He passed through the peach-painted parlor, turning up his nose at the pastel sofa and matching wingback chairs. Heavy curtains with peach accents pooled on the hardwood floor in front of the windows, a nod to the "Southern tradition" of excess material in curtains representing wealth and not taste. The furniture was oak and dainty matching the feminine feel of the room. His mother preferred the parlor, but tonight she wasn't in her favorite wingback chair with her whiskey. Beau figured she'd moved her drinking to her bedroom—the one she slept in down the hall from his father's room.

That other parents shared a bedroom had been a shock at the tender age of six. He thought all parents slept apart and rarely spoke. Sleeping over at friends' houses had shown him his family wasn't the norm; they were the exception.

He was about to step into the central hallway, close to the curved staircase, when a shadow of movement came from his father's study.

Beau tiptoed across the floorboards, keeping to the red and gold runner down the center, hoping it would mask his steps. He was just about to pass a gold and marble french side table when the damned floor gave him away. The groan echoed throughout the hall and he cringed, sure his father heard it.

"Beau, come in here."

Convinced he was in trouble for something—usually not living up to Gage Devereaux's excessive standards—he stiffened and gripped his meal to his chest, prepared to get it over with so he could get to his homework.

He pushed the heavy cypress door open, and the warm light from the room engulfed him.

With burgundy leather furniture, ash paneling, and an Oriental rug covering the old hardwood, the room was distinctively male. Even down to the wide walnut desk his father sat behind, the space reeked of authority.

"Where have you been?"

Relaxed in his red leather office chair, a thick folder opened on his desk, Gage frowned as his son approached.

Here comes another lecture.

With Gage Devereaux, it was always about talking, never about being heard.

"I had to stay late for a student council meeting after practice."

Gage pushed a small pile of papers off to the side. "And what about schoolwork?"

"I've got it covered."

The scowl on his father's lips summed up a lifetime of memories. Never a smile, never a kind word, only *work harder, do more.*

"You only think you do. That's your problem. You don't study hard enough."

Beau's stomach rumbled.

"You need to do more if you want to get into Tulane. Your ACT scores weren't exactly impressive. Neither are your grades."

Beau took a step forward, feeling brave. "I've got other skills the admission committee will look at."

"Are we talking football?" Gage sat back, clasping his hands. "That's not enough."

Beau gave an upbeat grin. "But it will help. Colleges look at sports stars before regular students."

"Being good at football isn't going to help you run this business. A degree is. You're also going to have to set more of an example in this town. I've been hearing some talk about you, your friends, and the river." Gage stood and came around to the leather chairs in front of his desk. "Is there anything I should worry about?"

"No. Nothing." Beau nervously shuffled his feet.

Gage sat on the edge of his desk, eyeing his son. "You're going to be running the family business one day. What this community thinks of you now will influence how you do business in the future. I've had to fight to uphold our family name. It's why I've pushed you so hard to not make my mistakes and earn the respect you will need to carry on the business."

"But people do respect me." His voice notched upward, reflecting his frustration. "I work my ass off. I attend all the benefits put on by the brewery. I'm captain of the football team, president of the student council, and I do the volunteer work at the local family clinic. What more do you want me to do?"

"And what about the anger? Your mother told me what you did with the computer. Are we going to have issues again?"

His father's hard tone directed his gaze to the rug. "No. I got it under control, sir."

"I don't think you do. There are those in this town who'll be watching your every move because they know eventually, I'll be passing the reins of everything I own—the brewery, the town, the businesses, and the investments to you. Remember that. The image your project, the deeds you do, that's what you're known for. Don't let them see who you really are."

"I know." Beau raised his head, giving him a confident smile. "You've got nothing to worry about."

Gage crinkled his brow and then glanced back to the pile of papers on his desk. "Go eat your dinner and leave me to my monthly invoices."

Anxious to get out from under his father's scrutiny, Beau hustled for the door. His father's voice rambled around in his head, giving him a headache.

He stood before the curved oak staircase at the end of the hall, unable to understand why his old man was so mistrusting of him. Beau never screwed up, and if he did, he covered his tracks.

At the top of the stairs, he peered down the long burgundy carpet running along the second floor. He saw a light shining beneath his mother's bedroom door. Gingerly, he walked across the carpet, praying he could get to the safety of his bedroom without encountering Elizabeth. He hated dealing with her late in the evening.

"Beau, is that you?"

He cursed under his breath.

A lock clicked open and then light from her open door beamed into the hallway.

Sighing, he answered, "Yes, it's me, Mom."

Elizabeth came into the hallway, wearing her yellow robe.

She examined the apple juice and container of mac and cheese in his hand. "Is that all your eating? Is everything okay?"

"Fine. I was just going to get started on my homework and grab a bite." He made a move to head down the hall.

"What is it? You don't want to give your mother a minute of your time?"

He halted, curtailing his desire to tell her what he was thinking. Approaching the open door, he noted its shiny new lock.

"You changed the lock again." He smirked. "Was that before or after I threw the computer across the kitchen?"

She went to touch him and he backed away. Elizabeth curled her hand into her chest.

"I got scared. The last time you got angry at me, I ended up with twenty-two stiches. I don't want to go through that again."

He shook his head, wondering how the cold bitch could even think of calling herself a mother. "I was seven when that happened. I didn't mean to hurt you. It was an accident."

"It wasn't an accident, Beau." She rolled up the right sleeve on her robe. "You attacked me."

The shiny thin scar on her forearm brought back memories he had tried day after day to suppress.

The ferocity of his rage at the time came back to him. It had been there all his life, like boiling water beneath the surface of a still lake. His muscles twitched as he pictured taking the butcher knife out of the block in the kitchen and going in search of his mother. She had taken away his favorite toy because he'd bitten a boy at school. He was going to show her.

He had climbed the stairs and crept down the hall to her bedroom door. Beau had turned the handle, being very quiet like in his favorite ninja movies. Her back had been to him as she sat on her big bed, talking on the phone.

The first blow had glanced off her arm, but the second ripped through her flesh, and the blood. He'd loved the metallic smell of it mixing with her floral perfume.

"I'm not that kid anymore."

Elizabeth rolled down her sleeve. "I hope not. I don't want to—"

"I said I'm okay!"

His shout echoed throughout the hallway. He hoped his father hadn't heard. Having his mother on his ass was enough.

She took a step backward. "Go eat your dinner and get to bed early. You know how you get when you don't sleep."

He tilted his head in the open door. She had turned down the comforter on her mahogany four-poster bed, but on the nightstand was an empty glass and bottle of whiskey. In the background, the blare of the television mounted on the wall filled an uncomfortable silence.

"How many have you had tonight?"

Elizabeth pulled at the lapels of her robe. "It's just a nightcap, sweetie, so I can sleep."

He hated the saccharine voice she used after a couple of drinks. Beau faced his mother, not hiding his tight grimace.

"Is that your excuse for the past ten years?"

The caring glint in Elizabeth's gray eyes faded. "I don't like your tone."

"And I don't like seeing you drunk, Mom." He let his anger seep into his voice. "Are you ever going to do something about it?"

"Don't lecture me." She shook her head, leaning against the doorframe. "We get enough of that from your father."

He motioned to the bottle on the nightstand. "Is that his fault or mine?"

Elizabeth pushed off from the doorway. "You already know the answer, Beau."

He stepped closer, the hate bubbling under his skin. "You

bitch."

She backed into her room, the hall lights accentuating the pallor of her cheeks.

I can smell your fear.

Elizabeth slammed the door in his face and the *click* of the lock put an end to their conversation.

Satisfied, he strutted down the hall. Nothing like terrorizing his mother to make him feel better.

He clenched the brass handle of his door as he thought of her pouring yet another drink. His anger eased, knowing she would retreat to her bottle to dull her pain. Ever since that night, she had found refuge in her whiskey.

The knot in his chest coiling tighter, Beau shoved his door open. Only a few more months and he would be free. He could put St. Benedict behind him and never come back.

Chapter Fourteen

The warm Louisiana sun crested the towering trees alongside the high school parking lot, chasing away the dewdrops on the blacktop. Beau eased his car into his shady spot next to the big oak and searched for Leslie's car.

Good. He'd beaten Dawn to school.

He'd dressed in khakis and a freshly starched shirt, wanting to look his best for her. It was time to put any rumors about their relationship to rest. He couldn't let a girl walk away from him. When the time was right, and Leslie was his, Beau would end it.

Across the parking lot, Sara appeared, wearing a flowery and fitted dress, showing off her boobs. She was with Dawn's irritating friend, Zoe. The two girls had their heads bowed as if deep in conversation. A cold sweat broke out under Beau's shirt.

What are these two up to?

He set out across the lot and charged up to the girls. "Hey, there."

Zoe frowned while Sara flourished a radiant smile.

Beau ignored Zoe. "So, Sara, did you get that last problem in chemistry? I could use your help."

Zoe sniffed and shook her head. "I'll see you at lunch, Sara."

Beau waited until Zoe was out of earshot before he said, "I just wanted to say, I had a great time on the river the other night. You're a good listener. I'm sorry if I bored you."

Sara flipped her long hair around her shoulder. "Not at all. I liked talking to you. Perhaps we could do it again sometime."

The invitation irritated him. The last thing he needed was Dawn finding out about his time with Sara.

"I'd love that." *Then I can shut you down for good.* "We could sneak away this weekend at the river during the party. I know a special place where we could talk in private."

A faint blush warmed her cheeks. "Sure. I'll be there."

He nodded after Zoe. "What were you two talking about? Didn't know you were tight with her."

"We're not. She was just asking me if I wanted to try out for the cheerleading squad. Taylor Haskins quit."

Taylor. A rush of adrenaline seized him. He had to make sure she didn't become a problem.

Sara waited in front of him, her tedious smile wearing on his nerves.

"Well, I gotta go."

She pouted, obviously not happy. "What's your hurry?"

He scrutinized the odd twist of her lips. "After what happened last time at the river, I don't think we should be seen together. Best to play it safe."

She spun away without saying another word.

Seconds later, the Moore girls' car entered the lot.

Perfect timing.

He set off across the green grass at a brisk pace.

Leslie eased into her usual spot close to the quad. He slowed down, not wanting to appear too anxious, wiped his hand across his damp brow and put on the amiable smile he knew would win her over.

Dawn climbed from the front passenger seat, her hair hanging free, her blue eyes clogged with mascara and her lips stained with thick red lipstick. His heart sank. She looked like a whore.

Ignoring his revulsion, he went up to her, determined to make a very public display.

"I've missed you, baby." He kissed her cheek.

Over Dawn's shoulder, he saw Taylor on the school steps,

glowering at him. Her ill-fitting clothes and pale skin made him wonder what the hell he had ever found attractive in her.

Dawn slinked out of his arms. "What was that for?"

"I wanted to start things off right between us."

Leslie stood from the car. His fingers dug into Dawn's arms when he eyed her saucy smirk.

"So, you're back." Leslie peered over the top of the car. "You're like bubonic plague, Beau Devereaux. You can never be eradicated."

I know just what I'm gonna put in that smart mouth of yours.

"Ignore her." Dawn handed him her book bag. "Walk me to class?"

His fists clenched the straps. "Absolutely, baby."

Dawn clung to his arm, smiling like a beauty queen wearing her newly won crown, eager to make sure everyone got a good look at their reunion.

Beau wasn't interested in the whispers and quick glances directed their way. He kept his focus locked on Taylor.

She remained hidden in the shadows along the side of the stone steps to the school, the tormented look of a captured animal in her eyes. The meticulously secured buttons of her shirt climbed all the way to her throat, reminding him of a nun. Gone was the nymphet wanting to "play hard."

He tuned out Dawn's chatter about plans for after school, nodding only when necessary. It was the terrified Taylor who piqued his interest. Hugging the side of the steps as he approached, she never turned away. The laughter of other students rose around them, a gentle breeze caressed the wisps of Taylor's hair fallen from her ponytail, and a faint whiff of clover from the quad wafted by. The smell reminded him of Leslie. Taylor backed to the side of the steps, cowering in the shadows.

He imagined his Leslie acting just as compliant, just as afraid.

I can't wait.

* * *

The bell rang and students crammed the halls. Beau weaved in and out as he rushed to the hallway right down from Taylor's locker. He settled into a corner, dumping his bag on the floor. Leaning against the cool metal lockers, he kept watching for Taylor. He knew she had no class for the next hour, having craftily coaxed her schedule out of Mrs. Bankston in the school office. He'd pleaded he needed to speak with Taylor about a community service project. Beau planned to skip trig to give them time together.

Her behavior bothered him—the change in clothes, attitude, and her quitting cheerleading would raise questions from those who knew her best. Questions he didn't want answered. A pep talk was in order to remind her of what was at stake if anyone ever found out what had happened.

The bell rang and the hall scattered with students rushing to class. He remained in his spot, his focus fixed on her locker.

The last frenzied screech of tennis shoes skidding on the tiled floor faded and the hall went still.

He waited.

The rumble of desks and shuffling of students came through the wall next to him. followed by a teacher's muffled call for students to take their seats.

He waited.

The door to the girls' bathroom creaked open. A head poked out, and Taylor searched the hallway.

Beau pressed up against the locker, hiding his figure behind the corner. A slight squeak of shoes on the floor made him look back around.

She was at her locker, working the combination, her back to him.

He snuck up behind her, careful not to make a sound.

He placed his hands on the lockers beside hers, effectively

trapping her in place.

"Taylor, how are you today?" His voice turned velvety as memories of her sweet submission flooded his mind. "I've missed you."

She arched away from him. "Leave me alone."

Beau put his lips to her ear. "What did I say last time we chatted about lying low? Stop staring at me like some sick stalker when you see me. Understand? We can't have people knowing about our special time together. You've kept your mouth shut, right?"

Her breath became in choppy waves. "I said I wouldn't say anything and I haven't."

Beau ran his fingertip down her neck, loving the way she stiffened. "Good. Let's keep it that way, shall we? I'd hate for something to happen to your daddy's career."

Taylor cringed as he leaned in, his breath brushing across her ear.

"Just remember, you go back on your word and I'll take you again. And this time, when I'm done, no one will ever find your body."

He pushed away from the lockers and strutted down the hall.

If she ever breathed a word of their encounter, he would carry out his threat. Taylor Haskins would end up as just another victim of the rough waters in the Bogue Falaya River.

* * *

Late for class, Leslie was jogging down the hall when she noticed Beau curled into a girl's back, a brown ponytail draped over her left shoulder. She stopped and hid behind a row of lockers, anxious to not be seen.

He stormed down the hall.

What the hell is wrong with him?

Beau had just rounded the corner when Taylor slammed her

locker door.

The two alone in the hall suggested something more than coincidence. But unlike other couples sneaking some quality time, Beau's anger and Taylor's shaking hands didn't scream secret rendezvous to Leslie.

First the hasty departure from the squad and now meetings with Beau Devereaux. Something is up with the girl.

"Hey, are you okay?"

Taylor displayed a weak smile, blowing out a shaky breath.

"Just got a lot going on."

"Was that Beau Devereaux?"

She peered around the hall, sidestepping Leslie. "I'm not sure."

The way she laced her fingers to hide the slight tremor in her hands struck Leslie as odd.

"Are you and Beau …?" Leslie left the suggestion hanging.

Taylor's head popped up and her eyes flew open. "No, no. We're nothing. Please, please don't mention you saw us talking to anyone. Especially Dawn." She clung to Leslie's arm.

"It's all right." Leslie spoke as she would to a terrified child. "I won't say anything to anyone."

Taylor bobbed her head and let her go. "Thank you. I can't let … I mean I don't want any problems with him. I prefer to stay as far away from Beau as possible."

A stab of suspicion went through her. Something had happened to Taylor and Leslie was certain Beau was behind it.

"Glad to hear I'm not the only one who hates running into Beau. That's something we have in common."

Taylor angled her head to the side. "But he dates your sister. How can you hate him?"

"Probably for the same reasons you do." She inched closer, hoping to win her confidence. "He's got everyone in this town believing he's some kind of saint, but he's far from that."

A veil of calm seemed to descend over Taylor. Her shoulders

relaxed, her trembling subsided, and a long slow breath escaped her lips. "Why can't Dawn see what a horrible person he is?"

Her fear, her hatred for Beau made sense, but Leslie couldn't put together why she had met with him in the empty hall.

"What did Beau say to you?"

Taylor's eyes darted around the hall, and she bit her lower lip. "Ah, I'm late for class. I should go."

She took off, leaving Leslie wondering what had upset her.

Derek rounded a corner in the hall as Taylor rushed past him. He glanced at her and then walked up to Leslie.

"Hey," Derek said, coming alongside her. "What are you doing out here? I thought you had calculus."

Leslie kept peering down the hall where Taylor had disappeared, trying to make sense of their encounter.

"I do, but I ran into Taylor Haskins."

"You run into Taylor all the time." Derek brushed the bangs from her eyes. "What's so special about that?"

"She was with Beau Devereaux." Leslie thumbed the locker behind her. "I caught them together in front of her locker."

Derek inched closer. "Did she tell you why she was with him? Seems funny those two being alone together. Is he going to start bothering her now and leave you alone?"

The comment gave Leslie pause. Could she be suffering the same abuse Leslie had endured for months? It would explain her odd behavior. In some ways, it mirrored Leslie's.

Derek nudged her shoulder. "So, what do you think?"

She came out of her stupor. "Think about what?"

"Camping out by the river this weekend?" He grinned, appearing excited. "We could fish and lay out under the stars. We haven't done that in a while, and it will be too cold soon."

She winced at the prospect of disappointing him. "I have to go to the lake house with my family this weekend. I've tried to get out of it, but Dad's not letting me or Dawn slide."

He put his hand on her shoulder. "Then you need to go to the lake house."

"But can we go when I get back? Maybe next weekend?"

Derek touched his forehead to hers. "That's a date." He stood back and waved down the hall. "Now get to class. You're not doing that great in calculus."

Chapter Fifteen

His muscles aching from practice, and his hair still wet from the shower, Beau pushed open the gym door and stepped outside into the rays of the late afternoon sun. The cool air clung to him like cobwebs and tickled his skin. He strutted from the door, lugging his heavy book bag over his shoulder as his stomach rumbled for food.

At the gate to the field, the shadows from the metal bleachers blocked the sun, sending a shiver through him. He halted. The sensation was more than passing from light to dark—it was as if he had changed from one world to another.

Something told him to look up, and when he did, he saw Taylor seated at the bottom of the stands, taking in the cheerleaders gathered below her. Their eyes met, and the chill returned with a vengeance.

Taylor got up from her spot and went to the steps leading to the oval track where Dawn and the other cheerleaders stood huddled in a group.

He hurried to the track, his tennis shoes crunching on the gravel while a bitter taste rose up the back of his throat.

Taylor pulled Dawn away from the others in the squad and whispered in her ear. Since Dawn's head was down as Taylor spoke to her, he couldn't gauge her reaction, and the knot in his stomach tightened.

If that bitch so much as ...

"Dawn, you ready to go?"

She raised her head; the smile she gave him radiated nothing but love and warmth. There was no hint of anger in her eyes, and he relaxed. Then he shifted his attention to Taylor, picturing her spread naked, bruised, and bleeding before him.

"Hey, baby." Dawn picked up her bag and motioned to Taylor. "You remember Taylor Haskins, right?"

Beau ignored Taylor's glower and took Dawn's hand. "Let's get out of here."

"What's your problem?" Dawn shirked off his grip as he tugged her to his car.

"No problem." His arm went around her. "We just got a limited amount of time together this afternoon. I don't want to waste it talking to some stuck-up girl."

"You think Taylor is stuck up?"

He opened her car door, feeling edgy. He needed to keep those two far apart.

"Let's not talk about her anymore." Beau pecked her cheek. "Now tell me what are you in the mood for? Pizza or burgers?"

She squealed. "Pizza!"

Once Dawn settled in the front seat, Beau shut her door and went around to his side of the car. He reached for his door handle and glanced at the field.

Taylor met his threatening gaze, but instead of backing down, she seemed empowered. She kept up her hostile stare as if to say, "I dare you."

He imagined taking her back to his cell and making her pay for her disrespect.

Just you wait.

* * *

The sun dipped behind the buildings along Main Street, stretching long shadows over the road in front of Beau's car. The businesses in the one-story shops crowding the sidewalks had a steady stream of customers buying clothes, hardware, shoes, antiques, art, and even getting a trim at Best Barber.

"So that will mean I have to find a new girl," Dawn explained, coming to the end of her lengthy explanation

"A new girl for what?" He peered ahead to the storefront—a neon piece of pizza flashing *Carl's* in white.

"Weren't you listening to me?" She swatted his arm. "Taylor wants to quit the squad." Dawn huffed in her seat. "How do you not want to do cheerleading anymore? That baffles me."

"I told you that girl was screwy." He pulled into a small parking lot. "You need to stay away from her."

Dawn scrunched her face. "Why don't you like her? She's nice."

He eased into a spot at the end of the lot, away from the side entrance to the eatery. "Some of the guys had a few run-ins with her and said she's a bitch. I don't want her influencing you."

"What guys?" Dawn's heart-shaped mouth twisted into a frown. "She never mentioned anyone to me."

"I've heard stuff in gym class." Beau kicked open his door, wanting to drop the subject. "Come on. I'm starved."

Through the glass windows along the side entrance, classmates and several members of the football team filled the booths and tables. He opened the door and a whoosh of pepperoni-flavored air-conditioning accosted him. A jazzy hip-hop tune blasted from the red, yellow, and green neon jukebox in the corner of the dining room.

He pulled back his shoulders and plastered on a fake smile. Years of listening to his father's lectures on how to present himself in public had become ingrained.

He put his hand behind Dawn's back, helping her through the center aisle and around the clog of tables set up between the steel-topped counter on the left, and orange vinyl booths on the right. The aroma of cooking cheese and meat teased him while the din of conversations and music unraveled his concentration.

"Beau, my man," Carl Jr. greeted from behind the counter.

"You going to lead the team to victory against Forest Glen High this Friday?"

Beau gave the short man with sunken eyes a confident nod. "You know it, Carl."

Carl set his flour-covered hands on the counter. "What can I get you guys?"

"Large pizza, the works." Beau held up two fingers. "Two iced teas."

"Coming right up." He pointed deeper into the restaurant. "Grab a table. I'll send someone over with your teas."

Beau ushered Dawn along the center aisle to the back of the dining room. Students and families occupied most of the orange booths and tables. He passed a collection of faded pictures on the walls of food selections served in the restaurant. Ceiling fans spun while images of coke floats and ice cream sundaes hung from the fluorescent light fixtures.

Dawn selected an empty booth right in the middle of the dining area, much to Beau's dismay.

He preferred to keep a low profile in public, not wanting anything to get back to his father, but she would have none of it.

Dawn scooted into the booth. "Carl Jr. must be happy he will have this place to take over one day." She scoured the faces of other diners. "Like you will take over the brewery and your father's businesses."

Beau slid in next to her, aggravated by the reminder of his father's plans. He hated thinking of a life stuck at the brewery. In five years, he envisioned himself no better off than Carl Bucelli Jr.—trapped in a dead-end job and under his old man's thumb.

The front glass doors opened just as the streetlamps outside came on. In a pair of black boots, wearing a high cut skirt and tight white T-shirt, Sara Bissell walked in.

She caught his eye, not for her looks but for how he craved to change them. To wipe the thick makeup away, blacken her eyes and split her bottom lip. Show her he was more than a man to be flirted with.

Around her was a gaggle of girls, dressed in similarly revealing clothes and with just as much makeup. Beau's appetite waned when Sara spotted him. The smile she gave him did nothing to arouse his passion, only his fury.

"That bitch is here," Dawn muttered.

He patted her thigh. "Play it cool."

Sara sashayed by their booth, her eyes connected with Beau.

"I'm gonna kill her." Dawn shimmied toward him, pushing him out of the booth.

He had to make Sara pay for rattling Dawn. Things were tense enough for him at home without adding this to his pile of bullshit.

He refused to move. "Baby, you need to calm down. I told you there was nothing with her."

Dawn gave another big push. "I don't believe you. Get me out of here."

He wanted to talk her into staying, so everyone would see they were cool. But he recognized the angry glint in her eyes and held up his hands.

"All right. We'll go."

Beau grabbed her hand and headed for the door.

A voice behind them called, "Leaving so soon, Beau?"

He turned around. Sara winked at him. He prayed Dawn didn't see it, but out of the corner of his eye, he glimpsed the open-mouthed shock.

Dawn was about to take a step toward Sara's table when he wrapped her in his arms and carried her out of the restaurant.

A mixture of *oh*s, *ah*s, and applause followed them out the door.

"Put me down!"

He ignored her and didn't stop until he reached the safety of his car, hidden in the shadows at the edge of the lot.

He deposited her by the passenger door. "Are you insane?"

Dawn attempted to get around him to head back inside. "Did you see her winking at you?"

"So what?" He held out his arms, blocking her way back into Carl's. "That's no reason to act crazy. There were a lot of people in there. How long do you think it would have been before the whole town heard about your little run in? How would I explain that to my dad? You know how he's up my ass about how I present myself in public." He gripped her right upper arm, digging his fingers into her soft flesh. "Damn it, Dawn, do you have no self-control?"

She tried to back away, but he only squeezed harder. "You're hurting me."

Her pale face became Leslie's. She smirked up at him, egging him on. His fingers cinched tighter, tingling with excitement.

"Beau!" a voice called across the lot.

Beau let her go, and she pressed up against the car; fear pinked her cheeks and her blue eyes watered.

Carl Jr. came running up to them. "Is there a problem?"

His anger cooled when his gaze settled on the man's flour-covered jeans and red apron. Was this his future? Every day for the rest of his life in slacks and a button-down shirt, stinking of beer just like his old man?

"No, no problem, Carl." Beau gestured to the restaurant. "I'm sorry we can't stay. I've got to get Dawn home."

"You want me to get your order to go?" Carl asked.

Beau wasn't about to wait around and give Dawn another chance to confront Sara. He'd had enough of both girls for one night.

Anxious to get her home, he reached into his back pocket and removed his wallet.

He slipped Carl a fifty-dollar bill. "Give our order to someone else. Next time, I promise we'll stay and eat."

Carl crumbled the bill in his hand. "I'll take care of you, Beau."

After Carl Jr. slipped inside, Dawn opened her mouth to speak, but Beau took her hand. "Don't say another word."

He put her in the car and slammed her passenger side door.

Once he peeled out of the parking lot, his fury shifted from Dawn to Sara. She had jeopardized everything with her brassy attitude.

Bitch is gonna pay—big time.

"We could have at least waited for our order."

Dawn's high-pitched voice intruded on a daydream of tying Sara to the pipes in the wall of his cell.

"What are you talking about?"

"You paid for our food. Why not wait for it? Running out like that just seems silly."

He hit the gas, needing to get her home and out of his hair. "You'd better be thankful I got you out of there before you did something stupid. Otherwise, Sara would probably be calling the cops and filing charges against you."

"For what?" Her half-hearted laugh irritated him. "Calling her whore? Threatening to rip out her hair? That's what I wanted to do."

"Then you would have committed assault, Dawn." He gripped the wheel, holding in his admonishment. "For being the daughter of an attorney, you're not too bright."

Her eyes widened, and she got that shocked deer-in-headlights look he hated. It meant a fight was coming.

"If you hadn't been hanging around that slut Saturday night, this wouldn't have happened!"

Beau punched the steering wheel. "I didn't do anything with Sara!"

She flinched and retreated into her seat.

For the first time, a taut expression of fear distorted Dawn's face. She clenched her hands, her knuckles showing white against his sienna leather seats, and hugged the door as if she would jump out at any moment.

Beau had gone too far. He'd let his anger show. His hand throbbed. With the pain came the regret.

Keep it together. She can't see you. Not yet.

"I'm sorry." He sat back in his seat, keeping his eyes on the road. "I lost my temper back there and I shouldn't have. But with Sara and you about to go after each other … I should have handled that better."

She moved back into her seat, settling down, and rubbed the red mark on her upper arm. "No, I should have ignored her, like you said." Her gaze softened and her clenched hands relaxed. "She just seemed awfully interested for someone you just said hello to."

"Forget about her." Beau put on a pleasing grin, wanting to assure her all was well. "Do you really believe I would want to go out with a slut like her?"

"No." A slight smile returned to her lips, but her eyes remained apprehensive. "I'm sorry I was a witch at the restaurant. I promise to do better."

In the beginning, her sweet disposition and promises to do whatever he wanted—be the girl he needed and follow his rules— had pleased him. Now, they grated on his nerves. Perhaps it was time to shake things up with her.

"You can make it up to me at the river this weekend. There are some things I want to try with you."

Her smile slipped. "Ah, I have to go to the lake house this weekend. My dad is being a real pain in the butt about having a family weekend. So, I can't hang out at the river with you."

The pang of regret in his gut didn't last long. There were others he could have fun with.

"I'm going to miss you."

She leaned across the console. "Promise to keep out of trouble and away from Sara Bissell while I'm gone."

He made his smile appear genuine; years of practice had taught him how to deceive people.

"I won't have anything to do with her."

The lie pleased her, but he questioned how anyone could be so trusting. Leslie would never have believed him.

His sour mood lifted. With Dawn out of his hair, his weekend looked bright.

Perhaps an evening with Sara is what I need.

Beau punched the accelerator. He would invite Sara to join him at the river and bring her to the cells. There, he would exact his revenge for the shitstorm she'd brought down on him. With Sara, he could try something new—and dangerous.

* * *

The *vroom* of Beau's engine carried up her sidewalk as he pulled away from the curb. The stars popped out in the sky above, and the lights from the other houses on her street cast a protective glow, chasing away the encroaching darkness.

But the tranquil ambiance did little to offset the unease raging inside her. Stunned by Beau's treatment at Carl's, Dawn didn't understand what had happened to the gentleman she had known.

She turned from the street and walked up the path to her front door, her upper arm still stinging from where he had held her. She checked the spot again. His red fingerprints remained.

She'd seen another side of him tonight. She knew he had a temper, but this had been different. It was as if he had unleashed a fury that scared her to death.

I bet Leslie doesn't have to deal with this crap with Derek.

The comparison brought her to a standstill on her porch steps. She admired the warm lights coming from the windows of the other homes and considered her relationship with Beau as compared to the one Leslie had with Derek.

They never seemed to fight, have problems with other girls, or even argue about their future. They were always laughing, talking, and happy together. Derek didn't push Leslie to have sex. Derek never wanted to party with his friends. He was always kind to her.

Maybe I picked the wrong guy.

Weak at the thought of a life without Beau, she sat on the steps. For the first time since seeing his face in the hallways of St. Benedict High, Dawn had reservations about continuing with Beau Devereaux. She'd dreaded the coming weekend at the lake house, but part of her wanted an opportunity to think.

What is happening to me?

It was the first indication her feelings for Beau might not be what they seemed. Had what she believed to be love been something else? A little time away from Beau could help her get some perspective. Perhaps even consider calling off the whole thing. Playing by his rules wasn't as fun as it used to be. It was time to create some rules of her own.

Chapter Sixteen

The rustle of people moving, the clatter of steps on the metal bleachers, laughter of children, and shouts of excited teenagers filled the football field of St. Benedict High School as patrons of the Cougars' winning game packed up to head home.

In his football uniform, fresh from the game, Beau escorted a clingy Dawn, still in her cheerleading uniform, to the blacktopped parking lot next to the field as her parents waited by the gate.

"Promise to call me every night, even when you are at the river."

Her sweet voice had the tinge of desperation to it, but he didn't care. Getting her out of his hair for a weekend was what he needed.

"I'll call day and night." He searched the field, hoping to see Sara. "You know I can't go a day without you, Dawn."

Dawn pulled away, and his eyes instantly went back to her. "Remember, I love you, Beau."

Love? Did she even know what the word meant? To him, love meant possession, rage, power—not some fuzzy warm fairy tale.

"I have to go. Coach always wants to do a recap of the game after we get off the field. He'll probably bring up my two TDs to Mitch." He kissed her cheek. "Can't miss that."

He took off running for the locker room, glad to have gotten away before she pushed for his feelings about their relationship. He didn't have any.

When he made it to the metal doors of the gym entrance, Sara was waiting. His anger for her still smoldered, but tonight he would take care of it.

"You and me at the river tonight?"

She gave an ambivalent half-nod. "What about Dawn? I saw you and her at the gate."

His gaze drifted down her red top and snug blue jeans. "She'll be gone all weekend. I told her we needed a break, so she's going away with her parents."

Sara's eyes lit up and she moved away from the doors. "I like the sound of that."

He admired Sara's hips as she sashayed away.

This day just gets better and better.

* * *

"Man, you nailed it tonight." Mitch pumped his fist in the air as Beau turned his car into the Rouse's Grocery Store parking lot for a liquor run. "When you hit me with that twenty-yard pass, I was like *boom*. We crushed it."

The fiery beat blasted from the stereo speakers, the cool fall air sifted through the cracked windows, and the high from the game radiated through Beau's system.

"It was sweet." Beau headed around the side of the store to the back-loading area.

"And now we're gonna have ourselves a wild time at the river." Josh leaned in from the back, his broad shoulder barely squeezing between the bucket seats. "So glad Dawn cut you loose for the weekend. I hate to say this, dude, but she's a downer."

Beau turned to the loading dock, not wanting to give away his true sentiments about Dawn, but he had to agree.

"Lately she's been different. I'm not sure what the problem is."

"You just tell her who's in charge and she will back down." Josh scanned the inky darkness around their car. "Chicks dig an alpha male."

"My sister reads them alpha male books like they're goin' out of style. All chicks do." Mitch batted his chest with his fist. "Be the beast, dude."

He wanted to laugh. *They have no idea.*

"You guys aren't in relationships." Beau parked next to the rear entrance. "It's not so easy just telling women what to do. You have to finesse them into thinking what you want is what they want."

Josh looked mystified. "How do you do that?"

Beau dialed down the music, itching to boast about his special talent.

"It's a question of power. You have to assert yourself in a relationship. You ask a girl what she wants, pretending to be considerate and all, but before she can have time to think about it, you put suggestions in her head. Where to go out? What she should wear? Who her friends should be?" He thought back to how easily he had conquered Dawn. "Pretty soon, her wants are yours. When you have the little things down, you can manipulate their thoughts and move on to bigger things like sex."

Mitch turned to him, his eyes wide with amazement. "Dude? You're creepin' me out. You really do that shit?"

"Shut up." Josh leaned in farther. "Go back to how you get girls to have sex with you."

Beau was well aware he wasn't dealing with the brightest of the bunch, but that was why he hung around them. What he did to girls, he could also do to friends.

"You weren't listening. You cajole. You sweet talk. You tell them what they need to hear, and then once they're addicted, you change the rules."

Mitch chuckled, his coarse laugh cutting through the air. "Sounds like the same crap you've done to win over everyone in town. The good boy, no drinkin', smokin', or drugs, do-gooder." He thumbed Josh next to him. "But we know better. You're a badass."

Beau shook his head. *You have no idea.*

Josh's brow furrowed. "So, what happens when you do all that stuff and they still refuse to sleep with you?"

Beau just smiled.

Bright fluorescent light bathed the car as the back door to the grocery opened.

Eddie emerged, carrying a box loaded with bottles.

Beau climbed from the car and met him at the trunk.

"Here ya go." Eddie held up the box. "Wish I was going with you guys. I remember the river used to be a blast."

Beau set the box in his trunk. "Yeah, still is. Thanks for the supplies, Eddie." Beau reached into his pocket and handed him some cash.

"Let me know whenever you guys need more." He looked at the two, one-hundred-dollar bills before tucking them into his shirt pocket. "Your liquor runs sure help pay the baby bills."

Beau shut the trunk. The ass-kissing store clerk disgusted him. One of many in the small town who saw his family as a meal ticket.

Losers.

"We stocked up?" Josh had a boatload of exuberance in his voice.

"Yeah, we're good." Beau started the car. "Let's make this a night to remember."

Chapter Seventeen

Dawn arrived with her family at their cabin on the shores of Lake Pontchartrain. The setting sun tossed ribbons of red, orange, and pink across the lake's modest waves. A log home designed with picture windows along the front sat nestled amid a circle of thick pines. A wooden deck jutted out over the edge of the lake with two Jet Skis secured to the dock.

A sleek, modern interior with a log décor added an earthy texture to the walls and beamed ceilings. The simple furniture, with forest green and burnt sienna upholstery, complemented the pine hardwood floor. A massive stone fireplace rose past the straight staircase leading from the combination living room and den.

Once settled in her upstairs bedroom, Dawn unpacked one of the two large duffel bags set on their twin beds. Through the window overlooking the lake, the last dregs of sunlight reached across the white plush rug.

She turned away from the window and cast a wary eye to her sister, wanting to broach the subject of her confusing feelings for Beau but unsure how to do it.

"You said goodbye to Derek?" She set a few shirts in her dresser.

"Yep." Leslie pulled out her blow dryer from her bag. "What did Beau say after the game?"

"Not much, but that's Beau." Hand on her hip, Dawn debated how to ask the question on her mind. "When you say 'I love you' to Derek, does he say it back?"

Leslie put the blow dryer on her bed. "Yes."

Dawn smashed her lips together. "And when you leave Derek

alone for the weekend, do you trust him?"

Her sister's musical laugh circled her like the bothersome caw of a crow. "Of course, I trust him."

Dawn went to Leslie's bed and flopped down next to her bag. "Then why don't I feel like I can trust Beau?"

Leslie took a seat next to her. "Maybe that's your heart telling you he isn't the guy for you."

The wall of hostility she'd put up whenever she dealt with her sister came tumbling down. She believed she was impervious to Leelee's comments and quips about Beau, but every single one had stuck in her head for months. Suddenly, she needed to know what Beau had done to her.

Dawn kept her eyes on her bag, afraid to look at her sister. "I've been thinking about the things you said. The things Beau told you." A lump formed in her throat; her lower lip quivered. "When did it start?"

Leslie's loud sigh sliced through Dawn like a razor blade. In that instant, she knew—she could feel it—Leslie had been telling the truth.

"After the first night you two hooked up at the river. He corners me at school, saying ..." Leslie shook her head. "Disgusting things."

Her heart broke into a thousand pieces; she knew why he'd harassed her. It was the same reason she'd refused to acknowledge.

"He wanted you that night at the river, not me. And he's been making you suffer for turning him down. Beau doesn't like for anyone to tell him no."

Leslie touched her hand. "I was trying to protect you. You seemed so happy with him in the beginning, so I let it go. Was I wrong to keep quiet?"

Dawn put her hand over Leslie's. "You can't always protect me, Leelee, but I probably wouldn't have listened until now. I had to see for myself what Beau is, but I believe you." She sniffled, trying not to cry. "And I'm going to talk to him, tell him to stop."

Leslie gripped her hand. "Be careful. There's something very wrong with him."

"Wrong with who?" Shelley came through the open bedroom door, carrying a duffel bag. "What are you girls so cozy about? Haven't seen you put your heads together about anything in months."

"We were talking about Derek and Beau." Leslie got up from the bed.

Shelley set the bag by the door. "Do I want to hear this?"

Dawn stood alongside her sister. "Leslie was just trying to help me make up my mind about something."

Shelley's eyebrows went up. "Can I ask what?"

"What's going on in here?" Her father walked into the bedroom, looking oblivious as usual. "Why isn't anyone downstairs ready to roast marshmallows?"

Shelley waved to her and Leslie. "Your daughter was just about to tell me she made up her mind about something having to do with Beau Devereaux."

Her father folded his arms, appearing stoic, but Dawn knew better. "Which one?"

Shelley frowned at her husband and pointed at Dawn.

John grinned. "What's the big decision?"

Dawn went back to her bed, the pressure of her parents' curiosity suffocating her. She hadn't even made up her mind yet and felt no need to share her problems with anyone.

"It's no big deal."

"Are you two having problems again?" Shelley took a step closer to the bed. "Because if you want to talk about—"

Her father held up his hands, demanding quiet. "New rule. For the duration of the weekend, there will be no more talk of boyfriends. No one is to mention the names of Beau or Derek until we are back in St. Benedict. Agreed?"

Dawn wasn't crazy about the idea, but reluctantly nodded along with Leslie.

John rocked cockily back and forth on his toes. "See? Problem solved."

He left the room, and a grimacing Shelley followed close behind him.

Dawn sagged into the bed. It was going to be a long weekend.

* * *

The moon shone down on the beach next to the Bogue Falaya River while the pounding bass from speakers sent ripples out over the black water. Beau felt the throb of music through his tennis shoes, mesmerized by the dance of light on the shallow waves and how the canopy of trees arched over the river seemed to sway with the beat.

He turned, nursing his bottle of water, already bored with the festivities. Revelers on the beach danced, most paired off in couples, while those gathered around the bonfires close to the water's edge talked or checked their phones.

A few of the guys from his football team had settled farther up the shoreline with a ping pong table and were doing shots of tequila every time someone missed the ball.

How had he found such simple minds fun? Before Taylor, the kids at the river had intrigued him. Now, they bored him to death.

Josh and Mitch sat on picnic tables not far from his spot, chatting with two scantily clad girls from Covington High who had heard about the party on Instagram.

Beau loved the notoriety, but not the bigger crowds. He preferred the beach filled with locals who knew who he was and that he ruled the river.

He checked the time on his phone, pissed about Sara. He'd searched for her, wanting to get her to the cells, and if she didn't appear soon, he would find another girl to take with him.

"Did you see those two hotties from Covington High we were

with? Beverly and Lindsey." Mitch slapped Beau's back. "Do those girls rock, or what?"

Beau checked out a few of the girls around them. "Not the best way to describe women."

"Okay? What do I say? They're pretty?"

Beau took in his friend's exuberant smile and the dimples in his cheeks. "Hey, if you're having fun with them, then great. I suggest you offer them the wine Eddie sent. But don't let them drink too much. Girls love it when a guy steps in and acts concerned about their welfare. Insist you want to get to know them sober, and I promise they will go out with you."

Mitch gave him a fist bump. "You're the best, Beau."

While Mitch hurried away, a leggy redhead caught Beau's attention. She chatted with the two girls he'd seen with Josh and Mitch. Slim hips, an upturned nose, and full red lips had him wondering how she'd look naked on his cot in the cells.

"Hey, baby," a sexy voice whispered in his ear.

Sara eased in front of him.

She'd swept up her hair in a ponytail and had on a deep shade of red lipstick. He yearned to slap the color away. His arms went around her, and he lifted her into the air, eager to get her alone.

"Where have you been?"

"Had to sneak out of my house to come." She kissed his lips. "Mom doesn't want me here."

"Why not?" Beau put her down.

"Other parents at the high school are talking about the drinking and stuff going on here. She heard about it and said I couldn't come anymore." She hooked her arms around his neck. "Like she can stop me from being with you."

"Damn." He scratched his head. So that's how his old man had found out. "I didn't realize word had gotten out. Might be time to tone things down."

"Are you kidding? Every kid in town wants to come to your river parties." She nuzzled his chin. "And after tonight, everyone in town will know about us, too."

"Whoa." Beau pulled his chin away from her, his desire to take her to the cells fizzling fast. "What are you talking about?"

Sara gaped at him. "You're dumping Dawn, right? I'm taking her place. Anyone who sees us here tonight will know it's true."

He unwound her snakelike arms from his neck. This possessive streak meant she would be trouble. He thought he had screened her well enough. Aggressive, outspoken—she had traits he admired in Leslie but lacked her fire, intelligence, and class.

He took a step back from her, his cool demeanor snuffing out the hint of aggravation in his voice. "I haven't called it off with Dawn. And if she hears you were hanging on me tonight, she'll break it off for sure. I can't have that. Got a rep to protect."

"What am I supposed to do?" Her loud tone attracted glances from a few people standing next to them on the beach. "Wait in the shadows until you're ready for a relationship with me?"

Beau folded his arms, an arrogant smirk on his lips. "Who says I want a relationship with you?"

Sara's brown eyes narrowed to two slits. "You want me to blab to your little girlfriend about asking me here tonight?"

His first instinct was to punch her, but he couldn't do that, not in front of others. Instead, he lowered his voice to a menacing growl. "Careful. You have no idea who I am."

But she wasn't put off and cocked her arm back to slap him.

He caught her hand before she could land her blow. "I could make you pay for that."

"Oh, yeah." She yanked her arm away. "You can't touch me, Beau Devereaux. I don't care how much money you have."

His brow crinkled. "I don't need money to hurt you. All I need is what I already own—the ear of everyone in this town."

She gave him her best "bad girl" stare. "Oh yeah. Who's gonna believe anything you have to say?"

Keenly aware of the attention they attracted, he stopped and reset. He stepped up to her, making sure to lower his voice so only she could hear.

"The entire St. Benedict football team will after I tell them the things you did to me tonight and are *more* than willing to do with them. What do you think a gang of horny and drunk guys will do with that information? Hell, I'll even give them a place to do it. A place no one will hear you scream."

"You bastard." She came at him with her claws out.

But Beau cuffed her hands and held her against him. "Don't you dare think you can outsmart me."

Sara wiggled out of his embrace, her cheeks a brilliant shade of red. "You're a sick shit."

He nodded. "Quite possibly, but for now I'm Dawn's sick shit, and you're never to speak to her or even look at her again. Break that rule, and my boys will mess you up so bad, you'll never be any good to a guy again. Got it?"

The color drained from Sara's cheeks and she backed away. She took off toward a line of trees surrounding the plot of beach.

She disappeared into the shadows, chased by the whispers and stares of other revelers.

Once she left, Beau's edginess returned. He had planned to teach her a lesson in the cells but had to settle for threats and intimidation. Not what he wanted, and certainly not what he craved, but it would have to do, for now.

He'd been dreaming of hurting Sara, and like a coiled spring, he was certain to explode if he didn't find another girl to give him the rush. Beau craved the high again. He was an addict needing another fix.

"You sure know how to throw an entertaining party. Beau Devereaux, right?"

The alluring redhead was back. He honed in on her deep red lipstick.

"How do you know my name?"

Her low-cut blouse offered a tantalizing glimpse of her cleavage. "Everyone knows who you are."

He sized up her potential for a night of fun. Eager and dressed to tease.

"And who are you?" he asked in his smoky voice.

She tilted her head, adding a luster to her dreamy hazel eyes. "Kelly Norton."

"From Covington High?"

Kelly pursed her red lips and gave a toss of her red long hair. "We've met before. My mom manages the apartment building your dad built in Covington."

The news pleased him immensely. Daughter of an employee—she would be less willing to talk for fear of losing the family income. He could do what he wanted to her without fear of repercussions.

"My father has several properties in Covington, Mandeville, and even New Orleans, but I remember that apartment building." On the hunt to reel her in, he set the trap. "Your mother is Beth Norton, right?"

Her eyes lit up and her smile expanded, adding a dimple to her chin. "Wow. You've got a good memory."

He put his hands in his pockets and stepped closer. With a sheepish grin, he moved in, wanting to quickly establish her trust.

"I work summers at the brewery, and part of my job is helping my father with the books. I've seen your mom's name a lot lately."

"So, you don't remember me?"

Her smile never wavered. He detected a glimmer of hope in the undercurrents of her voice.

"No, I remember." He stepped around her, circling her like a predator. "At the building opening last year. You helped serve the punch."

Yeah, he impressed himself with that one, but it had come back to him. The mousy girl in the pink dress who had been too afraid to talk to anyone—including him.

An uncomfortable silence lingered; well, not uncomfortable for

Beau but it was for her. She shifted her feet in the sand, tugged at her top, and played with her hair. She was nervous—nervous meant insecure and easy to manipulate.

Beau glanced back at two girls at the picnic tables with Mitch and Josh. "Are you here with them?"

"Yeah." She took another step closer to Beau. "That girl you were with before, is she your girlfriend?"

Definitely interested.

"No. She's angry because she isn't my girlfriend." He shook his head, pouting for effect. "She's too possessive for my tastes."

Kelly twirled a lock of her fiery hair around her finger. "Why kind of women do you like?"

He ached to touch her. "Smart. Funny. Interested in the long term. One-night stands aren't my style."

Kelly tilted her head and raised the right side of her mouth in the slightest grin.

"You expect me to buy that bullshit?"

A tingle shot through Beau's crotch. The comment was just what he would expect from his Leslie.

"What do you do when you're not going to Covington High?"

Her features softened a little. "I work at a vet's office. I love animals. Hope to be a vet someday."

"Animals, huh?" He liked that. It made her sound wild.

She inched closer, her lips parted. "What do you like to do when not playing quarterback?"

Suddenly, he wasn't in the mood for toying with her anymore. He wanted to taste her fear.

"Have you ever seen the inside of The Abbey, Kelly Norton?"

Kelly's bewitching smile spread, highlighting the alluring curve of her lips. "No. Can you show it to me?"

After a quick check to see who was around, Beau clasped her hand. "Come with me. I'm gonna give you the night of your life."

Chapter Eighteen

Crickets chirped and mist curled around him as Beau eased out of the crack in the wall to the cells. The chill in the air teased his sweaty skin, but the surge of power pounding through his blood was like liquid fire.

The rush consumed him. He knew in that instant he would find another victim, but his rational mind begged him to be careful.

Don't get caught.

He chuckled. Besides the money, his father still had hefty political clout in Baton Rouge, thanks to his notorious grandfather and years of murky business dealings. The family name had spared him in the past from legal proceedings and institutions. It would again.

Heading toward the fountain across the grassy field, Beau considered his next night of fun. Before he reached the forgotten angel, a flash in the corner of his eye made him turn.

Amid the trees, crowding the edge of the property, something darted in and out. He could just make out a long, white hooded cloak, fluttering and billowing at the edge of the woods. Then it disappeared.

His heart rocketed to his throat. *It can't be!*

All the stories he'd heard of the lady in white of The Abbey came rushing back at once, intensifying his panic.

Then he calmed. Someone had to be messing with him. It wasn't the girl. Kelly had taken off, a bawling mess, across the field several minutes before and he'd heard the slam of the iron gate. He was alone. Unless ... the guys had pulled a fast one on him.

But the guys don't know about your room in the cells.

Beau cut across the grass, anxious to get to the iron gate and back to the party. Almost to the path, he glanced back over his shoulder to the patch of trees where he had seen the ghostly presence. Nothing was there.

It was just your imagination. Or was it?

He made it to the party at the beach, relieved to be back among people, but the incident with the ghost had eradicated his high.

He hungered for it to return but would have to wait.

The music had stopped, the revelers had thinned, and those who were left were packing up to go. Most had midnight curfews, including Beau.

He set out across the sand, avoiding numerous bottles and piles of trash in his path. His heels angrily dug in as he walked. Beau was ready to collect Mitch and Josh and head out to make his curfew. He searched the weary faces around him until he spotted the black curls and broad shoulders of his friend.

Mitch sat on a picnic bench and chugged a beer. Two girls slept curled up next to him.

"Dude, what's this?" He slapped Mitch's knee and waved to the girls.

His friend lifted his beer to his lips, appearing unfazed. "They passed out a while ago."

He leaned over and checked their faces. "Who are they?"

"Beverly." Mitch got up and wobbled slightly, pointing to a slim brunette sleeping next to him. "And Lindsey. The Covington High girls, remember?"

Josh stumbled forward, coming from the bushes and tugging on his zipper.

"We were about to go look for you. It's getting late."

Beau ran his hands through his hair, his anger creeping upward. "Let's get out of here." He lowered his voice, mindful of the others around them. "I've got to get home to make my curfew. My old man will pitch a fit if I'm late."

"Where have you been?" Mitch asked, tossing his empty bottle to the sand. "I don't remember seeing you around."

Beau picked up the bottle. "How could you with all those shots you did? Besides, you were busy." Beau motioned to the unconscious girls. "What did you give them? They're out cold."

"Wine." Josh wiped a bit of sand from his shirt, grinning. "Thanks for the tip."

"I said tipsy, not dead drunk." Beau tossed the bottle to a garbage can several feet away, making it in on the first try.

Mitch glanced behind him to the river. "Where's that Kelly girl? I saw you heading off with her. You make it with her?"

Beau's heart sped up, remembering her whimpers as he raped her, but he downplayed his encounter to avoid unwanted attention.

"She wasn't my type. I left her by one of the bonfires."

"You should have given Kelly some wine." Josh snickered and stumbled, almost falling to the ground before Mitch caught him.

Lindsey sat up, weaving as she held her head. "Wait? Kelly left us?" She looked around the beach. "How are we supposed to get home? She was our ride."

Josh helped her from the bench. "Beau will take you home."

Beau's cheeks burned. He was ready to kill. "I've got to make my curfew."

Lindsey wobbly sashayed up to Beau, going for sexy but came across as pathetic. Still very drunk, she rubbed up against him.

"I'll do anything you want if you give me a ride home."

Beau pushed her away. "Thanks, but I'll pass."

His phone rang with a rap ringtone. He checked the caller ID and frowned. Dawn. Probably to check up on him. She had also left one text. He returned the phone to his back pocket. He would deal with her later.

Josh put his hand on Beau's shoulder. "What do we do with the girls? We can't just leave them."

Lindsey wrapped her arms around Josh's thick neck. "Take me home with you."

There were times his friends were more trouble than they were worth, but if he left the girls behind, people might hear about it. Best not to make waves and keep up appearances—just like his old man wanted.

"Get the girls. Carry them if you have to." Beau moved back toward the path leading to the parking lot. "I'll drive them home."

"But they live in Covington?" Mitch objected while following him. "It will take you another hour at least, and you've got your curfew."

"We can't leave them here." Beau checked the clock on his phone. "It wouldn't be gentlemanly."

"My hero." Lindsey left Josh and went to him, slipping her arms around his neck.

Her foul breath and slutty behavior sickened him. He wanted to slap her away and kick her senseless to teach her a lesson. Instead, he peeled her off him and pushed her back at Josh.

"It's time to go."

Once the girls were safely in his car with Josh and Mitch nestled in beside them, Beau headed out of the parking lot and turned on to the dimly lit road.

The trees whipped by as he picked up speed, creating undulating shadows reminiscent of the odd presence he had seen by The Abbey. Had someone meant to frighten him? But who? The drunk ramblings of Josh and Mitch intruded on his thoughts; their hyena-like laughter grated on his nerves.

They act like stupid boys.

The evening exemplified the difference between boys and men. Boys, like Josh and Mitch, chased girls who drank too much and gave in easily to their demands. But Beau was a man. He no longer had interest in a woman who surrendered. He wanted her to struggle, to cry, to beg, to resist, to scream—just like Kelly had.

* * *

Beau sighed as he quietly shut the glass doors to the mudroom and stepped into the rear hall of his parents' home. The exterior security lights filtered through the hall windows as he crept past the kitchen—the clock on the microwave read almost two.

Don't get caught. Gage will kill you!

In the main hall, all the lights were out. Even his father's study was dark. He tiptoed, holding his black tennis shoes, not trusting them on the old hardwood floor. Years of sneaking around at night had taught him where to walk on so as not to create a single sound.

Once he made it up the curved oak staircase, he peered into the darkness, searching for lights.

Fortunately, everyone appeared to be asleep. Beau snuck into his bedroom and shut the door.

He flipped on the light and looked around, studying the ornate mahogany trundle bed, high dresser with brass features, the carved desk with lions' heads on the corners, and the widescreen plasma TV he'd insisted on. But the posters of Bugatti cars and svelte Victoria's Secret models on his walls seemed childish. He would make some changes. It was time for his outsides to reflect his newfound insides.

After tossing his sand-encrusted tennis shoes aside, Beau crawled into his bed without removing his dusty jeans or long-sleeved shirt. He set his cell phone on his night table and wrapped his comforter around him. A light rapping came from his door.

Beau turned on his bedside lamp. "What is it?"

The door creaked open and his mother stepped inside. "You're home past your curfew."

After a ragged sigh, he raked his hand through his hair. "Yeah, I was making sure some drunk girls got home in Covington. I couldn't let them drive."

Elizabeth walked into the room. "Is that the truth?"

Beau cringed. "Yes, it's the truth! I wasn't doing anything wrong."

"You've been acting the way you used to—the rages, the tantrums. Now you're coming in late and shouting at me." Elizabeth gripped the edge of his bed. "Ever since this school year began, you haven't been the same."

He took in her bloodshot eyes, disgusted by the sight. "I'm surprised you noticed anything was different with me."

She tugged at the lapels of her yellow robe. "Don't push me. I went along with your father last time. He buried the incident under his money and connections. But do it again, and I won't remain silent."

"You're never going to let me forget that, are you?" He didn't hide his bitterness. "Every day you remind me with a look or a gesture." Beau tossed off his comforter. "You spend your days in the bottom of a whiskey bottle so you don't have to confront your son."

"Don't you dare speak to me that way."

"What? Have I offended your sense of decency? That's a laugh." He got up and went to her. "People are talking about you. The sad little wife of Gage Devereaux. You know how he feels about his precious family name. I guarantee he will get rid of you long before he ever pushes me out the door."

"God, you're just like your father." She backed away from him. "You even sound like him when you attack me."

"Then lay off the booze." He returned to his bed, wanting to end the conversation. "Find a man. It will get your mind off me."

Elizabeth rushed up to him, her fists tucked into her sides. "Does Dawn know about you? Has she seen the real Beau Devereaux? I'd hoped that poor girl was getting through to you, but she isn't, is she? Should I warn her to keep the family dog out of your reach? I can tell her what you did to mine."

You bitch!

The rush of adrenaline forced Beau from the bed. He charged

her, wanting to break her skinny little neck, but he refrained. The fear in her eyes delighted him. It gave him a rush, just like he got with Kelly and Taylor.

"If you ever say anything to Dawn, I'll kill you."

Elizabeth wasn't like his high school girls. Her fear faded and a steadfast resolve replaced it.

"Yes, I believe you would." She raised her head, becoming the society maven she always liked to portray. "I won't tell your father you were out past your curfew. He has enough on his mind."

He tempered his anger, not wanting to give his mother the upper hand. "I doubt he'd care." Beau strutted back to his bed. "All he needs is an heir for his empire, not a son."

Elizabeth gave him a stern rebuke with her cold eyes and then slipped out the door.

His head pounded after the confrontation. She always did that—enraged him to the point of madness. Ever since he could remember, he'd hated his mother.

Back in bed, he tried to sleep, but her comments lingered, and restless energy chased away his fatigue.

Unable to close his eyes, he turned to his cell phone. He snatched it up and read Dawn's missed call notice. Perhaps talking with her would help him settle down.

"Beau?" She sounded groggy after picking up. "Why are you calling so late?"

He lay back on his bed, his hand under his head, his calm returning.

What would she like him to say?

"I missed you tonight. I wanted to hear your voice."

"I miss you, too." Dawn's voice melted like butter over a flame. "Are you just getting home?"

"Yeah, Josh and Mitch met some girls at the river from Covington High. They were too drunk to drive home, so I took them. Made me miss my curfew."

"What did your folks say?"

"It's all good." He added a boastful lilt to his voice. "I have to set an example for the other kids in school."

She sighed into the phone. "You're a good guy, Beau Devereaux. Did you have fun at the river? Please tell me Sara Bissell wasn't there."

"She was there." He checked his fingernails in the light, thinking ahead, finding the right words to set his plan into motion. "I put her in her place when she tried hitting on me. She won't be messing with you or me anymore."

"What did you do?"

Her curiosity elicited a grin.

"I let everyone know what a slut she is. Hitting on me when I have a girlfriend, and not caring what she did with any of the guys at the river. I heard she went off with a couple of them."

"Wow." Dawn giggled and he smiled at the sound. "Wish I could have been there to see that. Her rep will be dirt come Monday."

Done with the subject of Sara, he searched for something to keep her talking. "Are you having a good time at the lake?"

"I'm enjoying myself. Leslie and I are actually getting along, if you can believe it. My parents are happy about that."

The mention of her sister set off alarm bells in his head. He sat up, his restlessness rebounding.

"What have you and Leslie been talking about?"

"Nothing much really. It's been cool spending time with her again."

Leslie in her ear was a bad thing. He didn't want Leslie's insubordination rubbing off on Dawn. He needed her compliant for a while longer.

"When are you coming home?"

"Sometime tomorrow night. We're going out on the boat in the morning."

"That sounds like fun." It didn't, but he figured it was what she would want to hear. "Wish I was there."

"I wish you were, too. If you go back to the river, behave please."

"I'm always good, baby." Beau tapped his finger on the bed, anticipating another night of fun. "After last night, I don't think the boys will be ready to party too much. They hit it pretty hard."

Dawn yawned again. "I'd better get back to sleep. I love you, Beau."

He hesitated, not sure what to tell her. Beau didn't love Dawn, but he didn't see the point in telling her that. He needed her for a little while longer.

"I'll call you tomorrow night."

Beau hung up with images of Leslie revolving in his head. When he told her how he felt, she would be on her knees, begging for him to hurt her, wanting to feel his hands around her throat.

That's real love. And she's gonna know it very soon.

Chapter Nineteen

A foggy tunnel loomed before him. Shadows played along the curved wall and beyond, he heard women's screams. The alluring sound urged him deeper into the darkness until a voice rang out.

"Beau, wake up."

The tunnel evaporated, and beams of light pierced the darkness around him. He opened his eyes and then his vision cleared.

His father arched over his bed. His thick brown hair damp, his face freshly shaven and his dark, harsh eyes glowering.

Damn!

"What is it, Dad?"

Gage Devereaux sat on the edge of his son's bed, seeped in the musky, woodsy fragrance of Clive Christian Number One, and oozing the sense of mastery he commanded whenever he walked into a room. His no-nonsense business manner permeated every aspect of his life.

"I got a call from Kent Davis at the Sheriff's Department this morning. It seems a girl who was at your river party last night was pulled over for driving erratically. They said she was very upset, looked like she had been roughed up, and had to call her mother to come and get her. Her name was Kelly Norton. Did you know her?"

Beau wiped the sleep from his eyes as his heart thudded. *Play it cool.*

"No, never heard of her. Does she go to St. Benedict?"

"No, Covington High." Gage checked the time on his gold Rolex. "I'm concerned because Kent's been getting a lot of complaints about the parties at the river. The noise, trash, and unattended fires are angering people who work and live along the river. You spend a lot of time there, and I want you to be careful."

"We just go there and hang out."

Gage stood up. "And drink. I'm not stupid."

He kicked his comforter away. "I don't drink. You told me not to. We just have fun, listen to music and talk."

Gage scowled, not looking convinced. "You aren't like the other kids. Your future is already planned, and you have the family's reputation to uphold. You will be a leader of this community. That position requires a certain sense of responsibility."

Beau suppressed a groan. "I know the drill, Dad, but can we have this talk another time? I'm beat."

His father grabbed the shoulder of his shirt and yanked him out of bed. "I want to make myself perfectly clear. When I tell you to mind yourself, tell you to stay out of trouble, you will obey me. I will not have you screw up everything our family has built."

Beau stiffened as his father held him, and he stared, terrified, into his old man's black eyes.

"Yes, sir."

Gage let him go and strutted to the bedroom door. "Get dressed. We're leaving in fifteen minutes."

Beau wanted to punch the wall. "You're serious?"

His father opened the door and glanced back at him. "You didn't think I would let you off for blowing your curfew last night, did you?"

He left the room, and Beau punched the air. "Dammit!"

* * *

Gage Devereaux pulled his red 750i BMW up to the front gate of Benedict Brewery. Beau sat next to him, his gaze fixed on the ten-foot-high wire fence surrounding the facility. It was part of the security his father had added when he'd moved his offices from his other businesses to the brewery, so he could run his little empire from one location close to home. Beau had been seven at the time and had just returned from a short stint at Children's Hospital in New Orleans. He believed the change would give him more time with his father. He had been wrong.

A private security guard, one of three on duty, waved from the guard house next to the gate. Beau caught a glimpse of the multiple TV screens inside where eighty cameras on the property monitored everyone coming and going from the site.

"New guy?" Beau asked as his father drove through the gate.

"We rotate new security guards through the facility every year or so. Only George Cason, my security head, stays on."

Beau glimpsed the single black smokestack rising out of the red-bricked processing plant.

"Seems a bit excessive for a brewery."

"Our family owns more than the brewery." Gage navigated a narrow cement road with landscaped gardens on either side. "We have other business interests to protect. In a few years, when you take over more of the day-to-day management of things, you will understand."

While the car passed two big metal buildings used for equipment storage, Beau's hopes for his future floundered behind his father's plans. It was all he had ever heard since he could remember— his life had been predetermined because of his name.

He had been in every building scattered across the fifty-acre facility at some point or another. Either working during the summer in the red-bricked packaging and shipping building, its loading docks filled with the fleet of green Benedict Beer delivery trucks. Or hanging over the giant copper vats in the processing center where the fermentation process took place. He'd even spent his freshman year of high school assisting in the sleek glass and steel research and development building, where his father's team of "beer fanatics" came up with new brews to keep the company vital.

Gage waved to a delivery truck as it pulled onto the road. "We've started sending out Fall Fest Beer for the Oktoberfest's going on around the area."

Beau tuned out his father as the sleek car eased into the reserved spot outside the gray clapboard, two-story office building.

"Come November, you'll be spending your afterschool hours in this building with me." Gage opened his door. "I've let you slide on your duties since football practice began, but once the season is over, you need to get serious about the business."

He bit his tongue as his father got out of the car.

This is such bullshit.

To the side of the building was a straight wooden staircase that climbed to a dark glass door on the second floor—his father's private entrance to his office.

Beau followed Gage up the steps and, once inside, peered down a hallway decorated with framed posters of beer bottles. Strawberry Ale, Bogue Falaya Rock, Crescent Dark Ale and the Devereaux Special Blend were just a few of the names Beau had memorized.

His father opened the door to his immediate right; Beau noted Connie Fricken's empty desk farther down the hall. Beau couldn't remember a day he hadn't seen Gage's longtime secretary at her post.

"Where's Connie?" He stepped into his father's corner office.

"It's Saturday. She's off."

Lucky her.

"I want to talk to you about college." Gage had a seat behind his impressive mahogany desk.

Carved with swirls and decorative designs, the desk wasn't as ornate as the one he had at home, but it was just as distinctive. His office was a replica of his study at home. He even had the same Oriental rug on the floor.

Beau sank into a cold leather chair, eyeing the certificates of merit, awards, and commendations earned by the brewery over the years, desperately avoiding his father's eyes.

Gage folded his hands on his desk. "I know you're setting your sights on getting on at Tulane to play football, but I think you need to reconsider."

Beau's irritation festered. "What? You don't believe I have the chops to make a college team?"

"I won't beat around the bush. No." He flourished his hand in the air. "You've got talent, like I did at your age, but it's not enough. You need to face that now and commit to your future."

Beau feared his father and the repercussions he could bring down on him if he refused to accept his fate.

"What if I don't want this future? Why can't I figure out what I want?"

Gage slapped the desk.

Beau flinched and sank deeper into his chair.

"I could really give a shit what you want. You're expected to take over the family businesses just like I did and my father did, and his father before him. This is the price you pay for being a Devereaux."

Emboldened, Beau leaned forward. "You can't make me do it. I'm gonna be eighteen soon. I can leave and be whatever I want."

Instead of shouting or taking a swing, his father drummed his fingers on his green blotter, staring down his son. He said nothing for what felt like an eternity. Gage's silence was more insufferable than his lectures.

Beau looked out the long picture window, down at the red rug beneath his feet, his fingernails, the edge of the desk, anything to avoid his father's disturbing gaze.

Gage stopped drumming his fingers. "Okay. I'm going to make a deal with you. I'll give you one shot at football. I think you will fail, but if you prove me wrong, I will relent and let you try playing college ball to see what you can do."

Beau perked up, not sure if he believed him. "You're kidding?"

"If you blow this shot, you will devote yourself to attending college and working summers here with me." Gage pointed a long, threatening finger at him. "And you will take your place as head of the company when I give it to you. No more talk about what you want. Your ass will be mine."

His rebellious streak resurfaced. "I'll prove you wrong."

Gage gave his son a cursory once over. "I've got a friend in the athletic department at Tulane. I'll give him a call. I'll ask him to send a scout to look at you for the next game."

He couldn't believe it. Joy shot through Beau like a bolt of lightning. He jumped in the air, almost toppling over his chair.

"Are you serious?"

Gage showed no emotion, not even a raised eyebrow. "They will determine if you're good enough to play. If they pass on you, you will give up this dream of playing football."

Beau went around the desk to his father, holding out his hand. "Yes, sir. If they tell me I'm no good, then I'll give up. But they won't, I know it."

Gage Devereaux studied his son, the doubt swimming in his eyes, but he did not shake his hand. "I think you're in for a rude awakening, Beau. And when that happens, you're to promise me one more thing. No more outbursts." His father stood, rising to his full height, just a smidgen over his son. "You will control your anger, and if you can't, I will take action this time." He then took his son's extended hand and shook it.

Beau didn't give a damn what his father said. He was going to impress the scout from Tulane and make the team. Then he could kiss the brewery goodbye and do what he wanted with his life.

Nobody's gonna tell me what to do.

* * *

"Can you believe my old man has got a scout coming to the game?"

Too excited to sit still, Beau paced in front of his bedroom window.

"Fan-fucking-tastic news." Mitch's voice grew louder with every word.

"Josh is game to celebrate tonight at the river. You in, Mitch?"

Beau had called each one of his teammates to let them know about the scout, hoping to motivate them to be in top form. If they played well, he would play well. Mitch and Josh were stoked.

"Anythin' you want to do. You know me, I'm always up for a party at the river." Mitch's voice rose a little. "Hey, have you heard about Kelly?"

Beau's enthusiasm sputtered. "Kelly? What about her?"

"Cops picked her up. Word is she got knocked around a bit at the river." Mitch hesitated. "My parents heard about it and started asking me all kinds of stuff about what we do there."

Beau tapped his finger on his phone, not happy the crazy bitch from Covington had rained on his parade.

"My dad asked me about it too. We'll just have to start being more selective about who we let into our parties."

Mitch's deep laugh came through the phone speaker. "Sounds like a winning game plan. What time we headin' out?"

"After dinner. I'll pick you up."

"Cool, I'll be waitin'."

Beau hung up and continued to pace. He couldn't sit still. Everything he wanted was within reach.

He wondered who else he could brag to and remembered Dawn. He debated texting her but wanted to hear the jubilation in her voice. It would make his victory even sweeter.

She answered on the first ring.

"Hey, Beau."

She didn't sound excited to hear from him, but he ignored it.

"Sweetheart, I have some great news."

"What's going on?" Her voice ticked upward. "Is everything okay?"

"It's fantastic. I just found out Tulane is sending a scout to the game Friday night to see me play. Can you believe it?"

He waited for her to shatter his eardrum with a jubilant scream, but she didn't make a sound.

"That's great, Beau."

Her flat, emotionless tone almost knocked him to his knees.

"What? Why aren't you happy for me?" His mouth went dry with disbelief. "This is a big deal. It could mean I—"

"I am happy for you," she cut in, her apathy oozed from the speaker. "It's just that I was hoping you were going to go to LSU with me. We talked about this."

He almost pitched his phone across the room.

Here he was, the opportunity of a lifetime handed to him, and all she could do was think of herself.

His grip tightened on his phone, willing his calm to remain in place. Perhaps she didn't understand what he was up against at a big school like LSU.

"I told you I can't get on the team at LSU. But at Tulane, I could shine. They love small school players, and I'll be a big deal there, instead of a nothing at LSU."

"But I'll be there." Her whiny tone shredded his placid poise. "Doesn't that mean anything to you?"

He let the seconds pass without giving her an answer. His fingers twitched to release his pent-up rage, but he held back.

"I thought you would understand, baby."

"I do, and I'm thrilled you will have a chance to play. I just wish we could be together at college. That's all."

She wasn't going to support him. He had believed Dawn a touchstone, someone he could count on to tell him what he needed to hear and to never question. The change indicated she'd outgrown her usefulness. Perhaps it was time to go after the woman he really wanted. His dreams of playing football were at hand—he needed the woman of his dreams by his side.

"I got to go."

He hung up before Dawn could say goodbye.

Dropping his phone on his bed, he muttered, "Time to find me a new cheerleader."

* * *

Dawn sat on her bed, staring at the black screen of her phone, debating if she should call him back. Perhaps she should have been more enthused about his news, but why did it have to be Tulane?

Leslie walked into their bedroom at the lake house, carrying a soda.

"Who died?"

Dawn slapped her phone on the blue bedspread. "He hung up on me. He's cut me off before, but he's never hung up on me. I thought he was a gentleman."

"Who? The asshole?" Leslie came up to the bed. "What did he do? Dent his BMW?"

Dawn listened to her sister's cocky attitude and shook her head. Why couldn't she be that way with Beau? Might be good for her to hang up on him once in a while.

"He called to tell me a scout is coming to the game Friday night to check him out. A scout from Tulane."

Leslie sat on her bed, a crease across her forehead. "I thought you two planned on going to LSU together."

Dawn got teary-eyed as she came to terms with the fact they would not be in school together. She sniffled and wiped her nose with the back of her hand.

"He made it very clear he wants to go to a school where he'll have a chance to play football, and LSU is not it."

Leslie dipped her head. "Sounds to me like the guy is putting football before you."

Her heart sank like a stone in a pond. Leslie was right. She had never wanted to see it before, but the truth stared her right in the face. Beau put football, his friends, and the river before her. The realization hurt.

This can't be love.

"Is it too much to ask that he think a little more about … me." She gazed up at her sister. "Am I being selfish, Leelee?"

"No." Leslie put her arm around her shoulders, tucking Dawn's head into her neck. "He will always put himself before you."

Her sister's embrace eased her heartache somewhat but did little to silence her regret. Beau's mood swings, the anger, his disregard for others, and how he hid it all behind a charming smile—how much longer could she put up with such a guy? Would a life without his constant rules, and expectations be so bad?

"Come on." Leslie coaxed her from the bed. "Let's go tell Mom and Dad about Beau's news. I'm sure Mom will be elated."

* * *

Sparkling pinpoints of sunlight skimmed the surface of Lake Pontchartrain, and a mellow breeze stroked the water's surface. Leslie studied her father as he stretched out on a wicker chaise lounge, reading messages on his phone. Shelley sat next to him, her nose in a book.

"Hey!" She announced coming onto the deck, dragging her sister by the hand. "Dawn has good news."

John lowered his phone and raised his eyebrows. "What is it?"

Dawn came out from behind Leslie. "Beau said a college scout from Tulane is coming to the game this Friday to see him play."

"It would seem Beau Devereaux is going to be a green wave and not a tiger." Leslie pumped her fist in the air. "I, for one, am very thankful."

Shelley put her book aside, her face impossible to read. "Dawn, as always, we'll be there watching you and Beau on Friday night."

She looked over at John. "Won't we, dear?"

"Of course." John nodded. "Wouldn't miss it."

"It would be nice if you went as well, Leslie." Shelley patted her husband's leg. "Don't you agree, John?"

Her poor father. How could he answer and keep the three women in his house happy?

"Yes, that would be nice." Dawn thankfully stepped in, saving him from a fate worse than hell. "But it probably won't happen."

Leslie folded her arms and smirked. "If Derek could sit with us, I would come."

Shelley's face turned a deep shade of crimson. It was John's turn to pat her knee, attempting to calm her down.

"Sounds like a fine idea to me, hon."

Slowly, the hard line across Shelley's lips smoothed. "If that's what it will take for Leslie to come and watch her sister cheer, then he's welcome."

Her father beamed. "We can make it a family event."

Dawn elbowed her sister. "Does that mean you'll come?"

Leslie grinned, glad to see her father happy.

"I have to see if Derek wants to go."

John stood. "Well, this will be a first. The entire Moore family at a St. Benedict football game." He dramatically placed his hand over his heart. "I might die of shock."

Shelley returned to her book. "That makes two of us."

Leslie chuckled. *That makes three of us.*

* * *

His muscles throbbed with excitement for the coming evening as Beau gripped the steering wheel. With the wind in his hair, his best buds by his side, a choice song blasting from his speakers, and a shot of living his dream in his grasp, life had never felt so good.

All eyes turned to his car as he drove down Main Street. Beau figured word had gotten out about the scout. Finally, it was his time to shine. Not as the senator's grandson, or Gage Devereaux's boy, but as himself—a high school kid with talent and a chance to go pro.

He pictured the sweet satisfaction he would get after the game when the scout praised his performance. The invite to play ball at Tulane would shut down his old man. Seeing his father eat his words would bring him more pleasure than raping ten Taylors.

"You called Eddie and let him know we're comin'?" Mitch demanded.

Beau held up his cell phone. "Just left him a text, but he'll have it ready. Eddie never lets me down."

Josh pointed out the window as they drove past the bright neon sign outside Carl's Pizza. "Hey, isn't that Bondage Bissell?"

Beau slowed down. Sara and a few cute girls in tight jeans appeared at the edge of the parking lot. She looked good in a short black skirt, showing off her trim legs.

"Let's see what she's up to," he mumbled, veering the car toward the lot.

Josh leaned in from the back seat, wide-mouthed. "Dude, after the way you blew her off last night? She might scratch your eyes out."

Beau liked the sound of the challenge in his voice. "She'll forgive me. I can get her to want me again. I'll even bet you guys I get her to come to the river tonight to celebrate with us."

Mitch held out his meaty paw to him. "Fifty bucks she turns you down."

With the gods of fortune smiling down on him, how could he lose? Beau took his hand. "You got a bet."

He steered his car into the lot and parked right next to the Nissan Pathfinder Sara perched against.

He leaned out of the window and could see the hate roasting in her eyes, but that didn't bother Beau. He got out of the car and went up to her, confident she would do exactly as he asked.

She tossed her brassy hair over her shoulder and sneered. "Look who it is, Mr. Pencil Dick."

Mitch and Josh laughed in the car behind him. The two girls with Sara tipped their heads to the side, checking out Mitch and Josh.

Beau didn't find the comment funny. He longed to teach her another lesson, one she would remember. He focused on her, a cocky grin affixed to his lips.

"You're not still mad about last night, are you?"

"Is threatening me your definition of foreplay? Boy, have you got a lot to learn about pleasing women."

If he'd been any other guy at St. Benedict, her interest in bondage would have been intimidating. But Beau understood the game of pain, considered himself an ardent student, and was certain Sara had not practiced what she professed to know.

"Then teach me how to please you. Show me how you want a guy to treat you. I'll do whatever you ask." His voice slipped into a smooth whisper. "Come to the river tonight, and we can slip away."

Sara hiked her hand on her hip. "No thanks, asshole."

Mitch and Josh had their heads sticking out of his driver's side window. Mitch raised his eyebrows as if insisting he concede. Beau wasn't done with her yet.

"We're going to have a big celebration tonight. A scout from Tulane is coming to watch me play Friday night. I'm on the verge of being famous."

"I'm not that big on football." She took a step back from him, appearing ready to walk away. "Nice try."

It was time to move in for the kill and offer her the one thing he knew she wanted. He rushed up to her and put his lips to her ear so no one else would hear.

"I can satisfy the curiosity burning inside you. The one keeping you up at night and asking how far you could go before you beg a guy to stop. Do you want to find out? Become a part of that special club where pain and pleasure are one."

When he backed away, Sara's mouth opened in an expression of stunned surprise.

"How do you know about ...?"

He grinned, taking in her face. He had been right about her—a wannabe who owned a pair of handcuffs but had never used them.

"You're not the only one in school who wants to try kinky things. Maybe we could try them together."

Sara said nothing but lowered her eyes.

Her relaxing posture told him she was debating his proposition. The outward hostility slid from her features, softening her lips and jaw muscles.

He gave her one more morsel to tip the scales in his favor. "Dawn won't be at the river tonight, if you're wondering. We called it quits today. She broke up with me in a text. I never expected her to turn into such a bitch."

Sara tucked a ringlet of hair behind her ear. "I did."

The high he'd been riding gained momentum.

"Say you'll come to the river."

Sara glanced at her friends, hiding her smile. "I'll think about it."

"We'll have fun," he whispered to her. "I promise."

When Beau climbed into his car, Mitch patted his shoulder. "I gotta hand it to you. You had her eatin' out of your hand."

"And you owe me fifty bucks." Beau steered the car back onto Main Street. "Now let's get this party started."

They arrived in the parking lot of Rouse's Grocery Store and drove around back to the loading dock.

Beau turned off the engine, popped the trunk, expecting to see Eddie coming out the back door at any moment.

Standing by the open trunk, he waited. But the minutes slipped by and Eddie didn't show.

"Hey, man?" Josh leaned out the back window. "Where is he?"

Beau retrieved his phone to text Eddie when the back door to the store opened and the bright lights illuminated Beau's car.

Eddie dashed up to him without the usual box. In his hands were two bottles.

"I couldn't score your booze tonight."

Beau browsed the meager supplies. "What the hell, dude?"

Eddie shoved the bottles at Beau. "The cops came by today asking about underage kids drinking at the river. You guys left the bottles behind. They tracked them here." He glanced back at the open door. "My manager is all over the checkout clerks about checking inventory and IDs on anyone buying alcohol."

Beau took the bottles and held them against his chest, his soaring spirits suddenly taking a nosedive.

"I need more than this."

Eddie took a step back, seeming uncomfortable with Beau's curt tone. "I can't get any more. Take those two bottles of vodka on me. When things calm down, and the cops stop coming by, we can go back to business as usual. Okay?"

Beau carefully appraised the store clerk and weighed his options.

"I'll let it slide, Eddie, but give me a heads up next time to make other arrangements. If you can't fill my orders, I've got another guy waiting to step up. He really needs the extra cash."

"No, Beau, no." Eddie rushed up to him, the light from the store accentuating his desperation. "I can get you what you need, but let the heat die down. Don't shut me out. I need that money for my girl and our baby."

Beau opened his car door, intent on getting back at the store clerk for letting him down. "It would be a real shame if you have to leave St. Benedict after your kid is born."

Eddie stared at him, with a scrunch-eyed look of bewilderment. "What are you talking about, leave? This is my hometown."

Beau passed off the bottles to Mitch, his zeal for the evening returning. "Yeah but, imagine how hard it will be to raise a kid here without a job and a misdemeanor offense for selling liquor to a minor on your record." Beau drove his point home with a smile. "They could take your license away for that."

Eddie shook his head. "No, you bought the liquor, Devereaux. Not me."

Beau kept up his grin as he got in the car. "I bought it from you, Eddie. There's a difference. One the parish DA will be real interested to hear about if my next run isn't just what I ordered."

Beau rolled up his window as Eddie came up to his car.

"What's his problem?" Mitch asked, nodding to Eddie.

Beau put the car in drive. "Eddie? He's just having a bad day."

He headed out of the lot as the bright light from the loading dock door faded behind them.

"This is it?" Mitch held up the bottles. "How we gonna party with two lousy bottles of vodka."

"That's all we're going to get." Beau navigated through the parking lot and back to Main Street. "The cops have been around. They were asking questions about our parties."

Josh leaned in from the back seat. "So what do we do?"

Beau came to a stop sign and checked the road, his mind abuzz. "Keep the parties to just people we know. No more out of town guests."

Mitch tucked the bottles under his front seat. "Good plan, but what do we do in the meantime for supplies?"

Beau was sick of Mitch's whining. "Get creative. Perhaps it's time for you to start scoring the booze."

"Yeah, right." Mitch put on his seatbelt, lowering his gaze. "I ain't you, Beau."

With an insolent grin, Beau turned onto Main Street. "Thank God for that."

Chapter Twenty

The gray light of dusk blanketed the town of St. Benedict. The curved wrought iron streetlights came on as Derek drove his mother's blue pickup truck along Main Street to Mo's Diner. He rubbed his thumb along a torn spot on the leather-clad steering wheel, hunting for a way to say what was on his mind.

"You look worried." Carol, wearing her yellow uniform, reached over and ruffled his thick brown hair. "You thinking about school?"

Derek inhaled a breath and held it. "Actually, I'm worried about you."

His chest contracted as he blew out the breath, glad he had finally found the nerve to say something.

"Me?" Carol chuckled. "I'm fine, sweetie. You've got nothing to worry about."

He examined the bags under her eyes and cheap uniform. There had to be more for her than a life of filling coffee cups and serving po-boys.

"Mom, you work too hard. You put in too many shifts."

She rested her head back against her seat, giving him an indulgent smile. "We gotta eat, Derek. And the diner isn't so bad. I get to pick my shifts, and the tips are good at night, and we've got everything we need, right?" She patted his hand.

Derek couldn't go off to college with a clear conscience thinking of his mother spending her days and nights at the diner. His biggest fear was once he was gone, she would work even more to avoid the empty house.

"Perhaps you should consider doing something else. Another

job, or maybe even getting a hobby."

"A hobby?" She ran her hand across her brow. "It's been a long while since I've done anything for me. You've been my motivation for so long. I'm not sure where to begin."

He had to know his mother had something other than him to fill her days. He wouldn't be around much longer to encourage her to pursue her interests.

"What did you like to do in high school? What hobbies did you have? Things you liked to do? You never speak much about when you were growing up in St. Benedict."

"Probably because growing up in St. Benedict was about the same then as it is now." She glanced out the passenger window. "Everyone went to the river, had parties, hung out at Ed's Diner, which is now Carl's Pizza. Not a whole lot has changed."

A thought popped into his head. "And the Devereaux family? Are they any different?"

She kept her face turned away, but he detected a change in her mood.

"Their influence is the same, yeah."

Derek pushed on for answers. "What about Gage? How was he?"

Carol gave a slight shrug, not appearing too interested. "He was the quarterback of the football team, like his son, and very popular."

Derek considered the slight tremor in her hands. "What happened between you and Gage Devereaux?"

The long, loud breath prepared him for something he might not want to hear.

"We were pretty serious, but his father never approved of me. I wasn't the right material to be a senator's wife, or so Edward Devereux believed. His mother, Amelia, was a snooty Uptowner from New Orleans. Her family was real blue blood, and she wanted Gage to marry into high society. They made him go away to college in Boston. He swore when he came home after his first year away, he would marry me. So, I went to LSU and waited."

Her quivering voice tore at Derek's heart. It was the saddest sound he'd ever heard.

She cleared her throat. "When he came back the following June, he refused to speak to me. I called, I went to his house, but I never found out why he cut me off. I fell apart and quit LSU, then got my job at the diner. It used to be his favorite coffee spot. I hoped one day he would stop by, order a coffee, and explain what happened. He never did. A year later, I met your dad."

"But you never forgot about Gage." Derek placed his hand over hers.

Carol raised her sad eyes to him. "Some pain haunts you. It digs in deep and awakens at those moments when you think you're just getting over it. Gage was like that for me for the longest time. Then I had you."

The glow of the white neon letters up ahead, spelling out *Mo's Diner,* brought a smile to his face.

His second home. The diner and the people working there had been the closest thing to a family he had known. Despite his happy childhood, his envy for all those cozy homes in the neighborhoods of St. Benedict persisted. He wanted to know what a real family was like—even if it wasn't his own.

He pulled the truck into one of the parking spots in front of the flat-roofed, one story building. Through the windows, he could easily see every customer inside. Seated at the blue booths and along the main glass-covered counter, they drank coffee, ate sandwiches, or enjoyed Mo's famous strawberry cheesecake.

He pictured his mother and Gage Devereaux inside as happy teenagers, stealing a few kisses in a corner booth.

"Do you think he forgot about you?"

Carol wiped her finger under her eyes. "I honestly don't know, and at this point in my life, I don't care. The boy I loved in high school isn't the Gage Devereaux everyone sees now. He's different—

darker, angrier, more like his father, the senator." She positioned the rearview mirror so she could check her makeup. "When I heard he married Elizabeth, I figured he'd forgotten about me. We've both moved on."

She tugged at her ponytail and ran her finger under her lower lip to wipe away a smear of lipstick. When she put the rearview mirror back in place, she smiled, the pain of the past erased.

"You want to come in and get some cheesecake before you head home?" She reached for the door handle. "You can chat with me while I work."

He was about to skip the offer, more intrigued by the sci-fi book waiting on his Kindle when a customer caught his eye.

Despite the mild October evening, she wore a thick black sweater, and sat on a corner stool hunched over a cup of coffee on the counter. Her brunette ponytail askew, with tufts of hair poking out at odd angles, she seemed very uncomfortable.

His mother tapped his shoulder. "I want you to promise me you won't go near the river. The cops are beefing up patrols there since they pulled over that girl."

There was something familiar about the stranger nagging at him. "Pulled over what girl?"

Carol gathered her big black purse, the umbrella sticking out of the top. "A Covington girl got pulled over last night. Kent Davis came in for coffee and told me about her. She'd been beaten up but refused to say who did it. She wouldn't even allow the police to take her to the hospital for an examination. All she would tell them was she had been at a party on the river."

He turned to his mother, revisiting what he knew about the river. "Leslie had a bad experience there once with some pushy football players. She never wants to go back, and I'm not part of Beau's crowd, so I wouldn't be welcome."

She leaned over and kissed his cheek before climbing out of the truck. "Glad to hear it. If you ask me, not being part of Beau

Devereaux's crowd is a good thing." She shut her door. "Pick me up at seven and we'll have breakfast."

"Okay, Mom."

Carol walked toward the double glass doors at the entrance to the diner, waving at him.

Derek waved back, uncomfortable with the idea of his mother working another twelve-hour shift. What could he do? After hearing her story about Gage Devereaux and why she'd taken the job at the diner to begin with, he understood her attachment to the place. But after all these years, it was time to let go and start a new life. He just wished he knew how to help her.

He was about to back out of his parking spot when the girl in the thick black sweater walked in front of his truck.

He sat back in his seat, flooded with astonishment. It was Taylor Haskins.

Her gray sweatpants, oversized sweater, and the flopping loose laces on her tennis shoes didn't bother him as much as why she was at the diner alone. Mo's wasn't the preferred hangout. Everyone gathered at Carl's. So why was she here?

He opened his door, grabbed his keys, and hurried from the truck.

"Taylor?"

She stopped. Her back to him, he could almost sense her cringing beneath the thick material of her sweater. She slowly turned to face him, pulling her sweater closer as if preparing her armor, and when her eyes met his, Derek became concerned.

Her stone-cold expression did not belong to the vibrant girl he remembered passing in the school halls.

"You're Leslie Moore's boyfriend."

He moved closer, taking in the darkness descending over the street. "Derek Foster."

She folded her arms and slouched her shoulders, appearing uneasy with the encounter. "Ah, yeah." She eyed the diner. "What are you doing here?"

He glanced at the windows. "My mom works here. I drop her off when she has the night shift."

Taylor nodded, pressing her lips together. "That's cool."

"Why are you here and not at the party on the river?"

Taylor paled, turning a sickly shade of gray. "I don't like it there. Those parties are … some crazy shit happens there."

Her words brought to mind Leslie's warning about the river. But, unlike his girlfriend, Taylor seemed terrified of something.

"I thought going to the river was mandatory for all cheerleaders."

"I'm not on the squad anymore." Taylor took a step back, her fingers nervously twirling her ponytail.

Her behavior bothered him, a lot. The girl standing before him was nothing like the cheerleader he'd seen leading pep rallies in the school quad during lunch.

"Are you okay?" He put a hand on her arm and she leaped back as if he had the plague.

"I'm sorry." She scoured the street. "It's getting late. I need to go home."

"Let me drive you." He wasn't about to let her walk home in such a state. He motioned to the truck. "You shouldn't be out here alone at night."

Her gaze went from him to the blue truck next to them, then back to him.

He could see the big vein along the side of her neck pulsing. She squeezed her arms closer while an ugly line darkened her forehead. She bit her trembling lower lip.

What happened to her?

"I have to go straight home. Okay?"

He thought the request odd. Where else would he take her?

"Sure." He went to the passenger door and opened it for her. "Get in and tell me where you live."

She stepped toward the car like a wild animal sizing up a trap—cautious yet hungry for the bait.

Once inside, she seemed to calm. After he shut her door, Derek went around to the other side and climbed in, his mind humming.

He started the engine and waited as she secured her seatbelt. It took her shaking fingers a while to get the belt locked in place.

"1125 Huntsman Road." She hugged the edge of her seat, closer to her passenger door. "That's where I live."

He nodded and put the truck in reverse. "I know where that is. Just before Devereaux Plantation in that new subdivision."

Again, the blood drained from her cheeks. She twisted her hands together. "Yeah, my house faces their black gates. I've got to look at them every single day."

"You're not a Beau Devereaux fan, are you?"

Taylor turned to her window. "What makes you say that?"

He dug his thumb into the same tear in the steering wheel, grasping for a way to get her to open up. "I get it if you don't like him. There's no love lost between Beau Devereaux and myself. I know everyone in this town thinks the sun shines out of his ass, but I know better. Leslie knows better, too."

She settled back in her seat, and for the first time, relaxed her hunched shoulders. "He thinks he's invincible."

"Invincible?" Derek chuckled as he remembered something he'd once read. "'The mighty have a longer way to fall than the helpless. That is why the impact of their demise resonates like a dying star throughout the heavens.'"

The smile on her lips was slight, but he figured it was a start.

"Did you just make that up?"

Derek eyed the last of the buildings as Main Street came to an end. "It's from a book, *The Dust of Giants*. I forget the author."

At the line of wide oak trees, he turned left, wondering how to keep her talking.

She leaned in a little closer to him. "What's the book about?"

"It's about the Titans—the giant gods who ruled before the Greek Gods of Zeus and Hera. They thought they were invincible, but eventually, their invincibility destroyed them. Believing you're above the laws of the universe will lead to a person's demise."

Her disdainful snicker compounded his concern.

"It sure does apply to the whole Devereaux family."

"Yep, sure does." Derek kept picking at the ripped leather. "Let's hope it's not too long before Beau Devereaux's invincibility eats him alive."

Taylor turned to him, her innocent smile taking on a devilish glow. "Wouldn't that be wonderful? To have the smug son of a bitch suffer just like those he's tortured. Makes you believe in Karma, huh?"

The chilly tone in her voice gave Derek pause. "Why do you say he's tortured people? Do you know something, Taylor?"

"Nah." Her evil grin widened. "I've just got a feeling."

* * *

The air brisk, the stars shining bright, the pounding techno-pop in the air—it was all for him. The river was Beau's playground and soon he would leave it behind. For his fellow team members seated on the picnic benches along the Bogue Falaya shoreline, football at St. Benedict High would be as good as it got for them. He would go on to be famous, but these guys would spend their days looking back and not ahead.

Just like my old man. Bastard. I'll show him I got more talent than he ever did.

The twitter of girlish laughter chased away all cares about his father. Pretty young things crowded their tables in an array of styles—from short to tall, blonde to black-haired, mahogany to lily white. He could have his pick, but he ached for someone with a little more wisdom in their eyes and adventure in their heart.

Sara wasn't among the girls at his table. She'd never showed, disappointing him. He struck up a conversation with a curvaceous sophomore with honey-colored skin and the prettiest heart-shaped, pink lips, but it wasn't working. Her innocence, and the way she constantly batted her eyelashes sent him from the picnic tables claiming he needed to grab a beer.

He wandered the beach, checking out the girls. He ached to take another to his cell. But he wanted a challenge, someone who could satisfy his thirst for pain. He debated between a perky cheerleader who reminded him of Dawn, and a serious-looking brunette with a perfectly round ass until he spotted a new face.

Older than the others, she had mature poise, whetting his appetite. She had to be in her twenties.

What's she doing here?

With dark hair and wide-set eyes, she came across as seductive and sensual. He especially liked the way she moved. She swayed in time with the music, rocking her hips like a wave rolling over the ocean. Fluid, smooth, and mesmerizing. The more he studied her, the more he wanted her.

He followed her around the beach until she ended up on the outer edge, away from the bonfires' light.

"We don't get a lot of your crowd here?"

She spun around, her full lips parted in a tempting smile. "My crowd?"

Her teasing tone aroused him. "All I ever see here is high school kids. Why are you here?"

She searched the beach around them, her eyes glistening in the light of a nearby bonfire. "I was at a campground further down the river. I heard the music and came to see what's up. But you're right. This isn't my scene. Sorry to intrude." She turned to go.

He hiked across the sand. "What's your kind of scene?"

She halted and glanced at him over her shoulder. "Something less ... noisy."

He took another step, his heart pounding. "What's your name?"

She faced him, looked him up and down, and then gave him a compelling smirk. "Andrea. What's yours?"

"Beau Devereaux."

She didn't bat an eyelash. Either she didn't know who he was or she didn't care. Either way, he was intrigued. He debated how to get her to his cell. She could be just what he needed to cap off his night.

Andrea folded her arms. "What would a lady have to do to get a drink around here, Beau Devereaux?"

He closed the gap between them. "Well, that depends on the lady."

She got a little closer. "You're cute. How old are you?"

Tantalized by the ivory color of her skin, he drifted his gaze down her skintight jeans. "Old enough to know how to please a lady."

Her eyebrows went up. "I doubt that." She arched closer, her voice barely a whisper. "Men have a hard enough time figuring out what women want. What makes you think you know, little boy?"

Now he was excited. The challenge in her voice, the way she teased him roused his hunger. "I've got a lot more experience than most men. I have very selective tastes."

She stood back, reappraising him.

He could sense her interest and her reservations. Tempted, she was still leery. He had to find a way to convince her to join him in the cells.

She chuckled, captivating him. "You're cocky, aren't you?"

Beau got up close, invading her personal space, letting her know he wasn't playing games.

"I'm eager and very motivated to try new things. I might surprise you."

A flicker of curiosity rose in her features.

He had her.

She scanned the trees surrounding the beach. "Is there a place we can go to get to know each other better?"

Beau turned to the far side of the beach where a cleared path led away from the sand. "You ever seen the inside of The Abbey?"

She sank her hands into the back pockets of her jeans, jutting her breasts forward. "I've heard about the old abbey around here, but I've never seen it."

He held out his hand; his every nerve on fire. "Let me show you."

Beau guided her through the revelers on the swath of beach until they came to the path.

"The Abbey dates back to the 1800s. The land was given to the Jesuit priests by a local family to build their seminary." The white spires rose in the starry sky ahead of him. "There are rumors about wild dogs seen hunting on the grounds late at night. And then there's a lady in white myth, but no one believes it."

She nestled closer to him, curling her hand around his arm. "Scary stuff."

He put his arm around her. "Don't worry. I'll protect you."

At the fountain, he stopped and turned to the brush-covered crack in the cell walls. "There's some place special I'd like to show you."

Andrea didn't resist when they marched across the high grass toward the cells.

His fingers itched, his heart sped up, and excitement gathered in his gut. Sensing he was close to his release, to capturing the power inflicting pain gave him, made his mouth water.

She's gonna be so sweet.

When he parted the brush covering the crack in the wall, she hesitated.

"It's in here?"

A slight tinge of apprehension. He liked that. It meant she was sober, somewhat cautious, and would put up a fight.

"We will not be disturbed. No one comes here."

She gave him a wary glance as she slipped through the crack.

He followed her and on the other side of the wall, took her hand. He guided her down the dark, dank corridor to his cell. The air heavy with moisture; the odor of rot and mold hung around them. She didn't flinch as the pinpoint of light coming through the cracks landed on the skeleton of a rat. Brave, too. Even better.

Once in the cramped room, he went around lighting the candles.

She waited at the doorway, the candlelight enshrouding her in a yellow halo. He admired the play of light and took her hand. The inviting smile on her soft lips enticed him. Unable to stop himself, he kissed her, a long, passionate kiss. She responded and her fervor for him added to the building excitement in his system.

It's time for some fun.

Beau flung his arms around her, practically carrying her to the cot. He carefully eased her onto the blanket, plotting his next move.

Andrea pressed her hand into his chest, pushing him back. "I'm not like other girls. I don't want you to be gentle and romantic. I'm not looking for anything like that tonight."

Shades of Taylor danced in his head. "Tell me what you want."

Her fingernails scratched all the way down his chest to his crotch. "You ever hit a girl?"

A wary thread snaked through him. Either she was twisted like him or a setup. He didn't trust anyone.

"What are you saying?"

Her fingers deftly worked the button fly on his jeans. "Some girls like to be spanked. Some tied up with ropes, or handcuffed." The fly undone, she slipped her hand inside his briefs. "I like to be raped." She bit his chin. "Rough, hard sex, with all the hitting and biting you can muster."

Beau should have been happy about his find in her, but a trickle of disappointment curbed his enthusiasm. She wanted to be hurt, wanted to have him abuse her—that didn't motivate him. The fear he got from those he assaulted aroused him more than this half-assed recreation.

She lay on the cot, her plump lips parted, eager for him, and though he wanted to button up his pants and walk away, he also wanted to show her *his* idea of rough sex.

Why pass up the opportunity?

He pushed her hands above her head. "I'm going to give you the night of your life."

He slammed her back on the bed and ripped her shirt open.

Andrea let go a wild loud cackle, sounding like some hideous cry from a cursed witch.

"Don't hold back, Mr. Devereaux."

Beau combed his fingers through her long hair, gripped it in his fist, and then yanked her head back. "I aim to please." He bit into the soft flesh at the base of her neck.

"There you go." She held him to her. "Show me no mercy."

Caught up, Beau roughed her up and slapped her face as he stripped her naked.

He bit her shoulders, breasts, and inner thighs, waiting for her to beg him to stop, but she never did. She took everything he gave her, winced through every bite but never uttered a sound. Andrea never asked him to stop, and the rougher he got, the more she seemed to enjoy it.

He bound her hands with her bra and secured them to the pipe in the wall. Her lower lip trickled blood, but she smiled through it.

He didn't care for this game. It wasn't fun. He missed the wide-eyed terror, the cries, the pleas, the whimpering. Her happy grin left him empty.

To offset the numbness her silence created in him, Beau took his violence to a whole new level with Andrea. The more he tried to make it like rape, the wider her grin got, heightening his anger. In a last act of desperation, he put his hands around her throat right at that climactic moment. He hoped to frighten her, shape her face in the mask of horror he'd grown to love, but it did nothing. Her smile continued as he choked off her air.

When her eyes bulged, and her lips turned a dusky blue, he let her go. Gasping and coughing, she never turned away.

"Don't stop. I deserve it."

The fury in him had not been satiated. Determined to have his release, Beau flipped her over, slapped her ass, and started all over again.

This time he didn't let up on his chokehold. She bucked beneath him as her fair skin turned red and then pale. Andrea kicked violently and jerked, fighting for air. For a split second, he pictured Leslie, and only then did he get off, reaping his satisfaction from the panic in her graying face. When he let her go, she collapsed lifelessly to the cot.

She lay motionless until the air entered her lungs in one loud, ragged gasp.

He rolled off her and lifted her chin. Her eyes were dotted red from a few broken capillaries. Proof he had pushed her to the edge of death.

What if he had gone further? What kind of rush would he have experienced if she had died? The idea floated around his head.

"Wow. That was insane."

Her hoarse but perky voice rattled him. He preferred a woman's whimpering to her accolades.

"That was the biggest rush ever. I thought I was going to die. I tried to get other guys to do that to me, but none would."

Beau's adrenaline surge fizzled. He pushed off her and rolled to the side, frustrated by the fact she wasn't frightened of teetering on the edge of death. His only enjoyment during the evening ripped away, he got mad. She'd been the one in power all along. It made him feel impotent. Subduing another, belittling them, hurting them, those were the things he hoped for but hadn't gotten with Andrea.

"If you wanted it like that, you should have told me from the start." He sat up on the side of the cot.

"Do I get a round two?"

Beau stood and worked his jeans over his butt. "I think we'll save round two for another time."

"I like your style, Mr. Devereaux."

"Don't call me that. Mr. Devereaux is my old man, not me."

Andrea cocked an eyebrow but didn't comment.

Beau studied the cut on her lip, the red handprints on her throat, and the assorted bite marks on her creamy skin. There was something intensely erotic about surveying the damage he'd inflicted. She was like a work of art, and he yearned to paint another.

"When can I see you again?"

Her lips curled into a wily smile. "I'll be in touch."

With a last peck on his cheek, Andrea darted out of the room and through the gap in the wall.

He pushed the vines aside and watched her run across the high grass toward the fountain.

The encounter bittersweet, he wanted the rush of being with her again, but not the letdown. How much better would the interlude have been with another less willing victim or even Leslie?

Tons better.

Images of Leslie's pale skin and blonde hair had meshed with Andrea's during the height of his passion but dwindled in the afterglow.

How much longer could he go on without her?

Every night he spent with another woman prepared him for the day he would be with her. No matter the depth of pain or type of torment he inflicted, his greatest rush would come with Leslie.

He rested his shoulder against the jagged line of broken stone.

Perhaps the time had come to make his move. The world was his, and with his life getting better with every day, it was the perfect time to bring Leslie into it.

The echo of twigs crunching floated down the corridor behind him.

Alarm tensed his muscles. He turned, peering into the darkness. Was someone in the cells with him?

Determined to defend his territory, Beau returned to his cell and snapped up a lit candle. He couldn't afford for anyone else to come to his spot; he had more work to do here.

In the corridor, he swept the candle from side to side, lighting up the narrow passageway. He checked the other rooms, kicked around some of the debris, but saw no one else. Could have been a rat or raccoon. He'd caught them in there before.

Beau settled down and wiped the damp from his brow.

Time to get back to the party.

He returned to his room, put the candle back on the ice chest and made sure everything was in place. He relaxed, chalking up the noise to nothing more than his imagination.

After he blew out the flame, he headed back to the damaged wall and slipped into the night.

Chapter twenty-One

U nder a cloudless sky, an invigorated Beau strutted across the parking lot at St. Benedict High ready to begin the week he was sure would change his life. Around him, students sat on car hoods, stood in small groups, or stretched out on the quad, whispering amongst themselves.

They've heard about my scout.

He waited for an onslaught of well-wishers to come up and praise his good fortune, but no one seemed to notice him.

Perplexed by the snub, he listened in as two girls, their heads together walked past him toward the school entrance.

"They said she was beaten up," a girl in glasses muttered.

"I heard she was high on a new drug mixed up in someone's bathtub," her friend replied.

Guys from his biology class sat on the hood of a green Toyota Corolla, deep in conversation. He stopped right next to them, pretending to adjust his book bag to pick up what they had to say.

"She was a Covington High girl," one skinny guy in a baseball cap said.

"Why was a Covington High babe at the river?" a member of his group asked.

Kelly. Everyone should have been gossiping about his coming success on the football field. Instead, they were obsessed with her.

But she's your success, too.

A surge of pride washed away his jealousy. Without him, no one would have anything to talk about.

He enjoyed the snippets he picked up here and there. Kelly had never told anyone about their interlude, and that boosted his confidence.

Leslie and Dawn's car entered the lot, and his optimism surged. With his girl back, his future set, and his secret safe, he felt sure the day ahead would be a good one.

Before the engine had shut down, Beau opened Dawn's door. The girl looking back at him was not the exuberant one he'd dated for the past several months. Her tense features reminded him of the snarling cougar she wore on the front of her cheerleading uniform.

"Hey, Beau."

Her flat tone sent a jolt through him. "What's wrong?" He took her hand. "Didn't you miss me? I missed you."

Dawn kissed his cheek, but her passion was gone. "Yeah, I missed you. We just got in late last night."

He didn't believe her. She was different.

Beau gazed at Leslie, who stood on the other side of the car, taking in the line of her profile, eager to smell her sweet skin.

"How did you like your weekend at the lake, Leslie?"

Her smirk reeked of her insolence. God, how he wanted to break her right there.

"Why? Disappointed I didn't die in a boating accident?"

Dawn shut her door. "Enough, both of you." Dawn took his hand and pulled him away. "Why do you do that? Why do you tease Leslie?"

Beau removed her bag from her shoulder, displeased with her line of questioning. It was what he expected from Leslie, not Dawn.

"You used to love it when I teased her."

Dawn brushed the hair from her face. "It was cute in the beginning, but then you did it all the time."

He pointed to the Accord, aggravated with the change in her. "I don't understand. You hate your sister."

"I never hated her. I just never talked to her. But this weekend, we had a really good time. I don't want to go back to fighting with her again."

Shit! He needed that wedge between them to keep a handle on Dawn and intimidate Leslie. This sisterly love crap wasn't part of the plan.

"Do you want me to kiss her ass? Is that what you're saying?"

She shook her head, scrunching her brow. "I want you to be nice to her, and to Derek. Can you do that for me?"

He never said a word. He didn't argue when he got angry—he got even.

When Beau glanced back at the car, Leslie stared at him with a menacing scowl.

"If that's what you want, baby, I'll be as nice as pie to your sister."

"Great." Dawn's bubbly demeanor returned as she walked ahead, a bounce in her step. "I told her you would be reasonable. She was the one who thought you wouldn't want to have anything to do with it."

"Your sister just doesn't know the real me." Beau chuckled as he thought of getting his hands around Leslie's neck. "I'll have to show her who I really am."

* * *

In the halls, the bang of lockers and excited din of conversation accompanied Beau on his way to the school cafeteria. He scoured the faces of the students whizzing by, paper bags, lunch bags, or thermoses in their hands. None of them were Dawn.

They had agreed to meet up to have lunch together, and she had always been on time in the past. Annoyed, he rammed his hands into the pockets of his khakis and waited.

With nothing to keep his mind occupied, it drifted back to Andrea. He'd relived their night over and over again, especially the part where he had brought her to the brink of death. Images of strangling her excited him more than roughing her up. Maybe it was time for a new thrill.

"What's up, Beau?"

Sara Bissell stood in front of him, in a long-sleeved, fitted black dress, tight around her boobs, and a silver chain of handcuffs around her neck. The jewelry brought a grin to his lips. He'd love to pull the chain tight around her throat and see what she looked like when the life left her eyes.

That would be a rush.

He rested his shoulder against the red brick next to him and checked out her long legs. "I missed you Saturday night."

"Yeah, I can guess just how much you missed me. Fifty dollars' worth, perhaps?"

He kicked at a scrap of paper on the ground, tired of her games. "What are you talking about?"

She sneered at him. "Mitch Clarkson is telling everyone you bet him fifty bucks to get me to come to the river. Is that what I am to you? A bet?"

Her raised voice attracted a few curious glances from the students heading into the cafeteria. The last thing he needed was for Sara's tantrum to get back to Dawn.

He grabbed her shoulders. "Yes, I bet Mitch I could get you to the river, but you never showed up." He shoved her into the brick. "And I'm glad you didn't come." He lifted her necklace with his finger and let it fall against her skin. "You don't know anything about bondage. I know it's all an act, Sara, because I've tasted the real thing. Would you like me to tell everyone in school what a fake you are?"

She wriggled under his hands. "You're an asshole."

He eased up against her, setting his mouth within inches of hers, aching to hurt her. "Yes, I am. But if anyone asks, I'm good ole Beau. The guy everyone likes, and if you jeopardize the image I've worked so hard to create, I'll show you what real bondage is. I'll tie you to a bed and beat you within an inch of your life."

Sara's cheeks heated. "Keep talking, big boy."

Beau let her go. A torrent of disgust rode through him, obliterating whatever had attracted him to her.

"You're a sick bitch."

She licked her lips. "Takes one to know one. And I can see what you've been hiding behind that little Mr. Perfect image. You like the rough game, and if you asked me, you've played it before with someone. Could it be that poor girl from Covington High they found on the road?"

He analyzed her face, searching for any hint of what she knew. He suspected it was nothing, but her accusation flustered him.

"Keep reaching. You know damn well, I never touched her." Beau backed away, pointing his finger. "Don't start shit with me you can't finish. Because I will make you regret it if you ever cross me."

Sara's head turned. "We have company."

Dawn stood a few feet away, gripping her lunch bag. She frowned at him and then marched through the cafeteria archway, almost running him over.

Sara snickered, sounding like a venomous snake flicking its tongue.

His apprehension skyrocketed. He couldn't risk losing Dawn. He was the one who had to let go first. His reputation would suffer big time if she dumped him.

"This isn't over," Beau muttered to Sara and took off after Dawn.

"Where have you been?" he caught up to her, slipping his arm around her shoulders. "I've been looking everywhere for you."

Dawn wiggled out from under him. "Well, you weren't going to find me hiding behind Sara."

"Her? That was just a little reconnaissance for Mitch. He's got the hots for her." Beau gripped her elbow, urging her to stop. "Hey, talk to me, baby."

With a loud snort, Dawn turned to him. "Beau Devereaux, you

expect me to buy that? You make it hard for me to trust you. Everyone says I'm a fool for staying with you."

The comment stirred his desire to throttle a certain someone. "By everyone, do you mean your wonderful sister?"

"Actually, my sister is pretty damn wonderful." Dawn pried his hand off her elbow. "She hasn't lied to me, cheated on me, or made me feel stupid, like some people."

Beau wiped his hand over his mouth, seething. "After school, let's talk. I think we have some things to iron out about our relationship."

"Talk? You hate having conversations about our relationship." She put her hand on her hip, giving him a defiant scowl. "Whenever I want to talk about something, you tell me, 'Don't worry about us, we're fine.'"

She even tried to imitate his deep voice, which irritated him even more.

"Well, now I'm ready to talk. I realize we need to."

"I can't." Her sassy attitude evaporated. "I've got cheerleading practice, and I told my mother I'd be home for dinner. Shouldn't you be concentrating on the scout for Friday night instead of worrying about me, or any other girl for that matter?"

The reminder of the scout quickened his pulse. He couldn't wait to put high school and girls like Dawn behind him.

"I'm not worried about playing football in front of a scout. I'm worried about us. You're everything to me, baby."

She didn't seem to melt, or smile, or even flutter her eyelashes like before.

"I have to go." Dawn stepped away. "I'm going to eat lunch with my sister."

He did so not want to hear that.

"You tell Leslie to stop saying bad things about me in front of you." He tried to temper his coarse tone with a pleasant smile. "She doesn't know me like you do."

"Would you leave Leslie out of this? You're always going on and on about her. You're dating me, remember?" Dawn pointed, in an uncharacteristically assertive way. "And she isn't putting anything in my head. You're the one making me second guess our relationship, not her."

Dawn stomped away, leaving Beau at the entrance to the cafeteria, dumbfounded. He tried to figure out what had happened to the girl he had under his thumb. His grip on Dawn wasn't what it used to be, and it was all Leslie's fault.

Why were all his problems boiling down to one rebel with the same face as Dawn?

* * *

Outside, under the canopy of blue sky, Dawn gripped her brown paper bag to her chest. She crossed the quad to the picnic benches set up beneath a few old oaks, offering shade from the strong sun.

The encounter with Beau left her heart a jumbled mess. Jealousy, betrayal, sadness, and a throbbing ache was all she felt for the guy. He used to make her toes tingle, her heart swell in her chest, and her feet as light as air. What had happened to them?

Ahead on a bench, Derek and Leslie cuddled together smiling and laughing. Love just oozed from them. She admired the way Derek caressed her sister's cheek, touched her hand, gazed into her eyes. It was genuine—real honest to goodness love and nothing like she had with Beau. She almost felt like an intruder, but she really needed the company and her sister's ear.

"Can I join you guys?"

Derek's eyebrows went up. "Sure." He pushed over on the bench for Dawn to sit down. "Happy to have you."

Dawn angrily tossed her bag on the table. "Glad someone wants me around."

Leslie's eyebrow went up. "That doesn't sound good."

Dawn suddenly didn't want to bring down their lunch. Her sister and Derek seemed so happy together. "Do you guys ever argue?"

Her sister opened her bottle of water. "Sometimes. No relationship is perfect."

"But when you make up, is the argument over, or does it keep coming back?" Dawn retrieved her sandwich from her bag.

Derek rested his arms on the table, frowning. "I don't understand."

Dawn searched for how to explain what arguments with Beau were like: a continuous rehashing of the same problems, always his problems with her, but never her problems with him.

"It's like you're playing a recording over and over. You try to offer solutions, but the recording doesn't register your solutions or even your opinions. It just replays the same words, and you can never change them, no matter how hard you try."

"Then walk away." Leslie unwrapped her hearty turkey sandwich. "If the other person in a relationship isn't listening to you, then they don't care about your feelings."

Derek took Leslie's hand. "I like listening to Leslie's advice and taking it."

Dawn noted the way her sister and Derek touched each other, spoke to each other in soft voices, and appeared so connected. Why had she never experienced such intimacy with Beau?

Leslie chuckled. "Sometimes you take my advice."

He let her go and picked up a bag of potato chips. "Well, sometimes you don't give the best advice."

Her sister inspected her sandwich. "Neither do you."

Derek threw a chip at Leslie. She snapped it up and stuffed into her mouth.

Derek laughed and kissed her cheek.

If she had told Beau he gave bad advice, he would have blown a gasket. Then again, he expected her to take his advice and never question it.

What to wear, what to say, how much to drink, and how he didn't like the makeup she wore. He even commented when she gained a few pounds. It had made her so terrified of putting on weight, she became regimented in her diet.

Her lettuce and tomato sandwich on low-calorie wheat bread was what Beau wanted her to eat, not what she wanted. She put her sandwich down, her appetite waning.

"Guess what?" Leslie tapped the table to get her attention. "Derek is going to the game with me. We're going to cheer you on."

She'd missed having her sister in her life. Ever since Beau had entered it, she had felt empty. The close bond with Leslie had frayed, but it was coming back, and she was glad. They could start over.

"So, who's this girl?" Leslie asked Derek.

Dawn perked up, always interested in gossip. "What girl?"

"Kelly, from Covington High." Derek leaned into the table. "When I gave my mom a ride to Mo's Saturday night for her shift, she told me Sheriff Davis reported a girl had been picked up by his men. She'd been beaten up and was coming from a party on the river."

Dawn shivered. *The river.* What the hell?

"That can't be true." She picked up her sandwich, her appetite renewed. "I'm at the river all the time. I've never seen anything bad happen to anyone."

Derek popped the can on his soda. "Taylor Haskins confirmed a lot of crazy stuff goes on at the river. She swore she was never going back."

"Taylor said that?" Dawn couldn't understand it. Taylor was her friend—or had been. Since she'd quit the squad, Dawn hadn't seen much of her.

"She never mentioned anything about it to me." Dawn sat back, holding her sandwich, too stunned to eat. Had she been so blind to miss bad things going on at the river? "Why have I never heard any of this before?"

Leslie reached for her hand. "Maybe Beau didn't want you to know."

The shade closed in around her. Dawn stood. "I gotta go."

She grabbed her lunch bag and hurried from the table.

It was as if a deluge of ice water surrounded her face and limbs. Every movement labored, every breath an effort, she didn't know where to turn or what to do. She scurried for the warmth of the sun wanting relief from the cold. She swore all eyes were on her as she made it across the quad.

I'm gonna kill him!

Chapter twenty-two

With the confining walls of St. Benedict High behind her, Leslie relaxed in her car, breathing in the humid honeysuckle-tinged air that blew in her window. She couldn't wait until the high school was a memory and the prison-like atmosphere created by Beau no longer existed. The only bright spot in her life—the wonderful guy in the seat next to her.

Unlike most days, he'd been relatively quiet during the ride, only engaging with her when she asked certain questions about classes or homework assignments they shared.

"What is it?" she finally demanded after a long silence. "You haven't said much."

Derek kept his eyes on the road. "I've been trying to come up with ways to get my mother out of the diner. I'd like to see her settled in a new, better job before I go to college, but I don't know how to help her, or even what she can do. All I know is, she works too hard."

"Maybe I could talk to my dad. He might know someone who could help her find a job."

Leslie turned down his street.

The wrinkles in his brow eased as his eyes radiated a brilliant warmth. "You would do that?"

The question knocked her for a loop. Of course she would do that. Didn't he know how much she cared for him?

"Why wouldn't I? Your mother is my family, too. I want to help her in any way I can."

She pulled up to the curb in front of his driveway and put the car into park.

Derek cupped her face. "You're the most extraordinary girl. I love you with all my heart, Leslie Moore. Do you know that?"

The hardships of her life, the pain, the worry, all melted from existence when he spoke those words. A sensation of freedom and the strength to overcome all odds flowed through her. She could conquer the world with him by her side.

"I love you, too, Derek. I could never picture my life with anyone else."

His forehead pressed against hers, he closed his eyes, as if praying. "Every day it's getting harder and harder to wait for you. I want you so much it hurts."

She took his hands and squeezed them, hoping to impart how his frustrations were hers. She longed to share every part of herself, but Leslie didn't want their love consummated in the back seat of her car or on his mother's living room sofa.

"I want you too, but until we have a place of our own, to take our time, we'll have to wait. Until then, we have high school to keep us occupied."

His rumbling chuckle sent a shiver through her as his lips brushed her forehead. "Yes, the trials of sex-obsessed, underwhelmed, electronically preoccupied, career-challenged, confused, and sometimes confounding temperamental teenagers will no doubt keep us occupied until June."

She loved how his mind worked. "After that, we'll have college."

He sighed against her. "You're going to kill me." He pulled away. "Thanks for helping me with my mom."

"Thank me after we see if my dad can help."

Leslie headed down Derek's street, and his house grew smaller in her rearview mirror. She fought the urge to turn her car around and return to his side.

Why not sleep with him? He loves you.

With every passing day, her determination to wait weakened. She was in love, in a committed relationship, and trusted him more than anyone. Perhaps it was time to find a private place for their special night together. But where would they go? There weren't a lot of choices for two broke teenagers in St. Benedict other than the river.

And I'd rather die a virgin than go there.

* * *

With jittery excitement, Leslie shut the door to her father's study. She traced the swirls of grain on the darkly stained wood, going over their conversation about Derek's mom. Her father had encouraged her to help others, and even though she didn't see much hope for Carol Foster's job hunt—especially in the small town of St. Benedict—her father's enthusiasm to join in the search encouraged her.

"I'll make a few calls and see what I can do," he had told her.

With a spring in her step, she couldn't wait to get upstairs and text Derek. To be able to bring him some hope for his mother's future, and lighten his worries, lifted her heart.

She reached the cushy carpet covering the second-floor landing and was about to make her way to her room when she spied Dawn's ajar door. The lights were out, but pitiful sobbing came from within. The sounds made all her good vibes vanish.

Some sister I am.

So caught up in Derek's concerns about his mom, she'd never bothered to check in with Dawn.

She knocked on the door. "Dawn? Are you okay? It's me."

Rustling grew behind the door, and then Dawn's face appeared in the crack.

Her red nose hurt Leslie's heart, but what distressed her more was the sadness in her sister's eyes.

Dawn sniffled as she pulled the door open a little more. "Do you think I'm a fool?"

Leslie pushed her way inside and held her sister in her arms, feeling even more like a wretch for ignoring her. "You're not a fool, Dawn. He's the bad guy here. He lied to you."

Dawn slinked away, wiping her nose on her shirtsleeve. "You knew what he was and tried to warn me, but I never listened." She marched back to her princess bed. "I should have seen it like you did." She snapped up a tissue from the box sitting on her pink comforter. "Some twin I am."

Leslie went to her side. "What are you going to do?"

"I don't know." She slapped her bed. "Part of me wants to break up, but another part doesn't want to be without a boyfriend. Especially with the big Halloween river bash coming up. I always dreamed of going." She raised her eyes to her sister. "Sounds stupid, huh?"

Leslie sat next to her, determined to make her sister smile.

"It's not stupid. And if you want to go to the party so much, go with me. Me and Derek. We'll be your dates. You don't need Beau."

A sharp twinge tore across her chest. She shuddered at the image of The Abbey's tall spires, but her sister's happiness was more important than her fears. She had to make the sacrifice for Dawn and go to the river. Maybe it would turn out to be a good thing. If Dawn could envision a life without Beau, then perhaps she would give him up and start anew.

Dawn crumpled up the tissue. "But you hate the river."

Leslie put her arm around her, feeling closer to her twin than she had in almost a year. "I can tolerate it for one night. If Derek is with me, it will be different than before. Who knows? I might even have fun. We both might."

Dawn rolled her eyes. "Beau is gonna die if he sees me there and I'm not with him."

Leslie nudged her shoulder. "He'll have to go through me first to get to you. And I'm not going to let him touch you. Remember what we always believed as kids—together we're stronger than apart."

Dawn wrapped her arms around her and all the fighting and snapping over the past few months melted away.

"What would I do without you?"

Leslie held her close. "You'll never have to find out. We'll be together for life."

Chapter twenty-three

Beau counted down the seconds in his head. Then the blare of the last bell of the day echoed throughout the halls of St. Benedict High. He scurried from his uncomfortable desk and hauled ass from his English Lit class. In the halls, Beau fist-bumped other guys in red cougar jerseys and shared an enthusiastic *whoop*. The biggest game of his life was hours away.

You're gonna wish you had stuck with me, Dawn.

Her brush off all week had been the only downer. He didn't want to let go. Sure, she looked like Leslie—who he wanted more with every passing day—but Dawn had also helped sustain his good-boy image. The squeaky-clean daughter of John Moore gave him the respectability he craved. Corrupting her had been a satisfying *fuck you* to his parents, who had deemed her worthy to date, but the week without her at his side in the halls had sent the gossip fanatics into overtime. He had to win her back soon if only to lose her in a very public fight so he could walk away clean.

At his locker, Mitch and Josh greeted him with high fives.

"Are you guys ready for the big game against Covington High?"

"I'm more than ready." Josh shifted his gaze to Mitch. "You ever call Lindsey to meet up after the game?"

Mitch nodded. "Yeah, she's comin' with Beverly. They're gonna join us at the river."

"Who's Lindsey?" Beau asked.

"Lindsey, the girl from Covington High? You gave her a ride home?" Josh reminded him. "She was with her friend Beverly."

He waved off the conversation. "Who cares about those girls?

~ 208 ~

We got a big game ahead of us. Focus, guys!"

"Beau?"

Mrs. Evers, the stout, middle-aged head of the English department, came up to his locker.

He turned to her, putting on his standard teacher smile—the one he used whenever he spoke to the faculty.

"Yes, Mrs. Evers. How can I help you, ma'am?"

She nodded to Mitch and Josh. "I just wanted to thank you for all the extra work you put in on the school newspaper last week. We just put the issue to bed and it's really wonderful."

Damn right it is. Busted my ass on it.

"I'm so glad you're pleased. I wanted to make it the best it could be."

"Keep up the good work." She leaned in and winked at him. "And good luck tonight. All the faculty is cheering for you to make a great show for the scout."

He tilted his head in his best a*ww shucks,* beguiling pose and deepened his smile. "That means so much, Mrs. Evers. Thank you and thank the other faculty members as well." He gripped his fist, attempting to look invigorated and not pissed off. "Go, cougars."

The most boring English teacher he had ever had to endure clenched her right hand and pumped it in the air, appearing comical.

"Go, cougars!"

After she walked away, Mitch patted his back. "Dude, you got them brainwashed."

"No, not brainwashed." Beau went back to his locker. "You keep asking me how I win people over." He shoved a book in his locker. "That's how. I kiss ass around here and do a ton of work I don't need to do, but it pays off. Mrs. Evers is tight with my dad and gives him reports on my school work. I keep her happy; he stays off my back."

Josh rubbed his chin, his eyes scrunched together. "And I thought it was just your sparkling personality. Dayum!"

Mitch ignored Josh and rested his shoulder on the locker next to Beau's. "What's goin' on with you and Dawn? Haven't seen you two hangin' together all week. Word around school is she's blowin' you off."

"That's bullshit." His entire body became wracked with tension. "We're still together. Since when have the people around here gotten anything right? They don't know me or my life."

This was all he needed. He had more important things on his mind than Dawn, but he also didn't like people thinking she had ended it. He would have to fix that ASAP.

Josh leaned in next to Mitch. "Shame you never scored with that girl the cops picked up. What was her name?"

"Kelly, wasn't it?" Mitch added.

Images of Kelly's tears and soft cries sent a fiery wave of lust crashing into his groin. Beau slammed his locker door.

"Guys, I need my mind on football, not on girls."

"Dude, you need to chill." Mitch slapped his back.

What he really needed was to find another girl and fast. He was jonesing for the sweet rush of power he'd gotten from taking Kelly. Every day, his need for more pain competed with his ability to keep up his well-practiced mask. He had never known such desire for anything in life, even football. How could something be so delicious and so devastating at the same time? He was like a heroin junkie hiding their addiction while struggling to show the world how normal they were.

"I have to concentrate." He touched his head to the cool metal locker, hoping for some relief. "I have to focus."

Mitch yanked him away from his locker and ushered him down the hall. "No, what you need is some hitting, yelling, running, and guy time. And there's only one place to get it—on the football field."

The corners of Beau's mouth lifted into an evil grin.

If only they knew.

* * *

Slumped against the hood of her car, her toes warmed by streaks of sunlight heating up the blacktop, Dawn scrutinized the students walking on the grassy quad or passing her in the parking lot. She wanted to crawl into a hole and die.

This sucks.

The funny looks, curious glances, and ever-present murmur of others had followed her all week. She knew what they were gossiping about. Since the first day she had caught Beau at the cafeteria entrance with Sara, she'd avoided him in the halls, after school, and even skipped cheerleading practice so she didn't have to see him at the football field. Staying away from him was popularity suicide, but she didn't care about what people thought anymore.

Gawd! When did I turn into Leslie?

A shadow suddenly appeared. It stretched across the blacktop and stopped in front of her, blocking the sun from her tennis shoes. She raised her head and discovered her sister standing a few feet away, her book bag slung over her shoulder.

Dawn looked behind Leslie, wondering where her other half had disappeared to. "Where's Derek?"

Leslie retrieved her keys from her bag. "He drove his mom's truck today." She arched an eyebrow at her. "I thought you were staying for cheerleading practice before the game?"

"Nope." Dawn picked up her bag from the ground, cringing at the mention of the game. "I told the squad to be back in time for the game. We don't need any more practice."

Leslie went up to her, a skeptical gleam in her eyes. "Where did that come from? You're always so anal about your squad being perfect."

"Lately, I don't feel like doing things so much. Like cheerleading. I wish I didn't have to cheer tonight."

Leslie folded her arms and directed a wicked stare at her, making

Dawn uncomfortable. "It's like you've been living under a rock for the past week. You hide in your room at home, your friends keep asking me where you are at school, and everyone is talking about you and Beau breaking up. On top of that, you aren't wearing your cheerleading uniform on a game day—you used to love wearing it. You used to be so determined to be the most popular girl in school. What's going on with you?"

Dawn searched the groups of kids around her, laughing and enjoying the late afternoon sun. She yearned to be one of them, without a care in the world, but her heart was too heavy.

"I don't want to be around people and listen to all their questions about me and Beau. I don't have the answers. All I know is I don't want to talk to him. I can't trust him anymore."

Leslie hit the remote and opened the car doors. "Not wanting to speak to Beau, I can understand, but your friends and cheerleading … I thought you loved cheerleading."

Dawn hugged her book bag like a shield of armor. "I loved the attention it got me. Particularly, Beau's attention. It was the big reason I joined. I didn't think he would notice me until I was somebody. I was so desperate for attention I slept with him that night at the river, no matter how bad it made me feel. I wanted Beau, and I thought life would be perfect with him. But it wasn't."

The weight of her confession didn't make her feel any better. Wasn't it supposed to be good for the soul or something? What a crock.

She yanked open the passenger door, angry with how stupid she'd been. "I guess I just realized the whole time I was with Beau, I was still the same desperate girl on the inside, trying to please everyone else but me. I'm not strong like you, Leelee. Maybe that's why Beau appealed to me so much. He could be strong for me." Her lower lip trembled, but she tried to hide her pain by stuffing her books into the back seat. "People around here may think Beau is some kind of golden boy, but I'm seeing him as he really is." She hesitated next to the car. "When I look at you and Derek, I realize how meaningless my relationship was."

Leslie came around the car to her side, her slight smile encouraging. "Sounds to me like you're growing up. I'm glad, but maybe take some time and discover who you are and what you want before you get involved with someone new. And keep cheering. You're good at it, and I think you might find you enjoy it."

"Then what?" Dawn shook her head as the riptide of all her future choices pulled her under. "I've been asking myself what I will do without cheering, Beau, my friends, or St. Benedict High. It's all kind of overwhelming."

Leslie stowed her bag in the back seat. "Yeah, we don't have much time left here." She rested her arm on the open passenger side door. "I've been thinking about next year at college. If I go to LSU and you go there, maybe we could room together for a semester or two. Might help us both adjust to all the big changes coming into our lives if we have each other."

Leslie was right. The future wouldn't be so scary if they could face it together. Six months ago, she would never have dreamed of rooming with her sister at college. Now, Dawn wanted nothing but.

"You're on." Dawn swiped the car keys from Leslie. "I'll drive."

Leslie grabbed for her keys but missed. "You hate to drive."

"No, I just let you drive because it's easier." She went to the driver's side door, her mood brightening. "I need to start doing things for myself. Don't you agree?"

"Glad to hear it." Leslie settled into the front passenger seat.

Dawn started the engine, eager to begin a new chapter in her life. She adjusted her rearview mirror and caught sight of a hulking red football jersey with a cougar in the center rushing up to the car.

"Oh no."

Beau stood behind the car, his hands on the trunk.

"We need to talk, Dawn."

She didn't want to talk. Dawn feared if she did listen to him, she might get sucked back into his lies. Beau Devereaux was a drug; one she had to avoid at all costs.

While the car was still in park, Dawn hit the gas and gunned the engine.

"Dawn, you can't run him over." Leslie grabbed her seatbelt.

She nodded to the rearview mirror, a zing of satisfaction egging her on. "No, but I can scare him a little."

Leslie spun around in her seat. "Just go. Don't confront the jerk."

Dawn put the car in reverse, backed up a few inches to clear the parking curb, and then put it in drive, making a hard turn to the left, avoiding coming in contact with Beau still waiting behind them.

Once she had a clear shot ahead, she hit the gas, a newfound sense of freedom coming alive as a stunned Beau was left behind.

He took off after them. Dawn drove through the parking lot, and he banged on the trunk, demanding her attention.

"Come on!"

He jogged behind them and motioned for them to stop, but Dawn kept going.

Leslie seemed to enjoy watching him struggle to keep up with the car gaining speed. She laughed and opened her window. "Better luck at the game, asshole!"

His figure grew smaller, but the fury in his face was unmistakable. A shiver ran through Dawn. She had pushed Beau too far, and he would seek his vengeance. Dawn had come to know his well-hidden bad side over the past few months, and she feared what he would do.

"You shouldn't have taunted him like that." Dawn kept a keen eye on the rearview mirror. "Beau has a real cruel streak, and never forgets a slight."

Leslie brushed off her concern with a smart smirk. "He's an idiot."

Dawn didn't like the apprehension tickling her chest. Beau appeared more like a guy about to lose control, and she needed to make sure none of the people she loved ended up in his line of fire.

Chapter Twenty-Four

Beau maneuvered his car into the parking lot next to the St. Benedict football field, his blood pumping in time with the rock song blasting from his speakers. In the metal stands, a good crowd already had their seats, and it was still thirty minutes until kick off. He hungered to find his scout before ducking into the locker room but figured he would get a good idea of who it was when he was on the field leading his team to victory.

Could this night get any more perfect?

He felt on top of the world, higher than he'd ever known—even better than his times with Taylor and Kelly. After grabbing a duffel bag filled with a change of clothes for the river party after, he strutted toward the gym, anxious to get to the game.

He was halfway across the lot when he noticed someone staring at him from the side of the stands. Taylor. Her baggy clothes seemed to hang off her. She'd lost weight. He could tell by her protruding cheekbones and the shriveled appearance of her neck. The hate in her eyes was still there. It was the only attractive quality she had left.

"What have you been doing to yourself, girl?" He yelled, swinging his bag in his hand. "You look like shit."

She never said a word but continued glaring.

He figured he was the reason for the change in her.

If she can't handle the rough stuff, she shouldn't have asked for it.

"Where's your cheerleading outfit?" he asked, getting in the last dig. "Or does it not fit anymore?"

He chuckled, proud of himself. He was almost to the gym doors when her high voice followed him.

"Ready for the night of your life, Beau?"

He stopped, not happy she had used his words. He glanced around to see if anyone had heard her.

"What's your problem?" He rushed up to her.

She backed away, stepping into the shadows of the stands, her face lost in the darkness.

He longed to follow her. The movement of the crowds above would make enough noise to cover her whimpering as he slapped her around a little, just to show her who was boss.

"Keep your mouth shut."

He turned to retreat to the gym doors, but she came back for more.

"Do you feel like a man, Mr. Hotshot Quarterback?"

She had come out of the shade and hugged one of the metal supports below the bleachers. Her diminutive demeanor and darting eyes were nothing like the brazen whore he'd taken to the cells.

He licked his lips, longing for another night with her.

"You're one psycho bitch, Taylor."

She inched closer, her head twisted on her stick of a neck as she gave him a deadpan stare.

Her bloodshot eyes sickened him and when she raised her upper lip, baring her teeth in a doglike snarl, he took a wary step back.

"Did you enjoy yourself in the cells the other night? You might want to be careful, next time. You never know who's watching."

Before he could ask her what she meant she walked away, heading toward Dawn and the rest of the cheerleading squad gathered in front of the stands.

That little slut!

She must have been spying on him. He thought he heard someone that night with Andrea. Had she seen what he'd done? But Andrea had wanted it, had asked for it, so he could never be accused of doing anything wrong.

What if she had seen Kelly …?

He ran his hand through his hair.

Think, Devereaux, think. What does the bitch have on you?

Beads of sweat gathered on his upper lip. He didn't need this right now. Not with the scout coming. He talked himself down, picturing how he would strangle the crap out of Taylor once he got her alone. He had a show to put on for the scout. Once Tulane was secured, he would beat what she knew out of her.

His fingers going numb as he gripped his duffel bag, he hurried to the gym entrance.

Before he stepped inside, a shadow crossed before the door. He turned, expecting another member of the team, and inhaled sharply when Kelly Norton slid in next to him.

In a granny dress buttoned up to her throat, she was no longer the seductive girl at the river. Her red hair was pulled back in a severe ponytail. She had on no makeup, and her pasty skin repelled him.

What had he seen in her? "Why are you here?"

She parted her pink lips, her stormy eyes on him. "I came to cheer on my team. Heard you got a scout coming to the game." She winked. "Night of your life, eh, Beau?"

His heart rate sped as anger bloomed in his chest. She was in league with Taylor. The two bitches had talked.

Shit!

A trickle of sweat rolled down his back.

She pouted her lips. "What's wrong, Devereaux?"

He got in her face, eager to remind her of their night together. "Don't fuck with me."

He was anxious to see the fear in her eyes. But there wasn't any.

Instead, she gave him a cocky grin and walked away.

Beau staggered into the locker room, hyperventilating. He gripped the wall just inside the door, struggling to calm down.

They were out to ruin his big night? He imagined their blood dripping off his hands. He would show them.

His head held high, he went to his locker, greeting a few

members of his team with high fives and encouraging shouts.

He dumped his duffel bag on the bench in front of his locker. His hands trembled when he reached for the zipper.

Pull it together. Self-control in all things.

* * *

Cleats nervously tapped on the cement floor, and an excited chatter floated in the stale air of the locker room. The clatter of safety equipment and the occasional bang of a locker all came together to unravel Beau's nerves.

Not even out on the field and he couldn't concentrate. His shoulder pads weighed a ton, his jersey itched, even his shoes weren't laced right. He was off, and he knew why.

"Are you ready to roll over Covington High?"

A thunderous war cry rose echoed throughout the locker room.

Beau ignored his coach. Taylor and Kelly consumed his thoughts. Had they talked to anyone else? Dawn? Leslie?

I'm gonna kill them if they blabbed to Leslie!

Or perhaps they wanted money. To blackmail him. Or worse, blackmail his old man.

"What's wrong?" Mitch waved his hand in front of his face. "This is the day you've been waitin' for, so snap out of it. Are you with me?"

Beau slapped his shoulder pads, pushing his worry away. "Hell, yeah."

Coach Brewer walked past Beau and went to open the gym doors to the field. "Let's go get 'em, boys!"

A whoosh of red jerseys rushed past. The coil of knots in his stomach stayed with him while he dashed out the doors and into the cool night air. Beau breathed in and out fast to right himself. It didn't work.

The glare of the lights on the field blinded him. Every game, it was the same. The blaring lights, and then the sweet aroma of the grass. It reminded him of Leslie. It had her same enticing essence.

The last thing to register was the crowd. Their roar was almost like that of a jet engine coming into land. He couldn't distinguish specific voices in the rush of sound, but he could hear all of them at once, calling for him to score.

Coach Brewer pulled Beau to the rear of the pack, kicking up some of the chalk marking the outline of the field.

"Don't be a hero, Beau. And don't do anything you think will impress that scout. Just stick to the plan and play like this is any other game." Coach Brewer slapped his shoulder pad. "These guys don't want show-offs; they want players."

He jogged in place, warming up his legs.

"Yes, sir. I got it."

Beau checked the clear sky, wishing away any rain, and then ran out onto the field, his legs two heavy anvils, sluggish and slow. His heart thudded and a strange ringing rose in his ears. He pushed the encounters with the girls from his mind, forcing images of touchdowns, perfect spiral throws and the cheer of his teammates into his head.

They won't talk to anyone. They have too much to lose.

He glanced at the home team's stands. Taylor and Kelly had their heads together right next to Dawn's line of cheerleaders, leading the crowd in a chant for victory.

This was too close for comfort.

A whistle's screech sounded. St. Benedict won the coin toss, so they opted to receive the ball.

On the field, for their first play after the kickoff, Beau fought to focus, but pictures of Taylor and Kelly kept popping into his head.

Set up on the twenty-two-yard line, Beau counted off the snap. He pulled back, saw Mitch down the field and threw the ball. The perfect spiral sailed over Mitch's head, and the referee blew the whistle on an incomplete pass.

"What the hell, dude?" Mitch complained when they were back in the huddle.

Beau's indignation flared. How dare he question him?

"You need to show a little more hustle to get the ball," Beau griped.

On the second play, Beau called for the snap and pulled back from the line, his mind a scattered mess with images of the river and Taylor. He made a sloppy handoff to his running back, David Acker, who fumbled the ball.

Beau cringed, knowing he'd screwed up.

Luckily, David fell on the ball and recovered it.

Back in the scrimmage, he had to cover his mistake. No point in letting his guys know he was frazzled.

"Nice move, David." Beau hit the guy hard in his shoulder pads, venting his frustration. "Get it together, will ya?"

"You get it together, Devereaux." David poked him hard in the chest. "You blew that pass."

Like a serpent rising to the music of a snake charmer's flute, his anger slithered through his limbs, clenching his muscles. He would show them who was the king on this field.

On the third play of the first drive, Beau shouted for the snap. He stepped out of the pocket and scanned his men scattered on the field. Mitch waved his arms, jumping in place to show he was open deep in the end zone. *Perfect!* His confidence surged. Beau cocked his arm back, lining up his throw, and then everything turned to shit.

A hard shove came from his left. The ground rushed up to meet him. He slammed into the grass, grunting as air left his lungs on impact. His vision blurred momentarily.

He rolled over, getting his bearings. The lights glared in his eyes. He sat up, then noticed a defensive lineman from the opposing team, sharing high fives with his teammates.

I've been sacked. Me? Nobody does that to me!

Exploding with rage, he scrambled to his feet and went after the lineman who had missed the block—Brett Massey.

He grabbed Brett's facemask. "You blew my touchdown!"

Brett Massey shoved Beau to the side. "Get off me, Devereaux."

Refs' immediately descended on them, pulling them apart. The punter for St. Benedict came on the field, sending Beau to the sidelines.

"Devereaux!" Coach Brewer shouted when he reached the bench. "What is wrong with you?"

Beau removed his helmet, his cheeks burning. "He blew his tackle and got me sacked."

Coach Brewer went into one of his speeches about playing as a team, but Beau didn't pay attention. He searched the stands, eager to see the girls.

Where are you two? What are you planning?

Coach Brewer grabbed his chin and snapped his head around to face him. "Stop worrying about the scouts and play ball. If you don't, you'll blow it. Do you understand?"

Beau wanted to laugh. He wouldn't blow it, but the others on the team sure would. He had listened to all he could of his coach's bullshit. He pushed the man's hand away from his chin.

"Careful. You don't want to make me angry."

Coach Brewer scrunched his weathered brow as he stared at Beau, seeming unsure of how to react.

Shaking his head, he pointed to the bench. "Sit down and get your head screwed on right before you go back out."

A nervous Beau sat on the bench, his interest focused on finding Kelly and Taylor. Dawn was on the sidelines, huddled with her squad, her trademark red ribbon securing her long ponytail. She avoided looking his way. Then, just to the right of Dawn, he caught sight of a beautiful pale face with deep blue eyes.

Leslie, along with that idiot Foster, had come to his game. The negativity choking him since arriving at the field disintegrated. If she was watching him play, he would do his damndest for her.

Right behind her, another face appeared, and his hope sank. Taylor had positioned herself right behind Leslie. Her glower reignited his rage.

The game is turning into my worst nightmare.

* * *

The murmur of various conversations from bored fans carried through the chilly night air to Leslie's seat. She rubbed her bare arms, wishing she had brought a jacket. With the home team's sluggish performance so far, the dull game hadn't captured her attention. Beau also wasn't living up to his hype, which didn't surprise her.

Derek took her hand, sending a blast of heat to her fingers and toes. She was glad he was with her. It would have been agony without him.

"Beau sucks," he whispered to her.

She patted his leg. "He does, doesn't he?"

John leaned over to them. "He's usually better than this."

"He'll get better." Shelley clapped her hands. "Come on, Beau."

Derek leaned closer to Leslie. "Your mother even cheers for Beau when he's not on the field. No wonder she's been looking at me all night like a tiger about to devour its next meal."

Leslie nudged him with her shoulder. "She's coming around. She called you by name in the car on the way over. That's a big step."

John angled his head closer. "I know how you feel, Derek. Sometimes I think she's going to eat me alive, too."

Leslie gripped his hand. "See there? You have a fan."

Derek cleared his throat. "Ah, Mr. Moore, I wanted to thank you for helping my mom. She was so nervous about her job interview today with the law firm you recommended, she couldn't stop shaking."

"Glad I could help." John patted his shoulder. "I think she would be a great fit there. I'm sure they'll love her."

Derek nodded. "I hope so. I've been wanting her to get out of the diner for years."

His smile lifted Leslie's heart. Knowing she had helped to make him happy meant the world to her.

"Interesting game, huh?"

The soft voice came from behind Leslie. She careened her head around to the next bench up from hers.

"Taylor?"

Bundled up in an oversized jacket, Taylor was barely recognizable. Her pale skin and blank stare disturbed Leslie.

What could make such a vivacious and pretty girl wither away like this?

"I didn't know you were sitting up here." Leslie worriedly checked around her. "You here with someone?"

Taylor hunched her shoulders. "I came with a friend. She goes to Covington High. She sat with her team."

Her soft voice sounded as fragile as she appeared. Something was off with the girl, but Leslie couldn't put her finger on it.

"Who is your friend?"

"Her name is Kelly. We have a lot in common." Taylor grinned, showing the first speck of life in her features. "You two should definitely meet."

* * *

Clouds gathered in the evening sky, and the breeze turned colder as the second quarter got underway. A restless rumble rose from the St. Benedict stands, drifting across the field to Beau. On the fifty-yard line, he had the ball again, getting ready to count off the snap. He yearned for some action to show his fans and the scout.

The ball snapped, and he pulled out of the pocket, his feet

dragging on the grass, but he struggled to pull it together. He spotted an open man close to the end zone, and the sluggishness plaguing him magically lifted.

You got this!

He threw the perfect spiral pass. It hung in the air, coming right down on his player. Joy bloomed in his heart. But right when his receiver stepped forward to catch the ball, Beau was forced to the ground by a brutal slam.

His vision blurred, and he caught his breath. He sat up, remembering the pass. He strained to peer down the field, willing his eyes to focus. A player from Covington High had the ball and sprinted to the visiting team's end zone.

What the fuck?

He couldn't believe his eyes when the guy kept running without a single whistle blowing the play dead.

Beau staggered to his feet, ready to rip into the ref calling the play. He marched over to the referee closest to him.

His acidic tone emphasized his outrage. "Ref, that was a late hit."

The referee shook his head. "Not from what I saw, Beau."

Wound so tight he couldn't take it anymore, he lashed out.

Beau pushed the referee. "What are you, blind?"

A whistle cut off the ref's reply. Players gathered around him, blocking his access to the ref.

"Chill, dude," Mitch cautioned.

"Settle down," his tight-end said as he ushered him back.

The head referee ran into the melee of players, shoving them out of the way. He held up his index finger to Beau.

"You've got your first warning, Devereaux. One more stunt like that, and I'll kick your ass out of the game."

The storm inside him raged. Like a wildfire fed by the wind, hate consumed everything in his head. His reason, his desire, his hope for the future had gone up in smoke.

"Me? What did I do?" His growl triggered a few shocked looks. "This is such—"

"Devereaux," Coach Brewer hollered from the bench. "Get over here."

Beau walked off the field, his cleats kicking up the grass. What kind of idiots were refereeing this game?

"You'd better wise up, boy." Coach Brewer yanked off his helmet. "You push a ref like that again, and I'll bench you for the season."

He bit his tongue. He had an image to keep up. "Yes, sir."

Coach Brewer poked him in the chest hard. "Park your ass on the bench. I don't know what happened to you out there but get it together."

Every muscle in his being shook. Every nerve fiber was on fire. He wanted to hit someone, hurt someone, even kill someone. He could not see clearly around him, everything melted into one blur of blind rage. Wound tight, craving for a release, he held it all in. He suppressed his scream, letting it burn the back of his throat.

Hyperventilating, he took his seat on the bench, then raised his head to the stands, hoping the sight of Leslie would help him.

There she was, chatting with someone behind her. Her shoulder turned, giving him a clearer view of the person. His chest heaved, and the peace he sought in her face became a raging inferno.

Taylor shifted her gaze to him as she spoke to Leslie. The grin on her lips had *I've got you*, written all over it.

Josh took a seat next to him. "What is going on with you?"

He didn't look at him but kept his eyes on Leslie. "I don't know."

"You need to chill, dude. You're costing us the game. Get your head out of your ass."

Something clicked inside him. Without giving it a second thought, Beau tackled Josh, knocking him to the ground.

His teammates grabbed at him and pulled him away.

Coach Brewer waddled up to him, pulling up his blue long shorts. "Devereaux, have you gone mad! What in the hell are you doing, going after one of my players like that?"

He tucked his chin to his chest, hiding his grin. "Sorry, Coach. We had a disagreement about a girl."

A dark shade of red tinted the coach's cheeks. "You better simmer down, son." Coach Brewer waved to the gangly second-string quarterback at the end of the bench. "Marty Evans, you're filling in for Devereaux."

Marty climbed to his feet, nervously looked at him, and grabbed his helmet.

Beau gaped at Marty's back as he jogged onto the field.

The hush from the St. Benedict stands echoed his disbelief.

What just happened? A fit of laughter came over him, surprising him. He didn't know if it was shock or disgust at his coach's choice to replace him, but he kept laughing as he walked up to his coach.

"Are you serious? I'm the best you've got and if you put Marty in there we'll lose this game."

A hush descended over the St. Benedict players lined up on the side of the field.

Coach Brewer eased closer, his big belly almost touching Beau.

"Devereaux, do yourself a favor—stay out of my face until this game is over."

When Beau finally had a seat on the bench, he scanned the stands. His father was chatting with a middle-aged man with gray hair and glasses.

Is that the scout?

Gage faced the field, his eyes ripping into Beau. He could hear the lecture he would get, but he didn't care. He'd catered to his father's rules for too long.

But when Gage Devereaux took Elizabeth's elbow and escorted his chicly dressed wife down the steps, his determination faltered. His parents had given up on him.

He would expect nothing less from his father. Fail to live up to his ideal, and Gage Devereaux wrote you off like a bad check. He did it to his mother, and after his behavior on the field, Beau suspected he would do the same to him.

The astonished looks and reactions from others in the stands sickened him.

Bastards are always hungry for a show.

His parents, the school, even the town had held him back. Maybe if he had gone to school in New Orleans and played at one of their big schools, he wouldn't have to beg for a scout to come to him. They would have heard of him already.

The emotional blow of his parents slinking away was nothing compared to the hurricane of hatred ravaging him. He wanted to hit, to punch, to kick, to bite, to destroy someone. Better than that, he yearned to kill. And if his coach didn't let him back on the field soon, Beau Devereaux would give the people of St. Benedict something to talk about for years to come.

* * *

The whistle blew starting the second half of the game. Beau paced the sidelines, kicking up the dirt and holding in his resentment. Thunder accompanied the clouds blanketing the sky, and the air was heavy with the promise of rain.

Convinced he would be called in to wipe out the fourteen-point lead of Covington High, he stayed off the bench, keeping his body warmed up and ready to go.

Minutes ticked by on the score board at the end of the field, and he agonized over every one of them. With three minutes to go until the last quarter, he'd decided it was time to turn on the charm and get back in the game.

"Coach." He arched his back and stood next to Coach Brewer, putting on his best ass-kissing frown. "I want to apologize for my behavior. I don't know what happened to me. I got hit hard twice and maybe I went a little crazy, but I'm good now."

Coach Brewer turned away from the game and gave him a skeptical side-eye.

"I'll be happy to clean up the locker room after the game, or anything you want me to do as punishment for my actions. I was wrong."

His coach kicked at the chalk by his feet. "Don't disappoint me, Devereaux." He nodded to the field. "Get in the game and send Marty out."

It was music to Beau's ears.

Mitch came up, pounding on his shoulder pads. "See? He's puttin' you back in. Let's turn it around."

His seething bitterness did not ebb while he put on his helmet; it skyrocketed. He had to sit by while the other team scored and now had to pull a miracle out of his ass to win the game and impress the scout. But he didn't complain; he smiled at everyone—just like his father would have wanted—acting like the Beau they all thought they knew.

On the field, he stayed focused, shutting out all other thoughts and keeping his anger in check. He threw short passes, connected with his open men, and his confidence returned as his team moved up the field.

His wrath retreated to the black hole inside him. Beau felt like his old self again. He settled into a rhythm. On third down, he backed out of the pocket and found an open receiver. It was one of his best passes ever.

Touchdown!

A tide of jubilation washed away all his discontent. St. Benedict was within seven points of catching Covington High.

Beau remained quarterback in the fourth quarter. The boost was just what he needed.

I'll show that scout, my father, even Coach Brewer. I've got the talent to go all the way!

On the first down, he passed the ball to Mitch for a thirty-five-yard play.

The bad beginning to the night forgotten, a rush of exhilaration hit him.

"You're back." Mitch butted his helmet when he returned to the huddle. "Keep it goin'."

Beau hoped to do just that but on the next play, the referee called offsides on a teammate before he got the ball off. He kept his cool and refocused.

He returned to the huddle and happened to glance at the visitor's sideline.

Kelly was there, chatting with one of the off-duty police officers working security detail.

He almost doubled over. Was she telling the cop everything Beau had done to her?

"Hey." Mitch slapped his helmet. "You with us?"

Beau joined the huddle but kept a wary eye on Kelly and the cop as he called the next play.

After the snap, he couldn't find an open receiver, so he ditched the ball to avoid another sack.

The blare of a whistle made him turn to his right. The line referee called him for intentional grounding.

Behind the referee, in the stands packed with cheering St. Benedict fans, he spotted Leslie. She looked right at him, wearing a strange smile.

Someone stood up behind her. Taylor, all alone on the bench, caught his stare. She aimed her finger like a gun and fired.

Beau snapped.

"Damn it, Kramer!" He charged the referee who made the intentional grounding call. "That's a bullshit call."

The lanky man blew his whistle at Beau.

"Keep it up, Devereaux, and you're out of the game!" Kramer

Wilson signaled for play to resume.

His fingers twitched, letting him know his ire was on the rise. He tried to lock it down, and before he went into the huddle, he glanced one more time to the stands. Taylor was gone, but Leslie remained with Foster by her side. His nerves calmed, then movement to the left caught this eye.

The older man he'd seen shaking hands with his father stood up, folded a notebook, and made his way down the steps.

The scout. He'd blown his shot.

Fuck!

"Beau!" Mitch called him to the huddle.

His flimsy lock on his anger broke. A myriad of black emotions pumped through him, urging him to move, to run. He barely got out the call for the play, he was so wound up.

On the line, he counted off the snap, ready to pound into the first person who touched him.

Out of the corner of his eye, Kramer Wilson stood to the side, waiting for the play.

Suddenly he knew who to blame for his lost dreams. Kramer's call had cost Beau his future and destroyed his ticket to the pros.

He took the snap, a plan hatching. But he had to be smart.

Don't let them know who you really are.

He backed out of the pocket and kept an eye on his open men. To the right, he saw Kramer heading downfield. He cocked his arm back, pretending to aim long for the end zone, even though no one was there.

His temper driving him, he zeroed in on Kramer Wilson, and let the ball fly.

It sailed through the air, a perfect spiral, gaining momentum. And as it came down, with not a single player on that side of the field to catch it, the football connected with the back of Kramer Wilson's head.

Beau hid his grin as the man went face first into the grass and didn't move.

Silence. The entire field was in shock.

There's your intentional grounding, asshole.

He relished the moment. He'd hurt him, in front of everyone, and no one would be able to say for sure if it was on purpose.

This was almost as much fun as taking a girl to the cells.

Coaching staff and players from both teams rushed to Kramer. Mindful of those watching him, he ran across the field to join the others, ready to convince everyone it had been a terrible mistake.

"Dude." Mitch ran alongside him. "You nailed him."

"The ball slipped." He slowed as they came to the small group tending to Kramer. "I didn't mean to hit him."

"Devereaux!" Coach Brewer was in his face, ripping off his helmet. "What in the ever-loving hell were you thinking?"

Beau glanced over his shoulder to see Kramer sitting up.

He pressed his lips together, hiding his smile. "The ball slipped, coach. I meant to connect with Mitch, and I must have gotten hit when I threw it."

All the years of his perfect golden-boy persona would pay off in that one moment. Who would believe Beau Devereaux would intentionally hurt anyone?

"Bullshit!" Coach Brewer leaned into him. "I've watched you throw balls for four stinking years. That was intentional." He pointed to the bench. "Go back to the locker room."

He clenched his fists, ready to fight, and then he saw all the players and coaches from both teams soaking in his every move.

Coolly, he backed away and walked off the field, keeping his head down. He wasn't about to show everyone how happy he was about clobbering Kramer.

The sound of his cleats hitting the gravel track echoed between the stands. He heard the whispers from the St. Benedict crowd as he drew near, then like a church bell on Sunday morning, someone's throaty laugh cut through the quiet. He glanced up and saw Leslie snickering.

He hurried the last few steps into the gym doors. Once inside the locker room, he let go of his rage and flung his helmet, taking out the clock on the wall.

Beau plopped down on the bench in front of his locker, his head in his hands. Faces from the game whipped across his mind. Taylor, Kelly, but most of all Leslie. Her outburst had proved the time had come to make her his. Her insolence needed to be tamed, and he was the only one who could do it.

The locker room door swung open and Coach Brewer waddled inside. He came up to his bench, his face the color of Beau's jersey.

"Devereaux, what in God's name has gotten into you?"

He didn't look up, keeping his eyes peeled on the coach's dirty tennis shoes.

"That referee you hit is okay but probably has a concussion." Coach Brewer waited for him to say something, then went on. "Do you understand what you've done?"

Beau had been pushed far enough and rose to his feet. "It was an accident. I never meant to hit him. I let go of the ball too soon, got tapped. I don't know, but it wasn't my fault."

"I'm not buying that." Coach Brewer scowled and pointed at the locker room door. "Everyone out there may buy your story, but I know what you can do. This entire game you've acted like you've lost your damn mind." Coach Brewer shook his head. "You're through, Devereaux. Leave your uniform on the bench and go. You're off the team."

Coach Brewer stomped out of the locker room.

Beau stumbled backward and plopped down on his bench, the dismissal thundering in his head.

They had four more games, big ones, and they needed him. Not that loser Marty.

He raised his head to the harsh fluorescent lights. The walls closed in. The air got thin.

He had to think. He had to breathe. He had to get out of that damned locker room and plan his comeback. But how to regain his status? How did he win back what was rightfully his?

Beau changed out of his uniform. When he went to put his jersey back in his locker, he hesitated. He wanted to keep it. He'd worked so long to earn it, but he decided it would look better to leave it behind.

While he walked to his car, the blare of the announcer calling the game lingering over the parking lot, it finally hit him—he'd lost his stardom. The tightrope of control he had fought so long to keep in check had betrayed him, and he had let loose.

Peeling out of the parking lot and speeding away from the school, Beau debated returning home. The last thing he wanted was another Gage Devereaux lecture. No, he needed to go to where he could recharge his batteries and release his frustration. To the one place on earth where he was always king—the river.

* * *

The first drops of rain came down on Dawn's head while she stared at the empty football field. The injured referee sat on the sidelines, a bag of ice on his head. The St. Benedict players, still scattered on the sidelines, waited for their coach to return from the locker room.

"Can you believe they kicked him out of the game for that?" Zoe tapped her red and white pompoms together. "That was a million to one shot. No one could do it on purpose."

Beau could.

She didn't bother to enlighten her. Zoe didn't know Beau; Dawn had a lot of experience with his chameleon-like personality. She'd never put it all together until she saw the football hit its mark. He had been good at portraying the model son, overachiever, squeaky clean teenager with a heart of gold, and then like the Incredible Hulk, his anger would turn him into a monster.

"You think they'll let him come back—?"

Zoe's question was cut off as whistles sounded across the field and players scrambled to get back out on the grass.

Dawn put her mind back on the game, but a lingering apprehension about Beau stayed with her.

The rain came down a little harder and her heart rose in her throat as minutes ticked until the end of the fourth quarter. She cheered with gusto as St. Benedict closed in for a touchdown. Then their drive got blocked and they had to settle for a field goal.

Anxious and exhausted from the roller coaster ride of an evening, she screamed when her team got the ball back with thirty seconds left on the clock. The rain stopped and the crowd put aside their ponchos and umbrellas, got to their feet, and shouted in unison with her squad for the home team to score.

Then, with ten seconds left, she held her breath as Marty Evans let go a Hail Mary pass to connect to an open receiver in the end zone.

Touchdown!

Ecstatic, she tossed her pompoms into the air, jumped, and yelled, and hugged her fellow squad members. The roar of the home crowd blotted out all other noise.

The players left the field, hurrying back to the locker room. Everyone lingered in the stands, reveling in the excitement of the game.

Dawn wiped her face with a towel, listening to the various theories moving through the stands about what had happened to their favorite hometown hero.

"He had an off night," one mother, holding an umbrella, offered.

"He was totally stressed over the scout," a freshman girl confided to her friends.

"Too much partying on the river," a faint female voice said next to her on the steps.

Dawn glanced up and caught Taylor standing at the railing and gazing out at the empty field.

Her loose-fitting clothes and faraway look confused Dawn. The Taylor she'd spent hours in cheer practices with had been a tough customer—no-nonsense, practical, and competitive. The change astounded her.

"What do you think will happen to him?"

Taylor had a seat next to her. "Nothing more than he deserves."

The anger in her voice took Dawn by surprise. Since when was Taylor so anti-Beau?

"I wonder where he went." Dawn searched the parking lot behind the home team's stands for his car.

"Aren't you meeting up with him at the river?" Taylor asked.

"No. I'm going home when I leave here." Dawn collected her pompoms, confusion mounting in her heart.

Why was it so hard to forget him? He had not looked her way once during the game and it had killed her, but then the way he'd acted …

"I'm not sure I want to go out with Beau anymore. After what I saw tonight … I've never seen him like that in public. He's always so careful to show people what he wants them to see. He slipped tonight, and I'm afraid what will happen next."

"I'm glad you're reconsidering your relationship." Taylor studied the crowds emptying the stands. "He's kept a lot from you."

Her stomach churned at the suggestion. But how did Taylor know anything about Beau?

"Are you talking about what goes on at the river?"

Taylor's cheeks lost their color. "You don't know how he is when you're not around. He's not what you think."

Dawn hugged her pompoms, feeling sick. "You mean the other girls, huh? I've suspected there were others for a while now. It's got a lot to do with why I want to end it. Is there something else?"

"Please stay away from him." Taylor gripped Dawn's forearm.

"He'll hurt you if you don't."

The grotesque mask of terror on her face shocked Dawn. Why should Taylor be so worried about her relationship with Beau? In her gut, Dawn's suspicions mushroomed. What did Taylor know? What could be worse than his cheating on her?

Perhaps she needed to find out for herself what was going on. Until she knew for sure, she doubted she would ever be completely free of Beau Devereaux.

Chapter twenty-five

Trees draped with Spanish moss created ghostly shadows along the sides of the rode as Beau drove to the river. The rain had cleared and the stars poked out from behind drifting clouds. The only sound in his ears was the hum of his engine and the thumping of his heart. Anger flowed through his veins, burning away every ounce of his restraint.

The faces of the girls who had demoralized him at the game, who had taken away his chance at stardom, drifted in and out of his head. He couldn't let them get away with any of it.

He hankered for a way to satiate his desire to hurt someone. The lot empty, he left his car by the entrance and made his way across the shells, the crunching of his shoes the only sound around him. He followed the path to the beach. Just as he was about to step through the thick brush running along the shoreline, the lone howl of a dog sailed through the air. He came to a grinding halt and listened.

No way! Is that what I think it is?

He checked the brush. He sure didn't want to end up eaten by one of those damned wild dogs. That would be a shitty way to go.

His toes hit the sand and disappointment shredded his hope. There were no early birds to the party. All was quiet.

He kicked at the water clawing the sand along the shore, thinking about what might have been. Could he redeem himself? Could he still find a way to play college ball?

Images of a life at the brewery or sitting behind his father's big desk left him feeling weak in the knees. He didn't want that life, and he would be damned if he would settle.

Suddenly the sounds of rushing water became like the roar of the crowd at the football game. He wanted peace and no reminders of what had just happened. There was only one place where he could be truly alone. He headed across the beach to the path leading toward The Abbey.

His feet pounded the ground, declaring his frustration. He needed another girl, someone else to destroy.

Beau turned right at the broken fountain, smirking at the praying angel.

"Nobody's listening, buddy."

He set out across the high grass, running his fingers along the tips of the shoots. The tickling sensation added to his throbbing need to pulverize flesh and bone.

He debated what to do with the rest of his life. Perhaps with his days free of the hassle of football practice, he could pursue other extracurricular activities. The kind used to enhance his burgeoning interest in pain.

Apprehension zinged through him when he stepped inside the cells. The warm light from flickering candles danced on the walls around him. Someone was in his room.

He hugged the wall, ready to tear into whoever had dared to steal what was his. He paused at the doorway and peeked into his room, trying to get an idea of what he was up against.

The flare of a lit cigarette in the shadows of the room caught his eye.

"Told you I would be in touch."

Andrea stretched out on the cot, a coat wrapped around her, staving off the chill in the room. The color of her hair intermingled with a red scarf draped around her neck as she reclined. A slender sliver of a smile welcomed him inside.

He wiped his hands together, imagining things he would like to do with that scarf. "I needed to see a friendly face tonight."

"I figured your friends would be at the beach by now and I

didn't want to be seen." She put out her cigarette in the wall behind her. "So, I came here."

Beau approached the cot, his desire to hurt her charging to life. "They're probably still at the football game."

She sat up and shimmied closer to him. "And why aren't you at the game?"

His heavy sigh resonated like a howling wind inside the small room. He leaned over the cot, apprehensive about saying too much. "That's a long story."

She traced her finger along the blue vein running up his left forearm. "You've got all night to tell me about it."

He ogled her tight jeans and her long legs. "I'm not in the mood for talking." He took a tendril of her silky hair between his fingers. "What I really need right now is to forget."

She stood from the cot, curling her arms around his neck. "You don't even want to talk about what's bothering you?"

Her hair sifted through his fingers. He was anxious to change the subject. "I know nothing about you. Where do you go to school? You never mentioned any place before."

"I'm not in school."

She smiled and he noticed the slight gap in her front teeth.

"Why were you hanging around here the other night?"

"It was by chance." Her deep green eyes gazed into his. "I was partying with friends on the river and wandered off. I'm glad I did."

Beau got excited at the thought of her being all his for the night. "Where are your friends? Did you come alone?"

She ran her hand up his chest. "Yep. I'm all alone." She took her lower lip in her teeth and then let it go. "And all yours."

Unable to wait any longer, Beau held Andrea by the back of the neck and kissed her. It was a long, slow, deep kiss. The kind he never liked to give, but with her, it just felt right.

A howl came from the direction of The Abbey.

Andrea pulled away, listening to the air. "Sounds like the wild dogs are close by tonight."

He nuzzled her neck, not giving a damn about the dogs. "You know about them?"

"I did a little research on this place. Talked to a few of the locals." She moved away from him. "There's quite a legend about it."

He watched her hips beneath her coat, getting turned on by the painful things he would do to her. "What legends?"

Andrea tossed her head. "The dogs hang around The Abbey waiting for the lady in white to claim them. She was a gamekeeper for the seminary school and a lover of one of the monks. She died on the grounds, betrayed by the man she loved. The dogs were kept to manage the varmint population. The wild dogs are said to be the offspring of her dogs."

Beau slipped the coat off her shoulders, eager to see more of her. "I've lived here all my life and never heard such stories."

She waited as he put her coat to the side. "Then you don't listen to the people around here. I also found an old newspaper article in your local library about the gamekeeper and how she was found hanging from a tree in a white hooded priest's cloak. It was all kept very hush-hush at the time by the Catholic Church. After the woman's death, her dogs were allowed to roam the grounds and live off the land. They're said to only appear when death is near."

Already bored with her story, he unzipped the fly of her jeans, eager to have his hands around her slender throat.

"That's just creepy."

She glanced at his hands as they tugged her jeans down her hips. "A guy who brings girls to these abandoned cells is into creepy."

Beau hesitated, confused. "What's wrong with the cells?"

He'd never considered himself weird. The cells had been a means to an end—a private quiet place to be with girls. But as he considered her statement, he liked the image the cells portrayed. It was his laboratory, like he'd read about in *Frankenstein*, where he could experiment and create his own monsters.

She cupped his cheeks and brought his mouth back to hers. "It's fine for us, but if you find a nice girl, don't bring her here."

He chuckled as he traced the outline of her jaw with his finger. "There's no such thing as nice girls."

Every girl who pretended to be nice hid a darker element beneath her pink cheeks. They were just as much into pain as he was.

Andrea took the red scarf and lassoed it around his neck. She worked her jeans the rest of the way down and kicked them away. Like an exotic dancer teasing a client, she hooked her fingers along the lacy edges of her pink underwear and slid them down her hips with an alluring grin.

His mouth watered with the things he would do to her. Her panties drifted to the floor, and he moved in. Spinning her around, he spooned into her back and kissed her neck. She smelled like a forest during the height of spring, adding to his desire to possess her.

On the cot, he removed the scarf from around his neck and dangled it in front of Andrea.

She held out her wrists. "Now you're talking."

"It's as if we're the same." He cinched the scarf around her wrists. "Don't you think?"

Their kiss was long and delicious. He broke away only briefly to wiggle out of his sweatshirt and jeans.

"I want to do everything with you, Beau."

That was all he needed to hear. He quickly collected a condom from his jeans and slipped it on. He settled next to her on the cot.

Initially, he was gentle. He caressed every inch of soft skin, but as his hunger grew, his need to hurt her did too.

She laughed with delight when he hooked the scarf on the exposed pipe in the wall and flipped her over. He caressed the curve of her ass, slapped it, and then she moaned. He didn't like the sound. To teach her a lesson, he spanked her again and again—each time harder than the one before.

Her body curled inward with every strike, and she trembled

beneath him.

"Night of your life, right, baby?"

Beau positioned her hips, thrust deep, and then closed his hands around her throat. He rode her, feeding his need for destruction. The command he had over her every breath made him squeeze tighter. She fought him, struggling under his weight, and his grip tightened. He thought of the game, the referee, Coach Brewer, and all the people he would have loved to strangle at that moment.

Andrea's face morphed and shifted. Her green eyes turned blue, and her plain features changed. Suddenly, it was Leslie who he rode; his hands were around her neck, his power over her absolute.

Spurred on by his fantasy, his thumbs squeezed into the back of her neck. The sounds of her throes on the cot heightened his pleasure. He could see Leslie's tears, hear Leslie's gurgling, feel her nails gouging at his skin, begging him to stop. But he didn't stop. He squeezed harder and kept on until she would be his.

A dull *snap* resonated in the room.

Andrea went limp. Beau felt her weight settle in his hands and it took him out of his vision.

He removed his hands and waited for her to suck in a breath, but she didn't move. He nudged her.

"Hey, wake up."

He shook her, but she still didn't move.

"Stop fooling around."

Beau climbed off her and rolled her on her back. She wasn't breathing. The dull luster in her eyes scared him to death. She wasn't pretending.

He stood from the bed; his heart racing and a cold sweat covering his skin.

"Shit! Shit! Shit!" He ran his hands through his hair, feeling like he would puke. "Think, Devereaux. Be smart about this."

He stared at her, her hair fanned out on the cot, and his thoughts turned to Leslie.

Beau threw his hands into the air, spitting as he screamed, "You bitch!"

Pointing at Andrea, he pictured Leslie. "This is your fault. You drove me to this. You're to blame for everything." He paced at the entrance to the cell, his chest on fire, his gut cramping as if stabbed by nails. "If you had given in to me that first night, I would never have touched those other girls, or Andrea. You cost me my football career. You've destroyed my life!"

Leslie's smile, the smell of her skin, the throaty charm of her voice—she was the reason for his suffering. She would pay for what she'd done.

Before he could deal with Leslie, he had to do something about Andrea.

He gathered up his clothes. "Get her out of here before the others find out what you've done."

Who the hell cares.

The adrenaline pumping through him slowed. No one would find out. There were no witnesses. No one knew Andrea had been there. All he had to do was get rid of her body and walk away.

A sense of calm eased through him.

You got this.

He took his time dressing. Then he collected Andrea's clothes and tied them into a ball.

Beau untied the scarf, his fingers lingering on the silky material. He raised it to his nose and breathed in the scent of her. Without a second thought, he put the scarf under his cot. He would keep that, to remember this night.

Her eyes were open, staring up at him. He closed them, but they didn't stay all the way shut. Unable to take her empty gaze, he turned her to the side. Her neck made a funny crunching sound. Yeah, that was weird.

Before taking her out of the room, he stepped outside to see if he heard any trace of the party beginning at the beach, but it was still quiet. No music, no laughing, no noise at all. Perfect.

In the cells, he thought he saw what looked like a white cloak heading down the corridor toward The Abbey. He was about to head after it when it disappeared. A cold breeze brushed past.

Where did that come from?

The hairs on his arms stood. Someone watched him from somewhere in the shadows—he could feel their eyes on him.

It had to be one of the girls from the game. They had tracked him down.

Ready to rip whoever it was apart with his bare hands, he took off down the corridor, going from room to room, convinced someone had witnessed Andrea's death.

He reached the door to The Abbey, finding no one. Had they slipped out before being caught? He tried the wooden door, but it wouldn't budge—the damp must have sealed it shut.

He peered down the corridor. So where had they gone?

Never mind. Get the body out of here.

Where could he put her? How could he hide the evidence?

The only thought that came to mind was the river. He had no shovel, no means of digging a grave. And graves could be unearthed, especially by hungry dogs. The river was the only place he could dump the body and have all the evidence wash away.

Beau picked up her clothes, then hoisted Andrea's body over his right shoulder. Maneuvering through the dimly lit hallway was not a problem, but when he came to the gap in the wall, he had a dilemma. Beau would have to pull her through the narrow opening.

He set her on the ground and breached the wide crack. Then, he grabbed her feet and tugged her through.

Outside, he thought he heard something. Beau paused, his heart racing, but there was only the wind.

Straining under her weight, he hurried through the grassy field while Andrea's head bobbed against his back.

At the path, he heard voices coming from the beach. The

revelers had arrived.

Hurry!

To his left, gaps in the trees offered glimpses of the rushing Bogue Falaya.

Beau stumbled down the embankment, carrying Andrea's body to the shoreline. A narrow strip of beach opened up before him. It was good enough.

At the water's edge, he callously dropped her on the sand, her bundle of clothes landing beside her. He found a Louisiana driver's license and forty dollars in her coat. The license he tossed into the river and then pocketed the cash. The only other items she had on her were a set of keys and a couple of condoms.

Since he'd not touched or even seen her car, there was no evidence there to worry about. With her keys and the condoms at the bottom of the river, he picked up her clothes.

He couldn't throw perfectly good clothes into the river. He had to make it look like an accident or an attack of some kind.

Rip them up.

The shirt was easy—the jeans, not so much. The coat took a lot of effort and he was sweating by the time he was done.

Once he saw the items turn the bend in the river, he went back for her.

Beau lifted her from the sand. Something appeared out of the corner of his eye.

He hesitated; someone watched from the line of brush along the shore.

A tall dog came out from the smattering of leaves. Black, with patches of fur missing, it had a long snout and skinny body. It sat on the edge of the beach, studying him.

They only appear when death is near.

Andrea's words echoed through his head.

He was afraid to move in case the animal attacked. So, he remained still. Andrea's body got heavier and heavier. He didn't know how much longer he could hold on to her.

Then the dog cocked his head and leaped into the brush, disappearing from view.

Gasping, Beau relaxed, and Andrea's body almost toppled from his arms.

A shrill laugh came from the direction of the party. The dog must have heard it and been scared away.

With the moonlight shimmering on her ashen skin, he pushed Andrea's body out into the river, mindful not to get his shoes wet. Her pretty hair spread over the water's surface, undulating behind her. The current took her faster than he'd hoped. Soon, she vanished around the bend.

All traces of her belonged to the river.

He rinsed his hands in the water as if he were washing away his sins. He envisioned Andrea being swallowed up by the strong current and never seen again. His crime was perfect. She'd come with no one and left with no one. The only person who knew of his interaction with her was now him. Beau was back on top. He could feel it in his bones.

Wiping his footprints from the sand as he backed away, he reached the end of the slender beach.

The brush to his right moved. It wasn't the wind. There wasn't any on the beach.

His exasperation quickly smothered his apprehension about Andrea's death. "Dammit, who are you?"

He went rushing into the brush. He swept leafy twigs and vines aside, determined to find out who had followed him. Anger drove him. He paid little attention to where he went. Beau couldn't see anything through the trees as he climbed the embankment.

The underbrush disappeared, and he was back on the cleared path from The Abbey. The pounding music rang in his ears. Or was that his heart? He wasn't sure. He kept on, jogging down the path, searching the brush around him, but all he could find was shadows.

Sweat covered his brow, and a spiral of panic rose in his belly.

There couldn't be a witness. He had committed the perfect crime. Who could have been there?

He thought he heard footfalls behind him. He glanced back over his shoulder as he kept moving forward. He searched for any hint of who it could—

He ran smack into something and almost toppled to the ground. "Beau?"

He caught himself and raised his head. The familiar deep melodic tone he knew well.

Mitch held out his hand, helping to hold him upright.

Grateful to see a familiar face, he patted Mitch's thick arm and wiped his brow. He took in his damp hair and the beer in his hand as he caught his breath.

"Dude, you okay? I've been looking for you. I saw your car in the lot."

He glanced back down the path toward the spires of The Abbey. "I was just walking around the old grounds and thought I saw … something."

Mitch's eyes narrowed, almost disappearing in the faint light. "Something? You mean, the ghost?"

Beau shook his head and motioned ahead to the path. "No, this was a person." His voice became strained. "And I'm going to find them."

Chapter twenty—Six

The satisfying sweetness of the chocolate filled Leslie's mouth while she scooped the last dregs of ice cream from her bowl. The tick of the icemaker in the fridge was her only companion in the darkened kitchen. She relished the time alone after the commotion of the game. With her parents off to bed, and her sister still not back, enjoying her favorite snack in peace was the perfect ending to a rather satisfying evening.

Her mother had been cordial to Derek during and after the game—awakening a smidgen of hope in her heart for their relationship. Beau was about to become an FBI most wanted fugitive, or at least on his way to a well-deserved suspension, and Halloween was almost here. It was the one holiday she and Dawn had always enjoyed together. Maybe this year they would get one last chance to celebrate it before leaving for college.

The bang of the garage door shutting roused her. Soft voices drifted down the hallway to her spot at the breakfast bar.

She put her spoon down and waited to see who had accompanied Dawn home.

A pair of blue eyes set against a porcelain face poked out from under a girl's gray hoodie. Bangs hid her diminutive smile.

"Taylor?" Leslie stood from her stool. "What are you doing here?"

She took in her unshapely clothes and lack of makeup—not at all what she expected from a former cheerleader. But nothing Taylor had done lately struck Leslie as ordinary.

"I asked her to spend the night." Dawn set her bag on the

breakfast bar. "We got to talking after the game, and she told me a few things about Beau."

Leslie picked up her sister's bag and handed it back to her with a scowl. "I think half the girls at St. Benedict could tell you a few choice things about Beau."

Taylor shifted her purse on her shoulder, hiding her eyes from Leslie. "People don't understand how dangerous he is. He's sick, profoundly disturbed. Your sister needs to stay away from him."

Leslie recognized something in her voice—the same terror she'd experienced with Beau.

"What did he do to you?"

Taylor twisted her fingers together, her eyes darting about the kitchen.

The girl's frantic movements told Leslie something bad had happened to her. But what?

She stepped forward. "It's okay. You don't have to say anything. But when you're ready ..."

Taylor sucked in a deep breath. "Thank you."

The *plonk* of Dawn's duffel bag hitting the floor made Leslie jump. Her sister seemed oblivious to Taylor's distress.

"I'll leave you with Leslie while I take a shower." She unzipped her bag and pulled out her pompoms. "I'm soaked through from the rain and I've got to dry these out before they wilt." She shook the pompoms and a few droplets of water settled on the stone floor.

Leslie, for once, was grateful for Dawn's cluelessness. She didn't want her to hear something distressing. She'd been through enough.

Before Dawn went across the den to the stairs, she glanced back at Taylor. "You can tell my sister your wild tales about Beau. I'll bet she will love telling me 'I told you so'."

Dawn hurried up the staircase, but Leslie could tell her sister knew something was wrong. Running out of a room when conversations got heated or too emotional had been Dawn's coping mechanism for years. Leslie was the one expected to handle the tough stuff; then she would give Dawn a watered-down version of the news to spare her the emotional upheaval. It was something she had always done for her sister—another way to protect her.

Once she heard Dawn make it upstairs, Leslie pointed to her ice cream bowl.

"Want some?"

Taylor nodded. "Yeah, that would be good."

Leslie took her time getting the carton of chocolate ice cream out of the freezer and selecting a bowl for Taylor. While scooping a large serving, Leslie eyed Taylor's clothes.

"You going for the grunge look there or is this more hip-hop?"

She pulled at her hoodie as if trying to hide her curves. "I like to be comfortable."

Leslie pushed the bowl of ice cream across the breakfast bar. "Not too long ago, you were like Dawn, wearing your cheerleading uniform to class whenever you could, keeping your hair down, not up and hidden away." She put the top back on the ice cream carton, her heart breaking for the lost little girl. "What happened to you?"

Taylor picked up her spoon, keeping her eyes on her bowl. "I'm okay."

Leslie returned the ice cream to the fridge and then went back to the counter.

Taylor dipped her spoon into the chocolate mound in her bowl.

Leslie was certain if she didn't get Taylor to open up, something bad was going to happen. But to do that, she needed the girl's trust.

Her hands folded on the counter, Leslie searched for a way to make Taylor know that she understood her fear.

"Beau has been harassing me for months. Ever since the night at the river when I turned him down. He's never let me forget it." Her lower lip quivered, anxiety crushing her chest. "He says he's going to take me to The Abbey and make up for the night I should have been his. He says sexual, ugly things to me." Leslie clasped her hands together, squeezing hard. "The worst part is, no one believes me. I think Dawn is coming around, but there's still a part of her not willing to let go of Beau. Crazy huh?"

Leslie sniffled, biting back her tears.

Taylor said nothing as she traced designs in her bowl with her spoon. "He's a bad, bad guy."

The voice didn't sound like her. It was colder, deeper, and for Leslie, a bit sinister.

"Beau has had a lot of girls there. And I know he has hurt some of them."

A numbing cold rose inside Leslie. "Hurt? What do you mean?"

Taylor continued to swerve and weave her spoon in the bowl, the eerie sound carried throughout the kitchen.

"I mean raped."

Leslie gripped the edge of the counter, digging her nails into the gray granite. "How do you know this?"

Her eyes were dead. There was no sadness, no terror, no fear in Taylor's face, just overwhelming hatred.

"I was at the river. Beau noticed me. I thought he was interested. And then he took me to his special place. That's what he called it. There was nothing special about it."

The subdued, unemotional way she spoke scared the living shit out of Leslie. She covered her mouth, infuriated.

"Oh, God, Taylor, no."

Taylor's flat expression never changed. She didn't even shed a tear.

"It went on for quite a while. He beat me, raped me, and when he was done, he told me he would get my father fired from his new job at the brewery if I said anything to anyone."

Leslie wanted to puke. Why didn't she notice the changes? The clothes, the withdrawal from friends and school? It was the pattern of sexual abuse she had read about before, even seen in her own behavior, but had not recognized in someone she knew.

I'm an idiot!

She ran through the agencies she had heard about. The ones who helped rape victims. She had to make sure—

"The funny thing is, the whole time he was hurting me, I kept thinking what did I do? What did I do to deserve this? Was it something I said, something I did, the way I looked? I kept asking myself why." Taylor dipped her spoon into the ice cream and brought it to her lips. She put the small portion in her mouth. The emptiness in her face lifted, and she smiled. "This is good."

Leslie's tears trickled down her cheeks as she watched the broken girl eat her ice cream. The barbarity of what she had endured, coupled with something associated with the pleasures of childhood, tore her apart.

"We have to get you help." She reached for her hand.

Taylor pulled away. "No. I don't need help. What I want is revenge."

* * *

From her spot at the top of the stairs, Dawn gripped the banister and suppressed her scream.

His special place. It had to be the cells. The same place he had taken her countless times before to make love.

Tears streaked her cheeks as she absorbed what Taylor had endured. Her humiliation and anger blended with Dawn's. She had loved Beau and trusted him. What kind of monster was she for loving such a sick guy?

Taylor's soft voice and the matter-of-fact way she had told her tale eventually sucked the strength out of Dawn's legs. She sank to the plush carpet and held on to the banister, crying in silence, not wanting to wake her parents or let Taylor know she had eavesdropped.

"Do you know of any other girls he has done this to?" Leslie asked in the kitchen.

Dawn held her breath, waiting for Taylor's answer.

"Yes. There are more."

The unvarnished delivery of the news sent Dawn curling into a ball.

You have to do something!

The strength returned to her limbs—so did her resolve to get even with the psychotic asshole who had destroyed the lives of so many. She could almost hear Leslie scolding her to leave Beau for the authorities. But Dawn couldn't do that. She felt responsible for what had happened to Taylor, her sister, and his other victims. Leslie couldn't protect her anymore. She would find a way to make Beau Devereaux pay for what he'd done, and make sure he never did it again.

* * *

The breeze coming off the water teased Beau's hot skin as he fumed about his situation. The loud music set up by his picnic bench wasn't helping. And the students from St. Benedict and Covington High around him made him sick.

Assholes!

His run through the brush to find whoever had been watching him as he'd let Andrea drift away haunted every second. He also couldn't stand listening to the constant retellings of Marty Evans' Hail Mary pass. A few mentioned Beau's sweet toppling of Kramer Wilson, but everyone hailed Marty the hero of the day.

If that little asshole gets my place on the roster at Tulane, I'll kill him.

The loss of his dream bothered him the most. How had everything turned to shit so quickly?

He knew why.

He pictured Leslie drifting down the river in place of Andrea and smiled. That had been the one highlight of his evening. Killing Andrea had given him a rush; even disposing of her body had been a thrill. What if he could recapture those moments with Leslie? But he would have to be careful. He'd gotten lucky with Andrea. He'd have to meticulously plan for his night with his dream girl.

The party, the game, and the loss of his future didn't seem so important anymore. Andrea's death had given him an odd sense of purpose. If he could kill her, what else could he do?

"You okay, dude?"

Josh kept his distance. He'd never realized the little dweeb was such a pansy ass.

"I'm fine." He sipped his bottle of water.

Josh took a brave step forward. "You scared the piss out of everyone on the field tonight."

"Not to mention that referee." Mitch rubbed his chin, hiding a grin. "You clobbered him."

Beau eyed two attractive girls in very short skirts strolling past. They didn't have Leslie's shade of hair color or her effortless way of moving. They wouldn't do.

"It was an accident. I never meant to hit the guy."

Josh had a seat next to him, cradling his beer. "Coach Brewer doesn't buy it. What do you think the school will do?"

School? How could he be bothered with something as mundane as school? He'd entered a whole new level of the game with Andrea's death. How would Biology and English Lit help him carry out all the deliciously wicked visions popping into his head?

A group of laughing girls came scurrying onto the beach dressed in tight jeans with fitted tops. Beau licked his lips, sizing them up, but the surge of sexual attraction he'd felt before wasn't there. He found himself more interested in their necks. Each girl he pictured with his hands around their throats, recreating the rush he'd gotten from killing Andrea. It was like a drug. He wanted to get high again.

Self-control in all things.

First, he had to get Leslie out of his system. After her, the world was his.

"Sounds like Marty pulled out a great end to the game." He

recapped his water, already bored with the party.

"Yeah, he was fantastic." Mitch eased his arm back, imitating the quarterback's Hail Mary pass. "You should have seen it."

Beau squeezed the bottle. "I should congratulate him."

"Are you serious?" Josh didn't sound convinced. "We figured you'd be furious about his game."

He gave them his practiced smile, the one he used to charm everyone. He had grown so far beyond their simple minds—they would never be able to comprehend his ability.

"Hey, I'm a team player. I'm over it. I just want the best for everyone."

The roar of a bonfire catching and the crackle of the wood filled the air. A cheer went up among the partygoers; the party had hit its stride.

Three girls dressed in Covington High T-shirts and jeans had a seat on the other end of the bench.

"Do you know those girls?" Mitch asked.

He found one of them somewhat tempting. With slim hips, flaxen hair, and pouty lips, she reminded him a little of Leslie.

Yeah, this is what I need.

His ringing phone distracted him.

He stood and retrieved his cell from his back pocket. *Dad* showed up on the screen. Beau didn't bother to answer. Whatever he wanted, he wasn't interested.

Just when he was about to slip the phone back into his pocket, he received a text message.

Get your ass home now. No excuses.

"Something wrong?" Mitch asked.

He slipped the phone in his back pocket. "I'm gonna have to take off. It's my old man."

Mitch winced. "Yikes. That ain't gonna be good."

Josh patted his shoulder, never taking his eyes off the girls on the bench. "Maybe he didn't hear about you nailing Kramer yet."

Mitch chuckled. "Gage Devereaux? Are you kidding? He knows everything that goes on in this town."

Not everything.

Beau nodded to his friends. "I'll see you guys later."

He slipped away, hustling to get back to the parking lot. His old man never texted him, never checked on him. The fact that Gage had contacted him meant he was pissed. Beau may not have given a damn about his father, but he needed to kiss his ass to keep getting his money.

He opened his car door, and another ping rang through the air.

> If you are not in the door in ten minutes, I'm coming to get you.

He started the car, cursing his father under his breath. It would seem his night was about to take a turn for the worse.

* * *

Beau steered his car along the drive, the bright lights of the house glaring into the darkness surrounding the property. Shadows teased him as he headed to the garage. He swore he saw Andrea's face in the gloom, serene and lifeless, as it had been when the river had taken her away.

When he entered the back door of his parents' home, Gage was there. His thick arms—carved by years of weightlifting—folded across his broad chest, his dark eyes smoldering.

"Where were you?"

He dropped his duffel bag on the ground, knowing he couldn't con his father like everyone else in the town. He needed to play it real.

"At the river. I wanted to apologize to my teammates."

His father's cold-blooded expression never altered. "After that stunt you pulled on the field, you should have come right home!"

"You heard, huh?"

His father pounced, wrenching his arm. "What have I told you time and again? People are watching us, they're watching you. That stupid lapse of judgment is all some will need to question your integrity, your state of mind. How hard have we worked to keep you focused, to keep people from seeing who you really are? And you blow it on a stupid football game."

Beau yanked his arm away. "It wasn't a stupid football game. And it was an accident. I never meant to hit the guy. I lost my grip on the ball. How many times can I apologize for a mistake?"

"You expect me to buy that bullshit?" He threw his hand in the air, his voice black with anger. "I've watched you, studied you. I know what you are capable of, and everyone in this fucking town is going to find out, too. Do you know what that will do to our business? To our reputation? You can't walk around reacting to everything and everyone without thinking your actions through."

Beau sagged against the hallway wall, crushed. "Is that all this means to you? A loss of revenue? You don't care that I've lost my shot at Tulane, do you?"

"You never had a shot at Tulane!" Gage slammed his hand inches away from his face. "That scout was there as a favor to me. He looked at your numbers, watched some films on you before he came to the field and wasn't very optimistic about your chances. You never had what it takes to make it in college ball, but I was trying to give you a chance. A chance you blew."

He tingled all over as he considered his father's betrayal. Beau knew his father was a scheming, ruthless businessman, but he'd never dreamed he would use the same tactics on him.

You bastard!

Gage pushed away from the wall. "Perhaps now you can settle into your studies, concentrate on going to LSU, and put football behind you."

He charged up to his father. "But I don't want to give up football."

Gage rested his hand on his hip, shaking his head, appearing more frustrated than angry. "You're off the team. Brewer won't take you back. He called me after the game. That's how I knew about Kramer. He suspects you threw that ball on purpose. I know you did. So there will be no more football. We'll find other ways for you to handle that problem of yours without playing sports."

His insides boiled. For years, he had listened to his parents whisper about "his problem." But Beau never saw his anger as an issue. It made him stronger and better than the other losers at school. And as he pictured Andrea floating away in the river, he knew his bouts of madness had given him another gift—purpose.

He rubbed his hands together to hide their twitching from his old man. "What about baseball in the spring? I always play shortstop."

Gage ran his hand through his hair, his heavy sigh permeating the tension in the air. "Right now, you'll be lucky if the school doesn't expel you for that stunt. Ms. Greenbriar called me, too, after the game. I had to do a lot of apologizing to keep her appeased. She plans on having you do community service and volunteer work for the school."

A flurry of expletives was on the tip of Beau's tongue, but he held back. He had a part to play.

"I understand." He picked up his duffel bag. "I'll do whatever they want."

"No more trips to the river." Gage snatched the keys out of his hand. "You're grounded. You'll work at the brewery on weekends and after school. Until you prove to me you have a handle on your behavior, you will live under my thumb."

Beau took the news with a somber nod. He was about to head up the hall when his father stopped him.

"Aren't you going to ask about the guy you hit?"

He'd never even considered the line referee. He did not give a damn about the man.

"How is he?"

Gage gripped his keys. "He's got a concussion. I picked up the tab on his ER visit, which you will work off at the brewery. I'm going to put you in the shipping department under Kramer. You can apologize all you want to him when you're there."

He gritted his teeth. *So be it.*

If he had to kiss every nobody's ass in St. Benedict, he would climb his way back to the top. And once there, Beau would make sure every living soul who had brought about his downfall would pay an agonizing price.

Chapter twenty-Seven

The gnarled green trees and bright blue sky did nothing to ease the pain in Leslie's heart. Taylor's admission had stayed with her. She'd barely slept, hardly touched her breakfast, and though she and her sister were on their way to pick up Derek to go shopping, her enthusiasm had sputtered. How could she enjoy herself when someone else was in so much pain? And what should she do with the information about Beau? He had to be stopped. But who could she turn to?

"You're awfully quiet?"

She glanced at Dawn behind the wheel, grateful she had been spared Beau's psychotic rages.

"Are you sure you want to go to the Halloween party at the river? Beau will be there. We could avoid him and maybe check out some of the other events—"

"No, I want to go to the party," her sister insisted. "Besides, I'll be in costume. He won't know it's me."

Dawn's resolve came through in her voice. Leslie wished she wasn't so damned stubborn.

"I'm not going to run with my tail between my legs whenever I see Beau. We're going to go and have fun." Dawn hesitated as she turned off Main Street. "What made you change your mind? I thought you wanted to go."

Leslie forced a smile to her lips, her heart heaving as she remembered Taylor's emotionless face.

"I wanted to make sure you were into this. We'll have to hustle to get our costumes ready."

Dawn chuckled, sounding upbeat. "It will be fine. You'll see. We will come up with some great costumes. I know it."

When Dawn pulled into the driveway, her smile wavered a little. "You're sure Derek wants to join us?"

Leslie undid her seatbelt, chasing the apprehension from her voice. "Of course. He wants the three of us to hang out, and what better way than shopping?"

Dawn sat back in her seat, her gaze sweeping over her sister. "You never doubt him, do you? You're always optimistic about your future together." Dawn slapped the steering wheel. "I couldn't even get Beau to talk about going to the same college, let alone getting married. But you two have it all worked out."

Leslie wished she could erase all of Dawn's disappointment, but a part of her knew it could have been worse. She could have ended up like Taylor. Leslie drove the thought from her mind, unable to comprehend something so horrendous happening to someone she loved.

"He wasn't the right guy for you. Let him go. You'll find him one day."

Tears gathered in Dawn's eyes. "No, I'm not like you. You've always known what you wanted. Ever since we were little, you had everything figured out while I was still struggling. You were the smart one, the interesting one, and I ... well, I was just trying to keep up."

Leslie turned off the ignition and raised her sister's chin, determined to get through to her. "I want you to listen to me. You're just as smart, as funny, and definitely as pretty as me. And you never had to prove anything to me or anyone else. We're sisters, twin sisters, and nothing you do will ever make me jealous. I want you to be happy. That's all I ever wanted. I knew you weren't happy with Beau."

A teardrop slipped down Dawn's cheek. "I'm sorry, Leelee. I was a bitch to you when I was with him. I shouldn't have been. You're my sister and I—"

"Hey," Leslie cut her off. "You never need to apologize to me."

A knock on the window made both girls jump. Dawn wiped her face when she saw Derek.

"Are you guys okay?"

Leslie opened her door and climbed out, anxious to chase away her blues. "We're great. Get in and let's go shopping."

Derek wrapped her in his arms and kissed her nose. "Shopping? You said we were going to hang out."

Leslie took an extra second to escape inside the warmth of his embrace. The world seemed a beautiful place when he held her. The ugliness, the hate, the anger didn't touch her in his arms.

"Hey." Derek held her back, studying her face. "What is it?"

She yearned to tell him but couldn't. It wasn't her secret to share.

"I'm just glad to see you."

"I've got news." He lifted her chin. "Mom got that job at the law firm. She'll be working as a secretary in Covington. No more diner."

Leslie's troubles washed away. "That's great."

He nodded. "Yep. She's so excited. I can't remember when I've seen her so happy." He kissed her lips. "Thank you."

"Hey, you two," Dawn called from the car. "Get in. We've got Halloween costume shopping to do."

Leslie peered up at the blue sky before she climbed back in the car, thanking the heavens for keeping everyone she loved safe.

"Are you guys sure you want me to go with you?" Derek asked as he secured his seatbelt. "You could just pick out costumes without me."

Dawn put the car in drive. "Leslie and I have already decided we're going to have matching costumes." She giggled as she looked back at Derek. "If you're not with us, we might choose pink tutus and ballerina shoes."

He furrowed his brow. "Yeah, that's not a good look for me."

Leslie relaxed in her seat, snickering at his remark.

In the distance, she caught the tips of the white spires of The Abbey peeking out over the treetops. The dread lingering in the back of her mind resurrected, displacing her jovial mood. There was something about the place. She didn't know what it was, but Leslie was sure of one thing—it wasn't good.

Chapter Twenty-Eight

He wiped the damp cloth over the pale blue wall to remove the last remnants of the sticky adhesive he'd used to put up the posters of Bugatti cars and Victoria's Secret models. The smooth plaster surface gleamed under the rag, and the paint his mother had selected—because she felt it would be calming for him—showed no signs of stress.

He stepped off the ladder and surveyed the stark walls of his room.

This is me.

The posters lay in a pile on his floor, along with his football trophies and athletic medals. He would box them up and take them to the attic.

Beau tossed the rag aside and went to the black duffel bag on his bed. His "Leslie bag" would be waiting in his cell for his night of fun with her at the river. He checked the nylon rope, handcuffs, duct tape, rags, hunting knife, and lighter fluid he had put in there. He zipped up the bag, proud of the accomplishment—his new beginning.

He needed to check his cell at The Abbey to make sure everything was in order for when the big night arrived. He didn't want anything to backfire. His father had harped for years that preparation was the key to success.

You were so right, Dad.

Though he was still grounded, he planned to go to the river tonight. He could sneak out. He'd done it dozens of times before. Beau couldn't join his friends and party—his father might get wind of it—but he could watch from the sidelines. It was a way to weed out who was loyal to him, and who was taking advantage of his absence. Then he would make the disloyal pay.

He'd even decided on an outfit, something to make sure no one would know it was him. A solid black ski mask, black jeans, and black jacket sat on the bed next to his black duffel bag.

A knock on his door startled him.

He shoved the jacket, jeans, mask, and bag under his bed.

"Come in."

Elizabeth glided inside, searching his bare walls. "What are you doing?"

"Just making some changes."

No longer in her yellow robe, she wore slacks and a floral blouse. She didn't have her usual drink in her hand, and she had even done her hair and put on makeup. Too much makeup as far as he was concerned.

"Why are you dressed like that?"

Elizabeth skimmed her hand over her shirt. "What's wrong with my outfit?"

He wondered what his hands would feel like around her neck.

"Nothing's wrong." Beau played it cool. How the bitch dressed wasn't his problem. "I'm just used to seeing you in your robe."

Elizabeth held her head up, reminding him of the ice queen he'd known all his life. The woman had as much emotion as a glacier.

She folded her hands and leveled her gray eyes on her son. "The robe is gone. I'm making an effort to get better. I want you to do the same. Maybe this is something we can do together."

Ah, he got it now. His asshole father had spoken to her about the game, and this was her solution. What was next? Family therapy weekends at Disney World? He could just see Gage Devereaux in a Mickey Mouse hat.

"Since when do we do anything together?"

Elizabeth wrinkled her brow and dipped her lips into an angry scowl. "Since your father asked me to make an effort. We've been talking lately. We want to make things better for you. I know our strained relationship hasn't helped your problem, so we're going to make an effort to be around for you more. I want to try this before we have to go back to seeing therapists and psychiatrists. I don't want that for you."

He folded his arms, seeing red. His mother had attempted to dry out dozens of times in the past. His father had made just as many futile attempts to spend more time at home with his family. They had both proven themselves liars.

"It's a little late for family time, Mom."

Elizabeth stepped into his room and her features softened. "I blame myself for last night. Maybe if I had been there more, if both of us had been around more for you, there wouldn't be so much hostility."

"Hostility?" Beau wished he had a knife in his hand to send the woman screaming from his room. "Is that what you think my problem is?"

"Oh, I know exactly what your problem is." Her contentious voice rang in his ears. "But I'm not going to give up on you. I'm not afraid anymore."

He crept closer, a sly smile on his lips. "You should be."

One sudden move and she would run for the door like a terrified puppy.

"It's not too late for this family." She held up her folded hands, begging. "If we try, I know we can fix some of the wrongs from the past. But you have to be willing to work with us. Will you do that? Will you agree to at least listen to what we propose? If not, your father will take other action."

Dammit!

If he didn't support his mother's suggestions, then his father would insist on therapy or worse, drugs. He'd been down that road before and swore he would never take another pill. The fog they created stifled his mind. It seemed Gage's concern for his family's safety had finally outweighed his need to protect the Devereaux name from dishonor. He had to play along so he could hold on to whatever freedom he had left. He had plans to finalize.

"All right." He made his tone somber to convince her he meant what he said. "I'll work with you and Dad. I'll agree to whatever punishments you see fit. I'm sorry about what happened last night at the game. I'm still not sure how it happened, but I'm willing to take responsibility."

Her slight smile was becoming. He couldn't remember the last time he saw his mother smile. Beau stood, maintaining the distance between them. The last thing he wanted to smell was her heavy floral perfume. It would only make him ache for Leslie's intoxicating aroma more.

She folded her arms. "I have to admit I'm surprised to hear you speaking this way. It isn't you."

"Me?" He held in his snicker. "You don't know me."

"I know you, Beau. I know every thought going on in your head. I've seen how you are, your coldness, your loathing. Don't think you can fool me."

She turned on her low heels and marched out of his room. The confidence in her step was a charade. Had to be. Elizabeth Devereaux spent her years at Devereaux Plantation terrified of two things: her husband and her son. One night of sobriety wasn't about to change anything.

After she shut his bedroom door, he paced the floor, feeling the walls closing in. His parents would restrict his activity like before, but he wasn't a kid anymore and his needs had matured.

Then there was his prize. He had plans for taking her, taming her, and teaching her the lessons she deserved.

He wanted to know where she was. Being with Dawn had given him a sense of access to Leslie, but without her sister hanging around, he had lost touch.

He picked up his phone from his night table, toying with the idea of calling Dawn. What should he say? Should he try and win her back to keep tabs on Leslie?

"Screw it."

He dialed her number and paced some more.

On the third ring, she answered.

"What do you want, Beau?"

It didn't sound like Dawn. She was edgier and colder. "Leslie?"

"Surprise!"

Her throaty tone slithered through his soul. He pictured the same laugh echoing in the cells. He would make her laugh like that right before he strangled the life out of her.

Strained by his desire to punish her, his murderous voice sounded foreign. "Put Dawn on."

"You're the last person she wants to talk to right now."

Her defiant lilt made him ache to punch something.

"I promise you will suffer one day."

"Like you've made others suffer?" Her eerie whisper slashed at his well-honed discipline. "Stay away from my sister and me, or I'll kill you, Beau Devereaux. I swear to God, I'll tear you to pieces." Leslie then hung up the phone.

He clenched his phone, hyperventilating. Her smile, her smell, her laugh circled in his head squeezing out every single thought like a vise. It was as if shards of glass surfaced in his stomach, chewing their way out. He could not let her win, ever.

After dropping the phone on the night table, he held his hands together and squeezed with all his might. Imagining all the power and pleasure he would gain from her end.

When his fury passed, he calmly sat on his bed, smiling.

When I'm done, I'll burn her and leave the rest for the wild dogs. No one will ever find any trace of Leslie Moore.

* * *

The skies outside Beau's bedroom window were black. Not even the stars poked through the veil of ominous clouds. He lay on his bed, his lights out to let his parents think he was asleep. He listened throughout the night for the closing of bedroom doors. First his mother's door, and then a short time later, his father's.

It was almost midnight. Everyone at the river would be drunk. It was time to make his move.

In his black jeans and a black jacket, he felt like the special ops guys. He had read a lot about their missions online, daydreaming about joining their ranks, but he had garnered something else from the articles—how to move around in the dark and not be seen.

He added a pair of black combat boots and threw them, and his ski mask, into his duffel bag. The clothes added to his sense of power. He was one step closer to taking his prize.

Gently closing his door, he hiked the bag over his shoulder and eased along the hallway, careful to avoid the spots where the floor groaned.

Once he was safely down the staircase to the main hall, he picked up his pace. He wiped the beads of sweat from his brow as he neared the mudroom. He was almost home free.

But the blinking red light on the alarm pad brought him to a grinding halt.

His father had set it—something he never did.

Son of a bitch!

He had to get out of the house. He couldn't put his plans in order for Leslie unless he went to the river and checked the cells.

Think. What's the code?

He remembered the five-digit code his father had given him a while back. The combination of his mother's and father's birthday. He just hoped his old man had never changed it. Holding his breath, he punched in the code and waited for the blare of the alarm, wondering what he would say if he got caught.

The alarm light switched from red to green without making a peep.

With a sigh of relief, Beau exited the house and slipped into the garage.

He inspected the collection of cars. His father's BMW, his BMW, his mother's Mercedes, and the red McLaren 570GT his father had bought but never driven. Such a waste.

The one car not parked in the garage was a black 4X4 Jeep used for hunting. They always left it outside the garage to leave room for the other cars. No one would notice if it had been moved, especially his father.

At the Jeep, he put on his combat boots while remembering his father always hid the keys.

After a quick glance up at the second-floor windows, he went through the Jeep, patting underneath the tire wells and checking the rack on top. When his hand glided over the spare tire rack in back, he found them, tucked into a small metal shelf.

Gripping the keys, he grinned.

You can't outsmart me.

* * *

The parking lot above the beach contained a multitude of cars, crammed into every available spot. It surprised him how many people were in attendance—considering he wasn't there.

He left his Jeep at the entrance to the lot, next to a patch of trees. He grabbed his black bag, put on his ski mask, and ducked into the woods.

He took up position behind a thick oak and caught sight of Mitch on a picnic bench, nursing a beer and surrounded by a couple of girls. He yearned to join him but couldn't afford to be discovered. Disappointed, Beau was about to head to the cells when he noticed a lone girl heading along the path leading to The Abbey.

Unable to resist, he kept to the trees and followed her along the path.

She had on a big black coat, a half-full bottle of vodka in one hand and a cigarette in the other.

"Ellen." Josh stumbled up to her, appearing drunk. "Where did you go?"

"You said let's take a walk to The Abbey."

"I wanted you to wait for me." Josh clasped her hand and led her through the old iron gate.

Intrigued, he followed them, staying far back on the path. Instead of taking a left and heading for The Abbey, Josh turned right at the fountain and crossed the grassy field to the cells.

That little prick.

The cells were his domain. No one came here and he made sure to tell all the boys to stay out, claiming it was too dangerous. The Abbey was their make-out spot, not his cells. But here was his best friend, breaking the rules.

Josh glanced back over his shoulder as he ushered the girl through the break in the wall. Beau seethed when they disappeared into the opening.

He hurried the last few yards to the entrance and listened before slipping inside.

The flare of a match came from his cell.

"My buddy has quite a setup. He doesn't know I know about his place, so shh." Josh's slurred words echoed through the corridor.

Shuffling and moaning followed. The harsh creak of the cot being moved on the stone floor came next.

He debated what to do. Should he rush the room, knock the girl to the side, and let into Josh with his fists? This was his place!

Self-control in all things.

Yeah, to hell with that. His so-called friend had crashed his territory. He had to act.

Beau adjusted his ski mask, making sure his face remained hidden, and closed in on his room. The distinct sound of panting carried down the narrow passageway.

From the doorway, the yellow light of a few lit candles flickered. Josh was on his cot with a girl's long legs spread underneath him.

He put his duffel bag down and quietly snuck into the room.

Beau waited, poised right over the cot, observing the sickening display. When the girl's eyes opened, she parted her lips to scream, but he was too quick. He grabbed Josh by the collar and threw him against the wall.

The girl sat up shrieking as Beau went after Josh. He held Josh by the throat, pushing him up the cracked wall, his jeans gathered around his ankles. Beau relished the fear in his friend's eyes.

Josh clawed at his ski mask, his eyes bulged while he fought to get any air.

Not as good as Andrea, but definitely uplifting.

The girl ran out of the room.

He let Josh fall to the floor, deciding he'd had enough. This was supposed to be a warning.

"What do you want, man?" Josh coughed as he clung to the wall, fighting to get to his feet. "Beau, is that you? What is wrong with you?"

He jabbed his finger in Josh's chest, not bothering to disguise his voice.

"Come back and I'll kill you."

Beau slammed his fist into the wall. Pieces of plaster broke off, tumbling to the ground.

"You're crazy!" Josh scrambled out of the room.

Beau turned to his cell; the anger in his veins swelled.

The bastard has defiled my special place.

He let go and kicked the cot out of the way, smashed the vodka bottle they had left behind against the wall, and shoved one of the candles to the floor. The blanket he ripped to shreds. He even pulled apart the pillow, filling the room with chunks of cheap foam stuffing.

Worn out and breathing hard, he crashed to the floor. The world he'd thought was coming together for him, was, in actuality, falling apart. There was only one thing that could appease him and make up for all he had endured—Leslie Moore.

Something red peeked out from the chunks of stuffing. He reached under the cot. It was Andrea's red scarf. He rubbed the silky material against his cheek. He'd forgotten he left it there.

You're lucky Josh never found it.

He dug his nails into his palms, punishing himself for his slip up. Maybe he wasn't ready to take her just yet. He had to get better organized.

The debris roused him. He'd have to come back, clean up and replace what Josh had sullied.

His internal clock urged him to return. He'd been gone long enough.

He tucked Andrea's scarf in his jacket and blew out the rest of the candles. In the corridor, he groped in the dark and found his bag.

Under the light of the burgeoning moon, Beau ran across the field. Creeped out as he peered into the pitch-black trees surrounding him. The incident with the ghostly figure had never left him.

At the fountain, he turned and rushed toward the gate.

When he ducked into the brush, he used the light from the bonfire to guide himself around the beach, frequently checking behind him to make sure he didn't get caught.

He got back to his Jeep without a problem. All that was left was to sneak back into his house, and crawl into bed.

Piece of cake.

Chapter twenty-Nine

He maneuvered his car around the packs of students chatting and hanging out. The sun was up, birds chirped in the trees, and everyone seemed to be in a good mood considering it was Monday. Beau didn't share their sentiments.

After parking in his usual spot, he climbed from his car. The first few stares he got didn't bother him. He expected to get a lot of crap for what had happened at the game.

But as he crossed the lot, several students scurried out of his way.

"Dude, ignore them." Mitch approached, giving him a fist bump. "They're just freaking out about the news."

He swung his book bag over his shoulder. "What news?"

"You didn't hear about the body the cops found on a riverbank this morning? They said it was a naked woman. They haven't identified her yet."

The sting of apprehension rippled across his skin. How had they found her so quickly?

"Where did they find her?"

"That's the thing. She wasn't more than two miles from where we party. Everyone is scared about going to the river for Halloween. They think there's a killer on the loose."

"There is no killer. You know how people like to party on the river. She was probably some drunk." Wanting to change the subject, Beau surveyed the parking lot. "Where's Josh?"

He couldn't wait to put the backstabbing asshole's nose to the fire and make his life hell.

Mitch eyed two freshman girls in short skirts. "He stayed home sick. He hasn't been right since Saturday night. After he hooked up with some girl, he came back to the bonfires all pale and sweaty. Just hope I don't get it."

"I'm sure he'll be fine by the game Friday night." Beau wondered how much Mitch knew. "You have fun at the river Saturday night?"

"Wasn't the same without you, but a lot of girls from Covington showed up."

The whirlwind in him expanded into a sea of black clouds. "You hook up with anyone? Go to The Abbey?"

"Nah, man." Mitch turned to the parking lot. "You know that place creeps me out."

Beau's heart raced when a white Accord entered the lot.

She's here.

"Aw, dude, you're not still hung up on Dawn, are you?" Mitch slapped his shoulder. "I thought you two called it quits?"

That Mitch didn't understand the reason for his excitement didn't bother him, but why would he assume he'd split with Dawn?

"What makes you say that?"

Mitch's jaw slackened. "It's all over school. Everyone is saying she dumped you."

The air left his lungs.

"Are you kidding me?"

Mitch held up his hands. "Don't shoot the messenger. I'm just telling you what's out there."

The black clouds inside him surged into a raging storm. The interest of his fellow students made sense. It wasn't the game they cared about—it was Dawn.

Eager to save his rep, he scrambled across the parking lot.

"Did your sister tell you I called?" he blurted before Dawn could get out of the car.

She leaned back in her passenger seat, seeming more annoyed than upset to see him. "Yes, Beau, she did."

The sarcasm was new. Probably Leslie's influence.

He held out his hand to her. "Then why didn't you call me back, baby?"

Dawn climbed out and recoiled, avoiding his touch. "Because we're through, *baby*. You can party at the river without worrying about cheating on me." She folded her arms, smirking at him. Just like her sister. "Yeah, I know about all the other girls. How long did you think you had before it all got back to me?"

He wanted to tear her limb from limb; the only thing holding him back was his razor-sharp discipline.

"What are you talking about?" He kept a wary eye on the parking lot. Students gathered around, taking in their discussion. "You're going to believe the gossip of all these jealous losers over me?"

"They're not losers, Beau." Leslie butted in, coming between him and Dawn. "Losers are the ones who hurt people, who hit people, who destroy lives by … You're a monster."

His fingers twitched. He needed to walk away before she shredded the tenuous grip he had on his self-control. Despite his desire to keep her as his, he could not allow her to live. Her strange power over him had to come to an end.

"You don't want to push me, Leslie." Beau's voice became cold, menacing. "You won't like what I become."

Dawn pushed him away. "That's enough! Leave Leslie out of this."

Beau edged closer. He couldn't let it end like this. No one broke up with him.

"You might want to reconsider breaking up with me. Piss me off, and I will destroy your rep. I'll make it so no other guy will touch you."

Dawn didn't flinch, didn't raise an eyebrow at his threat. She grabbed her bag from the backseat, unflustered. Nothing like the girl he once knew.

"Breaking up with you is the best decision I ever made. Stay away from me and my sister, or I will tell everyone what I know about you."

Panic shattered his confidence. What did she know? Had Taylor talked? Or Kelly? His insides heated into a congealed mess. He couldn't afford loose ends, not when he was so close to his ultimate goal.

He gripped her arm, hard. "What do you know?"

Leslie came around to her sister's side and slapped Beau hard across the face. "Let her go."

He didn't register the slap. He was too eager to know what Dawn meant. "What do you know, Dawn? Tell me!"

"Is there a problem here, Mr. Devereaux?"

In a gray wool suit and high black heels, Ms. Greenbriar stood on the curb in front of Leslie's car, hands on her hips.

Beau let Dawn go and flashed the principal one of his winning smiles. "No, ma'am. Just having a friendly conversation."

Ms. Greenbriar tapped her shoe on the asphalt. "My office now, Mr. Devereaux."

Beau backed away from Dawn as a ball of anger burned in his stomach. "Yes, ma'am."

Leslie's throaty laugh followed him from the parking lot. The rhythmic clip of Ms. Greenbriar's shoes on the asphalt acted like a metronome for his fantasy about Leslie, timing every blow to her slender body as he made her pay for her sins.

* * *

"Good. You're here," Gage said as soon as Beau walked through the garage door and into the house.

The fact that his father was home early, and waiting for him, intimidated the crap out of him. Any deviation from his tight schedule meant his father was mad—very mad.

He held a mug of coffee in his hands, the rich aroma filled the room.

"No need to stay after school anymore, is there?" Beau quietly set his book bag on the floor, preparing for another lecture.

Gage sipped his coffee, eyeing the bag. "Ms. Greenbriar called me after your meeting. Luckily, you didn't get suspended. I guess she bought your 'it was an accident,' bullshit. But I don't. Your probation with the school for one month will coincide with my grounding you for the same amount of time. Since you're no longer on the football team and have been banned from all extracurricular activities, your time belongs to me." He paused and Beau gulped, dreading what was coming next. "You're to go to the brewery immediately after school where you will work with me in the office."

His heart sank. This was worse than prison. "Every afternoon?"

Gage ambled toward him, his somber eyes not showing an ounce of compassion. "And weekends, too. When your probation is up at school, we can discuss terms for your return to your extracurricular activities."

Nausea swirling in his stomach, Beau gripped the edge of the copper breakfast bar. "What about the big Halloween party next weekend? I can't miss it. Everyone will be—"

"No more river." Gage's deep voice reminded him of a foghorn at night—cold and impassive. "A girl was killed at the river Friday night. The police think there might be a man hanging out there looking for victims. I can't have you anywhere near anything that brings even a hint of negative attention to this family. I have several business associates who would ask a lot of questions if the police showed up on my doorstep. Make them nervous, and I will make your life hell."

The statement generated a flurry of images about his father and underworld figures. He'd always suspected the Devereaux family business had a shady side. He wasn't the only one in the family with secrets.

Gage came up to him and slapped the copper bar. "I noticed the

Jeep had been moved Sunday morning. Care to explain?"

How in the hell had he known? He would have to mark where he parked the damned thing when he went out again.

"I didn't touch it."

His father hovered, exasperation written all over his face. "I'm locking up the keys to all the cars from now on. You can have your car to go to school and the brewery."

Beau's beloved freedom, the only thing making his life bearable, had just been yanked out from under him. *Someone shoot me!*

"Yes, sir."

Gage set his mug down on the bar. "Let me make this perfectly clear. I've remained quiet about your problem, made sure you stayed off the radar of CPS, kept you out of institutions, and got you the best shrinks to treat you under the table. But fuck up my business and I will arrange for you to be tossed into a psych facility and make sure you never get out." He stood back and picked up his coffee. "Go to your room and stay out of my sight for a while."

His father's threats proved what Beau had always suspected— he was just another holding in the long list of Devereaux business interests.

He collected his bag and slogged to the curved staircase. Never had his father made him feel so insignificant.

His humiliation rose to a crescendo as he bounded up the steps. How dare he be treated like some deranged lunatic? His father had no idea who he was.

He stomped across the second-floor landing to his room.

Eager for something to destroy, Beau searched the spartan décor of his room. He kicked the leg of his bed, slammed his fists into the comforter, and screamed into his pillow until hoarse. He wished he had a girl in his bed so he could pound into her.

Andrea's soft skin came back to him. The way it had molded around his fists when he'd beaten her sent a shiver down his arms. Beau recalled the way she looked floating down the river. He couldn't be tied to her death. He had watched enough CSI to know how to cover his tracks.

Despite his father's ultimatum, he would not stay away from the river. He still had to live out his dream. After Leslie, he would have to find another place to take women, but he would keep his cell. It could become his shrine—a place where he could relive his greatest triumph.

He rolled over on the bed, worn out from his tantrum, and slowly accepting his current situation. He would have to continue to kiss ass, behave like a model son, and agree to everyone's terms. When he was back in the good graces of his teachers, coach, and parents, he could return to hunting for new victims. Then he could begin a glorious new life filled with pleasure, power, and pain.

Chapter thirty

Beau sucked in the stale air-conditioned smell of the school hallway and slammed his locker door. He caught a few whispers of students passing by. Not as much as a few days ago, but the gossip about him, Dawn, or his probation still got to him. For the past week, he'd been a model student, abiding by every letter of his probation, and following his father's rules at home and at the brewery.

The confining schedule cut into his time observing Leslie. He had analyzed her every nod, smile, frown or faraway look to read her mood. He'd memorized the clothes she wore and what she ate for lunch. Beau kept close tabs on her at school—following her to her classes, staying out of sight and sitting not too far away at lunch. She ignored him, of course, but knew he was there. He could see it in her stony gaze.

Unfortunately, his father kept him very busy after school, which brought the pursuit of his Leslie fantasy to a slow crawl. So, he turned to another outlet to relieve his tension—the internet. He spent hours searching for ways to hurt a woman. Sites on rape, torture, and how to get rid of a body became a late-night thrill.

Mitch came up to his locker. "Any word if you are back on the team?"

"No, not yet." He didn't see the ass-kissing interloper scurrying behind Mitch like he always did. "Where's Josh? I haven't seen him for the past week."

Mitch shook his head, frowning. "Don't know what's up with that boy. He's missin' practice, skippin' classes. Been real nervous lately, too. Like he's scared or somethin'. He says he's got the flu, but I'm not buyin' it."

He remembered the sensation of choking his ex-friend. "Must be some flu."

Mitch slapped his back and guided him down the hall to the school entrance. "If I were you, I wouldn't worry about football. The team didn't do half as well without you at quarterback last Friday night." Mitch ambled along in his slow style as students went around them, eager to leave the school. "And it was an away game. Nobody came from the school."

"And the river?" Beau kept a nonchalant quality in his voice. "How was that?"

"Nobody went to the river last weekend. After they found that dead girl there, people have been stayin' away. Plus, the cops have been patrollin' like crazy."

"I'm sure it will cool down by this weekend." Beau scanned the hall for Leslie; he usually saw her about this time. "Won't be a proper Halloween celebration unless we're at the river."

Mitch stopped. "You're gonna be there? I thought you were grounded?"

He still had to convince his father to let him out of curfew for one night. But he would come up with a way to get to the party. He had to.

"I'm working on my old man to let me go."

Taylor trudged down the hall, hugging her book bag and wrapped in a lumpy black sweater.

You're next on my list, darlin'.

He gave her a long, cold stare, hoping to intimidate her. After her antics at the football game, he had been keeping an eye on her, too.

Before she turned into the bathroom, she shot him the finger.

Mitch chuckled. "What was that about?"

"What's it always about." He cracked a grin, anxious to start spreading a little gossip of his own. "She's mad I turned her down. When word got out about Dawn and me splitting up, she came sniffing around. I don't want anything to do with that twisted bitch."

With a slap on Mitch's back, Beau guided him to the entrance of the school.

While descending the steps to the quad, Sara sped past and purposefully knocked him with her shoulder.

Her eyes seared into his.

Hers was the next name on his list. When he cleaned house, he would do it in a big way.

Girls will be filling the river.

"What's her problem?" Mitch ogled Sara's short leather skirt and long legs.

"Man, didn't you hear?" He sneered at her back, formulating his smear campaign. "She got caught with some guys in the gym, having their own little bondage party. Ropes, handcuffs, you name it. There's pictures on Snapchat."

"No way!" Mitch gave Sara a second look. "I got to check that out."

Beau chuckled, knowing anything he told Mitch would get around the school faster than the truth. He needed to get some serious revenge on the bitch who had put him in the doghouse with Dawn.

"Be careful with Sara. She charges. Works for one of them bondage sites."

Mitch covered his mouth and his eyes grew. "Are you shittin' me? How come you know this?"

"She told me at the river." He headed across the grassy quad, ready to drive the stake through Sara's dead heart. "She confided in me. She does it to help pay the bills. Her old man's a drunk. My father is getting ready to fire him, but nobody knows yet so keep it under your belt."

Beau had a spring in his step as the sun hit his face. He would have her transferring to another high school by Thanksgiving.

"Oh, boy." Mitch directed his gaze to the parking lot. "Try and keep your tongue in your mouth this time when you see her."

The sun dipped behind a cloud, covering him in shadows. "What are you talking about?"

Derek, along with Leslie and Dawn, passed right in front of him, heading to the parking lot. While they chatted, Derek held Leslie's hand. He hated that. She belonged to him.

Dawn leaned over and whispered in her sister's ear, then giggled. The sound turned his stomach.

"When was the last time you two talked?" Mitch's deep voice intruded.

"Last week when you were there in the lot." He kept his eye on them as they got in their car. "The week apart did me some good. I've wanted to end it for a while. That girl likes to put her hooks in deep."

Mitch snapped his fingers in front of his face. "Then why you keep starin' at her when you're at school? You need to move on."

Mitch was right. He did need to stop following Leslie around school, especially if someone as dense as Mitch had noticed. Besides, he wouldn't get the information on her habits and lifestyle at school. One thing he had learned from football, if a defensive line keeps blocking your every attempt to pass, then they're reading your plays. You have to shake things up and do the unexpected.

"I gotta go." Beau yanked his keys from his pocket. "Got to head to the brewery. My old man will be waiting."

He took off across the quad at a slow jog, antsy to get in his car and follow Leslie. It was time to finish with his obsession. Once Leslie was dog food, and the others on his list joined Andrea in the river, he could move on with his life; pursue other women and explore other interests. By then, he would have to expand his sights beyond St. Benedict.

Good thing New Orleans is close by.

* * *

There was still enough sunlight branching across the sky for Beau to keep an eye on the Accord as it headed down the busier part of Main Street. He stayed back, not wanting to crowd them. Passersby on the sidewalk who recognized his car waved, and he returned the welcoming gesture. The windows down, a mellow tune coming from his speakers, he appeared the same casual Beau everyone knew.

Their car took a right at the neon pizza sign hanging over Carl's parking lot.

Perfect!

He followed their car into the lot and parked. Then he pulled out his phone, pretending to send a text as he waited for them to walk inside.

Through the large windows facing Main Street, he watched as they took a seat at a booth—Leslie and Derek on one side, Dawn on the other.

From his vantage point, he couldn't see Leslie's face but could discern a few of her hand gestures.

She didn't use her hands as much as Dawn, and he preferred it. It made her more sophisticated. He relaxed in his seat, his phone forgotten as the calm she gave him permeated his soul.

It didn't take long for his reconnaissance to frustrate him. He yearned to hear her voice, her laughter, so he would know how she sounded when happy. To remember it when he made her scream.

Would she be high-pitched like Taylor or more muffled shrieks like Kelly? Shame he'd never gotten Andrea to scream. Might give him something to compare to Leslie when the time came.

He clenched his steering wheel as he summoned the image of Andrea on his cot, her neck in his hands, bending, bending, and then, snap.

It was a wonderful sound. One he would recreate again and

again.

He yearned to leave Leslie a present. Something to let her know how he felt.

Beau spotted his book bag on the seat next to him. An idea blossomed.

He picked up the bag and rummaged for a pen and piece of paper.

The note he scribbled was short and to the point. Soon all his fantasies would be realized. How delicious would his life be then?

Before he climbed from his car, he cast his eyes to the white Accord.

Time to make my little Leslie sweat.

Chapter thirty-One

The smell of pepperoni and cheese, the screech of an eighties ballad from the flashy neon jukebox, and the murmur of conversation floated around Dawn. She sat in the booth, her stomach rumbling, wondering how long they would have to wait for their pizza.

"All I have left to get are the sombreros and our black masks." Leslie picked up her iced tea across from her. "Then you can get the red sashes."

"Why do I have to get the sashes?" she asked, turning her attention to the window. "Why can't I get the sombreros?"

"Well then, you get the hats and masks." The enthusiasm in Leslie's voice wavered. "Remember, you have to make sure the hats and masks are the same."

In the parking lot, just outside her window, Dawn spotted a familiar silver car. Beau was inside, staring at her, and making no attempt to leave his car.

What's he doing here?

Derek patted her sister's hand. "We don't have to be exactly the same, do we?"

"We're the three amigos. Our masks and sombreros have to match." Leslie sipped her iced tea. "I don't want anyone to figure out who we are."

"I'll protect you, sweetie." Derek chuckled. "The football team will be too drunk they won't notice us."

Dawn studied the car, remembering his chiseled profile. It was hard to believe such a good-looking package housed such a demented mind.

His rules and preoccupation with his image had never set off alarm bells, but after hearing Taylor's story, it made sense. The one thing haunting her was his anger. It had been there since the first night, simmering under the surface. The flared nostrils, white knuckles, and tightly pressed lips—his warning signs not to push him. She'd thought it was a guy thing, not a psycho thing.

She kept an eye on him. She didn't bother to tell Leslie and Derek he had followed them to the restaurant. Dawn didn't need to upset her sister or risk Derek ending up in a fight. Luckily, neither one noticed his car in the lot.

But why had he come here? To order pizza? She doubted it.

"Did you know about this?"

Derek's deep voice drew her attention away from the window. "Know about what?"

He squeezed Leslie's hand on top of the table. "Leslie says you are riding to the river together, and I'm to meet you there."

Dawn shot a cool glance at her sister, having no idea what he meant. "I, ah …"

Leslie interrupted. "I'm trying to talk Taylor into going and figured it would be better if the three of us went together to the party and Derek met us there."

Leslie's easygoing manner was fake. Dawn knew her better than anybody. She was up to something.

"Taylor has been having a tough time lately." Leslie turned to her sister. "She needs some girl time. It would be hard to talk with you around."

Dawn didn't agree with any of it but wouldn't argue with Leslie in front of Derek. She'd pick her brain about it later.

"I don't like it." Derek's frown cut deeper, turning into a disgruntled scowl. "It would be safer to have a guy with you. Especially after they found that dead woman near there."

Dawn wanted to warn him off from trying to tell Leslie what to do. She angled closer to him, but it was too late.

"What? You don't think we can take care of ourselves?" Leslie shook off his hand. "Why? Because we're girls?"

Dawn grinned at him. "Choose your next words carefully."

Derek wiped his upper lip. "I'm just worried about you and Dawn, and Taylor. I want to protect you, not limit your personal freedom because of your gender. Okay?"

The line between Leslie's brows softened. "I appreciate that. Really, I do. But we'll be fine. I can ride home with you after the party. Nothing will happen. I promise."

Derek shifted his attention to Dawn. "What do you think?"

She sat back, folding her arms. "I stopped trying to tell Leelee what to do when I was four. I suggest you do the same. You'll live longer."

Derek leaned in closer to Leslie, offering soothing caresses.

Dawn turned back to the window to check on Beau.

His car was gone. She glanced around the lot and along Main Street, but he was nowhere to be seen.

The wind kicked up as a few foreboding clouds cruised by. Something flapped on the windshield of her car. She squinted. It looked like a note.

A funny feeling swirled in her stomach.

Dawn checked on her sister and Derek, their heads still together, and decided not to mention anything to them. She wanted to get to the note before they did.

"Hey, guys." She slid to the end of the bench. "I'm gonna go to the bathroom."

Dawn got up and walked away.

With a quick glance over her shoulder, she snuck out the side glass door, behind their booth leading to the parking lot.

The wind picked up, brushing her hair in her face. Humidity clung to her skin, and the aroma of the coming rain permeated the air.

Dawn hurried across the parking lot to their car, anxious to not be seen by her sister. She quickly snapped up the note flapping in the breeze and dashed to the side of the building to get a closer look.

While the acrid taste of dread climbed the back of her throat, she fought to keep the wind from blowing the note away as she read it.

> I'm going to rip you up so good, Derek will never be able to fuck you again.

There was no signature, no scrawl of letters at the bottom—nothing.

A rumble of thunder rolled across the sky.

Dawn leaned back against the building and shut her eyes, her hard, quick pulse roaring in her throat.

What should she do? Who could she tell?

Beau had left the note for her sister. What gut-punched her was the depth of his interest in Leslie. The times she'd caught them together, the excessive teasing, the strange questions, the weird comments; Leslie had been the one he wanted that first night at the river—the one he still wanted.

The heady aroma of magnolias and honeysuckle from that night on the river came back to her. She had gone to the party with one goal—Beau Devereaux. In a short black dress that showed off her cleavage, she'd flirted with him, laughed at his jokes, and done all the things boys liked. But his interest was in her sister until she offered something he could not refuse.

"Leslie won't have sex with you. She's saving herself for someone special."

Beau had grinned at her. *"And who are you saving yourself for? Or have you already found someone special?"*

She recalled the tingle in her belly as he'd looked at her. The longing she had felt for him. He'd been her obsession since ninth grade.

"I'm saving myself for you."

Tears crested her eyes. Dawn believed when she gave him her virginity his infatuation with Leslie ended. She had been wrong.

She'd spent months with a guy who had never cared about her, a guy she'd never known. A hollow emptiness enveloped her; she had been an absolute fool.

Now the sick, psychotic bastard had set his sights on her sister.

Through her tears, she reread the note, and this time the bitterness rising in her throat did not go back down.

She retched, overcome with grief and anger. Standing up, she wiped her eyes and crumpled the note in her hand.

"You've destroyed enough lives, Beau Devereaux." She faced the door and took in a deep breath, collecting herself. "I'm going to end this, and make sure you never threaten my sister again."

* * *

The headlights stretched ahead as darkness engulfed the Spanish moss-covered trees on either side of the car. While she drove the last few miles home from Derek's house, Dawn gripped the steering wheel, her insides a mass of doubt and fear about what to tell her sister.

"What's up with you?" Leslie asked as she flipped Dawn's long hair behind her shoulder. "You never said a word after you came back from the bathroom at Carl's."

She relaxed her shoulders, not wanting to give herself away. "Just tired, I guess."

"You?" Leslie chuckled. "I don't buy it. You've always been the Energizer Bunny."

Dawn didn't like the comparison. There was something else she didn't care for—Leslie's lying.

"What was that BS you told Derek about Taylor back at Carl's? We never talked about riding with her to the river. I didn't think she even wanted to go."

Leslie sighed and faced her. "She doesn't. I made that up because I've got a surprise planned for Derek Saturday night. I need to get to the river early, ahead of him, so I can be ready."

Dawn turned down their quiet street. "What surprise?

Leslie rolled her eyes. "Something we've been talking about. I want to let him know how much he means to me and share some time together."

Dawn's waning patience cracked. "Are you going to have sex with him?"

Leslie pounded her folded hands into her lap. "If I am, that's my business. I just want to know you'll go along and take me to the river."

"Why? Are you going to have sex with him there?" Her insides turned to ice, afraid of what her sister had in mind. "There's nowhere at the river to be alone. Everyone's all over the beach unless you plan on doing it in the woods and even then, there's those damn dogs people have been—"

"I'm not having sex at the river. Gross." She blushed and relaxed her hands. "I'm going to meet him at the cells with a bottle of champagne. We found this room there once where we talked about being together. I wanted to surprise him with my plans. Then I'm taking him to a spot where we can be alone."

Dawn tensed. The porch lights to their parents' home loomed ahead. "What spot?"

"A motel in Covington. I saved up some money and—"

"When did you decide this?" Dawn hit the brakes hard after she pulled into their driveway.

Leslie lurched forward and grabbed the dash. "Dammit, Dawn. What are you doing?"

Desperate, she grabbed her arm. "Meet him at the river if you want, but skip going to the cells. It's a nasty place and you don't want memories of your first time to begin in something that looks and smells like a dungeon."

"How do you know that?"

She turned off the engine, avoiding Leslie's eyes. "Beau took me there once. I didn't like it."

Leslie leaned in closer. "Did you two ...?"

She wanted to tell Leslie the truth about everything that had gone on in Beau's special place, but she was ashamed. Her time with him, and what he had done to others there, made her feel dirty and ugly. She regretted every second she had spent with him, but to tell her sister would hurt too much. It would confirm what had always been her worst fear—that Leslie was the better twin.

"Just promise me you'll stay away from the cells. Take Derek straight to the Covington motel for the night." She smiled, putting on a brave face. "That's what Lisa Faucheux did with Lyle Burgundy."

"Lisa?" Leslie's mouth slipped open. "Really? But she's Pastor Faucheux's daughter. She tells everyone she's saving herself for her husband."

"Yeah, well, Lyle beat him to it."

Dawn opened her car door, relieved her sister's attention had been diverted from the cells.

She hoped she had done the right thing not telling Leslie about Beau.

It's for the best. It's my turn to protect her.

Chapter thirty-two

Beau shouldered his way through patches of students clogging the halls. He stomped his tennis shoes on the tile floor, expressing his anger at being turned down by Coach Brewer for a chance to return to the team. All around him, excited voices jabbered about the coming football game against Beddico High Friday night. He wished he could smash all their heads into the lockers and turn the floors into rivers of blood.

"Marty will pull out a win," one thick-shouldered running back on his team said as he walked past. "He's turning into a good quarterback."

"I heard the team doesn't want him back." A girl leaning against a locker blew a big bubble with her gum. "They do better without him."

The wildfire in Beau's stomach spread to every corner of his being. He was the quarterback of St. Benedict High, and he deserved his spot back on the team, but Coach Brewer had been adamant when he met with him in his office.

"Forget it, Devereaux. You have to complete your probation."

"But the season will be over by then," he had argued.

"Maybe you should have thought about that before you threw that ball at Kramer."

Beau needed to get away from the noise, the students, the tight hallways closing in and cutting off his air. He longed to get in his car and take off, head to the river for some time to think and prepare his cell for Leslie, but his father would hear about his skipping class. It seemed no matter where he turned, Gage Devereaux's chokehold on his life never let up.

He turned a corner, anxious to get outside when he came across Leslie at her locker.

She was a few feet away, but the jutting corner of the lockers kept her from spotting him. She looked beautiful in her sweater top and jeans. Her skin, perfectly white without an ounce of makeup, glowed and she had her lips pressed together in a classic Leslie scowl as she searched her locker.

Zoe, Dawn's obnoxious cheerleading friend, was at Leslie's side. The pretty girl was known around school for having a thing for gossip. What was she doing with Leslie? His Leslie was better than the pushy cheerleader.

"Dawn told me you and Derek got your costumes for this weekend." Zoe hugged her chemistry book to her chest, grinning at Leslie.

"Yep, we're all set." Leslie shut her locker door. "We've got our sombreros, masks, fancy red sashes, black pants and white tops. It should be fun. What are you going as?"

Zoe hesitated, her smile slipping. "Is everything okay with Dawn?"

Leslie's eyebrows came together. "Dawn? She's fine. Why do you ask?"

His morning was looking up. Any juicy gossip to keep his ex in line was alright with him.

Zoe moved in closer to Leslie, casting a wary eye to those students passing by. "She seems out of sorts. Preoccupied, if you know what I mean. She mentioned the three amigos costumes you guys were wearing to the river—cute. And she let it slip you and Derek were planning a romantic evening. She seemed really upset about it. Said you wanted her to drive over early to surprise him with champagne in the cells. Ew, really?"

What? He stiffened. It can't be? This was better than he'd hoped. She would come to him, to the cells. His prize was within his reach.

His head swam with delight, picturing all the delicious things he would do to her. He envisioned the rush she would give him. It would be better than Taylor, Kelly, and Andrea combined.

Leslie's scowl was back. "Dawn had no right to tell you about my plans."

Zoe held up her hand. "Look, I know you two haven't gotten along since she was with Beau but now that he's history, I think she's worried you will make the same mistake. I mean, the guy was a total douchebag."

He clenched the grip on his book bag, ready to tear it apart. *That bitch!*

Leslie appeared appalled by the suggestion. "How can I be making a mistake with Derek? All we want to do this weekend is to spend some time together alone."

"Doing what? Moon watching?" Zoe snickered.

It seemed things had progressed further with Leslie and the loser Foster than he realized.

"Oh, ha ha. Laugh all you want. But Dawn can't possibly compare her time with Beau to my relationship to Derek. I know he cares for me and isn't ready to rush into having sex."

"But are you two ever going to have sex?" Zoe pressed her hand to the book against her chest. "Me? I would have jumped him after the third date."

Leslie lowered her voice and he could barely hear her. "I want my first time to be special."

"Special?" Zoe chuckled. "You're in for a big surprise." Zoe hooked her arm. "Come on, let's get to class."

Zoe's eyes briefly connected with Beau. A wave of dread froze him to his spot. She didn't say or do anything as she glided past. Leslie never saw him, thank goodness. He didn't want her changing her plans. He wanted his prey to be calm and happy when she walked into his special place. It would make her final screams so much sweeter.

* * *

Dawn tugged at the red ribbon holding her ponytail in place while a brisk breeze blew by, sending a chill through her. The gravel in the parking lot next to the playing field crunched beneath her feet. She glanced ahead to her squad, getting ready for their last practice before the big game tomorrow night.

"Hey girl, you got a sec?"

Zoe pulled up next to her, sporting a sullen frown.

Dawn inwardly groaned. She knew that look. It went along with Zoe's yearning to share some piece of gossip she'd picked up around school. The last thing Dawn needed was more gossip.

We need to get this new cheer right. Not spend the hour having a gabfest.

"When was the last time you talked to Beau?" Zoe asked.

Dawn hadn't expected that question.

"I have no idea. Why?"

"He's been acting funny. Have you noticed it?"

Dawn scrunched her brow, trying to recall his activities throughout the past few days. She had noticed some strange things.

"He hasn't been hanging out with his buddies Mitch and Josh lately. They always go everywhere together."

"Word in the halls is he and Josh had a fight." Zoe shook her pompoms out. "I tried to talk to Mitch about it, but he shut me down. He's such an asshole."

Dawn peered ahead to her waiting squad. The girls were standing around, talking. Not a good sign. She needed to get them to work.

"Zoe, is there a point to this? Because, if you haven't noticed, Beau isn't my problem anymore." She made a move to go to the field. "We gotta get to practice."

Zoe rushed in front of her, her brow etched with concern.

"Today I caught Beau staring at your sister from behind some lockers. Leslie was telling me about her weekend at the river with Derek. If I didn't know better, I'd swear he was listening in."

The chill in the air closed in around Dawn. Dread gripped her throat, tightening her airway, and making it hard to breathe.

"What did he hear, Zoe? I need you to remember everything you two talked about."

Zoe's brow furrowed. "What's going on, Dawn?"

Dawn dropped her pompoms and held her friend's arm. "What did Leslie say?"

Zoe shook her head, the maddening apprehension in her eyes persisting. "I don't know. We talked about her sleeping with Derek. How she planned to make Saturday night special. You two going together early so she could go to the cells and how you weren't happy—"

"He heard that. The part about the cells?"

"Yeah, I guess." Zoe pried her fingers off her arm. "The way he was standing there was just plain freaky. He had this look in his eyes ..."

Dawn stepped back, her mind a blur. If he knew about Leslie's plans, he might try and interfere, fight with Derek, or even Leslie. She had to find a way to stop anyone from getting hurt.

"Is everything okay?"

Zoe's question brought her back. "Yeah. It's fine." Dawn took in the open field next to the gym where the football team was warming up. "Do me a favor, don't mention this to Leslie. I don't want her upset or ruin her night with Derek at the river. I hear you on Beau. He has been strange lately."

"What are you going to do?"

Dawn bit her lower lip. "I'm going to find out what he's up to."

"Be careful with that boy." Zoe picked up Dawn's pompoms and handed them to her. "Something's not right about him."

Dawn gave her friend a reassuring smile. "Not to worry. Beau would never dare lay a finger on me."

Chapter thirty-three

The glow from the security lights on the first floor of the plantation home filtered into Beau's bedroom window. He admired the blank expression on his new Michael Myers mask and tossed it on top of the contents in the black duffel bag on his bed. All the goodies he planned to use on Leslie were ready. Beneath the mask, Andrea's red scarf caught his eye. He touched the fabric, picturing it around Leslie's long neck.

A knock on his door startled him. Beau hurriedly zipped up the bag and shoved it under his bed.

He wiped a bead of sweat from his upper lip and then said, "Come in."

Gage pushed the door open and boldly stepped into his room.

He got a whiff of his father's expensive cologne. "You going out?"

"Business meeting in New Orleans." His father tossed something at him.

Beau caught the object in mid-air. He opened his hand. It was the keys to his car.

"I need you to go to the brewery tonight and get out the Halloween decorations for the employee party this Saturday. They're in the storage building. Have the security guard on duty help you load it into one of the brewery trucks and take them to the meeting room in the administration building."

He stared at his father, confused. "Why tonight?"

Gage fiddled with the gold Rolex on his wrist. "Because tomorrow after school you will be decorating the meeting room."

Beau frowned. Decorating was a girl thing.

"Anything else?"

He didn't bother to keep the cockiness from his voice, even though he knew it would anger his father.

Gage eased closer, his mouth pinched shut as if holding back his irritation. "I know you haven't been happy since being put on probation, but it's not forever. When you've served your time, you can go back to hanging out with your friends."

"Served my time?" His hands closed around the keys, squeezing the metal into his flesh. "Prisoners get time off for good behavior."

His father's sigh hung in the air. "What do you want?"

Beau perked up, hungry to win back some of his freedom. "The Halloween party at the river Saturday night. I want to go."

"No. You're going to the brewery party Saturday night with your mother. We're going to put on a good show for the staff."

He clenched the keys harder, the pain giving his anger wings. "I won't go for long. Just enough to be seen, say hello to the guys, and then I'll head to the brewery. If I'm one minute longer, you can call the cops on me."

His father's eyes crinkled at the corners. Something he did when considering a proposal.

"Since the police will already be patrolling the river, there will be no need. Kent Davis is sending a man to the beach Saturday night to assure parents their kids will be safe, and no drinking will be taking place."

That will kill the party. Good thing I have other plans.

"Then you have nothing to worry about. You can call Sheriff Davis and have his man arrest me if I'm not on my way to the brewery."

The cold indifference emanating from his father didn't surprise Beau. It had been there all his life.

"Okay. The party at the brewery starts at seven. By eight, your ass better be there or I will add another month to your punishment."

Beau's enthusiasm returned. He would have all the time he needed with his girl.

His grip eased up on the keys. "Yes, sir."

Gage looked him over. "Leah left roast for dinner. Make sure you eat it. You're getting skinny."

He glanced down at his flat stomach and baggy pants. He hadn't noticed the weight loss until then. His preoccupation with Leslie had kept him so busy, he'd forgotten about everything else. But who needed food? He would soon have her.

"I guess not working out with the team, I lost my appetite."

Gage nodded at him. "You'll start hitting the gym with me. You need to stay in shape. Otherwise, people will think you're sick and ask questions."

Beau grinned. "And we can't have that, can we?"

His father's cheeks reddened, and he arched menacingly over him. Gage had a good twenty pounds and two inches on Beau.

"Let's cut the crap, shall we?" His father's voice took on the low growl of a dog ready to strike. "You're my son and heir, which doesn't mean a whole hell of a lot to you, but it does to me. I have stood by you, put up with your crap, and kept my mouth shut when your behavior has embarrassed me and this family. I sometimes wonder if you have a shred of responsibility in you, or if you plan on spending your entire life with your head up your ass. I've done everything I can to keep you under control, but I'm not sure it's enough. I hope you prove me wrong and become a man people can rely on, but I have a feeling you may end up being their worst nightmare. If that day ever comes, I will cut all ties with you. You will be dead to me."

The admission wasn't a shock, but a relief. Beau had been well aware of his father's distaste for him ever since he was a kid, but after the incident, things had been rocky between them. Beau felt as if the last tether keeping him grounded to his life as Gage Devereaux's son had finally snapped. He was free to be who he wanted, do what he wanted, his family name be damned.

"I'm glad we cleared that up." He unfurled his hand from around the keys.

His palm was wet and stung like mad.

"Your mother will be waiting up until you get home from the brewery. She's going to call me as soon as you get in, so don't think you can go out and fool around with your friends."

Beau shook his head at his father's stupidity. "It's Thursday. Nobody goes out on a school night."

"Yes, I know." He turned for the door and strutted out of the room.

He should have been livid, but a strange calm cruised through him. Fate was on his side, giving him the chance to be with Leslie. It was the only way to explain how everything seemed to be falling into place.

The throaty roar of an engine called him to his bedroom window. Outside, he spotted the red McLaren leaving the garage.

"Business meeting, my ass."

The car, the clothes, the cologne—he had a date. Probably a new woman. He always dressed up for the first few dates. Then, when he got bored, he went back to his casual attire.

He's so predictable.

Beau remembered his hurting hand. He examined the keys. Flecks of blood showed up against the silver.

His finger tracked through his blood. He wanted to paint the world in the ruby shade. To show his father, mother, everyone at school he wasn't Gage's son anymore. He was his own man—a man to be feared.

Back at the bed, he retrieved the duffel bag and hoisted it over his shoulder. He had a stop to make before he went to the brewery.

He patted the bag. "My party will be the talk of the town."

* * *

The brush of tree limbs against his car was the only sound as he slipped into the gravel lot by the river. The beams from his headlights cut into the blackness, not landing on any other cars. Good. He was alone.

He parked on the far side of the lot, safe from any police patrols happening by. Initially, he thought the patrols a nuisance, but suddenly, he was grateful. They would keep the partygoers from the river, ensuring the contents of his duffel bag would remain safe in his cell.

He retrieved a flashlight from his back pocket and flung the bag over his shoulder, ready to set out for The Abbey.

Rustling leaves to his right startled him. Beau stood still, holding his breath.

After a few seconds, he shook his head and brushed off the noise. Who would be following him? No one knew he was there.

He set out across the lot and when he came to the sloping path leading to the river, he ducked into the brush.

Low-lying twigs scratched his hands and swiped his face as he moved through the dense foliage. When he stopped to adjust the heavy bag on his shoulder, a crash of something moving through the underbrush came from behind.

His heart climbed in his throat. Was it the police? Had he been caught?

He spun around, but no one was there.

A patch of green leaves on a bush shook. He shined his flashlight at the bush, the leaves stilled.

"Who's there?"

Nothing. Then black eyes, low to the ground, caught in the beam of his light. A round head, covered in black fur moved out from the brush. A large, skinny dog, his fangs dripping with saliva moved in closer.

What if there were more of them? What if the pack surrounded him like those velociraptors in that dinosaur movie?

He spied a thick stick on the ground. He kept his eyes on the approaching dog and slowly picked up the stick. The animal's growl got steadily louder.

Determined not to be intimidated by the mangy creature, Beau remained calm. Right before it got too close, he hurled the stick at the dog's head.

A yelp pierced the air, but the mongrel did not back down. It glared at Beau with an intense, almost human hatred in its black eyes.

This had become personal to Beau. He wasn't going to let some stray push him around. Beau picked up another smaller stick and threw it, followed quickly by another.

"Come on, you bastard."

He waited for the animal to charge. Instead, it turned and headed into the brush.

Smug with his victory, he sucked in a deep breath and turned back toward The Abbey.

"You got this, Devereaux."

At the iron gate, he raised his head to the night sky. The stars weren't twinkling, and there was no moon. Perfect.

He cut across the field of high grass, turning at the fountain.

A few feet away from the cells, the lone howl of a dog fixed him to his spot.

He waited to see if there was another. Seconds ticked by, but the only sounds around him were the chirp of the crickets and the occasional croak of frogs.

What had Andrea said? When the dogs appear, death is near.

He chuckled. Maybe the dogs knew what he had planned.

Inside the abandoned ruins, he directed the beam of his flashlight to the floor. A rat dashed by, startling him.

Beau kicked the defenseless creature. It landed a few feet away on a pile of leaves and dried twigs, stunned. He thought of things he could do to it, ways he'd like to torture it, but there wasn't time. He needed to set up his room and head back to the brewery.

The cell was in the same disarray after his encounter with Josh. Beau set his flashlight down and dumped his duffel bag on the cot.

From the bag, he pulled out several new scented candles—rose and honeysuckle

She would appreciate their aroma. He tried to find one at the store that smelled like her—springtime clover—but none seemed to have her essence. After lighting a few candles, he set them around the room, on the floor and ice chest, eager to capture the right ambiance. Once satisfied, he collected the black garbage bag he'd brought along with a small broom.

Beau took his time, sweeping up the wads of foam, broken glass, and torn fabric from the floor. He found the preparation for Leslie soothing. The way he felt before Christmas morning as a kid, knowing he would get what he wanted. He just had to wait.

With the room freshly swept, he retrieved the new blanket and pillow from his bag and set them on the cot. The last thing he took out was Andrea's red scarf. He gently laid it on the pipes jutting from the wall.

He left the other toys he brought in the duffel bag and placed it under the cot, pushing the bag out of sight.

The flickering light from the candles added to the eerie atmosphere in the room. Beau hoped Leslie would appreciate his attention to detail. Still, something was missing. It needed a homey touch, something to let her know how he felt.

Flowers. Yes, of course. He would pick up a bouquet of flowers and set them up in a nice vase on his ice chest. Daises. Leslie loved daisies. He'd seen Derek bring her bouquets at school.

Breathing in the musty odor of the room, Beau trembled with anticipation. He would act out every depraved fantasy, ending his obsession with Leslie. Then life would be perfect. The annihilation of Leslie Moore would be his greatest work of art, but not his last.

Satisfied, he tied off the garbage bag, blew out the candles, and headed back outside.

A glimpse of white slipping through the break in the wall caught his eye.

The hair stood up on his arms. He had not been alone.

He took off for the opening. Several precious seconds passed as he worked the garbage bag through the narrow crack. Once in the night air, he scanned the grounds.

A strange mist had appeared since he'd entered the cells. It hovered beneath the grass. The tall blades rose from the dense fog and wiggled like fingers, beckoning him to follow. Beau dashed through the weeds, creeped out by the ghoulish atmosphere.

Ahead, he saw something—a white cloak floating beneath the trees. His anger returned.

"I'll get you."

He reached the spot where he had seen the strange apparition and examined the ground with his flashlight. There were no footprints, no disturbance to the grass.

A long, low howl sliced through the air.

His heart pounding, he hurried in the direction of the gate, sweating under his long-sleeved shirt despite the chill in the air.

I have to find out who's following me!

He headed into the brush, cutting off his flashlight, ready to annihilate the conniving little bitch playing head games with him.

Beau carefully maneuvered through the brush and low hanging branches, not making a sound. But when he emerged in the parking lot, no one else was there. The pale light from the streetlight filtered through the trees and across the gravel surface, revealing no other cars.

He stood by a pine tree, attuned to every noise around him. He stayed still for several minutes, before his fear of being late to the brewery urged him to his car.

He tossed the garbage bag in the back seat, planning to leave it in the brewery dumpster.

He sat behind the wheel his aggravation gnawing at him. Someone had followed him. He ran through his list of suspects in his head.

What if it's the ghost?

The childish notion brought a chuckle to his lips. He started the car.

It was a person; it had to be. Any other explanation meant Beau's grip on reality was slowly slipping away.

Chapter thirty-four

"**I** can't wear this, Leslie!"

Derek stood over his phone from where he placed it on the rickety kitchen table, the smell of stale coffee lingering in the air. He secured the black mask around his head, debating how he would get through the evening wearing it and the large sombrero, without running into people.

"These pants have one pocket. How am I supposed to carry my phone, wallet, and keys?"

"Put them in your hat." Her velvety warm chuckle careened through him.

He loved her laugh. He loved everything about her. Her costuming skills, however, he was still iffy about.

"You do realize I will run into everyone with this thing." He picked up the hat and set it on his head. The comically oversized brim dipped to his chest. "Tell Dawn the hats are too big."

"Stop complaining."

The voice was higher, less throaty than Leslie's. He figured Dawn had joined her sister in her room.

"Is Dawn there?"

"She's here." It was Leslie again. "Completely dressed and ready to go." She sounded happier than he had heard her in months. "You're right. Those sombreros are too big."

Before her break up with Beau, he'd thought Dawn bitchy due to her preoccupation with her popularity, cheerleading, and obliviousness to her boyfriend's cruelty. But since then, she'd won Derek over with her sometimes flighty, always brash, optimistic viewpoint.

"Aw, come on you guys. They're fun." Dawn sounded close to the phone.

"Derek says he doesn't have enough pockets for his phone," Leslie told her sister.

"Then tell him to leave his phone in his truck. We'll have our phones. We have to be in the same costumes. He can't cop out and change his pants so he can carry his phone. So not cool."

Derek could almost picture the eye roll Dawn gave him.

Leslie came back on. "You heard that, right?"

He heard it. He didn't like it, but if Dawn insisted he wear the same outfit, he would do it. Their costumes represented their new friendship, and for Derek, the evening marked an important milestone—he'd won the trust of the entire Moore household. Even Shelley had warmed up to him. It gave him a sense of belonging; he had become part of a family.

"You need to get dressed, Leelee. We'll be late."

An uncomfortable twinge raked across his gut. "Late? I thought we weren't meeting there until seven. It's not even six yet."

"We're getting there early." Leslie's tone changed to right above a whisper. "I have a surprise for you."

He tossed his hat on the kitchen table. "What surprise?"

"Just meet me in that room we found behind The Abbey at seven. I'll show you what I have planned."

He played with a loose green thread in his sombrero, the uneasiness in his gut not letting up. "Why would you want to meet in the cells? I thought The Abbey creeped you out?"

"I can stand it for one night. Besides, it's only a place to meet. We won't be hanging around there for long."

"We won't?" He became suspicious. "Please tell me this isn't a scary surprise."

"No way! You're going to love it."

The front door opened. Carol Foster rushed inside, her arms

laden with file folders, a laptop bag hanging from her shoulder.

"Hey, Mom." Derek ran to help her. "What you got there?"

Carol handed him the pile in her arms. "Cases from the firm. Mr. Garrison wants me to go through them and type up the notes he made. He even gave me the office laptop to bring home. It will probably take me all weekend, but he's paying me, so I don't mind one bit."

Carol kicked the door closed and set her purse and keys on a table by the door.

"Is that your mom?"

"Hold on," he told Leslie as he carried the files to their kitchen table.

He set them down and picked up his phone. "Yeah, Mom just got home from work. She went in today to get caught up and came home with more work from the law firm."

Carol took off her gray pantsuit jacket and set it on the table next to the files. "Is that Leslie?"

He put the phone up to her.

"Leslie, tell your dad thank you again." She went to the coffeemaker and took the empty pot to the sink. "The job is wonderful. The Garrisons are giving me more and more to do every day."

"I'm so glad everything is working out," Leslie called to her. "I'll tell Dad when I see him later tonight. He and Mom went to the party at the brewery."

Derek watched his mother refill the coffeepot with water and chat with his girlfriend. To see her doing so well gave him a profound sense of relief. Her eyes brighter, her waiflike figure filling out her new pantsuit, she was more vibrant than he could remember.

He could finally look to the future with excitement instead of worry. How had he gotten so lucky? A great mom, a girlfriend who he loved, and a family who filled him with hope.

"Leelee!" Dawn shouted. "Get off the phone. You have to get

dressed now."

A strange rustling sound erupted over his speaker.

"Everything okay?"

"Leelee will see you at the party, Derek," Dawn said.

"Okay. Tell Leslie, I love—"

Click.

That's weird.

Carol spooned a measure of coffee in the top of the maker. "What was that about?"

He set his phone on the kitchen table. "I think Dawn was mad Leslie hadn't dressed yet for the party."

Carol flipped on the coffeemaker, checking out his outfit. "What are you? A pirate?"

"No." He picked up his sombrero and put it on his head. "Leslie, Dawn, and I are going as the three amigos."

Carol chuckled and lifted the brim of his hat. "Lose the sombrero; keep the mask. You're more convincing as a pirate."

Chapter thirty-five

A bouquet of fresh daisies sat in a green glass vase on top of his ice chest. He arranged the stems, wanting them looking perfect for when she walked into his cell. The burning candles filled the room with the sweet scents of honeysuckle and rose.

On the cot, set out precisely so he could easily reach for them, were a roll of duct tape, handcuffs, a hunting knife, lighter fluid, and the finishing touch for his night of fun—his Michael Myers mask.

Beau stood in the corner of the room, close to the entrance. He wiped one sweaty palm down his black pants, and then rubbed the smudge away from his black combat boots. He glanced at the mask on the cot. At the end, when the essence of life left her eyes, he would reveal himself. To make sure his face was the last she ever saw again.

He'd fantasized about the idea, but there were times he doubted his dream would come true. Like an Olympic athlete, he'd trained his entire life for this defining moment.

The sound of shuffling, like someone trying to get through the crack in the wall, came from the corridor.

She's here.

He retrieved the mask from the cot and quickly put it on.

An audible gasp drifted into his room.

The voice was definitely female.

Beau grinned. She was right on time.

A clap of energy surged through him. He peeked at her through the doorway, holding his breath, afraid to make a sound and scare her away.

She came down the corridor to the light. All in black, with a red sash around her waist, she had a sombrero on her head, a black mask around her eyes, and a bottle of champagne in her hand.

He waited as she inched closer, anxious to get his hands around Leslie's throat.

She stuck her head in the door and glanced around.

Beau stayed to the shadows, his back pressed against the stone wall.

He jumped her when she turned her head and slapped his hand over her mouth. The champagne bottle tumbled to the floor by the entrance, shattering with an explosive *pop*.

She struggled against him like he knew she would. The sombrero was squashed between them, almost making him laugh. With one hand around her mouth and the other around her neck, Beau dragged her to the cot. A quick jerk ripped off the flimsy hat. He took in her pinned up, dirty-blonde hair.

She screamed as he forced her to the floor. He snatched up the duct tape and then wrapped it snugly over her mouth.

Her mewing cries filled him with such satisfaction.

He peered into her deep blue eyes. "No one can hear you, my Leslie."

She fought against him even more. He liked that. Sitting on top of her, he retrieved the handcuffs from the cot, flipped her over on her stomach. Her hands secured he could now have his fun.

Beau undid a few of the pins holding up her hair. He played with her shoulder-length blonde tresses, reveling in the silkiness. Then, he picked up the knife, sizing up which end of her costume to start with—the top or the bottom.

Decisions, decisions.

He wanted to see her breasts. Beau carefully cut the black shirt away from her chest, making sure not to leave a mark on her, and then removed her bra. He would wait to see her entire naked body before he chose where to make his first cuts.

Her struggles lessened when the cold air hit her breasts. Her nipples perked up and he licked his lips, enjoying the display.

To cut her pants away took some skill, but by the time he snapped her underwear off, he felt proud of his accomplishment. He'd removed every stitch of her clothing without so much as a scratch.

Beau hoisted Leslie off the floor and placed her on the cot.

"You wanted your first time to be special. I'm going to give you the night of your life."

She didn't fight him as he secured her handcuffs to the pipes. He didn't like that. In his fantasy, he'd imagined her resisting so much more.

Inspecting her slender body and long legs, he smelled her skin, eager to fill his nostrils with her heavenly scent. Unfortunately, the heady scent of honeysuckle from the candles obliterated her faint perfume. Damn!

Irritated one pleasure had been denied, he wanted to feel her naked against him. He kicked off his boots, slid out of his pants, and discarded his underwear. His mask stayed on; it made him feel powerful.

She kicked her legs when he climbed on top of her. There was his girl. Her resistance aroused him. It was what he had longed for.

"That's it, Leslie. Fight me. Don't make it easy."

She thrashed harder, trying to free her hands from the pipe.

"Keep that up, and you might cut yourself." He laughed— sounding cold just like his old man. "I don't want you bleeding yet."

He savored the feel of her in his hands and raked his nails down her chest. Finally, he had the girl he'd been obsessing over for months. He wanted to make his enjoyment last.

From her ankles to her stomach, he deposited tender kisses, still trying to catch her scent. When he licked her nipples, Leslie kicked again. She caught him in the stomach, provoking Beau's rage.

"You're going to pay for that."

With a closed fist, he knocked her back on the cot. Blood

blossomed from her nose, dripping down the duct tape over her mouth. He delighted at the sight. He went back to kissing her thighs, but soon his kisses turned into bites. Beau sank his teeth into her flesh and she bucked in pain.

He went a little crazy, ripping into her breasts, tearing at her nipples. The taste of blood turned him on more than seeing her naked.

But the biting got boring, and he yearned to move on to the climax of the evening.

"Now to the good part. I've had a few virgins in my time, but I always wanted you."

Beau pried her knees apart, throbbing with anticipation. He had not brought any condoms with him, wanting to enjoy every inch of her.

Holding his breath, he braced her hips and thrust hard and fast into her, eager to make sure it hurt.

Leslie let go a muffled scream.

"How's that feel? Was it worth the wait?" He put his mouth to her ear. "All those times you laughed at me, all your comments, your bitchy attitude, I swore this moment would come. I promised you I would make you mine."

Eager to enjoy his fantasy to the fullest, he took Andrea's red scarf from the wall and cinched it around her throat.

Leslie gasped for air as blood continued to flow from her nose.

The metallic scent blended with the perfume from the candles around him as he rammed into her, tightening his grip on the scarf. He was high, like a bird, soaring with his ecstasy. He had conquered her impudence, broken her will, and it took away his anger.

Then the rush; the wave of power he felt with the others, but with her, it was so much more. This bliss he equated to heaven. What the angels sang about, the prophets preached, and the regular people hoped to attain. But he had captured it here with his Leslie.

"Can you feel it?" He slammed harder into her. "So good. This was meant to be."

Before he knew it, a flood of satisfaction overtook him. He let out a low, guttural scream as he released into her.

He collapsed on top of Leslie. The night had even been better than anticipated.

Panting, Beau pushed up on his elbow and noticed she was very still. He slapped Leslie's face repeatedly, wanting to make sure she stayed conscious. He had much more fun planned.

She trembled when he gripped her hips. The fear oozing from her was sublime.

Beau flipped her over on the cot. He ran his hands over her butt, relishing the smoothness of her skin, the purity of the color.

"Now, to the real prize. I've always wanted to take a girl's ass."

Leslie thrashed as he held her hips to his. To stop her wiggling, he yanked at the red scarf, jerking her neck back and holding the fabric in his teeth. He wished he could feel his hands around her neck but needed them.

He spread her butt cheeks apart, spat into his free hand like the video online had recommended to heighten his pleasure, and then forced himself inside her.

Leslie arched on the bed, screaming with all her might. He could feel her every muscle shaking. She crumpled onto the bed, giving in to him completely.

It was better than he expected. The power it gave him over her was the real thrill.

He didn't last long, and after he groaned into her back, he pushed her away.

His fantasy fulfilled, he sat on the edge of the bed, watching her sob into the cot. He didn't like the sound—he wanted silence, so he punched the back of her head.

After a minute, Beau became concerned because she wasn't moving. He shook her, but nothing. Not even a moan. He checked. She was still alive.

"Pity we can't have another go, but I have to make sure they don't find you."

He unhooked the cuffs from her wrists and discarded them. Lifting her battered and bloody body from the cot, he thought it a shame he couldn't keep her somewhere, to revisit again and again.

Might have to look into that for my future ladies.

Once he had positioned her on the floor, he set her hands over her chest like a corpse. She would be one soon enough.

He put his pants on and then went into the corridor. After collecting several handfuls of dry leaves and twigs, he drizzled them around her. He also added her cut up clothes and sombrero to the pile. For the final touch, he doused everything with lighter fluid.

A nice slow burn was what the internet advised to destroy a body.

Beau set a few of the candles on the floor next to the debris.

After gathering up his things and returning them to his duffel bag, he examined the room. He would miss the cozy little space. So many fond memories had been created there.

Leslie had not moved the entire time. He figured she was almost as good as dead. Just about to leave the cell, his bag over his shoulder, he glanced back at her.

"The best and last night of your life, eh, girl?" He removed his mask, making sure she saw his face, and then tossed it on top of her.

Snickering under his breath, he left.

Once outside the cells, Beau sucked in the crisp night air, invigorated. His fingers and toes tingled with his power. Why couldn't he feel like this all the time?

He eased forward, letting his eyes grow accustomed to the night, the grass knocking against the legs of his black jeans. His desire for another crept into his thoughts. But who would replace Leslie? Who would be his next prize?

Ahead, something moved at the edge of the fountain.

He squinted to get a better view. He wished he hadn't. Three large dogs had gathered at the fountain. Their eyes on him, they snarled and hunched their backs, ready to attack.

His euphoria spiraled into fear.

Beau took off at a run for the brush, determined to get out of there before the dogs came after him.

Chapter thirty-Six

D erek climbed from his blue pickup and checked Leslie's car, which was parked next to his. The lot pretty full—the collection of cars ran the gambit from a high-end Mercedes to his beat-up truck. The one car he did not see was Beau's. Perhaps he had caught a break and could enjoy an evening at the river without running into that idiot Devereaux.

With his sombrero in his hand, he followed the techno beat to the beach, ready to enjoy a night with his best girl.

And the surprise she had waiting for him? Hopefully, it involved something away from the noise of the party.

"Buck it up, Foster. It's a party. You're supposed to have fun."

A night of binging Netflix and popcorn was a whole lot more palatable than this.

His feet slipping on the well-trod pine needles, he got down the embankment to the beach.

When he landed on the sand, he adjusted his black mask and pulled the aggravating sombrero on his head. Ready to put on a good show for Leslie. Anything to make her happy.

He searched the crowds, but there were too many people to locate Dawn. He stuck to the line of trees and thick green bushes, avoiding the partygoers and anxious to get to Leslie in the cells.

At the divide where The Abbey property began, a handful of revelers with vapid gazes drew his attention away from the rusted gate. Their heads raised to the sky and their mouths open, a few even held up phones videotaping something.

He looked up, following their line of sight. A trail of smoke rose in the air. It came from The Abbey.

"Oh my God."

He pushed the gawkers out of his way, horrified. Derek tossed his hat and mask to the side and dashed through the gate.

Others joined him along the way. Princess Leia, Han Solo, Captain America, Iron Man, and Wonder Woman tossed their shields, golden lassos, and lightsabers aside, running across the high grass.

* * *

Beau rushed along, batting low-hanging twigs out of the way, still terrorized by the devilish creatures. He hugged the rim of the beach to avoid being seen by the partygoers. Seized by cramps, he stopped to catch his breath. He would come back with his shotgun and make sure he eliminated every one of those damned dogs. They would never interfere with his plans again.

Shouting arose from the outskirts of the party by the iron gate. His head popped up. What was that?

The thump of the music abruptly stopped.

"Fire! The Abbey's on fire."

His little pyrotechnic show must have spread past the cells. So be it. That old wreck needed to go up in a ball of flames.

He wondered what it looked like. It would be something everyone in the town would talk about for decades to come.

Beau pushed on through the brush, eager to get to the parking lot.

After he secured his duffel bag in his trunk, he checked his phone. He had plenty of time to make the party at the brewery. If he didn't, he had a hell of an excuse.

He combed his hands through his hair and straightened his shirt. Time to tell everyone he had just arrived. Act surprised like everyone else and enjoy the big show.

And Leslie?

A grin stretched across his lips. Beau pictured her charred remains pulled from The Abbey in the aftermath. Or perhaps the partygoers would reach her in time to remove whatever was left. He couldn't wait to see the tears in Foster's eyes, or the pain Dawn would experience at losing her twin sister. The thought of their grief made him happy, but not exuberant. He'd need another girl for that.

"But it might make for a very interesting evening."

Beau hurried, anxious to join the rest of the revelers at The Abbey.

* * *

Sick with fear, his heart a tangled mess, Derek ran as fast as he could across the high, clingy grass. At the fountain, he caught the spindle of smoke wafting upward into the black sky from the caved-in entrance to the cells. Flashes of orange light coming from The Abbey lit his way across the grounds. *Fire!* It would spread quickly through the dry, derelict structure, consuming everything in its path.

At the opening in the wall, he slipped inside, not caring what awaited him. His fear for Leslie pushed him through the thick smoke. Eyes burning, tears raking his cheeks, Derek walked blindly through the haze.

Small patches of red and orange flames spread along the corridor, carried by piles of debris. He followed the billowing smoke to a cell. Inside the most dilapidated section, in the room he and Leslie had found, the fire burned out of control.

Derek tore the sash from his waist and covered his nose and mouth. On the ground, in the doorway of the cell, he saw a naked woman. She lay on her stomach as if she'd tried to crawl to safety.

Leaves and twigs were tangled in her blood-soaked hair. Duct tape covered her mouth. Wounds, along with red and pink patches— some dotted with blisters—covered her skin. She reeked of some kind of accelerant.

His throat clenched.

God, not my Leslie!

He was almost afraid to touch her—afraid she would shatter into a thousand pieces and be lost forever.

"I'm here, baby. I'm here."

He scooped her into his arms, the smoke and his utter disbelief compounding his tears. Derek wanted to scream. His grief came crashing down on him, leaving him breathless. He almost fell to his knees but pushed on. He had to save her first, then he could fall apart.

His regret turned to dread. She wasn't reacting to him. She remained limp in his arms.

"Leslie? Wake up, baby. God, please wake up."

She didn't respond. Panicked, Derek carried her to the gap in the wall. In the seconds he had been with her, the fire had swelled and filled the corridor, heading toward The Abbey at alarming speed.

His muscles screamed as he carried her dead weight through the narrow crack. The vines, smoke, and bushes cutting off the entrance made him claustrophobic, but he kept on, for her.

Once clear, he gasped for fresh air, coughing up the smoke he had inhaled. His vision blurred, he could not see where he headed, but he ran. Carrying his lifeless Leslie in his arms, he summoned every ounce of strength he had and prayed for someone to help them.

At the edge of the grassy field, people gathered to watch the fire. Some held up cell phones, videotaping the event.

"Help me!"

Several individuals stopped filming when they heard him, but only two guys came to his aid.

Derek stumbled and fell to his knees. He inspected the battered creature in his arms. She was like ice.

Derek set her on the grass and ripped off his black shirt. After he gently covered her, he searched his pocket for his phone. He'd left it in his truck.

"Holy crap," one guy said. "Who is she?"

"Do either of you have a knife to cut this tape away?" he demanded.

The taller of the two boys brandished a Swiss Army Knife on a keychain.

Derek snatched it from his hand. "Call 911. Get an ambulance out here. Get the fire department. Get everyone."

While one of the boys dialed 911, the other helped Derek cut the tape away from her mouth.

He wretched when the tape pulled away some of her skin. "No!"

Her nose broken, blood drizzled from both nostrils. Her lips were swollen and split, her cheeks red, and her discolored jaw hung awkwardly to the side. He could not imagine what she had endured.

"Help me get the rest of this tape off her," he hysterically demanded.

The boy's hand stayed Derek's. "Let's get her to the parking lot first. The faster we get her to the paramedics, the better."

Derek nodded, knowing he was right, and carefully lifted Leslie into his arms. He held her close, willing her pain away. The thought of giving her to strangers sent a whirlwind of panic through him. He didn't want to give her up. What if this was the last time he could hold her? What if this was the last memory he would have of her?

"The paramedics are coming," the other boy said, jogging alongside them.

The crowd gathered at the gate parted as Derek approached. They gawked at the half-naked girl in his arms.

With the two strangers as his guides, Derek carried Leslie to the parking lot. The whole time, he kept repeating, "She won't die." An existence without her was unimaginable. He would not survive it. His life revolved around her. His heart belonged to her. Everything good in his world came from her smile.

At the parking lot, he took her to his truck. He had to get her warm. Then, she would wake up and everything would be all right.

When he heard the screech of sirens, he turned and began running to the road, Leslie in his arms.

"Hold on, baby. Help is coming."

The headlights of the ambulance came toward them. The boys with him waved and screamed for them to stop.

Two men dressed in blue jumpsuits hopped out of the back. They took Leslie from his arms; Derek almost fought to hold on to her. He didn't want to let her go.

"What happened?" one man called out.

"She was, ah …" Derek fought to keep from crying. "In the cells. They're on fire. I found her like this and put my shirt over her."

The two medics carried her to the back of the truck. Derek followed, needing to see her. If his eyes stayed on her, he wouldn't fall apart.

"Can you tell me anything about her?" the ambulance driver asked. "Do you know her name?"

Derek kept his eyes on the two men as they lowered Leslie on a gurney.

"Leslie, Leslie Moore."

"We need to go now, Rick," one of the medics called from the ambulance.

The driver moved Derek to the side and shut the back doors.

"We'll take it from here, son."

"Can I go with her?" Derek's voice cracked.

"You can follow us to the hospital." The driver then rushed to the front of the ambulance.

Derek stood shaking and unable to move until the ambulance sped away, its harsh yellow lights disturbing the darkness surrounding the road.

A hand slapped his shoulder. "Get in your car and follow her."

Without even glancing at the boys who had helped him, Derek ran to his old blue truck. Panic had his hands shaking so hard, he could barely get his door open.

Just as he pulled out of the lot, fire trucks sped past him.

But he didn't care about the fire. All that mattered to him was Leslie.

He hit the accelerator and the old truck chugged, gaining on the bright lights of the ambulance ahead.

"Please, dear God. Save my Leslie. I'll do anything. Just save her for me."

* * *

In a waiting room, stinking of smoke, Derek paced the scuff-marked floor. He vacillated between the scorching pain of guilt, the sour knot of fear, and the sickening grip of grief. Minutes felt like hours. Perhaps it was all just a bad joke—her promised surprise.

"Are you the young man who came in with Leslie Moore?"

Derek wheeled around and was hit by a pair of troubled hazel eyes. The name across the lab coat pocket read Dr. Jeffers.

"Is she okay?" Derek shuddered as the words escaped his lips.

The doctor's faint smile did little to reassure him. "How do you know her, son?"

"She's my girlfriend. We were supposed to meet up at the river. She had a surprise for me, but I must have missed her on the beach because when I got there—"

"Do you have a number where I can reach her parents?" he cut in. "I need to ask them some questions."

"I called her dad. I got his voicemail and left a message. He was at a party, but I'm sure he's on his way." Derek's lower lip trembled. He was going to be sick.

"What's your name?" Dr. Jeffers asked.

"Derek. Derek Foster."

"Derek, do you know if she has any drug allergies? Any medical conditions she might have told you about?"

Derek shook his head. "She wasn't allergic to anything. Last year, she got the flu. Other than that, she's healthy."

Dr. Jeffers scanned the faces of the other people in the waiting room. "Is there anyone with you?"

Something had happened? The doctor wouldn't ask if he needed anyone unless it was bad—very bad. Derek shook uncontrollably, the reality of losing her settling over him.

"No. I found her … in the cells. I followed the ambulance and …" His voice dried up. The lump forming in his throat made it impossible to go on.

Dr. Jeffers grimaced and lowered his head. When he looked, his hand clasped Derek's shoulder.

"I think you should come with me."

Derek's knees buckled. "What is it? She's gonna be all right, isn't she?"

Dr. Jeffers put his arm behind his back and urged him through a pair of double doors.

"Your girlfriend is very critical, Derek. I'm not sure how much longer we can keep her going. Maybe if she heard your voice, knew you were there, it would help her."

A long white corridor appeared before him. Derek's trembling got worse—a lot worse. He could barely stand.

In the corridor, the aroma of antiseptic blended with the stink of bleach and the smoke clinging to Derek's clothes. Conversations of staff, patients, and others in the hallway came and went, but he couldn't make out any words. His world shrank before his eyes until the only thing he could see were the white tiles on the floor and the reflection of the harsh fluorescent lights above.

"You're going to see her hooked up to tubes," Dr. Jeffers warned as he stopped before a door at the end of the hall. "They're keeping her alive. She's sustained a lot of trauma to her brain and …" He pushed the door open. "Just let her know you're here."

Derek fought back tears. Brain trauma. He might have been a high school kid, but he'd watched enough medical shows to know that was bad. What if his Leslie came back and wasn't his Leslie anymore? What would he do?

Digging his nails into his palms to keep from breaking down, he walked into the room. Then he froze, his legs like lead when he saw Leslie on a bed.

Machines with blinking lights surrounded her. The breathing tube in her mouth was foreign. Her pallid hands rested on her stomach with bright red lines cut into her wrists. Burns blistered her arms, while her bruises had turned a pale shade of blue.

This wasn't his Leslie. There was nothing he recognized of the girl he loved. She was so still, so empty of life. How could this be the same person? This didn't seem real.

Bile rose in his throat. He forced it back, bringing tears to his eyes.

Machines hummed and the monitor above the bed beeped with her every heartbeat. The noises whirled in his head to a deafening shrill. The lights above became too bright, and the heaviness in his heart sunk him deeper into a pit of despair he was sure he would never climb out of.

A heavy, numbing, throbbing sensation overtook his limbs, erasing all thought. He was overwhelmed and overcome.

"Is he family?" a nurse at the bedside asked.

"No, but I'll take responsibility," Dr. Jeffers said. "Let him stay with her."

The nurse pulled a chair closer to Leslie. "Have a seat."

Derek willed his legs to move, approached the bed, and became transfixed by the pattern of bruises on her cheeks. *Is that real?* The red mark around her neck left a patchwork design embedded in her skin. Her lips, her jaw, her nose were distorted and swollen. Her beautiful hair, now partially shaved, lay spread out on the pillow behind her.

"You can hold her hand," the nurse encouraged.

Something tapped against his cheek, and he wiped it away.

Tears. He hadn't even realized he was crying.

He lifted her fingers, caressing her skin. Still shaking, he slipped his hand into hers, hoping for some sign of life, something to let him know she was in there. She was like ice. He almost asked the nurse to get her another blanket, because her hands had never been so cold. Leslie's hands had always warmed him, strengthened him, uplifted him.

Memories of her laugh, her smile, her voice, her beautiful eyes inundated him. He curled inward, unable to breathe, unable to speak. It hurt so much.

"You can't leave me."

He didn't recognize his voice.

This can't be happening.

"We have our whole lives ahead of us. There's college and law school. We have to open our law practice together. And we are supposed to get married, remember? Who's going to teach me about feminist literature, watch movies with me on Friday nights, and make me smile?" Tears flowed down his cheeks. He couldn't stop them. "I'll be lost without you, Leslie. I can't go on without you. You are everything to me. Stay with—"

A loud, harsh buzzer rolled around the small room. Dr. Jeffers and the nurse raced to the bed, shoving Derek out of the way.

"Give her an Amp of Epi," Dr. Jeffers ordered.

More hospital staff stampeded into the room, moving Derek farther from the bed. He wanted to hold Leslie's hand, to beg her to fight, but he could not get near her.

"What is it? What's happening?" he shouted.

The monitor alarm above the bed continued to sound its godawful screech. People shouted. In the back of the room, Derek waited.

He was nothing more than an observer, helpless to interfere. He became a shell. Absorbing everything but registering nothing.

Shouts filled the room and he flinched with every raised voice.

Someone climbed into her bed, performing CPR. The pounding on his Leslie's chest horrified him. This was nothing like his life support class. His Leslie wasn't a doll. They were hurting her.

They added medicine after medicine to her IV while the doctor stood by and waited for the flat orange line to change on her monitor.

Derek prayed, he hoped, he called to God to save her, but the orange line never wavered. It stayed flat and ugly, bereft of life.

A hush settled over the room, and then Dr. Jeffers turned to Derek.

His eyes connected with the man, and he saw it. The sympathy he had seen since he was a kid. People sorry for his lonely life, for his struggling mother, for his absent father. His heart trembled.

No, God, please.

Dr. Jeffers raised his head to the clock on the wall. "Time of death, ten-fifty-three."

"No!" Derek cried out. "You have to save her."

Dr. Jeffers grabbed his shoulders. "She's gone. There's nothing else to do."

Derek ran out the open door and down the corridor. He had no idea where he was going; he just had to get away.

Then Derek ran right into someone. He bounced off them and fell back on the floor. He glanced up. John Moore stood over him.

Derek pulled up his knees and covered his head with his hands, wanting to disappear. "She's gone. She's gone."

The world came crashing down around him. The pain in his chest made him feel as if he had been split in two.

Someone helped Derek from the floor. Arms went around him and held him close. He cried onto a shoulder, and he inhaled a familiar scent. A spring meadow filled with clover—that was it. Through his tears, dirty-blonde hair registered. He pulled back, realizing who held him.

He had to get it together. Leslie was his, but she had a sister, a mother, a father who would grieve for her, too. The Moores needed him as much as he needed them.

His voice caught in his throat. "Dawn, what am I going to do? I won't make it without her."

She took his hands, squeezing them. "Derek, what happened?" Her hands were so warm, like Leslie's used to be.

"I don't know." Derek's deep breath rattled around in his chest. "When I arrived at the cells, there was smoke everywhere and when I went inside …"

"Why would she go there without me? I'm supposed to protect her. I'm in charge of keeping her safe, but she never gave me the chance. But why didn't she tell me about it? Why?"

Dawn's voice was different, deeper. It frazzled him. She sounded so much like Leslie. Derek wiped his eyes, wanting to see Dawn's face.

Then, slowly, her blue eyes came into focus, her nose, her lips, her lovely chin. It was everything she shared with Leslie, but then she tilted her head—her face was discerning, questioning, tough. This wasn't Dawn.

"Leslie?" Derek whispered.

The slight nod took away the strength in his legs. He wobbled and then sat on the floor, hyperventilating, overcome. She was alive. He glanced back at the room door. But Dawn was gone. Suddenly, his grief meant nothing next to the horror he had to share with family.

She stooped down to him, her arms around him, holding him close. "Tell me my sister is alive, Derek. Please tell me she's okay."

He held her, squeezing her harder than he ever had. "I don't understand. How are you here?"

Leslie trembled against him. "Dawn took my phone, the car, even the bottle of champagne I had for us. I went to a neighbor's and called you, but you never picked up."

"I thought she was you. Her hair was short like yours." He sat back and touched the ends of a curled lock. "I saw it."

"She cut it." Leslie's brittle voice sounded so frail. "I found her hair in the sink in our bathroom. Why did she do that?" She collapsed into his arms. "It was supposed to be me. I should be in there, not her. We're supposed to go together. Not like this. How am I going to live without her?"

Her sobs destroyed him, but a selfish piece of him rejoiced. He hated himself for feeling that way, but his guilt could wait. Leslie needed him.

Dr. Jeffers came into the hall. Cries rose around him as Shelley and John learned of their daughter's passing.

Derek never let go of Leslie. He whispered how much he loved her.

"Why did this happen?" she kept asking, but he didn't tell her.

His Leslie would find out the horrible truth soon enough.

Chapter thirty—Seven

Sobs, sniffling, and reverent whispers permeated the gym at St. Benedict High. Beau sat surrounded by teary students and faculty gathered around the basketball court. Some carried white roses in memory of Dawn Moore. The podium in the center of the court had a black sash across it. The rain tapping on the tin roof seemed an appropriate accompaniment for such a solemn occasion.

He, like the others there, was devastated. Dawn? It had been Dawn squirming and screaming beneath him. But she had short hair and the bottle of champagne. The high of his kill deflated the moment he learned Dawn had died.

If he was going to pursue this, he had to smarten up. And what if he had discovered her? Beau would have killed her anyway. She had been a means to get closer to Leslie, nothing more. He would have considered her practice.

Leslie wasn't at school, which really ticked him off. But with his anger came a speck of optimism. He could still take her. No one knew it was him, so he had another chance. He would also eliminate the Moore twins from his life for good. There was a silver lining to his disappointment after all.

"The river is off limits from now on," Sheriff Davis announced from the behind the podium. "The beach is closed, and the ruins of The Abbey are going to be patrolled day and night until Dawn Moore's killer is caught. Two women have died at the river. We fear a killer is on the loose."

"Is this a serial killer, Sheriff?" one of the female faculty members asked.

Sheriff Davis slapped his Stetson against his thigh, looking uncertain. "I don't know, but the federal authorities are coming in to help with the investigation. That's all I can say."

The rumbling of student conversations echoed throughout the large gym.

"This is bullshit," Beau muttered to Mitch. "Guys can still party on the river."

"Yeah," Mitch agreed. "But we'll have to find a way to get around the cops."

Beau's gut tingled at the challenge. It might make parties at the river even more thrilling. Then there was the matter of The Abbey. He longed to visit the scene of his crimes. Find out if he could still use the abandoned location to serve his needs.

"We can make it work."

The idea of returning to the river, and planning for a night with Leslie brought him back to life.

I can be king again.

The clatter of students climbing down from the bleachers awakened him from his daydreams. He followed the crowd to the gym doors after the impromptu meeting came to an end.

"Big game against Jesuit High coming up." Mitch butted his shoulder. "You think Coach might let you play?"

"Seriously doubt he'll let me finish the season."

"Go talk to him today during practice. He might feel sorry for you after …"

But Beau didn't hear the rest. Someone from the throng around them grazed by him and whispered, "I know," in his ear.

He stopped. A few students behind him gave him dirty looks when they almost ran into him. He spun around, searching for the culprit, his breath trapped in his chest.

"Dude, you okay?" Mitch slapped his back.

Students clogged the doorway. He nervously examined their faces, sweat beading his upper lip.

Something ahead caught his eye. The swing of a brunette ponytail secured with a red ribbon.

Beau stood on his toes to get a better look, rising above the students around him.

The girl wearing the red ribbon stopped, turned, and her blue eyes met his.

Taylor Haskins grinned at Beau and then ducked out the gym doors.

He elbowed students out of the way, anxious to catch up with her.

"Hey, watch it, Beau," a girl snapped at him.

He reached the doors, but there was no sign of Taylor.

Sweat dripped down his back and an unsettling prickling danced across his skin. Had she been the one watching him at The Abbey?

He had to find out what she knew and shut her down before she talked to anyone else.

* * *

Overcast skies dulled the skylights in the school library. The lack of light made it difficult for Beau to see his computer screen. He'd tried to change stations, but the bitchy librarian had turned him down.

Fed up, he was about to skip his computer class lesson and look up news articles about Dawn's death when he received an unexpected message on the school's in-house email system.

I know.

That was it. No name, no sender name, nothing.

The kick in his gut knocked him back in his chair. He sat up, avidly browsing the other computer stations around him.

Everyone had their heads down. He even checked for Taylor's red ribbon.

He sat again, rubbing his hand over his face.

"Okay, let's play."

Beau opened the messenger system and typed his password. When a blank screen came up, where his notifications should have been, his stomach clenched. An entire semester of class information had been wiped clean.

"What the hell?"

He retyped his login information twice, thinking there must be a mistake. But the same empty screen came back on. Even the newest message didn't show on his board.

Beau slammed his fists on his keyboard, cursing under his breath.

"Is there a problem?"

Any second, he expected to see Mrs. Peters arching over him. The old hag loved to patrol the computers for students searching for porn.

"I have an issue with—"

Sara Bissel leaned over his chair, smiling sweetly, a red ribbon holding up her ponytail.

He tried to speak but lost his voice. His eyes remained fixed on the red ribbon.

"What's wrong, Beau? Cat got your tongue?"

He wanted to smack her across the face, but instead he stood and grabbed his books. "You think you're smart? Just you wait."

He hurried from the library, unhinged by the encounter.

* * *

The last bell of the school day echoed through the hall. Lockers banged closed while students around Beau still buzzed about the tragedy at the river. The constant mention of Dawn's name and his unending performance as the grieving ex ate away at him.

Outside, he stormed across the wet grass on the quad, the cool

November air teasing his face. Eager to give Coach Brewer another try, he headed to the gym doors. He missed the game, the glory of being the quarterback, and the physical outlet. There was no better place to let go than on a football field.

He was about to head inside when he was distracted by a few cheerleaders on the practice field. He couldn't make out their faces, but it wasn't the entire squad of eight girls, only four. Why were they on the field and not in front of the stands where they normally practiced?

And why were they out there so soon after Dawn's death? Weren't they upset like everyone else?

Intrigued, he took a step closer to the field.

The wind picked up as he neared the stands. The breeze seemed to circle him, and the hair stood up on the back of his neck. An odd tickle ran across his palms.

Wanting to get a good look, he moved out from the shade of the stands.

The girls stopped in the middle of their cheer when they spotted Beau.

The red ribbons securing each girl's ponytail caught in a passing wind and twirled toward the sky.

He wasn't sure if he should waste time confronting them or go on to his meeting with his coach. Perhaps the ribbons were their silly way to commemorate Dawn.

When the wind died, the girls lined up, hands on their hips, and they chanted in unison.

"Hey hey, ho ho, we know what you did. We know. Can't hide the truth from our prying eyes. Vengeance will be ours tonight."

Stunned, he dropped his book bag.

What did that mean?

Someone stepped out from behind the line of girls. It was Leslie wearing Dawn's old uniform, glaring at him.

He stumbled backward. It could have been Dawn coming back

from the dead. But why would she be wearing—

Taylor joined Leslie. In her cheerleading uniform, with red ribbons in her hair, she marched toward him looking like the confident girl he'd known before their encounter.

His mouth dry, his stomach turning, he picked up his bag, ready to forget about his meeting with Coach Brewer.

A third girl appeared. Sara—also dressed as a St. Benedict cheerleader—stepped out from the front of the stands.

Shoulder to shoulder they progressed, their faces like stone statues.

Before they reached him, another girl linked arms with Sara.

Kelly Norton, a St. Benedict's red cougar on her chest, pointed a pompom at him. Her venomous little eyes reminded him of a cobra's right before the strike.

"I know," she called to him.

This was too much.

Before he could turn and run, a hand came down on his shoulder, paralyzing him with fear.

He expected Sheriff Davis to be there, ready to arrest him, but it was Mitch, dressed for practice.

"What's up with that whacked out cheer?" Mitch pointed his helmet at the field. "And I thought they weren't practicing today because of Dawn."

His skin was on fire, the air around him thinned; Beau was trapped by the girls he had hurt. They had talked to each other, shared their experiences. They knew what he had done. Even Leslie knew.

He had to get out of there.

"I've got to go," he muttered and took off for the parking lot.

"Hey, Devereaux? I thought you wanted to talk?" Coach Brewer called behind him.

Beau didn't stop to look back at his coach. He kept going as fast as his legs would carry him, hungry for the safety of his well-protected home.

The wind picked up in the empty lot. All the students not involved with after-school activities had taken off. The eerie silence added to his sense of vulnerability.

Beau stepped onto the blacktop. Someone was watching him from the shadows beneath the oaks scattered around the lot. He could feel it. He scoured the trees for the girls—nothing.

Keep it together. You're in control, not them.

He scurried to his car, looking over his shoulder and wrestling his keys from his front pocket. Once back at home, he would regroup and come up with a plan. They were out to get him, but they couldn't beat Beau Devereaux.

He muttered as he hurried along. "Stupid bitches think they can scare me?"

He was almost to his car when the keys slipped from his shaking hands. He bent down to pick them up.

"Where you off to in such a hurry?"

Sara stood in front of his driver's side door, blocking his escape.

She was one girl; he could take her on. He charged at her. "Get out of my way!"

"You seem flustered, Beau." Taylor appeared on his right.

He stepped back and bumped into someone.

"Whoa, dude, watch the uniform."

Beau spun around. Kelly was behind him.

"You can't touch me. None of you can. I can say what I want about each of you. It will be your word against mine."

"No, Beau," another voice said on his left. "No one is going to hear your side."

When he faced Leslie, his throat closed, cutting off his air. It was Dawn staring at him from beyond the grave.

"Get away from me. I had nothing to do with what happened to your sister."

Leslie's cold, hollow eyes burned into him. She eased closer.

"We know better."

Fed up, Beau cocked his arm back to take a swing at her when something pricked his neck.

He clasped the spot below his left ear. "Oww, what the hell was that?"

Kelly held up a syringe. "I swiped it from the vet I work for. I figured if it can knock a horse out, you haven't got a prayer." She recapped the needle and stuck it in the front pocket of her uniform. "Any last words?"

"You bitch!" Beau stumbled, becoming woozy. "What did you give me?"

Leslie stood in front of him. "Just a teaser of things to come."

It was getting hard to stand. "You won't get away with this." He sank to his knees.

Taylor stood over him. "Oh, yes, we will."

He pitched headfirst into the parking lot just as everything went black.

* * *

Beau awoke in blurry darkness; his mouth a desert. He blinked a few times, and when things came into focus, he wished they hadn't.

He was in the charred remains of The Abbey. Burnt pews and fallen beams littered the blackened, debris-covered floor. He could see the clear night sky through the hole in the roof. The acrid smell of smoke burned his nose. He tried to move but couldn't. Zip ties secured his hands and legs to a wooden chair. Around his feet flickered several candles.

"Seems fitting to bring you here," a female voice said in front of him. "Back to the scene of the crime."

He raised his head, woozy with the movement. Shapes formed beyond the golden aura of candlelight.

Kelly, Taylor, Sara, and Leslie, still in their cheerleading uniforms, stood in front of him. The red ribbons in their hair matched their heavy lipstick, giving each girl a macabre, Joker-like appearance.

Beau, still a little drunk from the drug, laughed. "So, what is this? Some kind of hashtag-me-too revenge club? You've got nothing on me."

"We've got *you*, Beau." Leslie leaned over the candles, her eyes aglow in the fiery light. "You could go to jail for murder one, do you know that?"

Her husky voice reawakened all the wonderful plans he had for her.

"I didn't hurt anyone."

Taylor stepped forward. "You lying piece of dogshit. What about me?"

"Or the sick, perverted time you had with me in the cells?" Kelly added.

Sara folded her arms. "Try and talk your way out of that, asshole."

They couldn't touch him, and he knew it. They had more to lose by talking and would never risk it.

"What are you going to do? File charges? With what evidence? And even then, who would believe you? You all got what you wanted."

"What about my sister?" Leslie slapped him hard across the face. "Did *she* get what she wanted? You killed her!"

The sting incited his outrage. His fingers twitched while he struggled against the zip ties. "I never touched Dawn. I cared for her."

"Cared? Like you *cared* for the girl who ended up dead in the river?" Taylor held up her phone in front of him. "Remember her?"

The video was grainy, but she had captured Andrea's face, her head tilted toward the camera while Beau trailed kisses down her neck.

"I didn't get a chance to hang around and get more. You almost caught me. Tomorrow morning this video will be sent in an anonymous email to Sheriff Davis. Then the police will find out you knew her."

Leslie took the phone from Taylor. "What do you think your daddy will do then?"

He looked from one girl to the other, his fear evaporating. "Nothing. I had sex with the girl. She happened to show up dead in the river. I didn't do it."

"No, Beau." Leslie shook her head. "We know you *did* do it. The same way you killed Dawn, destroyed Taylor and Kelly. The same way you tormented me and Sara. And you have to pay."

He was done with their games. They were only four stupid girls with nothing on him that would hold up. Ready to turn the tide in his favor, he rocked the chair back and forth, attempting to get free.

He pushed too hard and the chair tipped to the side, toppling over and scattering a few of the candles. Beau hit his head on a charred beam and yelped in pain.

With burning cheeks and fury, he fought even harder against his restraints. How dare they think they can treat him like this?

Kelly patted the top of his head. "You're going to have a long night on the floor like that."

"Get me up!" His shriek resonated throughout the ruins of The Abbey.

Taylor snapped a picture with her phone. "No, you will stay right there. So the police will know where to find you in the morning."

Taylor, Kelly, and Sara backed into the shadows while Leslie moved forward.

Her smirk exacerbated his rage. He ached to be free. The acidic burn of panic flooded his mouth. He thrashed, sucked in gulps of air, and strained until the zip ties cut into his wrists, Black spots formed in front of his eyes from the exertion.

Leslie knelt beside him. "You're going to spend a long time in prison, having done to you what you did to my sister and these girls. Enjoy hell, Beau." She stepped over him to join the others. "I just hope the dogs don't get you before the sheriff does."

Their figures melded with the darkness. They reached the burnt arch that was once The Abbey doorway, and he lost them completely.

When the only sound he could detect was the cold wind whipping through the charred beams above, Beau's outrage was replaced by fear.

* * *

Seconds turned into minutes. Beau continued to struggle, but the zip ties were too tight.

Think. There has got to be a way out of this.

He ran one scenario after another through his head, searched the ground for something to cut his hands free, then closed his eyes when a pounding headache shut down his capacity to think clearly.

Would they call the police, or was this just a game?

His mind drifted, plotting ways out of his predicament, the blackened ruins around him as silent as a tomb. A howl rang through the night and alarm heightened his senses. He became attuned to every creak and groan inside the structure.

Another howl, this one closer. He renewed his attempts to free his hands. When another howl sounded right outside the church, panic quickened his breathing.

Something glimmered at the entrance. White and flowing, it glided toward him. He thought the candlelight was playing a trick on his eyes, but then a figure in a long cloak appeared.

"It's you." He rested his head against the cold ground, the stench of ash and burnt wood in his nose. "Are you done having your fun, whoever you are?"

The cloak concealed the slender shape of a woman. He couldn't quite make out her features beneath the hood, but he knew she was real.

"I'll hunt you down and kill you ... slowly."

A low growl rose from a shadowy portion of the ruins. Followed by another, and another. Out of the gloomy corners of The Abbey, dogs appeared, the whites of their eyes shining against their matted coats. The snarling dogs gathered around the hooded figure.

She drifted closer, coming into the candlelight.

"You're the one who will die tonight," she whispered.

A black dog slinked up to her, resting its head under her hand.

Beau didn't like this. The dog had the oddest look in its eye—an almost human, vengeful glint.

"I don't scare easily, and you would never—"

The dog trotted up to him, its teeth bared in a grotesque snarl.

"Scared now?" She patted the dog. "You were right about the pack living here. But they're not wild, just very hungry. And they never forgive ... like me."

The dog frightened the crap out of him, but not the girl. He recognized her face as she dipped into the light.

"I'm gonna give you a night you'll never forget." She backed away, and the pack closed in.

Frantic, Beau wriggled in his chair, desperate to escape. Several of the creatures stood around him, their bared teeth gleaming in the candlelight.

"No!" His muscles quivered with fear. "Get away!"

The black dog drew closer to his face.

He stared into the fiendish black eyes, and the cold tentacles of abject terror slithered through his body, paralyzing him.

The dog opened its mouth—the stench of rot and death on its breath.

Beau screamed. The high-pitched sound echoed throughout the crumbling abbey.

And the candles went out.

Epilogue

A black body bag closed over the pale face of Beau Devereaux. God, he hated that sound. Kent Davis removed his Stetson from his head and wiped his brow. Around him, several officers combed the beach for clues as to how the kid had ended up there.

Two men in tan jumpsuits from the St. Tammany Parish Coroner's Office lifted the body bag and carried it across the beach toward the parking lot.

"Did you see those bites?" one of the officers on the beach asked Kent. "I've never seen a person chewed up like that."

Kent put his hat back on, disgusted. "The bites didn't kill him, Phil. Something else did."

A heavyset man with black glasses approached. "I'll get to his autopsy as soon as possible."

"Did you note the zip tie burns on his wrists, Bill? Looks like he was tied up somewhere." Kent needed another coffee to get him through this. "See if you can get me any fibers. We have to figure out what happened."

"What *happened*?" Bill repeated and removed his glasses. "You get a look at that kid's face? Whatever killed him, he was terrified by it. I've seen a lot of shit as coroner of this parish, but never that."

"Fear isn't a cause of death," Kent insisted.

The coroner returned his glasses to his nose. "No, but it's a clue as to what killed him. Or who killed him." Bill shook his head. "I'll have a preliminary report for you in the morning."

Kent stifled his urge to get the hell away from the creepy crime scene. He hated the nasty ones.

"What are you going to tell his old man?" Phil questioned.

He shook his head, sick at the prospect. "I have no idea. This is going to kill Gage. He had big plans for his son."

"Just goes to show no one is invincible," Phil professed. "Not even a Devereaux."

Kent studied the rushing waters of the Bogue Falaya River. "I guess someone forgot to tell that to Beau."

"He knew, Sheriff." Phil glanced back across the treetops to the remains of The Abbey's charred steeple. "By the look on that kid's face when he died, I'd say he got the message."

* * *

The cold November air streamed through Leslie's open car window as she eased into a parking spot outside the gray clapboard, two-story office building.

She cut the engine and turned to the duffel bag on the seat next to her. Memories of that night came rushing back. Memories she wanted to forget but knew she never could.

Bag in hand, she climbed from the car and headed for the straight wooden staircase alongside the building. On the second floor, she opened the dark glass door and stepped inside.

She peered down a hallway decorated with framed posters of beer bottles. She'd never look at a bottle of Benedict Beer again without thinking of the animal who killed her sister.

Leslie checked the secretary's desk down the hallway, not surprised to find it empty on a Saturday.

She slipped inside the open door to her right. The office had certificates of merit, awards, and commendations touting the excellence of the brewery. She found the décor distinctively masculine and a reflection of the man who sat behind the carved mahogany desk across the room.

Gage Devereaux never looked up, busily writing something as

she walked across the Oriental rug.

Leslie dropped the black duffel bag on top of his desk. "I'm returning this."

Gage put his pen aside and glanced at it but never acknowledged her.

He stood, unzipped the bag and pulled back the edges to inspect the contents.

Leslie watched him, seeing flashes of Beau in his face and his movements.

Gage reached inside and lifted the hem of a white cloak. His face a mask of stone, he leveled his dark eyes at her but said nothing.

She didn't expect him to.

He stuffed the cloak back into the bag and zipped it shut.

"When you came to me for help, and we planned that night." His voice had a cold, hard edge. "I promised he would never hurt you again."

Gage turned to the window behind him.

"And now, he never will."